BODIES FROM THE LIBRARY

3

Forgotten stories of mystery and suspense
by the Queens of Crime
and other Masters of the Golden Age

Selected and introduced by

TONY MEDAWAR

COLLINS
CRIME
CLUB

COLLINS CRIME CLUB
An imprint of HarperCollins*Publishers*
1 London Bridge Street
London SE1 9GF
www.harpercollins.co.uk

HarperCollins*Publishers*
1st Floor, Watermarque Building, Ringsend Road
Dublin 4, Ireland

This paperback edition 2021
1

First published in Great Britain by Collins Crime Club 2020

Selection, introduction and notes © Tony Medawar 2020
For copyright acknowledgements, see page 373

A catalogue record for this book
is available from the British Library

ISBN 978-0-00-838096-0

Typeset in Minion Pro 11/15 pt by
Palimpsest Book Production Ltd, Falkirk, Stirlingshire

Printed and bound in Great Britain by
CPI Group (UK) Ltd, Croydon CR0 4YY

MIX
Paper from
responsible sources
FSC
www.fsc.org   FSC™ C007454

This book is produced from independently certified FSC™
paper to ensure responsible forest management.

For more information visit: www.harpercollins.co.uk/green

CONTENTS

INTRODUCTION

'You and I, serene in our armchairs as we read a new detective story, can continue blissfully in the old game, the great game, the grandest game in the world.'

John Dickson Carr

One of the many joys of visiting the British Library and other repositories is coming across forgotten or unknown works by some of the most highly regarded writers of the Golden Age of crime and detective fiction, a period that can be considered to have begun in 1913 with *Trent's Last Case* by E. C. Bentley, and to have ended in 1937, the year in which Dorothy L. Sayers sent Lord Peter Wimsey on a *Busman's Honeymoon*.

This, the third collection of *Bodies from the Library*, continues our mission to bring into the light some of these little-known short stories and scripts, as well as works that have only appeared in rare volumes and never previously been reprinted. For this edition, there is a previously unpublished mystery featuring Ngaio Marsh's famous detective, Inspector Roderick Alleyn, as well as a long lost novella in which John Dickson Carr's satanic sleuth Henri Bencolin goes head to head with a brutal murderer. Stuart Palmer's Hildegarde Withers confronts 'The Riddle of the Black Spade', and six authors go in search of a character as they rise to the challenge of building a short story around the same two-line plot. Among the more famous detectives featured are Anthony Berkeley's Roger Sheringham, who does his bit to help defeat Hitler, and Senator Brooks U. Banner investigates a murderous scarecrow in a case from the pen of Joseph Commings.

And, in the year that marks 100 years of Agatha Christie stories, the inimitable Hercule Poirot investigates a murder foretold . . .

Tony Medawar
March 2020

SOME LITTLE THINGS

Lynn Brock

Inspector Clutsam of the Yard came into the office of the senior partner of Messrs Gore and Tolley on the morning of Thursday, June 27, looking peeved. He came because Chief Inspector Ruddell of the Yard had called to see Colonel Gore at three o'clock on the afternoon of the preceding Monday and had not been heard of since.

'Afternoon, Clutsam,' said Gore, brightly. 'Hot, isn't it? You'd find it cooler without that natty little bowler, wouldn't you?'

'Now look here,' growled the visitor. 'What did Ruddell come to see you about? The Isaacson necklace, wasn't it?'

'Yes.'

'Did he say anything to indicate any line of action he had in view concerning it?'

'Not definitely. I gathered that he wanted us to drop the case. He conveyed to me that he had some information which made us quite superfluous. However, as he had by then spent half an hour trying to pump me for information, I concluded that he was talking through his hat.'

'What time did he leave you?'

'A little before four.'

'Say where he was going next?'

'I gathered somewhere where there was beer. Monday

afternoon was also very hot, you remember, and unfortunately I could only offer him whisky. Which reminds me—'

Inspector Clutsam undid his face partially and accepted a cigarette and a whisky without prejudice. 'In that case, Colonel,' he said, 'you're the last person we know of who saw Ruddell alive.'

'That,' replied Gore, 'is a very real consolation to me for his loss.'

'S'nothing to be funny about,' snapped Clutsam.

'In life,' murmured Gore, agreeably, 'Chief Inspector Ruddell was not an amusing person. In death, I admit, he will be a very serious proposition for any sort of Hereafter to tackle. You think he is—er—deceased?'

'Think? Ruddell's been put away—I know it. There are plenty who'd do the job and glad of it. He's been bumped off—I tell you I know it. He was due back at the Yard on Tuesday morning for a conference with the Commissioner. He didn't stay away from that just to be funny. And we haven't been able to find him for two days. Someone's got him.'

'As we are on the fourth floor,' said Gore, reassuringly, 'we have no cellar. But you are at liberty to inspect our strong-room—'

'Why did you ask him to come here if you had nothing to tell him?'

'We didn't.'

'He told the clerk you did—that you rang him up at two o'clock on Monday and told him you had something special for him about the Isaacson necklace.'

Gore considered his cigarette thoughtfully. 'Now, *there's* an instance of the importance of little things, Clutsam. If Ruddell had mentioned to me that he had got that message, I rather think both you and he would have been saved some trouble. But he didn't. He just blew in as if he owned my office, talked eyewash for half an hour, lost his temper, and made an unsuccessful attempt to bluff us off the case. Pity; but, as it happens, it makes things more interesting.'

'What things?' snarled Clutsam.

'Oh—stolen necklaces and things. As a rule, they bore us horribly—necklaces do. As a matter of fact, in strictest confidence, we decided just twenty-five minutes ago to leave Lady Isaacson to you gentlemen at the Yard. I'm wondering now if we shall.'

'Stop wondering,' growled the visitor. 'You take it from me, Colonel, this Isaacson woman is a—'

'Now, that's just what Ruddell said about her,' smiled Gore, winningly. 'Have another little drink, and tell me why you people dislike this poor little lady so much. By the way, I hope you haven't been *very* unkind to her about that smash-up on the Portsmouth Road last month, have you?'

Lady Isaacson was the wife of a millionaire and a very showily-handsome young woman. She had been comparatively unknown to fame until, some six weeks previously, she had made a determined attempt to kill one of His Majesty's Ministers. Returning in the small hours of the morning from London to her Surrey residence near Farnham, she had crashed into a car going Londonwards, near Guildford. The Important Personage had escaped without injury, though his car had been badly damaged. But the incident had been given elaborate publicity by a certain section of the press, owing to the fact that the lady had been driving well over on the wrong side of the road at a furious pace, and, it was alleged, in a condition of intoxication. She had refused to disclose the name of a gentleman—*not* her husband—who had been her passenger at the time of the accident and on whose lap, according to the Important Person's chauffeur, she had been sitting; a detail which had added additional piquancy to the fact that she had been returning from a very notorious night-club. The loss, a few weeks later, of an immensely valuable diamond necklace, which had been stolen from her town residence in

Grosvenor Square, had revived the interest of the British public in this sprightly young person. The necklace had been insured for £120,000; but Lady Isaacson had issued a statement to the press disclaiming all intention to hold the insurance company concerned to its liability. She desired, she said, to discover if the police, who spent so much time in attending to other people's business, could attend to their own with any satisfaction to the public.

Inspector Clutsam had shut up his face again. It was quite clear that he did not intend to answer the last question. Upon consideration of the face Gore picked up an unsigned letter from a little heap upon his desk, tore it across and dropped it into the waste-paper basket.

'These little things—' he said. 'Now, you *know* you and Ruddell have been bullying Lady Isaacson to get out of her the name of that man who was with her.'

Clutsam made a noise of contempt as he rose.

'Why did you decide to take Ruddell's advice?' he demanded. 'We didn't.'

'Then why did you decide to drop the necklace affair?'

Gore reached for the *Morning Post* which lay on the top of his desk, and indicated a small paragraph tucked away at the foot of an unimportant page. 'Another little thing, Inspector. Let's see what you make of it.'

'A curious occurrence,' Clutsam read, 'is reported from Bath. William Brandy, an elderly tramp, was admitted to the Infirmary on Tuesday suffering from injuries to his head and eye. According to his statement, he was struck by a heavy object while asleep during the previous night on his way from Salisbury to Westbury and rendered unconscious. On awakening in the morning he found close to him a wash-leather bag containing a necklace of what he supposed to be diamonds, fastened by a gold clasp set with three emeralds. Upon examination, however, by a Bath firm of jewellers, the supposed precious stones proved imitations. No explanation is forthcoming of the circumstances which occurred shortly after midnight in a remote spot at a considerable distance from any road or habitation. It is feared that the unfortunate man will lose the sight of the injured eye.'

'Curious little story, isn't it?' Gore commented. 'You remember that Lady Isaacson's necklace had a clasp with three emeralds. Not that I suggest for a moment that *hers* is a fake . . . But *that's* why we thought of dropping the case—'

'It seems a damn silly reason to *me*', blew Clutsam. He dropped the newspaper disdainfully. 'Hell—I'm fed up. I've heard enough fairy tales in the last twenty-five years. I tell you what it is, Colonel. I'm sick of this job. Here I am running round like a potty rabbit for the last forty-eight hours, without a square meal or half-an-hour's sleep, with everyone yelling at me, "Have you got Ruddell? Why the what's-it haven't you? You get him or you get out. There's a man waiting for your job." And these beggars in the papers blackguarding you. People looking at you as if you were a mad dog. Hell, I'm tired of it. Here, can I use your 'phone for a moment? My kid's bad—diphtheria. I haven't been able to get home since Monday morning.'

The burly, dogged figure bent over the instrument and rang up a Balham number. 'That you, Alice? How's the boy? Worse. Yes—get another doctor at once. No, I can't go—*I can't*, old thing . . . Sorry, girlie . . . Get the second opinion at once—the best man . . . I'll ring up this evening . . . Stick it, kid . . .'

Clutsam straightened himself. 'The kid's got to go, the Missus says', he said, simply. 'Bit of good news for a chap, isn't it? Well, good morning, Colonel.'

A little thing—but it moved Gore. On the whole, his relations with the police, professionally, were rather trying. But no one knew better than he how hard was the task to which Clutsam and his colleagues, in uniform and out of it, were bound day and night—the ceaseless vigilance that alone made life for the citizen even tolerably secure. At the moment the man in the street and the man on the bench had their knives into the police. No doubt, in private life, Clutsam and his Alice had to suffer the averted eyes and *sotto-voces* of their neighbours.

Experience had taught Gore, too, what sort of a job it was to look for a lost man in London—long days, perhaps long weeks of false scents and monotonous failure—the search for a needle in a haystack of stupidity, falsehood and hostility. Also he was interested by William Blandy's misadventure.

He took Clutsam by the shoulders and pushed him down into a chair. 'Don't be in a hurry,' he said. 'That telephone message we didn't send has given me an idea. The cigarettes are there. It's only an idea—but there is the fact that the lift was not working on Monday afternoon, and that Ruddell went down by the stairs. Sit tight for a bit, will you?'

The bit lengthened to nearly half an hour before he returned; but he returned with news which brought the impatient Clutsam to his feet in a hurry.

'I think I've found where Ruddell went when he left here,' he said. 'Care to see?'

The building in Norfolk Street, which housed Messrs Gore and Tolley on its fourth floor, contained the offices of some score of assorted businesses. On the third floor, by the staircase down which Gore led Clutsam, were, at one end of a long corridor, the offices of a literary agent, at the other end those of a turf accountant named Welder, and, facing them, those of the 'Victory' Aeroplane Company. In the doorway of Mr Welder's offices the caretaker of the building awaited them, jangling his bunch of keys. They went in and surveyed the three meagrely-furnished rooms. Gore pointed to a window which he had opened.

'I rather think they got him in here somehow. And I rather think they got him out of here by that window, when they were ready—probably at night, when it was quiet.' He leaned out to point down into a narrow yard below. 'Some of the tenants here park their cars down there. There's a gate into the street. It would be quite simple to cart him away . . .'

Clutsam stared about him incredulously. 'Bunkum,' he snapped. 'There isn't a chair out of place. Ruddell would have wrecked this place before six men got him. There isn't anything to show—'

Gore pointed to a cigarette which lay under the table of the inner office. 'Just one little thing, Clutsam. Look at it. Been in trouble, hasn't it?'

Clutsam stooped and picked up the cigarette, which was badly bent and burst at its middle. But he derived no other information from it.

'You smoked one of that brand just now, Clutsam,' Gore smiled. 'If you'll forgive swank, it's rather an expensive brand. Also you notice that it has barely been smoked. Now, I gave Ruddell a cigarette just as he was leaving me on Monday afternoon. Of course, they tidied up. But they left this little thing. Careless of them! Why wasn't the lift working on Monday afternoon, Parker?'

The caretaker could not say. The lift had jammed at a little before three, but had been got right shortly after four. He had never seen Mr Welder, never known anyone to use these offices since they had been taken by Mr Welder a couple of weeks before. From the agents who had let the offices the telephone elicited no information except that Mr Welder had paid six months' rent in advance. They had never seen him.

'Let's see,' suggested Gore, 'if the people over the way can tell us anything about him.'

But the clerk in charge of the 'Victory' Company's offices— apparently the staff consisted of a clerk and the manager, Mr Thornton, who was away—had not seen anyone enter or leave Mr Welder's offices.

'Not on last Monday afternoon—about four?'

'I wasn't here on Monday, sir. The boss gave me a day off.'

'Ah, yes,' smiled Gore. 'That must have been nice. Mr Thornton himself, I suppose, was here that afternoon?'

'I believe so, sir.'

'On Tuesday?'

'No, sir. He went down to the works at Bath on Monday night. He's down there now, sir.'

'Ah, yes, yes, yes,' said Gore, affably. 'Many thanks.'

On the landing he looked at his watch. 'Two more little things, Clutsam. And here's a third. On the occasion of her first visit to us, Lady Isaacson was indiscreet enough to inform me that Mr Thornton had recommended her to consult us . . . Care for a run down the Bath road? I ought to be able to get you back to London by six.'

Inspector Clutsam was not a nervous man, but he was, for many reasons, glad when the big Bentley deposited him in Bath two and a half hours later. They failed to see Mr Thornton; he was 'up', it seemed, testing a bus. It was not known when he would come down.

But they saw Mr William Blandy—not at the Infirmary, which he had left that morning, but at a police station behind Milsom Street, where the arrival of the celebrated Inspector Clutsam created a feverish stir. Before they saw William Blandy, who had been brought in on a charge of drunkenness, they saw the necklace—a quite first-rate bit of fake.

'No pains spared,' Gore commented. 'Sixty-four diamonds, three emeralds, and twelve small diamonds in a clasp of Egyptian design—'

Blandy was produced—a haggard, depressed old down-and-out, still stupid with beer, which had made him peevish. The pupil of one bloodshot eye was still distended with atropine; he had torn off the plaster from an ugly cut on his forehead, which was still oozing blood. His story was that on Monday morning he had set out from Salisbury for Westbury and Bath, that he had lost his way trying to make a short cut across the Plain, and had ultimately lain down to sleep somewhere or other—he had no clear idea where, save that next day he had walked for two hours before reaching Westbury. He had been sound asleep when he had been struck by a mysterious missile which had rendered him unconscious. When daylight had come he had awakened, still sick and dizzy, and had found the wash-leather bag lying beside him. There had been no road near the spot, no house in view—as he himself expressed it, 'no blinking nuffin.' His eye had been very painful, and his forehead had bled a lot, but he had contrived to walk to Bath. He was very indignant over his arrest, which he denounced as part of the plan of the police to deprive him of his reward. Nothing could shake his belief that the necklace was the genuine thing.

'Quite sure,' Gore asked, 'that that ugly big cut on your forehead was made by this thick, soft, wash-leather bag?'

'Sure? Of course I'm sure.'

Gore turned to the station sergeant. 'Found anything else on him, Sergeant?'

In deference to Inspector Clutsam, the sergeant apologised profusely. The man had only been brought in an hour before. He fell upon the unfortunate Blandy at once, and, to his considerable surprise, extracted from various parts of his dingy person the sum of nine pounds odd in notes and silver, together with an expensive fountain pen. Blandy refused to say how he had come by this wealth.

'That's a very smart boot you've got on your right foot, my man,' said Gore. 'Let's have a look at it. Don't be coy.'

The prisoner's footwear made certainly the oddest of pairs. His left boot was a shapeless, split, down-at-heel old ruin, and presented the appearance of having been dipped in whitewash the day before. The right boot was a dapper, sharp-toed, even foppish, affair of excellent quality, still presenting, beneath its dust, evidences of recent polishing.

'Now, it's a curious thing, Clutsam,' mused Gore, 'but I recall distinctly that Ruddell was wearing an extremely doggy pair of boots on Monday afternoon. I wonder if by any chance—'

Clutsam had the boot off and examined it with bristling ruff. Then he fell upon the luckless Blandy with a ferocity which suddenly sobered that unlucky finder of windfalls. He admitted that he had found the boot, close to where he had found the bag—about a hundred yards away. He had also found the nine pounds odd and the fountain pen in a pocket wallet. He had thrown away the wallet and his old right boot. He was placed forthwith in Gore's car, which, followed by another containing a posse of uniformed searchers and two plain-clothes men on motor-cycles, made a bee-line for the high escarpments which rise against the sky to the south of Westbury, climbed them by a vile cart-track, which ended at the top, and came to a pause with the vast, flatly-heaving expanse of Salisbury Plain stretching away miles and miles to blue, daunting horizons.

The task of finding Mr Blandy's sleeping-place appeared, in face of that vast, bare expanse, rising and falling endlessly with the monotony of the sea, almost hopeless. The man had clearly the vaguest recollection of the route by which he had reached that point—the last point of which he was even tolerably certain. The *cortège* remained motionless, gazing dubiously at the dismaying scenery.

But fortunately another little thing presented itself for Gore's attention.

'That left boot of yours has been in wet chalk,' he said. 'There's been no rain for a fortnight. How did you manage it?'

'I got in some water, looking about,' Blandy replied, surlily.

Gore stopped his engine.

'He came along this track, he thinks, Clutsam. Well—there's only one kind of water on Salisbury Plain. We've got to find a dew pond with an old boot and a wallet near it. If you multiply twenty by twenty-five you'll get the size of Salisbury Plain in square miles. I'm afraid you won't get back to town by six, Inspector.'

They placed Blandy upon the track—little more than a sheep-track—and urged him forward. For nearly two miles he drifted slowly southwards, followed by his escort. But track crossed track; he went down into long, twisting valleys, and toiled up over long, baffling slopes, and became visibly more and more doubtful. At length he halted, completely lost. They left him at that point in charge of a man, and spread out to look for dew ponds.

It was just seven o'clock when an excited motor-cyclist rounded up the part with the tidings that Blandy's discarded boot had been found, as Gore had predicted, close to a large dew pond, about four miles south-east of the point at which they had debouched on to the Plain. Hurried concentration produced, after some time, some further finds—Chief Inspector Ruddell's wallet, a bunch of keys, a small automatic pistol with an empty magazine, one of Messrs Collins' pocket novels, and a silk handkerchief marked with the initials W.R.

At Gore's suggestion these articles were left where they were found, spaced out at varying intervals over a distance of nearly a mile, and marked by sentinels. Blandy was moved up to point out the exact spot where he had slept, and indicated the gorse bush in which the automatic had been found. He admitted then that he had found it, but had been afraid to take it. He agreed that possibly it might have been the automatic which had struck him.

Gore looked along the line of sentinels. 'Anything occur to you, Clutsam? I mean, from the fact that these things are all along one dead straight line—from this dew pond to where that farthest man is. Let's just see where Bath lies from here.'

One of the motorcyclists produced a map; Gore himself produced a pocket compass. A very brief inspection revealed the fact that the line of sentinels ran dead for the point where, invisible and thirty miles away to north-west, Bath lay among its hills. 'By Jing!' muttered Clutsam.

Gore turned about to face south-east again. 'Well, now,' he smiled, 'all we have to do is to go along our line until we come to Ruddell.'

The vast emptiness of the landscape chilled Clutsam's hope.

'Hell!' he murmured.

'Well,' demanded Gore, 'if you can find me in England a likelier place for a stunt of this sort, we'll go there. Of course, Ruddell's *your* bird, my dear fellow.'

'Well, we'll go on—for a bit,' agreed Clutsam at last.

The party spread out and advanced in parallel, with occasional halts to verify the line of march. The sun went down in a final crash of gold and scarlet, the landscape greyed; a chill little wind whispered of the coming night. The men began to mutter. Were they going to walk to Salisbury? As the miles crept up, even Gore himself began to think of a dinner that wouldn't happen.

But the end of the quest came with startling suddenness. Abruptly, from behind one of those rings of beeches that studded the desolation blackly, an aeroplane shot up, wheeled, and came rushing towards them. Twice it circled above their heads, then fled away to north-west, along the line by which they had come.

'Well, we shan't find Mr Thornton,' commented Gore. 'Perhaps not Ruddell. All the same, I should like to see if there's anything in that clump of beeches.'

They pushed on for a last mile and passed into the gloomy shadow of the trees. In there was an abandoned farm, silent and desolate. But in its living room they found the remains of a recent picnic meant for four people. And in a padlocked cellar of extremely disagreeable dampness and darkness they found Chief Inspector Ruddell, handcuffed and flat on his back on the slimy floor to which he was securely pinned down. Above his head a water butt stood on trestles, and from its spigot, at intervals of thirty seconds or so, a drop fell upon his forehead. For the greater part of three days and two nights that drop had fallen in precisely the same spot—between the victim's eyes. Ruddell was a man of iron nerve, but he was rambling a bit already.

Day was breaking when Gore deposited Inspector Clutsam outside his house at Balham. He waited until the big, burly man came hastening down the narrow little strip of garden again.

'Good news, Colonel,' he said. 'The kid's got through the night. They say he'll pull through now. I won't forget this. It'll be a big thing for me.'

'Good,' smiled Gore. 'But don't forget the little things. You never know . . .'

Whatever it proved for Inspector Clutsam, the Yard maintained a modest silence concerning the affair. But Lady Isaacson was quite frank about it in a little chat which she had with Gore next day. In their anxiety to identify her male companion in the night of the smash (they suspected that he had been the driver of the car), Ruddell and Clutsam had undoubtedly overdone their repeated examinations of the lady, who had determined to 'get some of her own back'. Thornton, a well-known flying man and, as Gore suspected, the hero of the 'smash up', arranged the plan and enlisted the necessary aides, three reckless airmen. An imitation necklace was procured and a vacant office opposite Thornton's taken; a bogus robbery of the real necklace was actually carried out, leaving careful clues as bait for the police. The next step was to enlist Messrs Gore and Tolley as stool pigeons, and get Ruddell to their offices at a known hour. At three o'clock on the Monday afternoon the lift had been put out of action, Ruddell was in Gore's office, and everything was ready.

As he went down the stairs, Ruddell had been met on the third floor by a young man who, under the pretence of having some information to give him, had persuaded him to enter 'Welder's' offices. There, in an inner room, the fake necklace had been produced and had completely deceived the Chief Inspector. While he was examining it, Thornton and his fellow conspirators had entered the outer room. As Ruddell came out, they caught him neatly with a noosed rope, gagged him, and handcuffed him—not without a severe struggle, despite the odds—and, when the building was quiet, had lowered him in a sack to the Yard, and quite simply carted him off to Bath. There he had been transferred to a big passenger plane and carried off a little before midnight to the lonely old farm on Salisbury Plain which had been rented for the 'stunt'.

The mysterious windfalls were simply accounted for. Above the Plain Thornton had had the pleasant idea of slinging the unfortunate Chief Inspector over the side of the plane by his waist and legs. In due course Ruddell's pockets had emptied themselves of their heavier contents, while the rope holding one leg had slipped and had pulled off one of his boots.

It had not been intended to carry the torture of the dripping drop to any serious point. The prisoner had been visited twice a day and was to have been released on the Friday. Lady Isaacson, who had made a personal inspection of her victim, was quite satisfied that she had got more than her own back in return for her ruffled self-respect.

'I'll say this for the brute,' she laughed, 'he never squealed from start to finish. Look here, what put you on to us?'

Gore rose, smiling, to finish the interview.

'Oh, one or two little things,' he said.

LYNN BROCK

'Lynn Brock' was one of several pseudonyms used by the Irish writer, Alister McAlister (1877–1943). Born in Dublin, McAlister was educated at Clongowes College, a Jesuit school in County Kildare once attended by James Joyce. After school he gained a scholarship to the Catholic University of Ireland in Dublin and on graduating in 1899 with a First in Ancient Classics, he set about becoming a playwright while working as a clerk at his alma mater. Although McAlister had some success with short stories, his first three playscripts were rejected—one by W. B. Yeats—but perseverance paid off and his first play was presented—as by 'Henry Alexander'—on 12 May 1905 by Edward Compton's Comedy Company. A one act comedy, *The Desperate Lover* is set in a bookshop in the eighteenth century, and its original cast included Compton's son Montague, later to become rather better known as the novelist Compton Mackenzie.

McAlister was nothing if not bold. After seeing the actor-manager Lena Ashwell perform in London, he sent her *The Desperate Lover* suggesting she might like to present it. Ashwell was impressed and commissioned a second play from him—the result, a three-act melodrama called *Irene Wycherley*, opened in 1907 at the Kingsway Theatre in London with Ashwell in the title role. The 'horribly grim but splendidly acted' play, credited to 'Anthony P. Wharton', was a huge success, even more so when it toured the following year with the celebrated actress Mrs Patrick Campbell in the lead, and the *Irish Independent* hailed Wharton as 'a brilliant fellow, a person of intellect, a writer of promise'.

McAlister's next play was *A Nocturne*, staged in 1908 as one of a quartet of one-act plays, and it was followed in 1912 by a 'most delightful comedy', *At the Barn*, starring the celebrated singer Marie Tempest. *At the Barn* was also a success and in 1921 a cinema adaptation appeared under the title *Two Weeks*. However, his next play—*Sylvia Greer*—was a flop, which McAlister appears to have anticipated because he did not allow his name to appear in any advertisements or even outside the theatre. In 1913 there was a brief run of a one-act thriller, *13 Simon Street*, and in 1915 *A Guardian Angel* and *Benvenuto Cellini*.

By this time McAlister was serving in France with the Motor Machine Gun Service of the British Army. He was wounded twice and in 1916, while he was lying in a Dublin hospital, his next play, inspired by the Maybrick case, was staged; the script of *The Riddle* was co-credited to another writer, Morley Roberts, although he had done little more than edit McAlister's original script. The production had a strong cast—including the playwright Dion Boucicault as a Machiavellian barrister and, as a woman once accused of murder, the great Irene Vanbrugh. The notices were good but McAlister was unhappy with Roberts' changes and, around a year later, the play was re-staged in Dublin in its original form, this time credited solely to 'Anthony P. Wharton' and with the original title, *The Ledbetter Case*. McAlister must have been very disappointed that this—the original version of his play—was less well received than *The Riddle*.

Although *Irene Wycherley* and other plays continued to be staged, McAlister's reputation as a playwright was beginning to fade. He therefore began writing fiction again, with short stories appearing in *Pearson's Magazine* and the *Empire Review*. His first novel, *Joan of Overbarrow* (1921) was a comedic romance—'If I had to choose between marrying you and dying in a pigsty, I should prefer to die in a pigsty'. Later books were more serious. *The Man on the Hill* (1923) anticipates the General Strike of 1926 while *Be Good, Sweet Maid* (1924) is a viciously misogynistic study of a woman novelist. In a lighter vein, *Evil Communications* (1926) is a series of sketches providing 'a rollicking study of village life', and *The Two of Diamonds* (1926) is a historical romance set in Second Empire France.

In the 1920s, crime fiction was very much considered a lesser branch of literature and for his first mystery, McAlister—then working as a publican in Surrey—adopted a new pseudonym, 'Lynn Brock'. His first Brock novel, *The Deductions of Colonel Gore* (1924), introduced Wickham Gore, a retired soldier turned explorer who returns from Africa to discover blackmail and murder among his friends. In an overcrowded market, Colonel Gore was an immediate success. His first case was followed up by a golfing mystery, *Colonel Gore's Second Case* (1925), and the extraordinary *Colonel Gore's Third Case: The Kink* (1925). Over the next twenty years, McAlister produced four more Colonel Gore books including *The Mendip Mystery* (1929), its sequel *QED* (1930) and the multiple murder mystery *The Stoat* (1940). The Lynn Brock name also appeared on some standalone novels, perhaps the best known being the revenge thriller *Nightmare* (1932).

At heart McAlister was always a playwright, and he wrote two final plays, presented as by Lynn Brock: in 1929 a farce called *Needles and Pins*, which received poor reviews; and in 1931, an adaptation of *The Mendip Mystery*.

One of only two uncollected short stories to feature Colonel Gore, 'Some Little Things' was first published in the *Radio Times* on 21 December 1928. I am grateful to the bookseller and archivist Jamie Sturgeon for drawing it to my attention.

HOT STEEL

Anthony Berkeley

''Itler wouldn't 'arf give something for a sight of what you're lookin' at now,' bawled the little foreman.

Amid the deafening din of a huge munition works, Roger Sheringham could hardly hear the words. He grinned amiably and nodded, saving his larynx.

'Come and see what this lot's doin',' invited the foreman.

Roger looked round for his host, saw that he had not re-appeared, and followed his deputy towards a little group of half-naked men who were wiping the sweat off their foreheads with the air of something accomplished.

Some kind of a lull in the general din made conversation possible, and Roger learned that they had been forging the barrel of a six-inch gun. He said the appropriate things.

'And I expect Hitler would give something for the sight of that, too,' he added with a smile.

The burly man nearest to him wiped his forehead again. 'Well, sir, even 'itler must know we're making guns in England by this time.'

To Roger this seemed a very reasonable remark, but the little foreman appeared to find it highly humorous. 'Ah, it isn't the barrels,' he shouted. 'It's what's in 'em.'

'Shells, you mean?' hazarded Roger, relieved to find that the burly workman appeared just as bewildered as himself before the foreman's wit.

'Shells?' replied that humorist. 'No, wot I mean, it all depends if you know what you're lookin' at.'

''E's looking at a gun-forging, same as you are,' rejoined the burly workman, with an air of finality. 'Come on, mates.'

Roger was not sorry to be rescued at that moment by his host.

Arthur Luscombe at school had been a large, heavy boy, with a passion for imparting unwanted information in a ponderous manner. Now, as the managing director and virtual owner of Luscombe and Sons, he seemed to Roger to have altered very little. Leading his guest with measured footsteps towards his private office, he appeared determined on sacrificing his valuable time to pouring into Roger's reluctant ears just about everything anyone could want to know about steel, and a good deal more than most did.

'Austenite-alloy steels . . . low elasticity . . . manganese steels . . . toughness . . . resistance to abrasions . . . high-tensile alloy steels . . . gun-tubes . . . resistance to shock . . . nickel . . . chromium . . . molybdenum . . . you're not listening, Sheringham!'

'I am,' Roger protested, as they turned in the managing director's office. 'You were talking about steel, I mean,' he added hastily, after a glance at the other's face. 'You were saying that some—er—alloys were harder than others, and . . . and some not so hard . . . I mean, greater elasticity . . . yes, and . . . I say, though, wouldn't Hitler give something to see what I've just seen?'

The managing director's response to this artless query surprised its maker. It was with a positive start and a look of something remarkably like suspicion that he snapped: 'What exactly do you mean by that?'

'Well . . . er . . . nothing,' Roger returned lamely. 'As a matter of fact, it wasn't even original. Your foreman said it, so I thought—'

'Johnson had no right to say anything of the sort.'

'But it doesn't matter, does it?' Roger asked, still more surprised. 'I mean, munition works and so on . . . naturally Hitler . . .'

'Yes, yes. Of course. Naturally. Still, Johnson . . . However, it's of no importance. Now, I can just spare another ten minutes, Sheringham. Would you care to see our sidings? I have to go there myself in any case.'

'I should like to, above all things,' Roger said agreeably.

Five minutes later he was trying to look intelligently at long lines of railway trucks, but over which Mr Luscombe threw the complacent eye of proprietorship.

'Most interesting,' Roger said, doing his stuff. 'And I suppose this is the—er—raw steel, or whatever you call it. Where does that come from?'

'Sorry, I can't answer that sort of question, Sheringham,' his host retorted, with (Roger thought) insufferable complacency. 'Official secrets, you know—Yes, O'Connor, what is it?'

Seeing his employer's attention distracted, the sidings foreman grinned sympathetically at Roger. 'Not that there's much official secret about it, sir,' he said, behind his hand. 'Anyone's only got to look at the labels on the trucks.'

Roger looked.

'Exactly. In fact, you get the stuff from Henbridge, wherever that may be—looks like a Government works.'

'Well, no, as a matter of fact we don't. We're getting our steel now from Allen and Backhouse, of Wolverhampton—this other label. That one's cancelled: some consignment from Henbridge to Allen and Backhouse, nothing to do with us.' The foreman saw Mr Luscombe returning, and hastily stepped back with an air of childlike innocence.

The rest of Roger's visit to the premises of Luscombe and Sons was uneventful. Indeed, it might very easily have passed out of his mind altogether. It is true that on getting home he had the curiosity to look up Henbridge in the gazetteer, and learned that it was a small village in the more inaccessible part of Cumberland, remarkable only as the site of the only coccodium deposits in England; whereupon he looked up coccodium in the encyclopaedia and gathered that it was a rare metal, resembling vanadium, but possessing certain unique properties, found only at Henbridge, in Cumberland.

It was just one of those coincidences, which so often do happen, which brought the name of Henbridge up in a conversation a few days later at Roger's club. It appeared that the man to whom he was talking lived there. Roger asked him about it.

'Used to be a grand little place—if you like 'em remote,' replied the other. 'Pitched up among the Cumberland fells and nearly a dozen miles from the nearest railway station. But it's all spoilt now. They've put up a huge great factory or something just outside, and the fells are covered with wooden huts. Just breaks my heart.'

'It seems queer,' Roger suggested, 'to choose a site a dozen miles from the nearest railway for a factory?'

The man snorted. 'But isn't it typical? Besides, that wouldn't worry them. They've brought the railway to Henbridge!'

'It certainly seems off,' Roger said mildly, and went away to look up trains.

'And you were as bad as any of them,' Roger was saying severely to a stricken Mr Luscombe a few hours later. 'Your works foreman was like a child playing with fire; couldn't help trying to be clever and drop hints that the stupid visitor wouldn't understand. He showed me there was some kind of secret going on; a simple remark of an irritated workman showed that the hands weren't in the secret, so it obviously wasn't a new hush-hush weapon; and then you gave me the biggest clue yourself.'

'I only told you a few elementary facts that you could have got out of any text-book,' protested the deflated remains of the managing director.

'It was the way you marshalled them. I know nothing of steel, but even I gathered that the hardest steels won't stand up so well to shock, and the ones that stand up best to shock have other drawbacks. You showed me that this fact, above all others concerned with steel, was most important to you. Naturally enough, perhaps, as one occupied in making gun-tubes, but there it was; the ideal steel alloy for a gun-tube had yet to be found, all the known ones lacked full efficiency one way or the other.

'Then your sidings foreman gave away that your suppliers have recently been changed, and I learnt that these suppliers are receiving consignments of what can only be coccodium. The inference is obvious. Experiments, using an alloy with coccodium to combine high resistance to both shock and friction have been successful, consignments of this coccodium steel are now reaching you, and are being tried out for six-inch naval guns. If Hitler had any idea of it, the works would be blown sky-high within 24 hours. So what?—And after all, why talk at all?'

'Look here, Sheringham,' pleaded the unfortunate man . . .

In the end Roger magnanimously promised to carry the matter no further. He decided that the managing director had learned his lesson—and it was quite certain that he would teach the others theirs.

ANTHONY BERKELEY

Anthony Berkeley Cox (1893–1971) is one of the most important writers of the Golden Age. Cox had a playful approach to the business of writing crime and detective fiction. His penchant for twisting tropes and confounding expectations undoubtedly played a major role in the genre's development away from a simple linear narrative—in which characters are introduced, a crime is committed, clues are solved and the criminal is detected—into a more complex form in which almost anything can happen. Cox's 'great detective', Roger Sheringham, is virtually the antithesis of Sherlock Holmes, arrogant rather than showily omniscient and unlikeable rather than unclubbable. Nonetheless, with only a few lapses from greatness, the detective stories that Cox wrote as 'Anthony Berkeley', as well as the smaller number of psychological thrillers published as by 'Francis Iles', should be on the bookshelf of anyone who professes to love crime fiction.

Cox was born in Watford, north of London, and educated at Sherborne, a boarding school in Dorset. After school he went to Oxford and after coming down in 1916 with a Bachelor of Arts degree from University College, Oxford, he enlisted in the British Army, serving in France. After being demobbed, Cox embarked on a career as a humourist, producing countless short stories and comic sketches for a huge range of magazines while, working with J. J. Sterling Hill, he expanded a twenty-minute vignette into a futuristic opera, *The Merchant Prince*. He also started to write crime fiction, exclusively so once he found it paid better than other genres. His earliest novels were published anonymously and Cox's career took off with the publication as 'Anthony Berkeley' of *Roger Sheringham and the Vane Mystery* (1927) and, as A. B. Cox, *Mr Priestley's Problem* (1927), which he went on to adapt for the stage the following year as *Mr Priestley's Night Out*. Cox was never without a sense of humour and in all of his Anthony Berkeley novels his tongue is firmly in his cheek, a tendency deplored by some contemporary reviewers. As well as incorporating humour and taking an iconoclastic approach to the genre's 'rules', Cox found the history of crime a ready source of inspiration, using several infamous crimes as the starting point for a detective story. He also broadcast on the BBC and its predecessor 2LO. Finally, as the self-styled 'first freeman' of the Detection Club, the dining society for crime writers that he and others had created in 1929, Cox played a key role in developing ideas to raise funds, including an anthology of crime writing as well as the Club's novel *The Floating Admiral* (1931) and other multi-authored stories.

Cox never made any secret of the fact that his motivation was money and at the end of the 1930s he stopped writing crime fiction when he found that he could be paid well for simply reviewing it, which he did up until shortly before his death in 1971. Since Cox's death his books have drifted in and out of print, but many will be familiar with his Francis Iles book *Before the Fact* (1932) in the form of one of Hitchcock's most successful films, *Suspicion* (1941) with Cary Grant and Joan Fontaine, as well as the late Philip Mackie's superb 1979 serial for the BBC of *Malice Aforethought* (1931), starring Hywel Bennett.

'Hot Steel' was one of two syndicated stories written specially to raise awareness of the dangers of loose chatter during the Second World War. The story was published in the *Gloucester Citizen* on 27 April 1943, with the postscript: '*Do you work in a munitions factory? If so, do you ever drop hints about the work you are doing? Don't! What may seem only a hint to you may be a whole explanation to someone else. And there are dangerous people about, you know.'*

THE MURDER AT WARBECK HALL

Cyril Hare

CHARACTERS

LORD WARBECK, master of Warbeck Hall.

THE HON. ROBERT WARBECK, Lord Warbeck's son.

SIR JULIUS PRENDERGAST, M.P., Chancellor of the Exchequer and Lord Warbeck's nephew.

LADY CAMILLA PRENDERGAST, Lord Warbeck's step-niece by marriage.

MRS BARRETT, wife of John Barrett, M.P., a colleague of Sir Julius.

JAMES ROGERS, a detective sergeant in the Metropolitan Police, assigned to protect Sir Julius.

BRIGGS, the butler at Warbeck Hall.

SUSAN, the butler's daughter.

Editor's note: *The British Parliament is a bicameral system: the lower house is the House of Commons and comprises elected members; the upper house is the House of Lords and comprises hereditary and appointed peers.*

NARRATOR: It is the afternoon of Christmas Eve. In the library of Warbeck Hall, a large, dilapidated country house in the

North of England, Lord Warbeck is reclining on a sofa, looking out at the steadily falling snow. He is a man of not much more than sixty, but with a face prematurely sharpened and aged by illness. Presently he rings a bell beside him. It is answered immediately by the butler.

BRIGGS: You rang, my lord?

LORD WARBECK: (*his voice is rather thin and tired, but quite firm*) Yes, Briggs, I thought I heard a car in the drive. Mr Robert arrived?

BRIGGS: Yes, my lord. He has just come in. I told him your lordship was asking for him. Shall I serve tea now, my lord, or wait for the ladies? They should have been here by now, but I expect the snow has delayed them.

LORD WARBECK: I think we'll wait for tea until they come, Briggs. Where is Sir Julius?

BRIGGS: Sir Julius Prendergast, my lord, is writing in his room. From his expression I should judge that he is contemplating an increase in the income tax.

LORD WARBECK: (*laughing*) Let's hope it isn't as bad as that! It's lucky for me, I'm not likely to live till next Budget Day, anyhow!

BRIGGS: Quite, my lord. That is—I'm sure, we all hope—

LORD WARBECK: That's all right, Briggs. Say no more about it.

BRIGGS: No, my lord. Er—there was one further matter, my lord.

LORD WARBECK: Yes?

BRIGGS: The—the person Sir Julius brought with him, my lord. Will he be having his meals with the family or the staff?

LORD WARBECK: The person? Oh, you mean the detective? Well, I hardly think even a Chancellor of the Exchequer needs protecting at meals in this house. With the staff, certainly.

BRIGGS: Very good, my lord. And will it be in order for him to be asked to assist with the washing-up?

LORD WARBECK: From my limited experience of Scotland Yard, I should say, undoubtedly.

BRIGGS: I am glad to hear it, my lord. Here is Mr Robert, now.

ROBERT WARBECK: (*a fresh, vigorous young man's voice*) Sorry I'm so late, father. I've had a simply poisonous journey here!

LORD WARBECK: Robert, dear boy, it's good to see you! How well you're looking!

ROBERT: And you're looking—(*he pauses, and then goes on in an anxious voice*) How are you feeling, father?

LORD WARBECK: The same as usual, Robert. I'm feeling quietly expectant, waiting for the aneurysm to blow up or whatever aneurysms do. I was told three months ago that I should not live till Christmas, and now with only a few hours to go I think I should do it. Indeed, I'm relying on you to tide me over till Boxing Day. It would be very ill-bred to expire with guests in the house.

ROBERT: Guests! You never told me there was going to be a house party!

LORD WARBECK: Certainly not a house party, Robert. Simply the ordinary family circle we have always invited here at Christmas—what there is left of it.

ROBERT: But father—

LORD WARBECK: As it is to be my last Christmas, I certainly don't propose to break with tradition now.

ROBERT: 'The family circle'—you don't mean that you've invited Julius!

LORD WARBECK: Certainly. Cousin Julius is here now—and, according to Briggs, is filling in time putting something on the income tax.

ROBERT: It's all very well to make a joke of it, but—

LORD WARBECK: Income tax is no joke, I am well aware. But Julius is the only near relation I have left alive, yourself excepted. I thought it proper to offer him hospitality.

ROBERT: And he thought it proper to accept it! The man who more than anyone has meant ruin to us—ruin to the whole country! I suppose you realise what the effect of the new Land Tax is going to be—when—

LORD WARBECK: (*bluntly*) When I die, Robert. Yes, I do. It will mean the end of Warbeck Hall. But until it does end, I mean to carry on.

ROBERT: (*loudly*) Well, I—

LORD WARBECK: Don't shout, Robert. It's a nasty habit you've acquired from speaking at street corners. Besides, it's bad for me.

ROBERT: I'm sorry, father. Well, who else is there in the 'family circle'?

LORD WARBECK: You can guess. Simply Mrs Barrett—

ROBERT: She's as bad as Julius. Oh, I know she was mother's best friend, but since she married that wretched self-seeking politician, she cares for nothing but pushing him up the dirty political ladder.

LORD WARBECK: Well, at least you won't be troubled with the dirty politician. He's abroad, she tells me. There is one more guest, Robert.

ROBERT: (*gloomily*) I suppose you mean Camilla Prendergast.

LORD WARBECK: Yes, I do mean your cousin Camilla, Robert. It would be a great comfort to me if before I go, I could know that your future was assured. She is very fond of you. I used to think that you were fond of her. But since you came out of the R.A.F. you seem to have changed. Why don't you ask her, Robert? If your engagement could be announced this Christmas, I should die a happy man.

ROBERT: Look here, father, I've been wanting to tell you, but it's difficult. I—

BRIGGS: Lady Camilla Prendergast and Mrs Barrett, my lord.

LORD WARBECK: Camilla, my dear! You're a sight for sore eyes! Have you a kiss for your aged step-uncle by marriage?

CAMILLA: (*clear, young voice*) Of course I have! (*Sound of kiss*) It's lovely to be back at Warbeck.

LORD WARBECK: Mrs Barrett, I daren't ask you for a kiss. You keep them all for your husband, I know. What sort of a journey have you had?

MRS BARRETT: (*middle-aged woman's voice—inclined to gabble*) Dreadful; dreadful! I thought we were never going to get through! And now we are here, goodness knows how we are to get out. The snow was so thick at Telegraph Hill . . .
(*Her voice fades out. Robert and Camilla speak in low voices close to the microphone. Faint sound of voices heard behind*)

CAMILLA: Well, Robert, how are you?

ROBERT: Oh, well, thank you. Are you well?

CAMILLA: Yes, thanks. (*Pause*) There doesn't seem to be much else to say, does there?

ROBERT: No, there doesn't.

CAMILLA: Look at the snow! It seems as if it would never stop. Wouldn't it be awful if we were kept here for days and days, with nothing to say but 'How are you?'

ROBERT: Awful . . .

MRS BARRETT: (*Fading in*) . . . Luckily the driver had chains or I don't think we would have ever got here.

BRIGGS: I am bringing in tea now, my lord. I have told Sir Julius that it is ready.

JULIUS: (*a self-confident, middle-aged baritone*) And I'm quite ready for tea! It's what one needs on a cold day like this.

LORD WARBECK: Ah, Julius! You have finished grinding the faces of the rich for the day, I hope. No need to introduce you to anybody here, I think.

JULIUS: I should think not! Camilla, you are looking more lovely than ever.

CAMILLA: Thank you! (*Laughs*) I'm glad somebody notices it!

JULIUS: And Mrs Barrett—your husband is doing a wonderful job for us in the negotiations at Washington.

MRS BARRETT: That doesn't surprise *me*, Sir Julius. I know he has the best financial brain in Parliament, even if—

JULIUS: Even if I'm the Chancellor of the Exchequer and he isn't, Mrs Barrett? Never mind, his time will come. We are all mortal, you know. Oh, Robert, I hadn't seen you, how are you?

ROBERT: (*very coldly*) How do you do?

JULIUS: You've only just arrived?

ROBERT: Yes. I had an important meeting in London yesterday.

JULIUS: Quite. The League of Liberty and Justice, I suppose?

ROBERT: (*defiantly*) And suppose it was? Is that any concern of yours?

JULIUS: I think it is the concern of everybody in this country who cares for democracy.

ROBERT: You call the present regime 'democracy'!

BRIGGS: Your tea, my lord.

LORD WARBECK: Thank you, Briggs. Put it here. No, no, man, *here*. Camilla, will you pour out for the rest? You have no idea how I envy people who can sit up to their meals! To have to feed lying down is the most messy, uncomfortable process I know.

CAMILLA: Let me arrange the cushions for you. That's better, isn't it? Does this mean that you won't be dining with us this evening?

LORD WARBECK: It does, Camilla. I shall, I trust, be asleep long before you have seen Christmas in. Robert will be your host on my behalf. I hope you don't mind.

CAMILLA: Not if Robert doesn't. Do you take sugar, Mrs Barrett?

MRS BARRETT: Two lumps, please. And that reminds me, Sir Julius—the increased duties on sugar. My husband feels very strongly that it would be a great mistake—

ROBERT: (*abruptly*) I don't think I want any tea. If I'm to preside at this festive affair tonight, I think I'd better have a word with Briggs about the wine.

MRS BARRETT: Well, really! As I was saying, Sir Julius, the sugar duties . . .

(*Her voice fades. Microphone follows Robert*)

ROBERT: I shall be in the smoking room if you want me, father.

(*Door closes*)

God! What a woman!

(*He is heard to take a couple of steps*)

Hullo! Who are you? Where do you come from?

ROGERS: (*clipped, official voice*) The name is Rogers, sir.

ROBERT: What are you doing hanging about in the passage?

ROGERS: Well, sir, hanging about is my job. My card, sir.

ROBERT: (*reading*) 'Metropolitan Police. Special Branch. James Rogers holds the rank of Sergeant in the Metropolitan Police. This is his warrant and authority for executing the duties of his office.' So that's it! Haven't I seen you before, at some time?

ROGERS: Yes, sir. On Sunday, September the 20th, between the hours of eight and ten p.m.

ROBERT: What?

ROGERS: Open air meeting, League of Liberty and Justice, sir. I was on duty.

ROBERT: That explains it. And now you've been sent down here to continue your spying, eh?

ROGERS: Oh no, sir. I'm on protection duty—looking after Sir Julius.

ROBERT: Protection! He needs it! I can tell you, when our movement comes into power, fellows like you will be out of a job.

ROGERS: Oh no, sir. That's what Sir Julius's crowd used to say. You'll want protection just the same. They all do.

BRIGGS: Excuse me, sir. Mr Rogers, your tea is awaiting you in the housekeeper's room.

ROGERS: Thank you, Mr Briggs. I'll go now.

(*He is heard to walk away*)

BRIGGS: Pardon me, Mr Robert. May I have a word with you?

ROBERT: Yes, if you must, Briggs.

BRIGGS: If you wouldn't mind stepping into the smoking-room, sir.

(*Sound of steps and door closing*)

ROBERT: Well?

BRIGGS: My daughter Susan, sir, is wondering—

ROBERT: Look here, Briggs, what on earth is the good of bringing up this business again now? You know what the position is as well as I do. I have promised you before and I can promise you now—

BRIGGS: Promises are all very well, Mr Robert, but that was some time ago and Christmas is upon us.

ROBERT: Yes, Christmas, with my father dangerously ill and the house full of people. It's utterly unreasonable to expect me to do anything now, Briggs. Things must go on as they are for the time being. After all, Susan isn't here and—

BRIGGS: Susan *is* here, Mr Robert.

ROBERT: Here! Of all the infernal cheek! What do you mean by doing such a thing, Briggs?

BRIGGS: Well, sir, Christmas is the season for family reunions— even for butlers.

ROBERT: Confound you! I suppose you thought this was a way of applying a little extra pressure?

BRIGGS: I trust that may not be necessary, sir. I—we—are relying on you to act like a gentleman.

(*Bell rings*)

Excuse me, I think that is his lordship's bell.

(*Sound of door opening*)

I beg your ladyship's pardon, I didn't see you coming in.

CAMILLA: Oh, Briggs, Lord Warbeck wants you to help him up to bed. He is rather tired.

BRIGGS: Very good, my lady.

(*Sound of door closing*)

ROBERT: I don't wonder father's tired if he's been listening to Mrs Barrett and Julius discussing the sugar duties.

CAMILLA: He managed to stand it longer than you, Robert, at any rate. Well, did the great discussion with Briggs go off satisfactorily?

ROBERT: Discussion, Camilla? What should we have a discussion about?

CAMILLA: About the wine for dinner tonight. I thought it was that that dragged you away from tea so reluctantly.

ROBERT: Oh, the wine! Yes, that's—that's laid on all right.

CAMILLA: I hope there's plenty. I mean to drink a lot tonight. I mean to get positively, completely blotto.

ROBERT: That will add enormously to your attractions.

CAMILLA: Well, they want adding to, don't they? I mean, they don't seem to have been very effective so far. (*Pause*) Robert, what is the matter with you?

ROBERT: Nothing, so far as I am aware.

CAMILLA: There *is* something, Robert. I wish you'd tell me. Can't you see I—I want to help you?

ROBERT: No thanks.

CAMILLA: Robert, you usen't to be like this. Something's happened. Something's come between us. I can't let you go like this. Look at me, Robert!

ROBERT: Leave go of me, Camilla! I warn you, leave go!

CAMILLA: Not until you've told me what it is. It's not too much to ask, to share your troubles, is it? Oh, Robert, if you only knew how I want—

ROBERT: (*brutally*) You want, you want! I know what you want, even if you don't!

CAMILLA: You're hurting me!

ROBERT: You want to be kissed—like this! (*Pause*) And *this*—and *this*! That's all for now, my lovely! I hope you're satisfied.

CAMILLA: Oh, you're hateful! hateful! I could kill you for this!

(*Door closes with a bang*)

NARRATOR: It is shortly before midnight. Sir Julius Warbeck, Mrs Barrett, Robert and Lady Camilla are in the drawing-room. All four have evidently dined well. Their faces are rather flushed and Lord Warbeck's excellent champagne has loosened their tongues. They have just finished a rubber of bridge and Sir Julius is adding up the scores.

(*Chatter*)

JULIUS: Let me see . . . Eight and six is fourteen, and carry one . . . That makes one pound four and five pence they owe us, Mrs Barrett. My congratulations!

MRS BARRETT: I'm sure you've added that up wrong! Give it to me. Seven and four's eleven, and ten's twenty-one—I told you so, it should be one pound four and ninepence! A pretty sort of Chancellor of the Exchequer you are!

JULIUS: (*laughs*) Well, well, one needn't be a dab at arithmetic to handle the state's finances, thank heaven! There was a Chancellor once who didn't know what decimal points were, and when he saw them—

MRS BARRETT: Yes, yes, Sir Julius, we all know that story. It's been the stock excuse of inefficient Chancellors ever since.

JULIUS: Are you suggesting that I am inefficient, Mrs Barrett?

MRS BARRETT: Oh no! I'm not suggesting anything.

JULIUS: Because if so, I was only going to say, that doesn't seem to be the view of that very loyal collaborator and colleague, your husband.

MRS BARRETT: My husband *is* loyal, Sir Julius—too loyal, I sometimes think, to consider his own interests. But since his name has been introduced into the discussion, may I say that I am sure I am not alone in regretting that the country's finances are not in *his* hands, instead of—

JULIUS: Instead of those of your humble servant, eh, Mrs Barrett? Well, well, it's all in the luck of the game. I can only say this, that should anything happen to our revered Prime Minister—which Heaven forfend—and it were to fall to me to form an administration, as it might—as it might—I should not need to look for my Chancellor beyond my old friend John Barrett.

ROBERT: (*somewhat tipsy*) Hear, hear, Julius! Hear, hear!

CAMILLA: Did you say one pound four and ninepence, Mrs Barrett? I've got it here exactly.

(*Chink of coins*)

MRS BARRETT: How honourable of you!

ROBERT: Afraid I haven't any cash on me, Julius. It's a commodity rather scarce in *this* branch of the family. Will you take a cheque?

JULIUS: Of course, my dear boy, of course.

ROBERT: All right, I'll give you one. You don't mind it's being drawn on the account of the League of Liberty and Justice, I suppose?

JULIUS: Really, this is an outrage! To suggest that I should take money from such a gang! Let me tell you, young man, your association with this so-called League is putting you in danger—in grave danger.

ROBERT: Thanks for the warning, dear cousin. At any rate, *I* don't need a flat-footed copper to give me protection. Where is he, by the way? Lurking outside the door, I suppose, with his little notebook and pencil in his hand. Let's have him in! Perhaps he'd lend me one pound four and ninepence!

CAMILLA: Robert, don't be so silly! I'll pay Sir Julius for you, if you like.

ROBERT: What a beautifully forgiving nature you have, Camilla! Almost thou persuadest me—but don't stand just there. You're right under the mistletoe, and I'm sure you don't want a repetition of this afternoon's sad scene. Let me get at the door.

(*Sound of door opening*)

Oh! It's you, Briggs!

BRIGGS: Yes, Mr Robert. It only wants a few minutes to midnight. I've brought the champagne to drink in the festive season.

ROBERT: That's the spirit! Let's keep up tradition while we may!

The last Christmas in the old home—thanks to cousin Julius! Fill up the glasses, Briggs, and give yourself one, too.

BRIGGS: Very good, Mr Robert.

(*Pop of champagne cork and sound of pouring*)

ROBERT: Where's the protecting angel, Briggs? He ought to be in on this.

BRIGGS: The detective-sergeant, sir, is refreshing himself in the servants' hall. I think that he will be more at home there. Your glass, my lady.

CAMILLA: Thank you.

BRIGGS: And yours, madam.

MRS BARRETT: Thank you.

BRIGGS: Sir Julius.

JULIUS: Thanks.

BRIGGS: Mr Robert, your glass. (*Meaningfully*) It is almost time.

ROBERT: (*more and more wildly*) Time marches on! But we've forgotten something, Briggs. The curtains are still drawn and the window shut. That won't do on Christmas Eve. We've got to let Christmas in!

BRIGGS: It's bitter cold outside, sir, and snowing hard.

ROBERT: What does that matter, man? There's a tradition at stake! Let's have those curtains back—

(*Sound of pulling curtains*)

—and the window open.

(*Sound of opening window*)

Now, hark! Can't you hear them? (*Pause*) Come close to the window, everybody. Closer! Camilla! Briggs! Lean out, everyone! Come on, Julius, the cold air won't hurt you! Can you hear them now?

(*Distant sound of church bells*)

Warbeck chimes! Ringing in Christmas, ringing out the Warbecks! Except for fat cousin Julius, who'll always be in on everything! Now listen, all of you! I've an announcement to make! An important announcement! You mustn't miss it, Camilla!

(*As he speaks a clock begins to chime the hour. It continues to strike twelve during the rest of the scene*)

Christmas! We must have our toast first. Where the hell's my glass? Someone's moved it. Where did I leave my glass, Briggs?

BRIGGS: It's on the card table, Mr Robert.

ROBERT: Ah, here it is. Are you all ready? Here's to Warbeck Hall, God help the old place!

ALL: Warbeck Hall!

(*There is the sound of a glass shattering*)

ROBERT: (*in a strangled voice*) What is it? I—

(*There is the sound of a body falling to the floor*)

CAMILLA: (*shrieks*) Robert!

JULIUS: What's happened?

MRS BARRETT: He's fainted.

BRIGGS: (*slowly*) He is dead.

(*The clock finishes striking*)

(*Music*)

NARRATOR: It is next morning. The scene is once more the library, but the sofa on which Lord Warbeck was lying the previous afternoon is now unoccupied. This time it is Sir Julius who is looking out of the window at the snow. There has been a further heavy fall in the night, and the countryside is everywhere deeply covered. Sir Julius turns from the window with a sigh as Briggs comes into the room.

JULIUS: Ah, Briggs, here you are! How is Lord Warbeck?

BRIGGS: He has stood the shock wonderfully well, Sir Julius, considering, but I am afraid he is not long for this world.

JULIUS: This is a terrible situation, terrible! Is there no chance of getting a doctor out to him?

BRIGGS: I should judge that it will take at least two days to clear the road, Sir Julius, even if there are no further falls meanwhile. But I doubt whether a doctor could do much for him.

JULIUS: This—this is a very embarrassing situation for me, Briggs.

BRIGGS: For you, Sir Julius? Quite so, no doubt. I confess I find my own position somewhat awkward. It is not a very easy one for any of us. Will you be requiring me any further, Sir Julius?

JULIUS: No, thank you, Briggs.

(*Sound of door closing*)

What am I to do? Oh, what *am* I to do?

(*Sound of door opening*)

ROGERS: Excuse me, sir.

JULIUS: Yes, Sergeant Rogers, what is it?

ROGERS: I have succeeded, sir, in making contact with the county police on the telephone.

JULIUS: Good, good. How soon will thy be here?

ROGERS: Well, sir, they are doing their best to get through, but it must take some considerable time, and meanwhile—sir—

JULIUS: Well?

ROGERS: I find myself in rather an awkward position, sir.

JULIUS: You're the second person who has made that remark to me already this morning. What's *your* trouble?

ROGERS: They have expressed a desire that I should meanwhile undertake the investigation into Mr Warbeck's death, sir.

JULIUS: Well, why not? You're a detective, after all, aren't you? I should think it's your duty.

ROGERS: Quite so, sir. But duties sometimes conflict.

JULIUS: Eh?

ROGERS: I look at it this way, sir. My duty is to protect you. Now, sir, the enquiries I have made so far—quite unofficially, of course—have established certain facts. Firstly, Mr Warbeck was murdered. Secondly, he was murdered by the administration of poison—probably cyanide of potassium—in his glass of champagne while he was opening the window of the drawing-room. Thirdly, *any* of the persons present might have poisoned the champagne while the attention of the others was distracted by Mr Warbeck's behaviour. And finally, sir—

JULIUS: Well?

ROGERS: Well, sir, I can't altogether shut my eyes to the fact that you are now the heir to Lord Warbeck, who himself may die at any moment.

JULIUS: But—

ROGERS: It would be a rather irregular situation, sir, if I were to find myself arresting the minister whom I had been detailed to protect.

JULIUS: This is preposterous! You can't imagine that I should kill anyone in order to get into the House of Lords?

ROGERS: I must confess, sir, the idea had occurred to me.

JULIUS: Then get it out of your head at once! As if I wasn't in a bad enough position already! Where is the telephone? I must get through to the Prime Minister immediately!

ROGERS: (*slowly*) The Prime Minister?

JULIUS: Yes, the Prime Minister! He must know at once. This business is serious. Why, it may wreck the Government!

ROGERS: (*slowly*) Yes, sir. I suppose if you put it that way, it might.

JULIUS: What are you gaping for, you fool? Where is the telephone?

ROGERS: (*Briskly*) I beg your pardon, sir, I was thinking. The police state that all the trunk lines are down, so you won't be able to get through to Chequers yet. But it doesn't signify. I must have a word with Mr Briggs. Will you excuse me?

(*Door closes*)

JULIUS: Has the man gone mad?

(*Sound of door opening*)

MRS BARRETT: Oh, Sir Julius, there you are! What a dreadful business this is! Briggs tells me that the roads are all completely blocked, and we may be shut up for days. What could have possessed that poor young man to kill himself, do you think? I do wish my husband was here, he would know what to do. I feel I am in such an—

JULIUS: An awkward position, Mrs Barrett. I know. But what makes you think that Robert killed himself?

MRS BARRETT: But he must have, Sir Julius, mustn't he? I mean, we all saw him.

JULIUS: Sergeant Rogers thinks that he was murdered.

MRS BARRETT: Murdered? Oh, how shocking!

JULIUS: Where is Lady Camilla?

MRS BARRETT: Oh, but you can't think that she could have done such a thing, surely, Sir Julius? Of course, I've known for some time that he *had* treated her very badly, but still—a young girl like that! No, if you ask me, if it was anybody, it would be Briggs. After all, he poured out the champagne, and only yesterday I did overhear him speaking to Robert in a most disrespectful way. Oh dear, it frightens me to think of it. I'm sure I shan't be able to eat any lunch if he waits at table!

JULIUS: Well, if it's any consolation to you, Mrs Barrett, Rogers seems inclined to think that I am the guilty party.

MRS BARRETT: (*with a laugh*) Oh, ridiculous, Sir Julius! (*Pause*) Still—of course—I do see what he means.

(*Sound of door opening*)

Camilla, dear, have you been with poor Lord Warbeck?

CAMILLA: (*in a dead tired voice*) Yes.

MRS BARRETT: Sir Julius and I were just saying—what were we saying, exactly?

JULIUS: I don't know that I was saying anything very much. Mrs Barrett was engaged in distributing suspicion for causing Robert's death between me, Briggs and yourself.

CAMILLA: I'm afraid I don't find that very funny. You see, I loved Robert—and yet, up to a few moments before he died

I was wishing him dead. Now I just wish I was dead—that's all.

MRS BARRETT: Oh Camilla, that's a very dangerous thing to say. Suppose the police were to hear you? That reminds me, Sir Julius, that man Rogers—is he safe? I don't like his looks at all.

JULIUS: My dear lady, Rogers is a police officer who has undertaken the duty of investigating this crime.

MRS BARRETT: Didn't you tell me he had been concerned with suppressing this League of Liberty and Justice that Robert was mixed up in? Suppose he thought the best way of suppressing the League was by—

(*Sound of door opening*)

BRIGGS: May Sergeant Rogers have a word with you, Sir Julius?

JULIUS: Yes, of course, Briggs. I'll see him in my room.

ROGERS: I would prefer to talk to you here, sir, in the presence of all the others, if you don't mind. I only want to put a question or two about last night's occurrences which will be of general interest.

JULIUS: I have no objection at all. Goodness knows, I have nothing to hide.

ROGERS: I am much obliged, sir. First, then, am I right in thinking that Mr Warbeck was in the act of proposing a toast when he died?

JULIUS: Quite right. The toast was 'Warbeck Hall', I remember.

ROGERS: That was just on the stroke of midnight, was it not?

JULIUS: I think so, yes.

CAMILLA: Yes. He was in the middle of saying something else when the clock began to strike.

ROGERS: Something else? What was it?

JULIUS: We don't know, of course. He said something about an announcement.

CAMILLA: Yes, that's right. He had an announcement to make.

ROGERS: Can you throw any light, sir, on what the announcement was that he was about to make?

JULIUS: I haven't the slightest idea. How should I?

ROGERS: Can anybody in this room tell me what Mr Warbeck
was going to announce when he died?

(*A pause*)

BRIGGS: Yes, I can.

JULIUS: You, Briggs?

BRIGGS: Yes, Sir Julius.

ROGERS: What was it?

BRIGGS: If you will excuse me for one moment, Sir Julius, I
have somebody here who can explain the matter better than
I can.

(*Sound of door opening*)

MRS BARRETT: What in the world is all this about?

BRIGGS: This way, my dear.

(*Sound of door closing*)

JULIUS: What on earth . . . ?

CAMILLA: Who is this woman?

BRIGGS: My daughter Susan, my lady.

CAMILLA: What right has she to be here?

BRIGGS: The announcement which Mr Robert was about to
make, my lady, was that of his marriage to my daughter.

CAMILLA: So that was it! (*Fiercely*) Married—to you!

SUSAN: (*uneducated voice, but with a certain dignity*) We were
married twelve months ago, my lady, at the Paddington
Register Office. I have my marriage certificate here to prove
it, if you want to see it.

JULIUS: Is there a child?

SUSAN: Three months old, Sir Julius. He's in the house now.

JULIUS: (*Eagerly*) He? It's a boy, then?

SUSAN: (*proudly and with emphasis*) Yes, sir—a lovely boy.

JULIUS: Thank heaven for that!

CAMILLA: Robert's son!

MRS BARRETT: I can't bear it! Oh, I can't bear it!

(*Sound of running feet*)

ROGERS: Stop that woman!

(*Sound of door slamming. Then sound of trying to open door*)

She's locked the door! Where does this lead to?

BRIGGS: The gun-room. I'll go round the other way.

(*Sound of door opening and closing*)

ROGERS: Open this door!

(*Sound of trying to open door*)

Open this door!

(*A loud explosion from outside. A pause. Then the sound of door being unlocked*)

BRIGGS: I was too late, Mr Rogers. Mrs Barrett has shot herself.

JULIUS: I don't understand. Do you mean that Mrs Barrett—?

ROGERS: Mrs Barrett, sir, was the murderer of Robert Warbeck.

JULIUS: I can't believe it. Mrs Barrett? She had no grudge against him, surely?

ROGERS: Not against him, sir, but against you.

JULIUS: Against me? I still don't follow.

ROGERS: Until a few moments ago, sir, you believed yourself to be Lord Warbeck's heir, did you not?

JULIUS: Yes, I did.

ROGERS: And likely to succeed to the title at any moment?

JULIUS: Quite.

ROGERS: I don't think you looked forward to the prospect of going to the House of Lords?

JULIUS: I should think not. It would have meant my resigning my post in the Government.

ROGERS: Because the Chancellor of the Exchequer must be a member of the House of Commons, is that not so?

JULIUS: Of course. Everybody knows that.

ROGERS: I don't know about everybody, sir, but Mrs Barrett certainly did. And if you were compelled to resign, who would succeed you in the Chancellorship, do you suppose, sir?

JULIUS: Why, of course—it would be Barrett! There's no question of that.

ROGERS: Exactly, sir. And Mrs Barrett was a woman who was prepared to do anything to further her husband's career. She chose this way to clear the obstacle which you presented from his path, by sending you to the House of Lords against your will. When you were so anxious to telephone to the Prime Minister just now, I suddenly saw what her motive was. But I had reason to think that unknown to either of you Mr Warbeck had left a son, so that in fact you were not the next heir to the peerage.

JULIUS: Oh, and what made you think that?

ROGERS: Well, sir, there are advantages to a detective living in the servants' hall, you know, sir. I ascertained the truth from Mr Briggs and arranged with him to confront Mrs Barrett with the child. I thought that when she realised that her crime had failed in its purpose she would give herself away—and so she did, with a vengeance.

CAMILLA: Poor woman, poor woman!

SUSAN: Ah, it's easy to say that of *her*, my lady, but it's those that are left behind that need pity most, I think.

CAMILLA: (*reflectively*) Those that are left behind . . . (*impulsively*) Susan, I'd like to come and see your baby, if I may.

SUSAN: You're welcome, my lady. He's ever so sweet, and just like his father.

JULIUS: Take great care of that child, young woman! Why, my whole political career depends on him!

CYRIL HARE

Best known to readers of detective fiction under the pseudonym 'Cyril Hare', Alfred Alexander Gordon Clark was born in 1900 in southern England. For around thirty years he led what might be described as a double life: as a highly respected lawyer; and as the author of nine superb novel-length detective mysteries as well as many criminous short stories.

Gordon Clark's legal career followed broadly conventional lines. He became a barrister in 1924 and practised on civil and criminal cases. During the Second World War he joined the Public Prosecutions Department and in later years served as a County Court Judge in Surrey, the county of his birth. Gordon Clark's first novel, *Tenant for Death* (1937), featured the Scotland Yard detective Inspector Mallett, while his fourth, *Tragedy at Law* (1942), introduced Francis Pettigrew, an ageing barrister who is based at least in part on Clark himself. Mallett and Pettigrew appear in several novels together but also tackle mysteries independently. While it features neither Mallett nor Pettigrew, one of Gordon Clark's best books is the elegiac *An English Murder* (1951), which was derived from the radio play, 'The Murder at Warbeck Hall'. Gordon Clark died in 1957.

The Murder at Warbeck Hall was first broadcast on the BBC Light Programme on 27 January 1948 as the second in a series of plays specially written for the BBC by Agatha Christie, Anthony

Gilbert and other members of the Detection Club, which 'Cyril Hare' had joined in 1946. This is its first publication.

THE HOUSE OF THE POPLARS

Dorothy L. Sayers

Adrian Belford, emerging from the offices of Messrs Golding & Moss, Financiers, hesitated uncertainly at the corner of Conduit Street and Bond Street. There was a heavy coldness at the pit of his stomach, and his tongue felt dry. He had, indeed, succeeded in getting the loan renewed, but for one month only, and at what a cost! He could see now Mr Golding's deprecatory smile, the spreading of his plump fingers with their heavy rings that winked in the lamplight. He heard himself saying, with an effort at easy bravado, 'It is good security, Mr Golding'; heard the smooth, thick sibilants of Mr Golding's reply: 'No thecurity ith abtholutely thound, Mithter Belford that dependth upon a lady'th caprithe—eh?' The swine!

If ever a fool, thought Mr Belford, had been called upon to pay heavily for his follies, he was that fool. There was his marriage to a plain and peevish invalid, far older than himself—only to find that the narrow hands whose clammy limpness had always displeased him could cling like limpets where money was concerned. Then there was that first unfortunate speculation in Megatherium Stock; then the long series of disasters attending his desperate efforts to recoup his losses; finally, the incredible suicide of mad Lord Ingleborough, whom everybody had expected to go lingering on for ever in his luxurious asylum. In two months' time the new Lord Ingleborough would be of age and would demand an account of the trust funds. In two months—

His limbs felt leaden, like those of a swimmer climbing out of deep water. Bond Street, with its close ranks of packed and palpitating traffic, roared in his ears, beat in his face, buffeted him. Men and women jostled upon the pavement, hurrying past him, pressing upon him. The glare of shop windows, a little diffused by the light October mist, was a cruelty to his eyeballs. Nothing was real. He, with his sick apprehensions, was the only living and suffering thing in a puppet show of painted masks and jerking movements and noise. He shrank back and shot his hunted glance to left and right of him. It was then that he noticed the restaurant.

It stood on the opposite side of Conduit Street, almost directly opposite the money-lender's premises. It was small and unpretentious, the lower half of its window discreetly veiled by a lace curtain, against which hung a framed menu. The upper half bore the legends: 'SANDWICH BAR—COCKTAIL BAR', silhouetted against the light within. Over the door hung a sign, bearing the single word 'Rapallo's'.

He glanced at his watch; it was a quarter to six. He had been over an hour screwing concessions out of the money-lender. Like an automaton he crossed Conduit Street and plunged into the restaurant. The door yielded easily to his touch and fell to behind him with a chuckling click. The place was suffocatingly warm, but it was quiet and almost deserted. A couple here and there sat eating American sandwiches at small tables. Occupying nearly half the available floor space was a vast semi-circular bar, gleaming with polished brass and mahogany. Behind it moved two barmen on soundless feet, taking down bottles from the glittering shelves, measuring, pouring, shaking. The lower murmur of conversation from the tables was punctuated by the musical tinkling of ice. Belford marched heavily up to the bar and demanded a large brandy and soda.

He drank it down and ordered a second, which he sipped slowly. He was beginning to feel better. The demure atmosphere of the place soothed him. The warmth of the brandy stole into his bones. The door clicked open and shut again with its cosy chuckle. A man joined him at the bar and asked for 'one of the usual'. The barman smiled slyly and secretly at him, as at a well-known patron and began his dainty manipulations. 'Like a chemist in his white coat,' thought Belford idly. He was reminded of his visit to the chemist that afternoon and patted his overcoat pocket to assure himself that the little bottle was still there.

The other man finished his cocktail and asked for a special variety of hot sandwich. When it came, he turned politely to Belford and requested him to pass the cayenne pepper.

'Have you tried one of these?' he added, pointing to his plate. 'They are a speciality here.'

Belford remembered that he had eaten next to nothing at lunch, and suddenly felt that he was hungry. He ordered the sandwich and sat absently playing with his empty glass. Presently he became aware that the stranger was talking—vague generalities about the political situation and the present state of England. He answered mechanically, trying in a subconscious way to 'place' the other man.

He was stout and dark, with a very high and polished skull, beneath which his features, chubby as a child's, seemed dwarfed into insignificance. He was dressed in a dark tweed suit with a stiff wing collar, which pushed the flesh of his chin up into a little pink roll. His hands were soft and white, and moved with delicate precision. On his watch chain he carried a curious emblem or charm, which led Belford to imagine that he might belong to some esoteric order. His hat, which he had taken off and laid on the bar, was a soft black felt, rather wide in the brim, and was the only part of his costume that departed in the least from the conventional. His voice was unusual, very soft and clear, with a kind of fluting sincerity.

'. . . And, of course, it is not capitalism that is the trouble,' he was saying. 'One cannot permanently equalise the distribution of wealth. If only those who had the money knew how to spend it. But they don't.'

Belford agreed.

'Rich men are dull dogs, mostly,' said the stranger. 'They hoard unwisely and they spend unwisely. The curse of Midas, my dear sir, was lack of imagination. If I were to be given a million pounds tomorrow, I should know how to make it yield a million pounds' worth of enjoyment. And so would you, would you not? If you were given a million pounds tomorrow—a hundred thousand, even—fifty thousand—'

'By God!' said Belford. 'I could do with it.' His sandwich was brought and he attacked it savagely. He found it good; curious and unexpected in flavour, but appetising.

The bald-headed man was talking again, but Belford interrupted him. He felt a violent need to unburden himself to somebody.

'Look here,' he said. 'How would you like to be me? I've got to get twenty thousand in two months' time or blow my brains out. I can't get anything more out of the money-lenders—I'm dipped too far already. And there's seventy-five thousand that belongs to me—that in justice and decency belongs to me—and I can't lay hands on it. What do you think of that?'

'That's hard,' said the stout man.

'My wife's ten years older than I am. I married her for her money; I admit it, and she knew it. What else would a man have married a plain and sickly middle-aged woman for? Mind you, I did my bit of the bargain. It wasn't my fault if the kid died and my wife turned into a permanent invalid. Why should she grudge me the very smell of her money? The income's all right and helps to keep the place going, but if I even suggest she might lend me—*lend* me a few thousands of the capital—you'd think I was asking for her life.'

The stout man nodded sympathetically and interjected an order to the barman.

'You'd better have one of these too,' he added. 'They're another speciality. They're not for the suburban palate, but they'd cheer up a five-year-old corpse.'

Belford said: 'All right,' and drink was put down before him. He lifted his glass and said, 'Here's how.' The stuff was queer, certainly—intensely bitter with fire beneath the bitterness. He was not sure if he liked it. He took it down quickly, like medicine.

'She says it will come to me when she dies, but what's the good of that? Creaking doors hang the longest. I've got to have money somehow. I daresay I was an ass to speculate, but it's done now and I can't undo it.' He bit savagely at his upper lip. 'Speculation—if she knew what I needed it for, she'd leave the stuff to a cats' home. She's religious. Religious! Let her husband go to prison rather than—'

He checked himself.

'Mind you, I don't say it's come to that. But what does she want the money for? What good's it to her? Missionary societies and doctors' stuff— that's all she gets out of it. That's a pretty wife for a man, isn't it? What am I to her? A cross between a male nurse and an errand boy, that's all. Forced to kowtow for fear of being cut out of her will. Running about with pills and potions and getting up at night to fill hot water bottles. Five hundred a year would give her all she wants—and she's worth seventy-five thousand.'

'What's the nature of her illness?'

'Damned if I know. Her doctor—oily hand I call him—gives a long name to it. Something to do with the kidneys or the spleen or something. And nerves, of course. They all have nerves nowadays. Also insomnia and all the rest of it. One of these damned tablets every blessed night in the year—not drug-taking, of course, oh, dear no! My wife is a religious woman. She wouldn't take drugs. Only a harmless pill to ensure natural sleep.'

He dragged the little bottle of veronal from his pocket and flung it on the bar counter. His head felt queer and he was conscious of a curious sensation of interior lightness, as though he were losing touch with realities. He realised dimly that he was talking too much. That odd cocktail must have been pretty potent.

The stranger smiled.

'Not altogether so harmless,' he said. 'One might easily take an overdose of that. She probably will one day. They often do, you know.'

'Think so?' said Belford. 'But she'd go to hell for that, you know. Straight to hell. "Where their worm dieth not".' He laughed. 'Worms, eh? That's a nice thing to think about.'

The stranger leaned towards him. Belford became intensely, seriously aware of his face, with every detail, every line, every tiny pore of the skin marked and individualised, like the pen strokes on a map. It was not a face—it was a continent. It was as wide as Asia, and he was an explorer upon its vast and uninhabited surface. For endless aeons he had been marching along its waste expanse, pitted with holes, ribbed with gullies. He stood at the mouth of a dark cavern, filled with trees, smooth and cylindrical, like hairs. He peered into it, as he had peered since the beginning of time, whose huge heartbeats he heard—tick tock, tick tock—incredible ages apart. Yet all around him the stealthy life of the restaurant went on. The barman was measuring a rainbow cocktail—pink, green, yellow—Belford suddenly realised the intense, the anxious importance of the comparative weight of liquids. Atoms, molecules, heating upward against the furious downward pressure of gravity. If the pink were to overflow into the green, the universe would be flung into chaos. He saw the bleak immensity of space, peopled by whirling planets over innumerable millions of miles, and all dependent upon that pink and green and yellow pinpoint—the ultimate focus of creation. He laughed. It was funny, it was enough to split your sides that he, and he only, should be in possession of that stupendous secret.

'Two months.' The stranger's voice floated over the abyss, clear as water. 'She will take an overdose before the two months are up. We can ensure that much for you, you know.'

The car sped through street after street, where swarms of men and women swam past like sea-creatures in a tank. At every bump it rose like a ship, riding huge combers. They were moving fast, they were racing at the speed of light. One hundred and eighty-six thousand miles a second. He could watch time spinning backwards, like a cinematograph film reeled out the wrong way. Yet nothing was blurred in their headlong flight. Lamp-post succeeded lamp-post, each one rigid as a soldier on parade, each one with its own mysterious character and importance. His companion was seated beside him, his face averted. He loomed gigantic, his shoulders had the exuberant mass of a sleeping elephant. Belford could hear the billowing outline of his back, like a symphony. It rolled out in striding harmonies. A persistent and birdlike trilling puzzled Belford for a moment, till he traced it to an artificial flower in a silver holder beside him. He felt feverish.

'It's rather hot, isn't it?' he said.

The stranger put down the window immediately. The air, rushing in, was cool and invigorating, like river water at dawn. Belford was filled with an utter peace and confidence. He had never before seen the beauty of the world so clearly. The smooth leather of the car's upholstery was a caress to his fingertips. He felt it slowly, luxuriously. It dipped to a hollow, held down by a round button. The exquisite significance of that button penetrated him with an inward ecstasy. He could feel the sense-processes and the thought-processes working swiftly and surely within him. The nerves sent up their urgent message, tingling along his arm. He felt the instant flurry of eager interpretation quickening the cells of his brain, threads of grey matter crossing and inter-crossing. This was what God felt—this endless awareness, stretching to the outer rim of universal consciousness. If a sparrow fell to the ground, he could feel it. He was sensitive to the movements of a microbe or a star. What absurdity to speak of small or great, as though greatness or smallness had any existence! He knew now that what the saints and sages had said was true—but none of them had ever known it as he knew it.

It was funny. It was absurd. Millions of men arguing and disputing—when *he* could tell them the whole truth of his own, intimate knowledge. But then, everything was funny. Everything had its absurdity, just as it had its beauty and its horror; there were no horrible or beautiful or absurd things; each one was horrible and beautiful and absurd at once, and quite separately. He must tell people about this. The telephone speaking-tube, curled over its iron bracket—it was ridiculous; it was the quintessence of absurdity. Gusts of laughter rolled up and suffocated him as he contemplated that preposterous speaking-tube. He pointed it out to his companion. Its curve as it hung there was a triumph of the incongruous. He shouted and whooped with laughter. One guffaw came breaking over the other like waves on a rocky shore. 'The laughter of the gods.' Stray phrases of Greek, forgotten since his school days, came back to him shining, clear-cut and luminous as jewels.

Exhausted with his own exuberance, he lay back in his corner. Every time the wheels turned, the cycle of existence turned through a thousand years. He was God, and he was unutterably lonely. And he was afraid. The stranger had turned and looked at him, and in that look he had seen unspeakable menace. Framed in the dark window of the car he now saw the river. He saw not merely its surface streaked with silver and hung over by brooding trees. He saw beneath the water where the bodies of the dead swam darkly, watched by the flat, round eyes of hungry pike. Small fish, too, devouring one another, struggling for life between the rank stems of the water-weeds, pursuing the dim unlovely things that grew fat upon contamination and sewage. The moon was coming up over a long bank of cloud. The cloud was steeped in silver behind, and he saw through and over it, but on the hither side it was black. Terror held him in chains of iron, so that he could not cry out.

The river had gone, and the moon. The car had stopped. He climbed out of it and stood before a high stone wall, extending right and left for ever. The chauffeur was unlocking the gates. They were enormous. They soared away above his head, so that his neck ached when he tried to see the tops of them. They were green in the headlights. Written across them in bold white letters were the words:

SMITH & SMITH

and underneath, in a smaller script:

REMOVALS

His companion took him by the arm and led him forward. They moved very slowly; each step lasted a week and stretched for a mile. On either side of him, tall poplar trees stood in a whispering avenue. How they talked, leaf chattering to leaf in a continual sibilant chorus! The wind shook them and a leaf fell, slowly, turning and twisting and floating in a dance of inexpressible grace and loveliness. Tears came into his eyes to think that so much wonder could exist. It was heart-rending, and it was beautiful. And all in a moment he was a small boy walking with his nurse along the Cherwell Banks in the grounds of Magdalen College, smelling the sweet, astringent smell of the poplar leaves.

The scent rose from the wet earth all about him. His soul ached at it. Then, miles away, glimmering out at the end of the avenue he saw the house of the poplars and knew that he had reached the ultimate significance of all his past and future. Here, since first he stirred in his mother's womb, the house had stood and waited for him.

He passed over the threshold.

Three men sat about a table. One of them was tall and thin, with sparse red hair and a straggling sandy beard. He sniggered when he spoke.

'This is Dr Schmidt,' said Belford's companion.

'Delighted,' said Dr Schmidt. 'It is very good of my friend Mr Smith to have brought you.' He sniggered. 'On my right is Mr Smyth. He spells it with a Y.'

Mr Smyth smiled. He had a narrow, dark face marked with a long white scar as though it had been splashed with acid.

'It is a pleasure,' said he, 'to welcome a new client. Mr Smythe will agree with me, I am sure. He spells his name with a Y and an E.'

The fourth man grunted. He was square and sallow, and his strong hands had short fingers and hairy knuckles.

'Mr Belford requires a little assistance,' said Mr Smith. 'He is troubled with a wife. A wife can be so unnecessary. It is obviously a case for removal.'

'We undertake removals,' said Dr Schmidt.

'They are a speciality of the house,' said Mr Smyth.

'Perfect discretion, and distance no object,' muttered Mr Smythe.

'What are the lady's habits?' enquired Dr Schmidt. He sniggered again. 'How often do I not warn people that it is unwise to contract habits, but they do not listen.'

'The lady's habits come into your department, I fancy, doctor,' said Mr Smith.

Belford listened as though from a great distance to the details of his own story. The bottle of tablets was in the hands of Mr Smith. Probably he had kept them ever since Belford had handed them to him that evening, centuries ago, in Rapallo's. But this was a trifle, after all. His attention wandered to the little tune that was being tapped out by the pattern of the tablecloth. It had a note like a xylophone, very bell-like and delicate, and it rippled out a tinny pastoral melody full of the scent of cowslips and newly-budded hawthorn.

Dr Schmidt was speaking.

'Ten-grain doses. Fifty tablets and fifty nights. And two months to go. That is easy.'

Mr Smith turned to Belford.

'Listen,' he said. 'If your wife were to take a fatal overdose within the next fifty days, would it be worth five hundred pounds to you?'

Extreme clarity of mind came back to Belford in a rush. He spoke precisely, articulating each syllable. It pleased him to feel vowel and consonant marching so orderly from teeth and tongue.

'It would be exquisitely worth it,' he said. 'I stand to receive seventy-five thousand pounds under her will. That would square Ingleborough and put me straight with my debtors. I could easily spare five hundred pounds.'

He made a gesture with his hands. Five hundred pounds in minted gold, running and jingling over the table. Not paper money, but gold. Under his feet he saw deep into the earth, where miners stooped and sweated to drag out the ore for him. Steamers and the noise of the dockyards—leagues of ocean—the work of the world bringing the wealth of the world to his feet. He saw the pictures best without ever losing sight of the quiet room and the four faces clustered beneath that lamplight. Only, on the screen of his imagination, the moving map of the something was mightily unrolled.

'Very good,' said Mr Smith. 'You have your cheque book with

you? You will write us a cheque for £500, payable—we will allow a margin—fifty-six days from now. That will bring us to the 17th of December—eight weeks precisely. The removal, you understand, may take place earlier, but in no case later than fifty-six days hence, when the cheque will be presented. That is fair, I think. If, between now and the day of the removal you should change your mind, you have only to leave word for me at Rapallo's; but when once the removal has occurred it would be unwise to endeavour to stop the cheque. We take our precautions, of course. Have you been abroad lately, by the way?'

'I was in Germany last May.'

Dr Schmidt sniggered and rose from the table.

'You need not hesitate to sign,' went on Mr Smith. 'It is our pleasure as well as our business to provide these easy little accommodations for our clients. Make it out, please, to Smith & Smith. Thank you—that is admissible. It is remarkable how readily these trifling difficulties can be removed with a stroke of the pen.'

Belford contemplated his signature. The bold outline of the B pleased him, the swaggering lift and drop of the l and f, and the flourish of the final d. Ludicrous, that he should have suffered so long and so acutely, when that powerful pen-shape on a slip of pink paper could set him free.

'Anything more?' he asked.

'Only your name to the Removal Order,' said Mr Smith.

He sighed again, happily. The paper began 'Order to Remove'—then came a blank space, with a dotted line at the bottom on which his freshly written name stood out blackly. Mr Smith took the paper from him and filled in at his dictation his wife's name and address and a date—'on or before the 17th of December'. The laughter that had seized on him before had him in its grip again. He bellowed, clinging to the table for support.

'Do you know what time you came home last night, Adrian?' demanded Mrs Belford, peevishly. Without waiting for a reply she went on, 'It was a quarter past three in the morning. I will not have these hours kept in my house. There is no godly or respectable occupation that could detain you so long. What can the servants think of you?'

Belford smiled. He knew that it had been past three o'clock when he returned. The white face of the clock on the landing had struck him as exceptionally ludicrous with its hands all askew and its two round winder-holes goggling at him like reproving eyes. Time had stood still for him during the centuries which it had taken him to climb the interminable staircase. He had slept in the House of the Poplars, and dreamed—what dreams! Even now he chuckled over these fantastic dreams.

'It's nothing to laugh at,' said Mrs Belford. 'I can only imagine that you were—intoxicated. It is most disgusting. Did you even remember to bring home my tablets?'

This staggered Belford. Had he done so? Or had he left them in the hands of the sniggering German doctor? He put his hand to his coat pocket, drew out a small package, wrapped in white paper and sealed at both ends with sealing wax. He stared at it. He so distinctly remembered having unwrapped it in the restaurant.

Mrs Belford twitched it from him.

'At any rate, I am glad you were not so lost to decency as to leave that behind.' She broke the seals and extracted the bottle, setting it upright on the bedside table. 'Fortunately, I still had two or three tablets in the old bottle. Otherwise, I suppose, I might have lain awake in agony all night as far as you were concerned.'

'Why don't you get the stuff from Mullings, instead of depending on me?' enquired Belford, impatiently.

'I have told you before, I do not care to have my affairs known to the local chemist. Mullings is a perfect centre of gossip. And that is not the point. Is there any reason why you should object to performing a trifling service for your own wife?'

'None whatever,' said Belford, cheerfully. He felt curiously well and happy that morning. Whatever it was that he had drunk at Rapallo's, it certainly left no hangover. The only reminder of his curious mental condition the night before was a tendency to see the funny side of everything. It was with difficulty that he checked a guffaw.

'I suppose it is useless to ask you where you were or what you were doing?' pursued Mrs Belford.

'I met a man and dined with him. We talked business.' Belford was amused. He looked down at his wife and, with a recurrence of that extraordinary clarity of vision, his eyes seemed to pierce her sallow skin and watch the sluggish and diseased blood as it pumped along the arteries, gathering up God-knew-what poisons by the way.

'See that it doesn't occur again,' said Mrs Belford. 'If this kind of thing is going to become habitual, I shall be forced to take steps. My dear father, who amassed his little fortune by hard work and sober living, would turn in his grave to think of its passing into the hands of a drunkard and debauchee.'

Belford again controlled his twitching laughter-muscles, and apologised. 'The happy hypocrite.' What a good phrase that was, and how well it expressed him. He ran down the stairs on escaping from the sick-room. Indeed, he seemed to float. His feet scarcely touched the treads. He was so buoyant that he could have skimmed right out of the front door on the wings.

His delicious hilarity lasted all day. He astonished his typists and clerks by his pleasant humour. He had only one disagreeable moment, when he took out his private cheque-book to pay a small personal bill. There was a blank counterfoil. He stared at it. Had he really given that cheque for £500 to Smith & Smith? His memory was not at fault; he remembered clearly everything that had happened, up to his falling asleep in the House of the Poplars. He remembered it—but he had not really believed in it. But the cheque was gone. 'Order to Remove'—'on or before

17th December'—'If you should change your mind, leave a message at Rapallo's'—'It would be unwise to change your mind after the Removal has occurred.' A nauseating feeling of horror rose up from some black deep of his subconsciousness. But it passed, and left him laughing at himself.

Three or four times during the next six weeks he returned to Conduit Street and walked past Rapallo's. Once he went in and ordered a sandwich and a glass of beer. A different pair of barmen were on duty, and he saw nothing of any Mr Smith. He came out without leaving any message. If he had had any fixed intention of doing so, the ominous sign of 'Golding & Moss, Financiers', just visible over the lace curtain, would have deterred him. In any case, it was absurd to suppose that Smith & Smith, or Brown, Jones & Robinson, could possibly influence his wife to take an overdose of medicine. As for the cheque, if he had really drawn it, it could make no difference. Bankruptcy and disgrace are bankruptcy and disgrace; and £500 one way or another was a drop in the bucket.

And, after all, the weeks went by and nothing happened. He began to make necessary arrangements. He drew out what remained of his current account and mentioned to his wife that he had business which called him to Germany. He left on November 20th. He went to the hotel in Berlin where he had stayed before. One must have an address, if one were not to arouse premature suspicion. Later, if nothing happened at the last moment to render it unnecessary, he could disappear quietly.

For he still had dreams. They came to him at night, or walking under the lime trees, past the restaurants where still a few tables stood outside in the crisp autumn air. The leaves being late that year, sometimes a solitary one, blown from the dry twig where it lingered, would flutter with lingering, exquisite grace to his feet, reminding him, so that he seemed to smell the resinous sharp scent of poplars.

He dreamed that one morning they would bring a telegram

to his bedside, summoning him home, because his wife had been taken ill suddenly in the night. He would take the steamer. He would drive through the foggy London streets. And when he got to his house, he would find the blinds drawn down.

On the morning of December 2nd, they brought a telegram to his bedside, summoning him home. His wife had been taken ill suddenly in the night.

It has not occurred to Belford that there would have to be an inquest. It all passed off, however, extremely well. The deceased lady had been a sufferer from a painful complaint affecting the kidneys and had been accustomed to take each night a tablet containing 10 grains of veronal, to allay pain and induce sleep. A second medical man agreed that veronal was a powerful hypnotic and usually harmless in the pharmacopeial dose. Dr Lovett affirmed that he had repeatedly warned Mrs Belford against taking more than the prescribed dose, particularly as the disease from which she suffered made her particularly susceptible to veronal poisoning. As a matter of fact, the ordinary minimum fatal dose of the drug was 50 grains, so that, if the patient had accidentally taken two tablets instead of one, the consequences should not have been serious. He had, however, out of precaution, made it clear to her that the single tablet was not on any account to be exceeded within the 24 hours, and she had appeared perfectly to understand this.

The bottle was produced. The maid, Maggie Brown, recollected that this had been brought home by Mr Belford on the morning of October 25th. It was then intact, with its mouth sealed over with wax, just as it came from the chemist. She had seen the original wrapper with the chemist's label lying on the bedside table. Mrs Belford had not begun to take the tablets till two days later, having still two tablets left from the former supply.

A representative of a firm of chemists in the City identified the bottle and the label. He remembered selling it to Mr Belford in person on October 25th. The mouth of the bottle had been stoppered with wax, as it had come from the wholesalers. The bottle contained 50 tablets, each containing 10 grains of veronal.

The analyst gave evidence. He had examined the body of deceased and found that she had died from taking an overdose of veronal. From the amount of the drug found in the viscera he concluded that she had taken at least 100 grains, or about twice the minimum fatal dose.

He had also analysed the tablets remaining in the bottle, and had found them to contain each exactly 10 grains of veronal. There were five tablets left in the bottle. If Mrs Belford had started taking the tablets on October 28th and had taken one each night regularly, there should have been 15 remaining. If Mrs Belford had taken ten tablets instead of one on the night of December 1st, that would account for the amount of veronal estimated to have been present in the body.

The coroner said that this appeared to be a very clear case. Deceased, who seemed to be in her usual health on December 1st, had been found dead on the morning of December 2nd of acute veronal poisoning. From the circumstance that there were 10 tablets fewer in the bottle than there ought to have been, there seemed to be no room for doubt that the unfortunate lady, failing to obtain her accustomed relief from pain and sleeplessness, had unhappily taken an overdose, the effects of which had been intensified by the kidney complaint from which she suffered. No blame could attach to Dr Lovatt who, unable to wean his patient from the drug that gave her so much relief, had frequently warned her against its misuse. There was no evidence whatever that Mrs Belford had at any time had any intention of doing herself an injury. On the day before her death, she had spoken cheerfully about the return of her husband from Germany. Mr Belford, with whom they must all feel the deepest sympathy, had testified to the uniformly harmonious relations between himself and his wife, and there was no evidence that the deceased had any domestic or financial trouble playing upon her mind.

The jury brought in a verdict of Death by Misadventure.

On December 18th, Mr Belford, having adjusted matters satisfactorily with all his creditors, came down to breakfast with a good appetite. Beside his plate lay a type-written envelope. He opened it and saw, with a curious pang of apprehension, the printed heading:

SMITH & SMITH—REMOVALS.

(There was no address.)

> Dear Sir,—with reference to your esteemed order of the 25th October for a Removal from your private address, we trust that this commission has been carried out to your satisfaction. We beg you to acknowledge your obliging favour of five hundred pounds (£500) and return herewith the Order of Removal which you were good enough to hand to us. Assuring you of our best attention at all times,
>
>   Faithfully yours,
>
>   Smith & Smith

He turned curiously to the enclosure. It bore his signature, but he had no recollection of having seen it before. It ran:

> I, Adrian Belford of (here followed his address) hereby confess that I murdered my wife, Catherine Elizabeth Belford, in the following manner. Knowing that she was in the habit of taking each night a tablet containing 10 gs. of veronal, a compound of diethyl barbituric acid, I opened a bottle of these tablets and removed 10 of them, substituting a single tablet, containing 10 gs. of a new barbituric acid compound which, giving a

similar chemical reaction to veronal, is ten times more powerful in hypnotic effect. The result of this would be that, on taking this tablet, as she was in due course bound to do, my wife would consume a dose of 10 gs. of the new compound equal to 100 gs. of the ordinary tablets, or twice the minimum fatal dose. The fatal tablet was prepared for me, in anticipation of these events, by the Gesellschaft Schmidt of Berlin, during my visit to Germany last May, of course in ignorance of the purpose for which it was required. My reason for committing this crime was that I had misappropriated certain trust monies belonging to the Ingleborough estate, and desired to replace them from the estate to which I was entitled under my late wife's will.

I make this confession, being troubled in my conscience.

Adrian Belford

17th December 193—

With shaking hands Belford thrust letter and enclosure into the fire.

DOROTHY L. SAYERS

Dorothy L. Sayers (1893–1957) needs little introduction. Though she wrote comparatively few novels and short stories, they form an impressively consistent and enjoyable body of work, second only perhaps to that by Agatha Christie.

Without Sayers, Sherlockian scholarship would not be the flourishing pseudo-academic field it is today. And the Detection Club—founded by her contemporary Anthony Berkeley—would have languished as nothing more than a dining society for crime writers without the many collaborative books and radio serials that Sayers initiated as one of the Club's most active members and as its President. Without Sayers' reviews and penetrating insights into the art and artifice of the detective story, the genre would surely not have developed internationally as a field of academic study. *And* without the protean aristocrat Lord Peter Wimsey there would almost certainly be no Campion, no Dalgliesh and no Lynley, to name but a few of the detectives whose character and approach bear some mark of Sayers' sleuth.

Sayers also wrote widely in many genres and, for some of her admirers, her crime stories and her studies of the genre are merely a distraction from even greater achievements: her analyses of Christian doctrine and her translations of Dante. For the majority, however, the reverse is certainly true.

There is the Wimsey canon—twenty-one short stories and eleven novels, several of which were memorably televised, first with Ian Carmichael (*Lord Peter Wimsey*, 1972–1975), and subsequently with Edward Petherbridge (*A Dorothy L. Sayers Mystery*, 1987). There are also the delightful stories of Montague Egg, a travelling wine salesman, and various non-series stories, the foremost being the extraordinary 'Blood Sacrifice'. As with the best of her contemporaries, Sayers draws on tropes of the genre—the impossible crime, the invisible weapon and so on—to create puzzles that remain as entertainingly baffling today as when they were first published, in some cases nearly a century ago. And as with Charles Dickens, her work is peppered with memorable characters, not the least of whom is the detective novelist Harriet Vane, in many ways a self-portrait of Sayers.

'Smith and Smith, Removals: I. The House of the Poplars' by Dorothy L. Sayers is a previously unpublished manuscript held by the Marion E. Wade Center, Wheaton College, IL, USA, which has the largest and most comprehensive collection of published and unpublished resources by and about Sayers worldwide. The original manuscript is twenty-eight handwritten pages with revisions by Sayers; the Wade Center manuscript number is DLS/MS-187. It was the first of two stories written by Sayers in the 1920s featuring the removals firm of Smith and Smith. The other, 'The Leopard Lady', was collected in *In the Teeth of the Evidence* (1939) and filmed with Boris Karloff for the American television series *Lights Out* in 1950.

THE HAMPSTEAD MURDER

Christopher Bush

It can be an absorbing undertaking, when the means are available, to trace to their original sources events which have proved momentous and to discover how trivial were the small beginnings that set them in motion. Even the hydrogen bomb can be traced directly back to a murder in Sarajevo. All our lives are shot through with the most incredible of coincidences. You happen to change the direction of a walk and you meet someone who changes the direction of your life.

The Hampstead Murder was a case in point. A man in Scotland wrote a letter to *The Times* and, by chance, *The Times* found it interesting enough to print. Because of that letter, which had nothing whatever to do with murder, a woman was strangled in a London suburb. You may not recall that murder. It created no excitement and never got into the headlines. The woman was found with a noose around her neck, and the killing could have been accomplished in a matter of seconds. As murders go, it was exceptionally swift and abrupt.

Considering its ownership there was nothing unusual about the room where she was found. It smelled faintly of pot-pourri, and its charming furniture included some delightful period pieces. Its china and pictures had quality, its carpet was Chinese and its chairs were Chesterfield-soft and seductive.

Then there was the woman, in a charming afternoon frock,

with a face like a surprised Madonna and hair like an aureola. She was wearing about a thousand pounds' worth of jewellery, which would unquestionably have proved tempting, in short, to a burglar. There was no blood, no signs of a struggle. No vulgarity, but everything quiet and restrained, except for that deadly circle around her neck. Even the murderer was only a part of that general background—a quiet man, writing peacefully at a Queen Anne bureau.

Later, of course, there was to be the comparative vulgarity of a trial, even if it ended in a matter of minutes with the knowledge that the murderer was hopelessly insane. And the reason of it all—let me repeat—was a letter that was written to *The Times*.

To get to that letter we must leave the charm of that drawing-room in Hampstead and come nearer town to Porter Street, Mornington Crescent. In Victorian times the Crescent had dignity and aloofness. Porter Street still retained something of that dignity even if its Georgian houses had become offices and flats. It was in one of these flats that Lutley Prentisse was working on a certain June morning.

It would be more true to say that he should have been working. In front of his swivel chair were table and typewriter but he sat there with the tips of his fingers together and his brow wrinkled in thought. You would have needed no particular shrewdness to have guessed that he was a writer.

But he was a writer with a difference. His name was far from well-known. He had three novels to his credit, two having as their theme extramarital intrigue and the other concerned with one of those coteries to be found on the French Riviera. The last only had sold quite well—a matter of gratification to its author purely from pride of workmanship. Money is always useful, but his private income was about two thousand a year after taxes, and the handsome royalties he received from his publisher made no great difference.

The fact of the matter was that he had drifted into writing

almost without knowing it, and primarily to escape from boredom. The first two years after his marriage had been a routine of which he had tired—Switzerland in mid-winter, the Riviera in Spring, golf in England in the summer and weekends at various house parties, with a week or two at Deauville or Le Touquet in early autumn. After that town—the club, theatres and the multitudinous rush and jigsaw fitting-in from morning till night.

All that was the life that suited Dorothy Prentisse so well. At golf Lutley was a shaky sixteen. She could give a low handicap man a good game and from the men's tees at that. Her tennis was almost first-class. She played a really good hand at bridge—a bit aggressive, perhaps, but rarely a loser unless cards and partners were impossible. Lutley was a cautious bidder if ever there was one. He was good, however, for what he said, and never less.

But he took things less seriously. In golf the game counted, not the figures—or at least that was how things had been before his marriage. Maybe it was the almost venomous earnestness with which Dorothy did things that first began to make them pall.

In some ways you might have thought them an ill-sorted couple. He was short and sturdy, with quiet brown eyes, and a kind of intellectual shyness. She was tall for a woman, handsome in a glittering way and with qualities that would have made for attractiveness only to a man quite different from Prentisse—knowledge of the jargons and sporting chatter, and with it that shrewd judgment that knows when to be only a highly ornamental background.

At Cambridge Lutley had read history and, until his marriage, had contributed occasionally to various reviews. That particular writing had been a part of his leisure, but later, when the hectic life of his first married years had begun to seem aimless and even boring, he had thought with regret of the pleasure his earlier labours had given him. Out of it had come his attempt at a first novel, and its publication.

All this was just before the last war when money was money and life less demanding. As for his marriage, he had met Dorothy at the house of George Foster, an old Cambridge friend, and it so happened that she had been at school with George's wife, Miriam. Dorothy's father had just died—he had been vicar of Purfield Warren—and she had come into a reasonable sum of money.

Six months after that first meeting they were married. He was then thirty-one and she twenty-eight, though she claimed to be younger. It was a love match on his side if not on hers. Her friends agreed that he had married a most attractive woman, her enemies that she had done exceptionally well for herself. But it would have been hard to judge objectively the success or otherwise of that marriage. Lutley, one could see through: the woman he had wed was far more inscrutable. In public a softly-murmured 'Darling!' and a playful tap are no particular signs, especially when the other hand holds a liqueur glass drained for the eighth time.

When Prentisse at first, and almost surreptitiously, returned to his writing, his wife seemed neither to mind nor to be interested. After all, she had plenty of outside interests. On her first discovery of his new activity it had been: 'Darling, how frightfully clever of you!' and then, at intervals, 'Oh, you poor dear, I hate to see you working so hard! Why don't you stop now and rest?' Then, on the publication of his first novel, 'Darling, it's too frightfully thrilling for anything!'

Thereafter it might have been said by the unkind that her tolerance or possible encouragement of his efforts was not unconnected with material considerations. But Prentisse apparently doted on her and generously provided that his earnings should be hers in the form of special presents.

But the Spring of 1947 had seen a slight deterioration in the warmth and closeness of their relationship. He was engaged on a new book which he definitely knew was good, and he refused to take his work to the Riviera. Dorothy had however kept to the routine and had gone to Menton with a small circle of friends that included Peter Claire and Miriam Foster.

Claire, a handsome, country club type man of about thirty-five, was a very old friend. Prentisse, in his own unde-monstrative way, was very fond of him. The Prentisses saw a lot of him when he was in town and he often dined at the Hampstead house.

It was because he did not want to keep that house open during his wife's absence that Prentisse had taken that Porter Street flat. Dorothy was away till the very end of May and then something happened. Her only sister had been taken seriously ill and she had gone down to Carnford to be with her.

That was not so unsettling for Prentisse as it might have been, for the book was not quite finished. A few days would see it with the publisher and he stayed on at the flat. In the morning he usually put in his best work, but that particular morning he was annoyed, and worried over what seemed a very trivial thing.

Before him was the morning's edition of *The Times* and it was at a certain letter that he was scowling. A policeman had written rather indignantly on the treatment of his profession by writers of detective novels. The police, he affirmed, were treated like buffoons and authors rarely troubled to make themselves familiar with the real workings of either Scotland Yard or the C.I.D. departments of provincial forces.

But it was not the police and their methods that were worrying Lutley Prentisse, but the whole principle which the letter called in question. He himself had always been careful to use in his books such local colour as had been familiar and things with which he had had at least a working acquaintance, but in that novel, now almost finished, he had brought in something with which he was not familiar at all—a private detective agency.

The chapter that dealt with it had been written and he had taken a great deal for granted, not caring much whether or not an absolute verisimilitude had been achieved. A detective agency, for instance, would have an office. Well, such offices were surely pretty much alike, and in his novel its appearance had been guessed at. And so with the head of the firm, and the conversation, and all the things that go to make what one calls local colour.

Some people would have regarded the whole thing as utterly unimportant. There could be little connection between that letter and the chapter in question. They would have argued that a private detective was most unlikely to read that particular chapter and that the man in the street, provided the book as a whole kept him reading into the small hours, would not care the proverbial tuppence about the niceties of local colour.

But such a view was contrary to Prentisse's meticulous mind. He was also a man of impulses and curious obstinacies. That was why he suddenly made up his mind that the right thing to do would be to visit a detective agency and check up that chapter in the light of such new impressions as he might form. But the resolve brought also an annoyance.

There was the chance that his guesses in that chapter had been reasonably correct and that the chapter would not have to be re-written. But whether that were so or not, time would be wasted and just when he was fired with the urge to finish the book. To ignore the letter seemed sheer carelessness. That letter from the policeman might start a spate of inquiries into local colour. Heaven knew what people and professions would be writing to the Press about the gross errors they had unearthed. He could almost see one such letter—

Dear Sir,

Referring to the matter of local colour, I was very amused to find in a novel by Lutley Prentisse entitled 'Tingling Symbols' a statement that . . .

In any case that morning he was unable to settle down to work and just before noon he went along to his club. He ran into George Foster and they lunched together.

'Was that Peter Claire I saw getting into a taxi just as I came in?' Prentisse happened to ask.

'That's right,' George said. 'I was talking to him just before. He's going down to Cambridge tomorrow to play for the Pilgrims against the Wanderers. A two-day match. Did you want to see him?'

'Well, in a way—yes. I wanted him to give me an introduction to his brother. He's a Chief Constable, as you probably know, and I hoped he might give me some local colour and save some rather tiresome inquiries.'

George Foster was probably the only man to whom he would have told that morning's worries. George didn't seem at all unhappy about it.

'I don't think a Chief Constable would help very much,' he said. 'Why not go to the fountainhead? I know a really good firm of private detectives who did an excellent job for a friend of mine. You go along and see them. Just make up some yarn or other. Just a simple job that won't cost very much. That ought to give you the whole bag of tricks.'

Foster happened to remember the name of the firm and the approximate address, and that Friday afternoon Prentisse made a bold decision and went to Took Street. The taxi driver happened to know the number and on a door on the first floor Prentisse found what he wanted.

PERRING AND HOLT
PRIVATE INQUIRY AGENTS

He knocked, and the door was opened with instant and agreeable promptitude by a receptionist.

'Can I see one of the principals, please?' he asked.

'Take a seat, sir, please,' the young lady replied. 'I think Mr Holt is free. Have you a card?'

A couple of minutes and he was in Holt's room. It was a smallish office crammed with filing cabinets and reference books. There was the usual flat-topped desk and swivel chair. Holt, a dapper-looking youngish man, rose and held out a hand.

'How d'you do, Mr Prentisse. Take a seat, will you? Cigarette? . . . And what precisely may we do for you?'

'Well, er—'

Holt smiled reassuringly. 'Secrets are safe with us, sir. We're used to handling affairs of the utmost delicacy, and in the strictest of confidence. You can rely on us implicitly.'

Prentisse had to think quickly. The thoughts he had had were now in thin air. It would be crude to admit that he was in that room solely for the purpose of picking brains. When he did speak it was only to make time.

'It's a fairly trivial matter,' he said.

'It doesn't matter to us, sir,' Holt assured him. 'Whatever the work, we can undertake it. And in strict confidence.'

His manner was suave and impressive. Prentisse thought of the use he had made in his novel of an imaginary detective agency and decided on something along the same lines.

'Well'—there was still a certain diffidence in his manner—'I take it you're prepared to keep people under observation? Not necessarily to do with divorce, of course.'

'Most certainly.' He drew a pad towards him, and the pen was poised. 'Name, sir?' he inquired.

'Lutley Prentisse.'

Holt smiled. 'Not your name, sir,' he said. 'The name of the person it will be our task to watch.'

Prentisse smiled too, but not at that mistake he had made. An idea had come to him, and wrapped up in it were all the elements of the ludicrous.

'Ah, yes, of course. The name is Peter Claire.'

'Address?'

'Three, Oudenarde Mansions, Kensington.'

'And what exactly do you want, sir—and when?'

'Just a report in confidence, by Monday, of what he does from now until then. You can manage that?'

'Most decidedly. Where do you wish the report delivered?'

'Five B, Porter Street, Mornington Crescent. About noon, if you can manage it.'

That was virtually all. As he walked down the stairs Prentisse was both gratified and mildly amused. He had been in the office of a detective agency and what he had seen and heard would involve only minor alterations in the carefully written chapter.

As to the amusement, it would certainly be uproariously funny if Peter, during his stay in Cambridge, discovered that a private detective was on his heels. And then suddenly he halted, and frowned. Annoying, too. The least thing he could do was to get hold of Peter and warn him. A knowledge of what was going to happen would make the joke the property of Peter as well as of himself.

From his flat he rang Oudenarde Mansions. Claire's man, Daniels, answered the telephone. Mr Prentisse was just a few minutes too late. Mr Claire had just left by taxi. Yes, Daniels was certain he had gone to Cambridge. He'd definitely taken his golf bag and a weekend suitcase.

'You know the hotel he'll be staying at?' Prentisse asked.

'I don't, sir,' Daniels said. 'All I know is that he'll be back early on Monday.'

So that was that—though Prentisse was still glad he'd hit on Claire as a stalking-horse for Holt's detective. A less intimate friend of the family would be highly indignant when he learned what had been going on. And Claire *would* learn, though now he must wait until Monday. So Prentisse sat down at the typewriter and wrote for Claire's exclusive enlightenment an account of the whole thing.

> . . . *And that's how it happened. It will be extremely amusing if you chance to spot the sleuth. In any case I'll send you the report, innocuous though it will be. Until Monday then.*
>
> *Yours as ever,*
>
> *Lutley.*
>
> *P.S. Why not have dinner with us on Monday? I'm expecting Dorothy back from Carnford. Her sister's much better.*

He went out at once and mailed the letter and as he walked back to the apartment he wondered if Peter's reactions would be altogether what he himself had expected. Not that Peter hadn't a sense of humour in a rather hearty way.

That evening he worked hard at the detective agency chapter and rewrote where the afternoon's call on Holt seemed to require it. By Saturday he had the chapter well in hand and that afternoon he treated himself to a matinee.

In the evening he dined at his club and then went back to his apartment and outlined the final chapter of his novel. On the Sunday morning he went to the Hampstead house. Dorothy had everything arranged. Lunt, butler and general man, was there, as were the cook and the maid. It was from the house that he rang Carnford Hall.

Phipps, the butler, answered. 'I'm sorry, sir, but Mrs Prentisse isn't back yet from church. She should be in at any moment. Yes, sir, the mistress is practically herself again. The doctor's very pleased. Just a moment, sir. I think I hear Mrs Prentisse now.'

A minute later Dorothy Prentisse was on the line.

'That you, darling? How sweet of you to ring! Yes, I'll be back early in the morning. I'm glad you found everything as it should be. But you shouldn't have asked Peter to dinner. Well, I'd been looking forward to us having our evening together alone . . . A special reason? Well, we might find some special excuse and put him off. He won't mind . . . Till tomorrow then, darling. 'Bye.'

Bright and early on Monday Holt himself arrived at the Porter Street apartment. He was like a man who had been given a job to do, and knew that he had done it well. From an unsealed envelope he produced several closely typed sheets.

Prentisse gave them a glance, tried to look impressed, and asked how much. Holt's account was for just over eighteen pounds and Prentisse wrote him a cheque.

It was a lot of money, Prentisse thought ruefully, for the view of an office and a few minutes with Holt. It rather looked, in fact, as if Peter would have the laugh. Which reminded him. Peter would be at Oudenarde Mansions and he'd better be rung up at once. And then Prentisse couldn't help wondering just how that sleuth of Holt's had got to work and he took the typed sheets from the envelope and began casually to read.

> *The party was picked up almost on arrival and followed to Liverpool Street Station where he took the train for Wenton Junction. He was met by a small black sedan driven by a lady and the car was followed to Justin Friars, six miles away, where it entered the grounds of a smallish country house known as Friars House. Phillipson followed me and he and I shared the supervision from then on.*

Prentisse stopped reading. He had wondered why Peter had not gone to Cambridge and he smiled to himself as he knew why. After all, Friars House was Peter's, and Justin Friars was only some twenty miles from Cambridge. He knew it well enough. He had been there once or twice when he and Dorothy had been staying at Carnford Hall. It wasn't more than a ten-minute run in a car. As for the woman, she was probably Peter's married sister. Or wasn't she still in India? Maybe she and her husband were home on leave. Curiosity made him read on.

> *There seemed to be no servants whatever in the house but observation was difficult. The couple did not appear until about eight-thirty that evening when they walked round the lawns and the borders and back through the long walk to the house. The woman was tallish, fair and about thirty by all appearances. Once or twice the couple were seen to embrace during their tour of the garden.*

Prentisse was horrified. The woman was definitely not Peter's sister and who she might be he had no idea. What he did know was that in beginning a joke he had committed an enormity. He had intruded unwarrantably into another man's private life and the fact that it had been done under a lamentable misapprehension would not make it appear the less reprehensible. His face was flushed as he realised what he must at once do.

He rang Oudenarde Mansions and it was Daniels who answered.

'Sorry, sir, but the master's just gone away.'

'Away? What do you mean?'

'What I said, sir. He got back at about eleven o'clock and almost at once he ordered me to pack his bags for the South of France. He didn't know how long he'd be away.'

'Good Heavens! Any idea why he went off like that?'

'No idea at all, sir,' Daniels replied.

'Very extraordinary!' Prentisse said. 'There should have been a letter for him from me asking him to dinner tonight. Did he read it? It was on pale blue paper.'

'Yes, sir, I remember it. He read it as soon as he came in.'

'Very extraordinary!' Prentisse said again. 'Let me know as soon as you hear anything from him.'

'I will, sir,' Daniels promised.

Prentisse hung up. He was angry and he was worried. What on earth could have possessed Claire to have made him go off like that? If it was that letter, then he surely should have had sense enough to know that his secrets were implicitly safe.

He picked it up and once more began reading.

> *A light went on in a bedroom at about ten o'clock and we brought a ladder from the garden and placed it near the open window when the lights went out. We had to act with enormous care but hearing was perfect. There were the following scraps of conversation.*
>
> *(1) 'Are you sure Phipps can be trusted?'*
>
> *'Yes,' the woman said, 'I'll square it with him on Sunday morning again. I'll have to be there in any case when he'—name not identified—'rings. He'll be sure to ring about noon.'*
>
> *(2) 'Darling, we'll have to be most careful from now on. You really mustn't go making faces at me behind his back.' He is apparently the unidentified name of 1.*
>
> *'It's all rather funny in a way,' Claire said. 'He's not a bad old stick, really. I don't think we'll be running any risk.'*

Something had already stood still with Lutley Prentisse. He read the rest of those sheets and as if his eyes no longer saw any words. When he laid the last sheet down he stood for a moment, hand gripping the table and his face a queer grey.

At first his movements seemed rational. He took the tube to Hampstead and made his way to his house and spoke rationally enough to the staff. Mrs Prentisse had gone out for a moment, he was told, but should be back practically at once. He went out himself and at a music shop bought a gut 'cello string. When he came back, Mrs Prentisse was there.

Five minutes later Lunt brought in tea. He found Mrs Prentisse lying dead on the carpet and Prentisse sitting writing at that

Queen Anne bureau. Lunt, white-faced and aghast, could get no answer from him. So he ran out to the road and got a message to the police. When they came it was still as if Prentisse did not hear. He let them take him by the arm and lead him away. The sergeant had a look at that paper on which he had been writing.

'Heavenly days, have a look at this, Inspector! What do you suppose it means?'

The inspector had a look. It didn't mean anything to him either. It was just a phrase, written over and over again.

'To the Editor of *The Times*, Dear Sir.'

CHRISTOPHER BUSH

Charles Christmas Bush was born on Christmas Day 1888 at Home Cottage in Hockham, a village in Norfolk in the east of England. Christmas Bush, as he was known as a child, was of Quaker descent and his family had lived in the area for over 400 years. He was educated in the village school and, in 1899, won a three-year scholarship to Thetford Grammar, where he gained distinctions in Religious Knowledge, English and Geography while winning prizes for English and German. In 1902 he won a further two-year scholarship and in 1903 his Form Prize. Outside school, Bush was a competent sportsman, playing competitive draughts and opening for the village cricket team; he also sang with his friend Ernest Hensley at the Primitive Methodist Chapel alongside his sister Hilda and her friend Ella Pinner, whom Bush would eventually marry.

In 1904, despite his Quaker upbringing, Bush secured a temporary position as assistant master at a Catholic school in North Worcestershire. In 1905, he returned to Norfolk to be an assistant master at Swaffham Boys' School and he became a published author when 'Life in the Black Country' appeared in the *Norwich Mercury*. He resumed singing at chapel and also played cricket, opening for 'Swaffham Singles' and, lower down the order, for 'Great Hockham Reading Room' a team that included his brothers in conviction, the two Ernests. Later that year, Bush matriculated as an undergraduate at King's College, London, where he studied modern languages, and on graduating he returned to teaching, this time at a school in Wood Green, North London. Around this time Bush also married Ella Pinner, although what happened next is unclear. Curtis Evans, the authority on Bush and other Golden Age writers, has determined that while the two remained married until Ella's death in the late 1960s, they do not appear ever to have lived together. Evans has also established that when Bush returned from four years' military service during the First World War, including a year in Egypt, he returned to Wood Green School and fathered a child by a teaching colleague, Winifred Chart. Their son, born out of wedlock in 1920 and largely unacknowledged, would grow up to become the composer Geoffrey Bush, co-author with Edmund Crispin of the excellent puzzle short story 'Who Killed Baker?'

Romantic entanglements aside, teaching had always been Bush's ambition. However, he did not find it fulfilling and in the mid-1920s, as the result of a bet, he wrote a novel which much to his delight was accepted and published. Set in 1919, *The Plumley Inheritance* (1926) concerns a treasure hunt and a mysterious murder, which prove to be connected. While not uncriticised by contemporary reviewers—'Mr Bush has two strings to his bow, and the story might have been a better one if he had restricted himself to one'—the book sold well. It was followed by *The Perfect Murder Case* (1929), whose manuscript the publisher required Bush to halve in length, and then two titles in 1930: *Dead Man Twice* in the summer and *Murder at Fenwold* for Christmas. Buoyant, Bush decided in 1931 to become a full-time writer and he eventually produced over seventy books, including some sixty novels as Christopher Bush. These feature several recurring characters, including Major Ludovic Travers who appears in all of them, and have been reprinted by Dean Street Press. Many of the best are set in English villages but Travers also solves crimes in France in *The Case of the Three Strange Faces* (1933), *The Case of the Flying Ass* (1939) and *The Case of the Climbing Rat* (1940). Bush also wrote four excellent Second World War mysteries, including three—*The Case of the Murdered Major*

(1941), *The Case of the Kidnapped Colonel* (1942) and *The Case of the Fighting Soldier* (1942)—that were partly inspired by his time at C19, a D-Day marshalling camp on Southampton Common in Hampshire, and also his service with the Home Guard, which Curtis Evans has established included serving as an officer at Pennylands prisoner of war camp in Ayrshire.

Writing success brought wealth and, in the early 1930s, Bush fulfilled a promise to his mother by buying the cottage where he had been born. He added two wings transforming it into Home Hall, which is now a boutique hotel. He also bought 'Horsepen', a fifteenth-century house in the village of Beckley in East Sussex, where he would live with his partner Marjorie Barclay for around twenty years.

While Bush is best-remembered for the crime fiction published under his own name, he also wrote a Ruritanian adventure, *The Trail of the Three Lean Men* (1932), published as by 'Noel Barclay', combining a variant of his given forename and Marjorie's surname. He adopted another pen name, the euphonious 'Michael Home', for a series of novels set in and around the East Anglian village of Heathley, a thinly disguised version of his birthplace. The first of the series, known as the Breckland novels, *God and the Rabbit* (1933), is a semi-autobiographical story about a boy who wins scholarships and becomes a schoolmaster while supporting his strait-laced mother from London and his dissolute father, a poacher. In later years, Bush would claim that, as had happened with *The Perfect Murder Case*, the publisher had required the manuscript of *God and the Rabbit* to be cut by half. True or not, the novel was very well-received and a second quickly followed. *In This Valley* (1934) is a melodrama about a Methodist farmer and his son, an ambitious man with two women in his life, suggesting autobiographical elements in this novel too. In all, there are around twenty Michael Home novels, including *David* (1937), a biblical biography, and three overtly autobiographical books, *Autumn Fields* (1945), *Spring Sowing* (1946) and *Winter Harvest* (1967). As well as the Breckland series, there were several Home novels involving Britain's military intelligence services, including two featuring Major John Benham of MI5: *The Strange Prisoner* (1947) and *The Auber File* (1953).

In 1941, after leaving the Home Guard, Bush made headlines locally for restoring the medieval wood carvings on the exterior of Horsepen, working to a Tudor design as specified by advisers from the Victoria & Albert Museum. He was also active in civic matters in the nearby town of Hastings as a member of the Twenty Club 'for men and women prominent in literature or art' and he was a patron of local artists and galleries, on one occasion donating to an exhibition 'A portrait of Mr Michael Home by Mr Christopher Bush'. And he was also prominent in the Detection Club, to which he had been elected in the late 1930s.

In the early 1950s Bush and Marjorie moved to the Great House in Lavenham in Suffolk where, while continuing to write, he again became a pillar of the community, opening art exhibitions and giving talks about being a writer. A modest man, Bush had no time for what he called 'literary arrogance', seeing himself as simply 'a public entertainer whose chief duty is to be thoroughly competent at whatever line of writing he decides to adopt'. But while many of Bush's novels have good ideas and interesting settings, others seem to some to fulfil the criticism levelled at lesser lights of the Golden Age by H. R. F. Keating—a former President of the Detection Club—that their work is characterised by 'ingenuity of plot, cardboardity of character [and] chunter of story'. Nonetheless, Bush remains popular and has been praised in particular for his ability to create and deconstruct the unbreakable alibi, a trait shared with the 'alibi king' himself, Freeman Wills Crofts.

With Marjorie's death in 1968, Bush lost his enthusiasm for writing. He died on 21 September 1973 at the age of eighty-four.

One of two versions of 'The Hampstead Murder', this text was published in the November 1955 issue of *The Saint* magazine.

THE SCARECROW MURDERS

Joseph Commings

It was the murder that drew Senator Brooks U. Banner to Cow Crossing, a town in the upper reaches of New York State. The study of crime had been Banner's hobby for years. Now Banner, a whopping big man, stood before the flimsy office door over the post office and gave it a brisk drubbing. The moulting gold-leaf lettering on the door read: *Judge James Z. Skinner*.

Skinner himself opened the door. Behind him his office was stuffy and smelled of mouldering papers. Dusk was shadowing all the corners and Skinner had been getting ready to close up shop for the day. Skinner recognized Banner at once, probably from Banner's many colourful political billboards.

'Senator Banner!' said Skinner, half surprised and half delighted. He spoke with a fruity voice.

'Yessiree, bub. Life-size, in the flesh, fulla beans, and raring to go.' Banner chuckled and came in. A liver-coloured leghorn was pushed back on his grizzled mane. He carried his frock coat over his arm, for the evening was still too warm to wear it. His silk shirt was mottled with sweat. He stood up straight, but his baggy grey britches looked ready to sit down. On his feet were a pair of brogans spotted with clay.

'I just horse-and-buggied into your burg, friend,' he said with a boom. 'I'm on a tub-thumping junket. After each sentence of my speech I pitch a forkful of hay. That puts the farmers behind me one hundred per cent. I think I'm gonna need the farm vote to carry me back to Washington this fall.'

Skinner bobbed his narrow head soberly. 'Your oratory is welcome in the hinterlands. Demosthenes on the stump. *Usus loquendi.*' He smiled bleakly. He was the law in Cow Crossing. He was in his sixties, long and weedy, with carefully parted grey hair and eyes like the heads of new ten-penny nails. Winter or summer he wore an antique beaver hat that reminded one of an abdicated kingdom: it had a fallen crown. He had the hat in his hand.

Banner eyed the old man sharply. 'I was in the next town when I heard that Cow Crossing had been glorified with a murder. It tempted me like a kid is tempted with custard. I had to come. Puzzles have teased me ever since I tried to take my socks off with my baby booties still on. They tell me you're the johnnie I have to see.'

'Yes,' said Skinner. 'If there's any law in this place, I'm it. I'm the *lex loci*, so to speak. People see me when they're married, they see me when things go wrong, and they see me after they're dead, only then they don't care.' He took a flat silver case out of his pocket. 'A fresh cigar?'

Banner remembered he had a corona between his teeth. It looked as if the rats had been at it. He took it out of his mouth and glowered distastefully. 'I'll own up to you,' he said. 'I never smoke seegars. It's all window-dressing.' He pegged the gnawed fag-end into a spattered cuspidor. 'About this murder, judge, what's the score?'

Skinner said there was not much to tell. He related all the known circumstances. In the shallows of the creek some fishermen had discovered Beverly Jelke's body. Farther upstream they found her clothes piled neatly on the bank. The body was in a common black bathing suit. Half her head had been blown away by the charge of a double-barrelled shotgun.

Apparently the victim had been swimming about ten feet off shore in the deep water near where her clothes were found. The murderer had fired from the heavy brake that overhung the banks at that point.

Hudson Jelke was Beverly's younger brother by a year. He was in his early twenties, with a face as pasty as dough, shaggy-haired, and unshaven. He had greedy eyes. He had lumbered into the mortuary that hot August afternoon and claimed the body. He had taken the dead girl's hand in his own. For a moment, the judge said, it looked like an affectionate gesture, but Hudson went ahead to strip the heavy ring off one of the fingers.

Skinner had said, 'Do you have to be so ghoulish, Hud? Can't you wait?'

'It's an heirloom,' responded Hudson. 'It's mine now.'

When he left, Hudson had all Beverly's personal belongings. He went back to the farm, knowing that all of it belonged to him now.

Banner shifted his feet in the gloomy office. 'Got any wild guesses who killed Beverly Jelke?'

'No idea.' A little cough cleared Skinner's long throat. Then he went on, in a gossipy manner, about the Jelkes. 'This is a pretty sparsely populated region, Senator. The Jelke farm—they call it Blackmarsh Grange—is about eight miles out of town and there are no farms in between. There were two Jelkes, Beverly and her brother Hudson. Hudson married a French Canadian girl from just over the border. There's an uncle living there too, and a hired man.'

Banner waited.

Skinner went on, 'Blackmarsh Grange is a big sprawling place, named on account of the dismal quagmire that was originally on the land, but most of that has been filled in. In the last couple of years the Jelkes haven't been happy. They've produced merely enough to get by on, and the brother and sister have been having one long hot argument.'

Banner was attentive. 'Argument?'

Skinner said, 'About selling the Grange. I offered them five thousand for it—a fair price, considering. Beverly wanted to sell right off and hie herself out of here and start fresh in one of the bigger cities. But Hudson was all against it. He had something to say about selling the farm. And he wasn't going to budge an inch. They came close to blows over it more than once.'

Banner grunted. 'Now that Beverly's dead, Hudson'll have it all his own way.'

Skinner's nail-head eyes dulled. He said slowly, 'That's the size of it.'

'And,' said Banner, 'you won't get the farm for love or money.'

Banner couldn't see Skinner's expression, for the judge had turned away to flick dust off a law tome with a flame-coloured bandanna.

'I'm anxious to see that crowd,' went on Banner.

Skinner looked at him. 'The Jelkes? You mean you want to help me solve this murder?'

Banner shrugged his bulky shoulders. 'Skunks and rabbits, they have habits,' he said.

They rode up through the long lane of dark poplars in the judge's buggy with the wobbly top, pulled by a spavined horse. The old buildings spread over acres. Lights were on in the kitchen and the front parlour.

Skinner, who had phoned the local constabulary and ordered no interference with Senator Banner's prowlings, had added a hawthorn stick to his rig since leaving the office. He courteously rapped the head of the stick on the front door. A girl in a printed house dress popped out at them.

'Come in,' she said at once.

They moved through double sliding oak doors into the parlour. There was a heavy brass lamp on a tabletop that was glazed with turpentine and beeswax. In the light Banner saw that the girl was small and slight. She had dark brown hair that she had begun to neglect and it was getting stringy. Her arms, bare from the elbows down, were sunbrowned till the skin looked like tan satin. Banner liked her wholesomeness. Skinner introduced her as Celeste Jelke, Hudson's wife.

'So you're the little girl the judge's been telling tales about,' said Banner as he shook her firm hand. She turned shyly away and called for Hud.

The doughy-faced, shaggy young man with the greedy eyes tramped in and stared suspiciously at Banner as the judge made them known to each other.

'I'm sorry we can't offer you any supper, Senator,' said Hudson coldly. 'We just finished.'

'I'll raid your ice chest,' Banner stated blandly. 'I'm needing a shakedown for the night. The hotel in town is fulla drummers.'

Hudson's brow blackened. 'You're damn cagey, ain't you? We all know what you're up to. Come right out and say it's about Bev!'

Banner grinned. 'That's throwing in your blue chips, son. We understand each other. *Tray bone*, as we used to say to the Frenchies in the Big War. We all wanna see punished the person who killed your beloved sister.'

Hudson was brutal. 'I didn't love her.'

Celeste's hazel eyes grew round at his audacity.

'If everyone's as truthful as you,' said Banner sourly, 'we won't have much trouble cleaning house. This's like catching another man with your wife: the situation calls for action.'

Celeste spoke up. 'I do have something to tell you. That double-barrelled shotgun we kept behind the kitchen door—it's gone.'

'Have you looked for it?' said Banner.

'High and low,' Hudson replied.

There was an uncomfortable silence.

Then Banner said, 'Haven't you got an uncle?'

'He ain't here,' said Hudson curtly. 'He's out prowling around.' He made it sound sinister.

A sinewy young man in overalls came into the parlour. His

hair and eyebrows were bleached by the sun. He stopped and took a smoke-blackened clay pipe out of his mouth and looked at the others with blank ocean-aqua eyes.

Celeste said quickly, 'Senator, this is our hired man, Wayne Markes.'

'How dee do,' said Wayne.

Hudson seemed to take a perverse delight in making others uneasy. He said, 'Wayne's got things on his mind, Senator. He's thinking all the time about that girl student over at Foxchase Hall.'

'What's that?' Banner asked. 'A school?'

'Yeah. A finishing school for girls. It's the nearest place to ours. Her name is Joan Vicars, ain't it, Wayne? He met her down by the creek a couple of times. He thinks it's love.'

Wayne's cheeks were as red as a Valentine heart. 'The Senator ain't interested in that, Hud,' he said resentfully.

'Ain't he, though?' Hudson persisted.

'I ain't,' said Banner. He patted his punchbowl tummy. 'Which way's the kitchen?'

'I'll get something for you,' Celeste said hurriedly. 'Wayne, straighten out one of the rooms upstairs for the Senator.'

Wayne went back out through the sliding doors. Hudson followed Celeste into the kitchen.

All this time Skinner had kept a keen-eyed vigil on Banner. 'There isn't much to go on, is there?' said Skinner.

Banner hitched up his pants. 'What kind of a damsel was this Beverly Jelke?'

'Not bad looking, not bad at all.' Skinner paused to think about it. 'I knew her all her life. She was a tomboy, always running around barefoot and going fishing. Her favourite pastime was horseshoe pitching and she was expert at it. She was clever—and heartless . . .'

There were plenty of rooms in the house. After a cold supper, Banner followed Celeste up a dark stairwell. Celeste lit a dim light in the upper hall. They passed one locked door. It was Beverly's room.

Banner eyed the steel-springed cot, the feather mattress, and the fat pillow. Inconveniences never fazed him. Celeste said good-night softly and left him. He tossed his toilet articles on top of a pine bureau. From his pocket he had taken a straight razor with a bone handle, a shaving brush, and a toothbrush for his upper plate.

He jimmied off his shoes and threw them away from him. They landed like kegs of nails. He dropped his clothes in piles on the floor. There was a crazy quilt on the cot. The night was getting cool. He pulled the quilt over him and went to sleep.

At a quarter to one Banner bounced like a gutta-percha ball into a sitting position. The echoes of a shot were still reverberating. He swung his feet over the side of the cot, feeling for his pants. As he tangled himself up in red suspenders* he heard doors slam and feet running inside the house. He kicked his feet into the widely-flung brogans and scrambled down the stairs without a shirt on.

The others were already clustered on the porch step. Celeste sobbed hysterically. Banner pushed his way through and looked down on the step.

In the moonlight Hudson Jelke lay sprawled with part of his scalp and his face blown away by buckshot.

Wayne Markes got a quilt and covered the body with it.

Skinner, who had also decided to stay overnight, phoned to Cow Crossing for a wagon to take the body away. Banner, consoling Celeste in a fatherly way, took her to her room and made her lie down. He came downstairs again to study the ground in front of the porch step.

Skinner came out and looked stupidly at Banner. Two murders were getting to be too much for the legal lights of Cow Crossing.

* braces

'There're some footprints,' said Banner. 'We'll have to wait till it gets daylight to follow them.'

'Do you think we can?' questioned Skinner doubtfully.

Banner was grim. 'We can use a coupla hounds.' He raised his head as if to listen. Skinner and Wayne listened too and understood.

The dogs were strangely silent. The sound of the shot had stirred them up a bit, but they soon grew still.

Wayne said, 'We had a house-breaker come one night and the hounds bellered till dawn.' He shook himself. 'All right if I take a look around, Senator?'

'Suit yourself,' said Banner.

The hired man melted into the dense shadows.

In time a wagon came with a fussy coroner who bawled everybody out merely for being there. Finally Hudson's body was taken away to keep his sister company.

Banner and Skinner went into the farmhouse. They could hear Celeste still crying in her room. Skinner went up to offer a few words of comfort.

Wayne came into the parlour looking ashen under his sunburn. 'I just saw something,' he gulped. Banner eyed him narrowly. 'I was wandering among the fruit trees,' went on Wayne. 'I saw something moving—flitting. It seemed to have a human shape. And it was luminous!'

'Luminous?'

'It gave off a glow.'

'Did you get near enough to—'

'No, no, it was gone in a flash.' Wayne turned abruptly towards the door. 'I'm going to bed.' Banner heard his feet stumble on the stairs.

No one knew if Banner went back to bed again that night or not. He didn't.

The first pink of dawn sifted through the heavy screens on the parlour windows. Banner heard a sound of pots and pans in the kitchen. He went in and found Celeste preparing breakfast. She had cried herself out and now managed to present a weak smile.

Skinner and Wayne came down shortly afterwards. Skinner looked more than his sixty years. Wayne was as fresh as if he had had a full night's sleep. That's what age does to you, thought Banner.

'Get us a doublet of hounds,' Banner said. Wayne brought a pair on chain leashes to the front of the house.

The footprints of the killer were plain in the early light. The hounds caught the scent and they bayed like muffled bells.

The footprints went on and on, past the storage shed and out towards the open fields. The trackers pressed into a clump of sassafras, the hounds sniffing confidently. The murderer's heavy ungainly shoes made perfect impressions in the loam. They crossed some shale where the prints disappeared, but the pace of the hounds never slackened.

They came to the edge of a field newly ploughed for winter wheat. The dogs stood motionless and stopped baying. There was bafflement in their melancholy eyes. They whimpered and quivered.

'What the devil's the matter with them?' snapped Skinner irritably.

He saw that the others were looking ahead at the footprints that went off across the freshly turned soil. A single line of prints they were. And they led straight to a gaunt scarecrow that stood some forty feet off, idly flapping its empty arms at them.

They trudged back to the house silently. Banner couldn't get the scarecrow out of his mind. He had gone out to it and stood looking at it, flabbergasted. The trail had stopped there.

The scarecrow was well dressed, as scarecrows go. It had on a frayed-brimmed straw hat. Its face was an old flour bag with two lopsided holes punched in it for eyes, a triangular nose, and a crayon mouth that resembled the teeth of a rake. The coat hung limply from stick shoulders. At the sleeve cuffs were pinned soiled white cotton gloves. The legs of the loose pants fluttered gently in the morning breeze. A pair of battered shoes with heavy soles stood within a foot of each other under the scarecrow. They fitted the tracks.

The footprints had made fools of them. Each print was sharp and clear. It hadn't been a case of using the same prints twice, for going and coming.

Banner said suddenly, 'Was that scarecrow always in that field?'

'No,' said Wayne. 'That's the one that used to be in Beverly's vegetable patch.'

As they drew near the house a man came out of it to meet them. He was as fleshless as a hoe-handle, and had hair like singed cotton and a dehydrated face. In short, he was the ugliest gaffer Banner had ever seen.

Banner leaned his head towards Skinner. 'Who's this, judge? Gloryanna! He's as ugly as a—' He stopped short, for something had clicked in his mind.

Skinner grinned without humour. 'Why don't you go ahead and say it, Senator? As ugly as a *scarecrow*! We know that. His appearance has been against him ever since he was a kid. He isn't as bad an actor as he looks. He's Hudson's uncle, Magnus Fawlkes.'

'What did you find?' croaked Uncle Magnus as he met them.

Banner said, 'The murderer's out in the field. Anyone can go arrest him. He ain't gonna run away. But how can you jail a wraith, an empty suit of clothes? It's the scarecrow . . . Let's eat.'

They all went in to a profusion of eggs and bacon and cornbread. Banner regretted that there was no black coffee. But Celeste had made excellent hot cocoa.

Banner thought hard. He didn't talk to Uncle Magnus, who got the story from the others piecemeal.

Banner suddenly cut in. 'Where were you buzzing last night, Unk?'

Uncle Magnus turned a pair of haddock eyes in his direction. 'After I heard Beverly got killed,' he said, 'I went settling affairs.'

'In other words,' said Banner, 'I can take that or leave it.' He jabbed his fork into the yolk of another sunny-side-up.

'I don't mean nothing,' said Uncle Magnus, 'but I'm not sure a city man like you'll get any place among us yokels.'

'Who's a city man?' grunted Banner. 'Listen, Karloff, I was born on a farm. I left it 'cuz it was too quiet. I like lotsa noise. There's lotsa noise hereabouts, what with shotguns going off at regular intervals.'

Celeste began to gather up the breakfast plates.

Banner said to her, 'Those groceries stick to the ribs, young 'un. Thank yuh kindly, ma'am. I'll help you with the crockery.'

Celeste was scandalized. 'Oh, no, no, Senator. Please sit still. I'll take that. Oh.'

But Banner wasn't easily discouraged. He trotted into the large kitchen with a tottering pagoda of cups and saucers and plopped them into a dishpan of hot soapy water. It was a new experience for Celeste to wash dishes with a senator. He was full of funny stories and soon she was laughing. Before she knew it she was telling Banner about Uncle Magnus.

Uncle Magnus, she said, had a grievance against nearly everybody, for all his life he had been either shunned or made fun of. 'You won't believe,' she said, 'that he once tried to make love to me.'

'Why, the nasty old home wrecker.'

'Oh, no. That was before I was married. He wanted to marry me. Of course I refused him as gently as I could.'

So Uncle Magnus and his nephew were once rivals for Celeste's hand, and now the nephew was dead. Was it the revenge of the scarecrow?

It was dusk and they began to light the lights. Celeste was sitting in the parlour with Banner and Skinner. Skinner seemed reluctant to leave the farm. Celeste's hands were twisting nervously in her lap. Her fingernails were chewed short.

She looked straight into Skinner's metallic eyes. 'Blackmarsh is mine now, isn't it, judge?'

'Legally, it is,' nodded Skinner.

'Then I'm going to sell it to you,' she blurted. 'I want to get away. I want to get rid of this place tonight. Will you still buy it?'

Skinner glanced quizzically at Banner, who didn't say anything. 'It's a little unusual,' said Skinner, 'what with everyone involved in a murder case. But I'm the law and I can make it stand. My offer is five thousand dollars, as you know.'

Celeste stood up. 'That's more than plenty.'

'I'll have to go to Cow Crossing to get the money,' Skinner said eagerly, getting up. 'Excuse me.' He took his mangy beaver off the hat rack, grabbed up his hawthorn stick, and presently they heard his horse and buggy crunch down the gravel drive.

Celeste looked appealingly at Banner. 'It's been a hard day. Do you mind if I go upstairs for a rest, Senator?'

'Run right along, baby bunting.'

She smiled gratefully at him. He followed her out of the parlour and watched her go quickly up the stairs, into the dark. Near the top he saw her hesitate and he plainly heard her startled, 'Oh!'

His bulk travelled up the stairs at a surprising clip. He stood by her side. 'What is it?' he asked.

'I—I stubbed my toe,' she said. Were there lies in her round eyes?

'Are you sure?' he questioned.

She laughed nervously. 'I'm all right, Senator.' She crossed the dark hall and switched on the dim bulb. He watched her walk to one of the rooms and go in and close the door quietly.

He went back down the stairs again. 'Something's wrong here. Damn it. It's all wrong. But there ain't gonna be any artful dodging tonight.'

Uncle Magnus and Wayne were playing snip-snap-snorem on the oilcloth of the kitchen table. And both were yawning.

'Thinking of hitting the hay early tonight, neighbours?' asked Banner.

They said they were about ready to turn in.

'Tonight,' said Banner, 'I'm gonna lock you all up.'

'Lock us up!' the men repeated at the same time.

'As a precaution,' said Banner. The two card players looked at each other. 'As a safeguard for yourselves and the others. Who has the bedroom door keys?'

'Celeste,' said Uncle Magnus. They got up and stretched.

Banner went upstairs and knocked on Celeste's door. She let him in. She was wearing a navy flannel robe over her nightgown.

Banner said, 'I'm locking all the bedrooms tonight, Celeste. They tell me you have the keys.'

'Key,' she corrected. 'All the doors have the same sort of lock. Hudson had a key. This is it.' She took a thick-bodied key off her dresser and put it into his hand.

He went over to her window and examined it. There were storm shutters that could be closed from the inside and locked. On the outside of the window a heavy screen was nailed solidly to the casing. To get out that way the occupant of the room would first have to punch a hole in the screen.

'When I go out I'll lock this door,' he said. 'If it ain't too warm for you, bolt those shutters.'

She didn't ask him why. She said good night timidly, and as he went out he saw her move toward the window.

He locked her door. Then he took a heavy chair and jammed the back under the doorknob as an added measure.

All the bedrooms were along the same hallway, some on one side and some on the other; but there were no connecting doors between rooms.

Banner went in to bid both Uncle Magnus and Wayne separate sleep-tights. He looked at both of their windows. They were like Celeste's; the shutters and the screen nailed to the window-frame from the outside. He locked both their doors too and put chair-backs under the doorknobs. Now just let anyone try and get out.

He was down in the parlour playing idiot's delight, a game of solitaire, when he heard the horse and buggy rattling up the drive.

Skinner came in. 'Where's Celeste?' he asked.

Banner riffled the deck of cards. 'She's gone beddy-bye. You'll have to save it till morning.'

'Oh, lord,' groaned Skinner wearily. 'Do I have to go all the way back to town tonight?'

'No,' said Banner. 'Take the same room you had last night. Go out and unhitch your dapple grey.'

When Skinner came back into the house Banner led him upstairs. Banner said, 'The people are sleeping in this house tonight under certain conditions—behind locked doors. I'm locking yours.'

Skinner looked stunned. 'Then you think that I—'

'I'm not thinking anything,' said Banner gruffly. 'I'm just doing.'

Assuring himself that Skinner could not get out through the window, Banner turned the key in the lock. Another chair-back went under a knob.

He padded down to the end of the hall to the stairway and looked back at the four bedroom doors barricaded with chairs.

There was one other door that he went to and tried. It opened on Beverly's room and it was fast. He left the hall light burning.

Going into the parlour, he surveyed the scattered cards on the glossy tabletop. 'I'm licking you this time,' he vowed. Idiot's delight began again.

Time had slipped by. Banner might have dozed over his game. A quake shook his whole big body and he found himself blinking at the sallow face of the grandfather clock.

It was past midnight.

What had brought him up so sharp?

The house was as still as a catacomb. Then he heard something that chilled him to the very marrow.

In the upper hall where the bedrooms were situated, someone was walking.

Someone was walking in the hall—*and yet he had locked them all in!*

He could hear the sound of each shoe as it came down on the hall runner. It was a clumping sound, as if the shoes were hanging loose on feet that were mere bones—or sticks!

Listening, he reached out and ran all the rows of cards together. He felt glued to the chair, unable to get up.

Then came a scream. It was Celeste. And the shotgun roared.

Banner heaved himself up clumsily and the heavy table rocked. The glass lamp teetered dangerously and then toppled to the floor. The smashing of the bulb brought blackness crashing down. Banner groped across the fallen lamp and found the sliding doors. He pushed them wider and scrambled for the stairs.

He came puffing to the top.

The dimly lit hallway was exactly as he left it. The four chairs were still propped against the four doors.

A spasm of bewilderment shook him. Then he heard weak rapping on the inside of Celeste's door. He plunged towards it, pulling the key out of his pocket. He flung the tightly jammed chair aside and keyed open the door.

Celeste was on the floor, half unconscious, her breath coming shallowly. A faint trickle of blood showed deep red on her whitened face.

Automatically Banner shot his eyes to the window. The storm shutters were bolted on the inside. The boxed-in air reeked of discharged gunpowder. But there was no shotgun.

He bent over Celeste, noting that it was a grazing head wound she'd suffered, while dimly into his consciousness came the steady sound of hammering.

The three male sleepers, trapped in their rooms, were pounding on the doors.

Banner ignored them. He brought water in a basin and

bathed Celeste's face. It didn't look so bad with the blood washed away. Still her scalp was torn and there were powder burns.

She stopped groaning and opened her eyes. She clutched blindly at Banner's arm with both hands. 'The scarecrow! It was in here! It shot me!'

'Easy now, child. How'd the scarecrow get in?'

She looked dumbfounded. 'I don't know. I don't know. I left the light on after I locked the shutters. I went to bed. Finally I went to sleep. I woke up with a start. *It* was standing right there at the foot of my bed. I almost died of fright. But when I saw the shotgun pointing at my head it made me throw myself forward to wrench it out of the thing's hands or to spoil the aim. It seemed to go off right in my face. I guess I fainted. When I was myself again I was alone in the room, trying to get out.'

She was frightfully weak from shock. Banner left her on the bed while he went to examine the shutter bolt. There was nothing tricky about it. The screen outside the window was intact and the lock on the door hadn't been tampered with.

Banner went out into the hall, took the chairs away from the other doors, and let the three men out. They peppered him with questions. All he said was, 'The scarecrow got into Celeste's room.'

'This finishes me with this house,' said Uncle Magnus. 'I'm taking Celeste to a doctor.'

'Wait a minnit,' snapped Banner. 'No wandering off, Unk, till I give you the checkered flag. We're all sticking together, like the Rover Boys.' He led them back to Celeste's room. 'Unkie'll take you to town,' he said to Celeste.

'I want to go and never come back,' she said. 'But there's one thing I haven't told you, Senator . . . You know that time when I was going up the stairs? You asked me why I'd stopped.'

'Yep.'

'It was something I *saw*.'

'What'd you see?'

'It was—just a white figure. That's all I can tell you. It was gone in an instant. When you asked me what happened I wasn't sure I really had seen anything. I thought perhaps I was so nervous I'd imagined it. But now I don't think so.'

Banner nodded soberly. He said to Skinner and Uncle Magnus, 'You two stay here with Celeste. Wayne, we'll hitch a horse to the shay.'

They went out of the house and started toward the stable. They drew up short.

Ahead of them on the path stood the empty grotesque scarecrow. It stood on its pole, taunting them.

Banner heard Wayne breathe heavily beside him. 'The hounds,' he was muttering. 'They never barked.'

Celeste and Uncle Magnus, to the pound of horse's hooves, were gone towards Cow Crossing.

The three remaining men huddled like sheep in the parlour. Banner went to a wall phone and said to a sleepy operator, 'Wake up, Rip, and gimme Foxchase Hall.'

Wayne looked at him in mute surprise.

Banner got one of the lady instructors on the wire after a lengthy wait. 'Lissen, Trixie,' he said, 'I'm calling the roll. You've got a gal there named Joan Vicars. Am I right or wrong?'

'You're incomprehensible, whoever you are,' was the reply. 'But you're right. She's a member of my American Literature class.'

'Is she in the school now?'

'Of course she's in the school now.'

'I'm still taking stock, sister. Put her on.'

'I'll transfer your call to her dormitory.'

Banner heard a click and a dull buzzing. Then a lazy blond voice came on the line.

'Who's this?' said Banner.

'A girl.'

'Joan Vicars?'

'Nope, one of her classmates.'

'Girlie, put Joanie on.'

There was a pause. Then the girl said, 'I can't. She isn't here.'

'Where is she, playmate?'

'Lord knows,' said the girl. 'Who're you? Her old mandarin?'

'No, this's Senator Banner.'

'I guess I can tell you what we think. She got pretty mushy with a farm boy named Wayne Markes. All last week she was starry-eyed and telling us she planned to elope with him. When she didn't come back the other day we all guessed she'd gone and done it. We've been covering up for her. Isn't that romantic—or are you just an old fuddy?'

'I'm an old fuddy,' he said. He hung up. He wheeled on Wayne. 'Did you elope with Joan Vicars ?'

'Elope!' cried Wayne. 'No such luck. I haven't seen her for days.'

'The gals at Foxchase Hall think you've spirited her off.'

'Well, I'll see about that.' Wayne jumped up impetuously and started for the door. There he paused, expecting Banner to halt him gruffly. Banner was carved from rock. Wayne bolted out. They heard him running.

That left Banner and Skinner at the Grange.

'Better stick with me,' said Banner, starting to follow Wayne out. Skinner stuck with him. They went past the storage shed, where Banner picked up a bull's-eye lantern. The horses stirred in the stable when they went in, the whites of the animals' eyes gleaming.

Banner climbed into the loft and kicked the straw around. He came down again and eyed the pile of horse blankets.

In a few minutes they went out into the night again.

'Skinner,' said Banner, 'the scarecrow is gonna make one more attempt.'

Skinner's voice sounded as if it were riding the edge of a razor. 'Who—'

Banner's hand fell heavily on the lean shoulder. 'You, Skinner.'

Skinner's laugh was sickly. 'You're clowning.'

'No, I'm not. You're next. Knowing that, we've gotta hamstring the scarecrow.'

Skinner almost sobbed. 'If you know that much, you know who the scarecrow is.'

'I do, pal.'

'For mercy's sake, Senator Banner, who is it?'

Banner shook his head. 'It's no use. You wouldn't believe me.'

They were halfway to the house in a wide open spot.

Banner said, 'You're bait, Skinner. As long as I'm with you, you're safe. That goes for me too. The scarecrow won't tackle two of us. But I'm gonna leave you alone—'

'No,' begged Skinner, 'don't leave me!'

'Scaredy cat. I'll only pretend to. We'll go back to the parlour. Then I'll tell you I'm returning to the stable. I'll go out and run around to the side of the house, and come in the window. Then we'll wait for the scarecrow. The scarecrow's forced to act tonight—now—if anything's to be accomplished.'

Banner helped Skinner, shaking and white-faced, back into the parlour, where Skinner flopped weakly in a chair. Banner prowled to the window and loosened the screen. Then he went to the sliding doors and said in a voice that must have carried all the way to the barn:

'It's no use your staying, Skinner. I'll put your dobbin between the shafts and you can jog back to town.'

'Yes,' said Skinner in a choked voice.

'Pull these doors closed after me,' continued Banner loudly. 'It'll only take me ten minutes.'

Skinner got up and slid the doors closed. Banner went out on the porch and let his footsteps die away in the direction of the stable.

In an incredibly short space of time Banner, puffing and

blowing, appeared at the side window. He came wriggling into the room like a walrus. 'This's what comes of eating too much strawberry shortcake,' he whispered, smothering a chuckle.

Skinner was collapsed in the rocker by the table in the centre of the room. Banner pulled a chair close to the sliding doors, now closed, sat down, and began to wait.

One minute went by. Two minutes. Three minutes . . .

Skinner, rooted to his chair, looked horrified at the crack slowly appearing between the two doors beside Banner. There was not a sound. The crack got wider. White-gloved fingers pushed their squirming way in and then a hand rested between the doors.

Banner never moved.

The white-gloved hand was withdrawn and gradually the double barrels of a shotgun slid through, the invisible gunner drawing a bead on Skinner's head.

Then like lightning Banner's hand shot out and seized the barrels and forced them up. The shotgun roared and buckshot riddled the ceiling. Banner slammed one of the double doors back and followed the gun out into the front hall.

Skinner uprooted himself. He had to see. He was behind Banner.

Then his senses almost failed him.

Struggling in Banner's iron grip, her face distorted with rage, was Beverly Jelke!

Daybreak was spreading over the sky like a pale stain. Banner faced Skinner in the jurisconsult's office above Main Street.

Banner said, 'Everything indicated that the body found in the creek was Bev's. Her clothes were on the bank, her ring was on her hand. Generally, the physique and colouring were Bev's. But exact identification of the features wasn't possible, 'cuz, as you had told me, the buckshot had smeared most of the face.

'Wayne saw a luminous figure in the fruit trees. Bare flesh

gives off a glow in the moonlight. The person Wayne saw was naked . . . Then there was the peculiar stillness of the hounds, though the hideous scarecrow cavorted all over the place. There's only one answer to that. The hounds knew who the scarecrow was. It was a person they were thoroughly used to.

'But it was the attempt on Celeste while all the doors were locked that settled it for me. *Nobody* could have gotten out of those four rooms. That proved the murderer was still on the outside. The murderer, then, was someone who had complete run of the grounds and whom the dogs regarded as a master. Everyone at the Grange was eliminated except one person— Beverly Jelke. That's why I told you the answer was unbelievable. But taking it as true, whose body was found in the creek?

'Remember that Wayne caught sight of Bev running naked through the trees after the second murder. Why was she naked? 'Cuz she had left all her clothes on the bank. Why didn't she put on her victim's clothes? 'Cuz her victim had been wearing nothing but a bathing suit; she had come down to the creek in a bathing suit.

'Who finds the creek that convenient? It wasn't anybody from the Grange. They were all accounted for. The nearest other place is Foxchase Hall. It was one of the schoolgals! And we knew that Joan Vicars had come down to the creek occasionally. Could it be Joan Vicars they found in the creek? I checked later and found her missing.

'We can see now that Bev needed clothes. She couldn't get back into the house immediately. All that was available was the scarecrow rig. She put that on. Bev, as heartless as she's painted, had killed Joan to pave the way to the more important murder of her brother.

'To murder Hudson, she made some disturbance outside the farmhouse while all of us were asleep, and when he came to the porch to investigate she let him have it with the kitchen shotgun. Before she vamoosed she removed a bedroom key from Hudson's pocket. It had been her key. Hudson had taken it from the body in the mortuary along with the rest of Bev's effects earlier that day.

'Then Bev began to play tricks. She left a broad trail from Hudson's body. This trail petered out in some shale at the edge of the ploughed field. At least we couldn't see any more footprints at that point, but the hounds were still able to follow the trail by the scent. Then Bev hit us between the eyes with the footprints in the newly ploughed field.

'What she did was simple. She wanted us to see with our own eyes where the trail led, so that we'd call off the hounds. She was standing there dressed as the scarecrow. She had to get that scarecrow forty feet inside the field with only one set of shoe tracks leading up to it. First she made a cross-piece of a couple of dead branches to hang the ragged clothes on. Then she took off the scarecrow shoes she was wearing and continued *barefoot* out into the field for another forty feet.

'She took off her clothes and set up the scarecrow the way we found it. All except the shoes. She put the heavy shoes on again and walked *backwards* to the edge of the field, where she started from. She stepped carefully on each bare footprint—the ones she'd made walking into the field. We didn't think right off that large shoe tracks can completely blot out slighter bare footprints . . .

'We have Bev standing nude on the rim of the ploughed field, the scarecrow forty feet from her and a pair of shoes in her hand. How'd she get the shoes out under the scarecrow? Horseshoe pitching is her favourite sport. You told me that. She could put them in pretty close at forty feet, couldn't she, Skinner?' Banner chuckled.

'During the day she hid out in the stable or the barn and kept herself covered with straw and horse blankets. She ate raw carrots, kale and broccoli from her vegetable garden.'

Skinner interrupted, 'But why—Why did she want to kill me?'

'She wanted to get away from the farm with the five thousand you were willing to offer for it. Since Hudson was dead, he could no longer raise an objection to the sale. Celeste would wanna sell out and you'd bring the money to the farm. Bev had to have that money to start over again somewhere else; there was no use going away without it. She knew she had to kill you for it.

'Bev had finally slipped into the house and into her room by the time you and Celeste had come to that sale agreement in the parlour. Bev had dressed herself in some of her own clothes. She was up on the stairs, listening to us. She knew you were gonna get the money that night. Then Celeste ran quickly up the stairs and Bev ducked back into the dark to hide herself. But Celeste caught a glimpse of Bev, though she didn't know who it was. For all Bev knew, Celeste had spotted her and knew she was still alive. So Bev had to put your killing on her waiting list. She had to erase Celeste first.

'As you can see, there really was no problem of getting out of the locked rooms. The scarecrow was outside all the time. The shoes on her feet sounded loose as she walked down the hall, for they were far too big for her. She removed the chair I had put up and entered Celeste's room with the same key she'd taken off Hudson's body. She intended to blast Celeste full of buckshot. But Celeste defended herself. Bev couldn't stay for a second shot. She had to get out and leave things the way I'd set them before I could stomp up the stairs.

'Bev was hard pressed. To get the money she had to kill you before you left the Grange last night. Her hand was forced. So she fell into my trap. Come into my parlour, said the flies to the spider.'

JOSEPH COMMINGS

Born in New York in 1913, Joseph Commings is today almost forgotten outside a diminishing circle of aficionados of impossible crime fiction. After a brief spell as a journalist, he began his sporadic and very varied writing career during the Second World War on overseas postings with the US Air Force. Initially, he wrote to entertain his comrades and, on being demobbed, he must have been delighted to find a ready market in the so-called 'pulps' such as *Western Trails*, *Hollywood Detective*, *Mystery Digest* and *Killers Mystery Story Magazine*. His crime fiction is characterised by undeniably improbable situations, unfeasibly trusting witnesses and extraordinarily clever solutions. In one story the murderer might appear to be a vampire and in another a giant, but what truly lifts his work out of the run of the mill is Commings' sense of humour.

Commings' best-known character is Brooks Urban Banner, a Senator in the Democratic party who is also a criminal lawyer and a practising magician. Banner is modelled very much in the style of John Dickson Carr's heroic sleuth Dr Gideon Fell (himself inspired by G. K. Chesterton) and is 'extra large' in every sense: he weighs nearly 300 pounds, has a mop of shaggy white hair and dresses loudly. Fond of tall tales, the Senator claims to have had all manner of careers—including hobo, locksmith and comic book enthusiast—which provide some of the arcane knowledge that allows him to unravel the baffling mysteries with which he is confronted. While he doesn't appear in any novel-length investigations, there are over thirty Banner short stories. Fifteen of these were gathered together by the late Bob Adey, the authority on impossible crime stories, and form the collection *Banner Deadlines* (Crippen & Landru, 2004); a second volume is forthcoming. Commings' non-Banner stories—of which there are at least forty, some written under pseudonyms—are mostly mysteries, sometimes with an unusual setting, but none captures the eccentric genius of the Banner canon.

As a writer, Joe Commings is sometimes criticised for an overly frivolous approach to the business of murder. That was of course quite deliberate. In a letter to the *New York Times Book Review*, published in 1941, Commings protested that the vast majority of publishing houses were uninterested in publishing anything humorous and therefore unwilling to accept his 'whimsical wares'. As he was unwilling to write in any another way his work remained largely confined to the pulps while a few novel-length manuscripts also failed to find a publisher.

In his fifties, Commings supplemented his income from crime fiction by writing pornographic paperbacks with titles like *Man Eater* (1965), *Operation Aphrodite* (1966) and *Swinging Wives* (1971), as well as a study of sex crimes whose aim seems to have been titillation more than education.

In the early 1970s, Joe Commings suffered a stroke and his writing career came to an end. He moved to a care home in Maryland where he died in 1992.

'The Scarecrow Murders' was originally published in *10-Story Detective* magazine in April 1948.

THE INCIDENT OF THE DOG'S BALL

Agatha Christie

(From the notes of Captain Arthur Hastings O.B.E.)

I always look back upon the case of Miss Matilda Wheeler with special interest simply because of the curious way it worked itself out—from nothing at all as it were!

I remember that it was a particularly hot airless day in August. I was sitting in my friend Poirot's rooms wishing for the hundredth time that we could be in the country and not in London. The post had just been brought in. I remember the sound of each envelope in turn being opened neatly, as Poirot did everything, by means of a little paper-cutter. Then would come his murmured comment and the letter in question would be allotted to its proper pile. It was an orderly monotonous business.

And then suddenly there came a difference. A longer pause, a letter not read once but twice. A letter that was not docketed in the usual way but which remained in the recipient's hand. I looked across at my friend. The letter now lay on his knee. He was staring thoughtfully across the room.

'Anything of interest, Poirot?' I asked.

'*Cela dépend.* Possibly you would not think so. It is a letter from an old lady, Hastings, and it says nothing—but nothing at all.'

'Very useful,' I commented sarcastically.

'*N'est ce pas*? It is the way of old ladies, that. Round and round the point they go! But see for yourself. I shall be interested to know what you make of it.'

He tossed me the letter. I unfolded it and made a slight grimace. It consisted of four closely written pages in a spiky and shaky handwriting with numerous alterations, erasures, and copious underlining.

'Must I really read it?' I asked plaintively. 'What is it about?'

'It is, as I told you just now, about nothing.'

Hardly encouraged by this remark I embarked unwillingly on my task. I will confess that I did not read it very carefully. The writing was difficult and I was content to take guesses on the context.

The writer seemed to be a Miss Matilda Wheeler of The Laburnums, Little Hemel. After much doubt and indecision, she wrote, she had felt herself emboldened to write to M. Poirot. At some length she went on to state exactly how and where she had heard M. Poirot's name mentioned. The matter was such, she said, that she found it extremely difficult to consult anyone in Little Hemel—and of course there was the possibility that she might be completely mistaken—that she was attaching a most ridiculous significance to perfectly natural incidents. In fact she had chided herself unsparingly for fancifulness, but ever since the incident of the dog's ball she had felt most uneasy. She could only hope to hear from M. Poirot if he did not think the whole thing was a mare's nest. Also, perhaps, he would be so kind as to let her know what his fee would be? The matter, she knew was very trivial and unimportant, but her health was bad and her nerves not what they had been and worry of this kind was very bad for her, and the more she thought of it, the more she was *convinced* that she was right, though, of course, she would not *dream* of saying anything.

That was more or less the gist of the thing. I put it down with a sigh of exasperation.

'Why can't the woman say what she's talking about? Of all the idiotic letters!'

'*N'est ce pas?* A regrettable failure to employ order and method in the mental process.'

'What do you think she does mean? Not that it matters much. Some upset to her pet dog, I suppose. Anyway, it's not worth taking seriously.'

'You think not, my friend?'

'My dear Poirot, I cannot see why you are so intrigued by this letter.'

'No, you have not seen. The most interesting point in that letter—you have passed it by unnoticed.'

'What is the interesting point?'

'*The date, mon ami.*'

I looked at the heading of the letter again.

'April 12th,' I said slowly.

'*C'est curieux, n'est ce pas?*' Nearly four months ago.'

'I don't suppose it has any significance. She probably meant to put August 12th.'

'No, no, Hastings. Look at the colour of the ink. That letter was written a good time ago. No, April 12th is the date assuredly. But why was it not sent? And if the writer changed her mind about sending it, why did she keep it and send it now?'

He rose.

'*Mon ami*—the day is hot. In London one stifles, is it not so? Then how say you to a little expedition into the country? To be exact, to Little Hemel which is, I see, in the County of Kent.'

I was only too willing and then and there we started off on our visit of exploration.

II

Little Hemel we found to be a charming village, untouched in the miraculous way that villages can be when they are two miles from a main road. There was a hostelry called The George, and there we had lunch—a bad lunch I regret to say, as is the way at country inns.

An elderly waiter attended to us, a heavy-breathing man, and as he brought us two cups of a doubtful fluid called coffee, Poirot started his campaign.

'A house called The Laburnums,' he said. 'You know it? The house of a Miss Wheeler.'

'That's right, sir. Just past the church. You can't miss it. Three Miss Wheelers there were, old-fashioned ladies, born and brought up here. Ah! well, they're all gone now and the house is up for sale.'

He shook his head sadly.

'So the Miss Wheelers are all dead?' said Poirot.

'Yes, sir. Miss Amelia and Miss Caroline twelve years ago and Miss Matilda just a month or two ago. You thinking of buying the house, sir—if I may ask?'

'The idea had occurred to me,' said Poirot mendaciously. 'But I believe it is in a very bad state.'

'It's old-fashioned, sir. Never been modernised as the saying goes. But it's in good condition—roof and drains and all that. Never grudged money on repairs, Miss Wheeler didn't, and the garden was always a picture.'

'She was well off?'

'Oh! very comfortably off indeed, sir. A very well-to-do family.'

'I suppose the house has been left to someone who has no use for it? A niece or nephew or some distant relative?'

'No, sir, she left it to her companion, Miss Lawson. But Miss Lawson doesn't fancy living in it, and so it's up for sale. But it's a bad time for selling houses, they say.'

'Whenever one has to sell anything it is always a bad time,' said Poirot smiling, as he paid the bill and added a handsome tip. 'When exactly did you say Miss Matilda Wheeler died?'

'Just the beginning of May, sir—thank you, sir—or was it the end of April? She'd not been in good health for a long time.'

'You have a good doctor here?'

'Yes, sir, Dr Lawrence. He's getting on now, but he's well thought of down here. Always very pleasant-spoken and careful.'

Poirot nodded and presently we strolled out into the hot August sunshine and made our way along the street in the direction of the church.

Before we got to it, however, we passed an old-fashioned house set a little way back, with a brass plate on the gate inscribed with the name of Dr Lawrence.

'Excellent,' said Poirot. 'We will make a call here. At this hour we shall make sure of finding the doctor at home.'

'My dear Poirot! But what on earth are you going to say? And anyway what are you driving at?'

'For your first question, *mon ami*, the answer is simple—I shall have to invent. Fortunately I have the imagination fertile. For your second question—*eh bien*, after we have conversed with the doctor, it may be that I shall find I am not driving at anything.'

III

Dr Lawrence proved to be a man of about sixty. I put him down as an unambitious kindly sort of fellow, not particularly brilliant mentally, but quite sound.

Poirot is a past master in the art of mendacity. In five minutes we were all chatting together in the most friendly fashion—it being somehow taken for granted that we were old and dear friends of Miss Matilda Wheeler.

'Her death, it is a great shock to me. Most sad,' said Poirot. 'She had the stroke? No?'

'Oh! no, my dear fellow. Yellow atrophy of the liver. Been coming on for a long time. She had a very bad attack of jaundice a year ago. She was pretty well through the winter except for digestive trouble. Then she had jaundice again the end of April and died of it. A great loss to us—one of the real old-fashioned kind.'

'Ah! yes, indeed,' sighed Poirot. 'And the companion, Miss Lawson—?'

He paused and rather to our surprise the doctor responded promptly.

'I can guess what you're after, and I don't mind telling you that you've my entire sympathy. But if you're coming to me for any hope of "undue influence" it's no good. Miss Wheeler was perfectly capable of making a will—not only when she did—but right up to the day of her death. It's no good hoping that I can say anything different because I can't.'

'But your sympathy—'

'My sympathy is with James Graham and Miss Mollie. I've always felt strongly that money shouldn't be left away from the family to an outsider. I daresay there might be some sort of case that Miss Lawson obtained an ascendency over Miss Wheeler owing to spiritualistic tomfoolery—but I doubt if there's anything that you could take into court. Only run yourself in for terrific expense. Avoid the law, wherever you can, is my motto. And certainly medically I can't help you. Miss Wheeler's mind was perfectly clear.'

He shook hands with us and we passed out into the sunlight.

'Well!' I said. 'That was rather unexpected!'

'Truly. We begin to learn a little about my correspondent. She has at least two relatives—James Graham and a girl called Mollie. They ought to have inherited her money but did not do so. By a will clearly not made very long ago, the whole amount has gone to the companion, Miss Lawson. There is also a very significant mention of spiritualism.'

'You think that significant?'

'Obviously. A credulous old lady—the spirits tell her to leave her money to a particular person—she obeys. Something of that kind occurs to one as a possibility, does it not?'

IV

We had arrived at The Laburnums. It was a fair-sized Georgian house, standing a little way back from the street with a large garden behind. There was a board stuck up with 'For Sale' on it.

Poirot rang the bell. His efforts were rewarded by a fierce barking within. Presently the door was opened by a neat middle-aged woman who held a barking wire-haired terrier by the collar.

'Good afternoon,' said Poirot. 'The house is for sale, I understand, so Mr James Graham told me.'

'Oh! yes, sir. You would like to see over it?'

'If you please.'

'You needn't be afraid of Bob, sir. He barks if anyone comes to the door, but he's as gentle as a lamb really.'

True enough, as soon as we were inside, the terrier jumped up and licked our hands. We were shown over the house— pathetic as an empty house always is, with the marks of pictures showing on the walls, and the bare uncarpeted floors. We found the woman only too ready and willing to talk to friends of the family, as she supposed us to be. By his mention of James Graham, Poirot created this impression very cleverly.

Ellen, for such was our guide's name, had clearly been very attached to her late mistress. She entered with the gusto of her class into a description of her illness and death.

'Taken sudden she was. And suffered! Poor dear! Delirious at the end. All sorts of queer things she'd say. How long was it? Well, it must have been three days from the time she was took bad. But poor dear, she'd suffered for many years on and off. Jaundice last year she had—and her food never agreed with her well. She'd take digestion tablets after nearly every meal. Oh! yes, she suffered a good deal one way or another. Sleeplessness for one thing. Used to get up and walk about the house at night, she did, her eyesight being too bad for much reading.'

It was at this point that Poirot produced from his pocket the letter. He held it out to her.

'Do you recognise this by any chance?' he asked.

He was watching her narrowly. She gave an exclamation of surprise.

'Well, now, I do declare! And is it you that's the gentleman it's written to?'

Poirot nodded.

'Tell me how you came to post it to me?' he said.

'Well, sir, I didn't know what to do—and that's the truth. When the furniture was all cleared out, Miss Lawson she gave me several little odds and ends that had been the mistress's. And among them was a mother of pearl blotter that I'd always admired. I put it by in a drawer, and it was only yesterday that I took it out and was putting new blotting paper in it when I found this letter slipped inside the pocket. It was the mistress's handwriting and I saw as she'd meant to post it and slipped it in there and forgot—which was the kind of thing she did many a time, poor dear. Absent-minded as you might say. Well, I didn't know what to do. I didn't like to put it in the fire and I couldn't take it upon myself to open it and I didn't see as it was any business of Miss Lawson's, so I just put a stamp on it and ran out to the post box and posted it.'

Ellen paused for breath and the terrier uttered a sharp staccato bark. It was so peremptory in sound that Poirot's attention was momentarily diverted. He looked down at the dog who was sitting with his nose lifted entreatingly towards the empty mantelpiece of the drawing-room where we were at the time.

'But what is it that he regards so fixedly?' asked Poirot.

Ellen laughed.

'It's his ball, sir. It used to be put in a jar on the mantelpiece and he thinks it ought somehow or other to be there still.'

'I see,' said Poirot. 'His ball . . .' He remained thoughtful for a moment or two.

'Tell me,' he said. 'Did your mistress ever mention to you something about the dog and his ball? Something that perturbed her greatly?'

'Now it's odd your saying that, sir. She never said anything about a ball, but I do believe there was something about Bob here that was on her mind—for she tried to say something just as she was dying. "The dog," she said. "The dog—" and then something about a picture ajar—nothing that made sense but there, poor soul, she was delirious and didn't know what she was saying.'

'You will comprehend,' said Poirot, 'that this letter not reaching me when it should have done, I am greatly intrigued about many things and much in the dark. There are several questions that I should wish to ask.'

By this time Ellen would have taken for granted any statement that Poirot had chosen to make. We adjourned to her somewhat overcrowded sitting-room and having pacified Bob by giving him the desired ball, which he retired under a table to chew, Poirot began his interrogations.

'First of all,' he said, 'I comprehend that Miss Wheeler's nearest relations were only two in number?'

'That's right, sir. Mr James—Mr James Graham whom you mentioned just now—and Miss Davidson. They were first cousins and niece and nephew to Miss Wheeler. There were five Miss Wheelers, you see, and only two of them married.'

'And Miss Lawson was no relation at all?'

'No, indeed—nothing but a paid companion.'

Scorn was uppermost in Ellen's voice.

'Did you like Miss Lawson, Ellen?'

'Well, sir, she wasn't one you could dislike, so to speak. Neither one thing nor the other, she wasn't, a poor sort of creature, and full of nonsense about spirits. Used to sit in the dark, they did, she and Miss Wheeler and the two Miss Pyms. A *sayance*, they called it. Why, they were at it the very night she was taken bad. And if you ask me, it was that wicked nonsense that made Miss Wheeler leave her money away from her own flesh and blood.'

'When exactly did she make the new will? But perhaps you do not know that.'

'Oh! yes, I do. Sent for the lawyer she did while she was still laid up.'

'Laid up?'

'Yes, sir—from a fall she had. Down the stairs. Bob here had left his ball on top of the stairs and she slipped on it and fell. In the night it was. As I tell you, she used to get up and walk about.'

'Who was in the house at the time?'

'Mr James and Miss Mollie were here for the weekend. Easter it was, and it was the night of Bank Holiday. There was cook and me and Miss Lawson and Mr James and Miss Mollie and what with the fall and the scream we all came out. Cut her head, she did, and strained her back. She had to lie up for nearly a week. Yes, she was still in bed—it was the following Friday— when she sent for Mr Halliday. And the gardener had to come in and witness it, because for some reason I couldn't, on account of her having remembered me in it, and cook alone wasn't enough.'

'Bank holiday was the 10th of April,' said Poirot. He looked at me meaningfully. 'Friday would be the 14th. And what next? Did Miss Wheeler get up again?'

'Oh! yes, sir. She got up on the Saturday, and Miss Mollie and Mr James they came down again, being anxious about her, you see. Mr James he even came down the weekend after that.'

'The weekend of the 22nd?'

'Yes, sir.'

'And when was Miss Wheeler finally taken ill?'

'It was the 25th, sir. Mr James had left the day before. And Miss Wheeler seemed as well as she'd ever been—bar her indigestion, of course, but that was chronic. Taken sudden after the sayance, she was. They had a sayance after dinner, you know, so the Miss Pyms went home and Miss Lawson and I got her to bed and sent for Dr Lawrence.'

Poirot sat frowning for a moment or two, then he asked Ellen for the address of Miss Davidson and Mr Graham and also for that of Miss Lawson.

All three proved to be in London. James Graham was junior partner in some chemical dye works, Miss Davidson worked in a beauty parlour in Dover Street. Miss Lawson had taken a flat near High Street, Kensington.

As we left, Bob, the dog, rushed up to the top of the staircase, lay down and carefully nosed his ball over the edge so that it bumped down the stairs. He remained, wagging his tail, until it was thrown up to him again.

'The incident of the dog's ball,' murmured Poirot under his breath.

V

A minute or two later we were out in the sunshine again.

'Well,' I said with a laugh. 'The dog's ball incident did not amount to much after all. We now know exactly what it was. The dog left his ball at the top of the stairs and the old lady tripped over it and fell. So much for that!'

'Yes, Hastings, as you say—the incident is simple enough. What we do not know—and what I should like to know—and what I *mean* to know—is why the old lady was so perturbed by it?'

'Do you think there is anything in that?'

'Consider the dates, Hastings. On Monday night, the fall. On

Wednesday the letter written to me. On Friday the altered will. There is something curious there. Something that I should like to know. And ten days afterwards Miss Wheeler dies. If it had been a sudden death, one of these mysterious deaths due to "heart failure"—I confess I should have been suspicious. But her death appears to have been perfectly natural and due to disease of long standing. *Tout de même*—'

He went off into a brown study. Finally he said unexpectedly:

'If you really wished to kill someone, Hastings, how would you set about it?'

'Well—I don't know. I can't imagine myself—'

'One can always imagine. Think, for instance, of a particularly repellent money-lender, of an innocent girl in his clutches.'

'Yes,' I said slowly. 'I suppose one might always see red and knock a fellow out.'

Poirot sighed.

'*Mais oui*, it would be that way with you! But I seek to imagine the mind of someone very different. A cold-blooded but cautious murderer, reasonably intelligent. What would he try first? Well, there is accident. A well-staged accident—that is very difficult for the police to bring home to the perpetrator. But it has its disadvantages—it may disable but not kill. And then, possibly, the victim might be suspicious. Accident cannot be tried again. Suicide? Unless a convenient piece of writing with an ambiguous meaning can be obtained from the victim, suicide would be very uncertain. Then murder—recognised as such. For that you want a scapegoat or an alibi.'

'But Miss Wheeler wasn't murdered. Really, Poirot—'

'I know. I know. *But she died*, Hastings. Do not forget—*she died*. She makes a will—and ten days later she dies. And the only two people in the house with her (for I except the cook) both benefit by her death.'

'I think,' I said, 'that you have a bee in your bonnet.'

'Very possibly. Coincidences do happen. But she wrote to me, *mon ami*, she wrote to me, and until I know what made her write I cannot rest in peace.'

VI

It was about a week later that we had three interviews.

Exactly what Poirot wrote to them I do not know, but Mollie Davidson and James Graham came together by appointment, and certainly displayed no resentment. The letter from Miss Wheeler lay on the table in a conspicuous position. From the conversation that followed, I gathered that Poirot had taken considerable liberties in his account of the subject matter.

'We have come here in answer to your request, but I am sorry to say that I do not understand in the least what you are driving at, M. Poirot,' said Graham with some irritation as he laid down his hat and stick.

He was a tall thin man, looking older than his years, with pinched lips and deep-set grey eyes. Miss Davidson was a handsome fair-haired girl of twenty-nine or so. She seemed puzzled, but unresentful.

'It is that I seek to aid you,' said Poirot. 'Your inheritance it has been wrested from you! It has gone to a stranger!'

'Well, that's over and done with,' said Graham. 'I've taken legal advice and it seems there's nothing to be done. And I really cannot see where it concerns *you*, M. Poirot.'

'I think, James, that that is not very fair to M. Poirot,' said Mollie Davidson. 'He is a busy man, but he is going out of his way to help us. I wish he could. All the same, I'm afraid nothing can be done. We simply can't afford to go to law.'

'Can't afford. Can't afford. We haven't got a leg to stand upon,' said her cousin irritably.

'That is where I come in,' said Poirot. 'This letter'—he tapped it with a fingernail—'has suggested a possible idea to me. Your aunt, I understand, had originally made a will leaving her property to be divided between you. Suddenly, on the 14th April she makes another will. Did you know of that will, by the way?'

It was to Graham he put the question.

Graham flushed and hesitated a moment.

'Yes,' he said, 'I knew of it. My aunt told me of it.'

'What?' A cry of astonishment came from the girl.

Poirot wheeled round upon her.

'You did not know of it, Mademoiselle?'

'No, it came as a great shock to me. I thought it did to my cousin also. When did Auntie tell you, James?'

'That next weekend—the one after Easter.'

'And I was there and you never told me?'

'No—I—well, I thought it better to keep it to myself.'

'How extraordinary of you!'

'What exactly did your aunt say to you, Mr Graham?' asked Poirot in his most silky tone.

Graham clearly disliked answering the question. He spoke stiffly.

'She said that she thought it only fair to let me know that she had made a new will leaving everything to Miss Lawson.'

'Did she give any reason?'

'None whatever.'

'I think you ought to have told me,' said Miss Davidson.

'I thought better not,' said her cousin stiffly.

'Eh bien,' said Poirot. 'It is all very curious. I am not at liberty to tell you what was written to me in this letter, but I will give you some advice. I would apply, if I were you, for an order of exhumation.'

They both stared at him without speaking for a minute or two.

'Oh! no,' cried Mollie Davidson.

'This is outrageous,' cried Graham. 'I shall certainly not do anything of the sort. The suggestion is preposterous.'

'You refuse?'

'Absolutely.'

Poirot turned to the girl.

'And you, Mademoiselle? Do you refuse?'

'I—No, I would not say I refused. But I do not like the idea.'

'Well, I do refuse,' said Graham angrily. 'Come on, Mollie. We've had enough of this charlatan.'

He fumbled for the door. Poirot sprang forward to help him. As he did so a rubber ball fell out of his pocket and bounced on the floor.

'Ah!' cried Poirot. 'The ball!'

He blushed and appeared uncomfortable. I guessed that he had not meant the ball to be seen.

'Come on, Mollie,' shouted Graham now in a towering passion.

The girl had retrieved the ball and handed it to Poirot.

'I did not know that you kept a dog, M. Poirot,' she said.

'I do not, Mademoiselle,' said Poirot.

The girl followed her cousin out of the room. Poirot turned to me.

'Quick, *mon ami*,' he said. 'Let us visit the companion, the now rich Miss Lawson. I wish to see her before she is in any way put upon her guard.'

'If it wasn't for the fact that James Graham knew about the new will, I should be inclined to suspect him of having a hand in this business. He was down that last weekend. However, since he knew that the old lady's death would not benefit him—well, that puts him out of court.'

'Since he knew—' murmured Poirot thoughtfully.

'Why, yes, he admitted as much,' I said impatiently.

'Mademoiselle was quite surprised at his knowing. Strange that he should not tell her at the time. Unfortunate. Yes, unfortunate.'

Exactly what Poirot was getting at I did not quite know, but knew from his tone that there was something. However, soon after, we arrived at Clanroyden Mansions.

VII

Miss Lawson was very much as I had pictured her. A middle-aged woman, rather stout, with an eager but somewhat foolish face. Her hair was untidy and she wore pince-nez. Her conversation consisted of gasps and was distinctly spasmodic.

'So good of you to come,' she said. 'Sit here, won't you? A cushion. Oh! dear, I'm afraid that chair isn't comfortable. That table's in your way. We're just a little crowded here.' (This was undeniable. There was twice as much furniture in the room than there should have been, and the walls were covered with photographs and pictures.) 'This flat is really too small. But so central. I've always longed to have a little place of my own. But there, I never thought I should. So good of dear Miss Wheeler. Not that I feel at all comfortable about it. No, indeed I don't. My conscience, M. Poirot. *Is it right?* I ask myself. And really I don't know what to say. Sometimes I think that Miss Wheeler meant me to have the money and so it must be all right. And other times—well, flesh and blood is flesh and blood—I feel very badly when I think of Mollie Davidson. Very badly indeed!'

'And when you think of Mr James Graham?'

Miss Lawson flushed and drew herself up.

'That is very different. Mr Graham has been very rude—most insulting. I can assure you, M. Poirot—there was no undue influence. I had no idea of anything of the kind. A complete shock to me.'

'Miss Wheeler did not tell you of her intentions?'

'No, indeed. A complete shock.'

'You had not, in any way, found it necessary to—shall we say, open the eyes—of Miss Wheeler in regard to her nephew's short-comings?'

'What an idea, M. Poirot! Certainly not. What put that idea into your head, if I may ask?'

'Mademoiselle, I have many curious ideas in my head.'

Miss Lawson looked at him uncertainly. Her face, I reflected, was really singularly foolish. The way the mouth hung open for instance. And yet the eyes behind the glasses seemed more intelligent than one would have suspected.

Poirot took something from his pocket.

'You recognise this, Mademoiselle?'

'Why, it's Bob's ball!'

'No,' said Poirot. 'It is a ball I bought at Woolworth's.'

'Well, of course, that's where Bob's balls do come from. Dear Bob.'

'You are fond of him?'

'Oh! yes, indeed, dear little doggie. He always slept in my room. I'd like to have him in London, but dogs aren't really happy in town, are they, M. Poirot?'

'Me, I have seen some very happy ones in the Park,' returned my friend gravely.

'Oh! yes, of course, the Park,' said Miss Lawson vaguely. 'But it's very difficult to exercise them properly. He's much happier with Ellen, I feel sure, at the dear Laburnums. Ah! what a tragedy it all was!'

'Will you recount to me, Mademoiselle, just what happened on that evening when Miss Wheeler was taken ill?'

'Nothing out of the usual. At least, oh! of course, we held a séance—with distinct phenomena—distinct phenomena. You will laugh, M. Poirot. I feel you are a sceptic. But oh! the joy of hearing the voices of those who have passed over.'

'No, I do not laugh,' said Poirot gently.

He was watching her flushed excited face.

'You know, it was most curious—really *most* curious. There was a kind of halo—a luminous haze—all round dear Miss Wheeler's head. We all saw it distinctly.'

'A luminous haze?' said Poirot sharply.

'Yes. Really most remarkable. In view of what happened, I

felt, M. Poirot, that already she was *marked*, so to speak, for the other world.'

'Yes,' said Poirot. 'I think she was—marked for the other world.' He added, completely incongruously it seemed to me, 'Has Dr Lawrence got a keen sense of smell?'

'Now it's curious you should say that. "Smell this, doctor," I said, and held up a great bunch of lilies of the valley to him. And would you believe it, he couldn't smell a thing. Ever since influenza three years ago, he said. Ah! me—physician, heal thyself is so true, isn't it?'

Poirot had risen and was prowling round the room. He stopped and stared at a picture on the wall. I joined him.

It was rather an ugly needlework picture done in drab wools, and represented a bulldog sitting on the steps of a house. Below it, in crooked letters, were the words '*Out all night and no key!*'

Poirot drew a deep breath.

'This picture, it comes from The Laburnums?'

'Yes. It used to hang over the mantelpiece in the drawing-room. Dear Miss Wheeler did it when she was a girl.'

'Ah!' said Poirot. His voice was entirely changed. It held a note that I knew well.

He crossed to Miss Lawson.

'You remember Bank Holiday? Easter Monday. The night that Miss Wheeler fell down the stairs? *Eh bien*, the little Bob, he was out that night, was he not? He did not come in.'

'Why, yes, M. Poirot, however did you know that? Yes, Bob was very naughty. He was let out at nine o'clock as usual, and he never came back. I didn't tell Miss Wheeler—she would have been anxious. That is to say, I told her the next day, of course. When he was safely back. Five in the morning it was. He came and barked underneath my window and I went down and let him in.'

'So that was it! *Enfin!*' He held out his hand. 'Goodbye, Mademoiselle. Ah! Just one more little point. Miss Wheeler took digestive tablets after meals always, did she not? What make were they?'

'Dr Carlton's After Dinner Tablets. Very efficacious, M. Poirot.'

'Efficacious! *Mon Dieu!*' murmured Poirot, as we left. 'No, do not question me, Hastings. Not yet. There are still one or two little matters to see to.'

He dived into a chemist's and reappeared holding a white-wrapped bottle.

VIII

He unwrapped it when we got home. It was a bottle of Dr Carlton's After Dinner Tablets.

'You see, Hastings. There are at least fifty tablets in that bottle—perhaps more.'

He went to the bookshelf and pulled out a very large volume. For ten minutes he did not speak, then he looked up and shut the book with a bang.

'But yes, my friend, now you may question. Now I know—everything.'

'She was poisoned?'

'Yes, my friend. Phosphorus poisoning.'

'Phosphorus?'

'Ah! *mais oui*—that is where the diabolical cleverness came in! *Miss Wheeler had already suffered from jaundice. The symptoms of phosphorus poisoning would only look like another attack of the same complaint.* Now listen, very often the symptoms of phosphorus poisoning are delayed from one to six hours. It says here' (he opened the book again) '"*The person's breath may be phosphorescent before he feels in any way affected.*" That is what Miss Lawson saw in the dark—Miss Wheeler's phosphorescent breath—"a luminous haze". And here I will read you again. "*The jaundice having thoroughly pronounced itself, the system may be considered as not only under the influence of the toxic action of phosphorus, but as suffering in addition from all the accidents incidental to the retention of the biliary secretion in the blood, nor is there from this point any special difference between phosphorus poisoning and certain affections of the liver—such, for example, as yellow atrophy.'"*

'Oh! it was well planned, Hastings! Foreign matches—vermin paste. It is not difficult to get hold of phosphorus, and a very small dose will kill. The medicinal dose is from 1/100 to 1/30 grain. Even .116 of a grain has been known to kill. To make a tablet resembling one of these in the bottle—that too would not be too difficult. One can buy a tablet-making machine, and Miss Wheeler she would not observe closely. A tablet placed at the bottom of this bottle—one day, sooner or later, Miss Wheeler will take it, and the person who put it there will have a perfect alibi, for she will not have been near the house for ten days.'

'She?'

'Mollie Davidson. Ah! *mon ami*, you did not see her eyes when that ball bounced from my pocket. The irate M. Graham, it meant nothing to him—but to her! "I did not know you kept a dog, M. Poirot." Why a *dog*? Why not a child? A child, too, plays with balls. But that—it is not evidence, you say. It is only the impression of Hercule Poirot. Yes, but everything fits in. M. Graham is furious at the idea of an exhumation—he shows it. But she is more careful. She is afraid to seem unwilling. And the surprise and indignation she cannot conceal when she learns that her cousin has known of the will all along! He knew—and he did not tell her. Her crime had been in vain. Do you remember my saying it was unfortunate he didn't tell her? Unfortunate for the poor Miss Wheeler. It meant her death sentence and all the good precautions she had taken, such as the will, were in vain.'

'You mean the will—no, I don't see.'

'Why did she make that will? The incident of the dog's ball, *mon ami*.

'Imagine, Hastings, that you wish to cause the death of an

old lady. You devise a simple accident. The old lady, before now, has slipped over the dog's ball. She moves about the house in the night. *Bien*, you place the dog's ball on the top of the stairs and perhaps also you place a strong thread or fine string. The old lady trips and goes headlong with a scream. Everyone rushes out. You detach your broken string while everyone else is crowding round the old lady. When they come to look for the cause of the fall, they find—the dog's ball where he so often left it.

'But, Hastings, now we come to something else. Suppose the old lady earlier in the evening after playing with the dog, puts the ball away in its usual place, and the dog goes out—*and stays out*. That is what she learns from Miss Lawson on the following day. She realises that *it cannot be the dog who left the ball at the top of the stairs*. She suspects the truth—but she suspects the wrong person. She suspects her nephew, James Graham, whose personality is not of the most charming. What does she do? First she writes to me—to investigate the matter. Then she changes her will *and tells James Graham that she has done so*. She counts on his telling Mollie though it is James she suspects. They will know that her death will bring them nothing! *C'est bien imaginé* for an old lady.

'And that, *mon ami*, was the meaning of her dying words. I comprehend well enough the English to know that it is a *door* that is ajar, not a *picture*. The old lady is trying to tell Ellen of her suspicions. The dog—the picture above the jar on the mantelpiece with its subject—'Out all night' and the ball put away in the jar. That is the only ground for suspicion she has. She probably thinks her illness is natural—but at the last minute has an intuition that it is not.'

He was silent for a moment or two.

'Ah! if only she had posted that letter. I could have saved her. Now—'

He took up a pen and drew some notepaper towards him.

'What are you going to do?'

'I am going to write a full and explicit account of what happened and post it to Miss Mollie Davidson with a hint that an exhumation will be applied for.'

'And then?'

'If she is innocent—nothing—' said Poirot gravely. 'If she is not innocent—we shall see.'

IX

Two days later there was a notice in the paper stating that a Miss Mollie Davidson had died of an overdose of sleeping draught. I was rather horrified. Poirot was quite composed.

'But no, it has all arranged itself very happily. No ugly scandal and trial for murder—Miss Wheeler she would not want that. She would have desired the privacy. On the other hand one must not leave a murderess—what do you say?—at loose. Or sooner or later, there will be another murder. Always a murderer repeats his crime. No,' he went on dreamily 'it has all arranged itself very well. It only remains to work upon the feelings of Miss Lawson—a task which Miss Davidson was attempting very successfully—until she reaches the pitch of handing over half her fortune to Mr James Graham who is, after all, entitled to the money. Since he was deprived of it under a misapprehension.'

He drew from his pocket the brightly coloured rubber ball.

'Shall we send this to our friend Bob? Or shall we keep it on the mantelpiece? It is a reminder, n'est ce pas, mon ami, that nothing is too trivial to be neglected? At one end, Murder, at the other only—the incident of the dog's ball . . .'

AGATHA CHRISTIE

Agatha Christie (1890–1976) became in her lifetime the world's most celebrated mystery novelist, a status she retains today, one hundred years after her first novel was published and more than forty years after her death. Her work encompasses detective stories, thrillers and tales of the supernatural as well as plays and some light romantic fiction. Her work continues to be filmed, with Kenneth Branagh's new version of *Death on the Nile* (1937) appearing in 2020 with a cast including Gal Gadot, Armie Hammer and Annette Bening, and, at the time of writing, her plays are being performed not only in London and New York but in theatres all around the world. There are websites and events devoted to her work, the foremost being the annual International Agatha Christie Festival, held in her birthplace, Torquay, each September to coincide with her birthday.

Almost uniquely among crime writers of the Golden Age, Christie created two equally famous detectives, the misleadingly genteel Jane Marple and the retired Belgian detective Hercule Poirot, who remains extraordinarily popular almost despite the fact that 2020 marks the centenary of his first case being published, *The Mysterious Affair at Styles* (1920). Poirot, self-styled as 'probably the greatest detective in the world', appeared in thirty-three novels and over fifty short stories, compared to Miss Marple's canon of twelve novels and twenty short stories. Yet, when asked by a fan in

1971, Christie said, 'On the whole, Miss Marple is my favourite. She fits more naturally into a normal world and one can give her more natural surroundings.'

Among her contemporaries Christie's favourite writers included the sorely neglected Ellery Queen and John Dickson Carr, of whose work she once said: 'In spite of a good deal of technical knowledge myself, I hardly ever solve one of his mysteries, though when I come to the end I feel I ought to have noted several points which had been given to me, but which I did not see.' While her favourites among her own work varied over the years, in 1971—not long before her death—she identified them in a private letter as *The Murder of Roger Ackroyd* (1926), *And Then There Were None* (1939), *The Moving Finger* (1943), *Crooked House* (1949)—a book whose writing she described as 'pure pleasure'—and *Ordeal by Innocence* (1958). Christie herself recognised that the author isn't the best judge of their own work but, while readers might not agree entirely with her selection, most of them would surely appear on everyone's list.

Much has been written about the secret of Agatha Christie's success but quite simply she had an astonishingly fertile imagination and a profound understanding of human nature. Time and again in her work, she shrewdly anticipates how her reader will engage with her characters and ruthlessly exploits the assumptions they will make about them and their actions to misdirect attention away from her solution. While some suggest that Christie always fixes on the least likely suspect, the precise opposite is more often true. That is why her solutions come as such a stunning surprise to her readers—and why she remains pre-eminent.

'The Incident of the Dog's Ball' was first published in *Agatha Christie's Secret Notebooks* (2009), the first of two volumes (subsequently combined in the revised *Complete Secret Notebooks*) in which the foremost authority on her work, John Curran, provides an essential study of the writer and her writings.

THE CASE OF THE UNLUCKY AIRMAN

Christopher St John Sprigg

Garnett climbed into his light aeroplane soon after the first rays of dawn lit Cape Town aerodrome. His flight had been announced, but it was not realised he would start so early. The only two people to see him off the tarmac were the aerodrome manager and a middle-aged man with one glass eye and a bilious, yellow complexion.

'You've fixed everything, have you, George?' asked Garnett of this person anxiously, as he leaned his elbow over the cockpit door.

'Absolutely! Don't get windy. You simply can't go wrong.'

Garnett nodded, pulled down his goggles and snapped up the engine switch. A mechanic swung the propeller and five minutes afterwards the biplane was bucketing over the aerodrome.

The airman was a lean youth with dark brown eyes and a slight but perpetual frown. He was a sound pilot but had not yet succeeded in making an outstanding record flight. Discontent, or perhaps worry, was clearly visible on his face as, one hand caressing the 'stick', he pulled a map out of his thigh pocket and set his course across the bare stretches of Cape Province.

He was out to break the solo record from the Cape to Croydon, flying the Central route. Messages from the air—he was carrying wireless—recorded his progress for a few hours. He had gained a slight lead on the record.

Shortly before reaching Bechuanaland*, his voice was picked up, sharp-edged with anxiety, announcing that oil was streaming from a leak in the piping.

He was next heard of near Lichtenberg, reporting that his oil tank was now practically empty and he would have to land.

Garnett brought off an excellent landing in a field, tramped two miles to a house, and here managed to send a messenger into Lichtenberg. A garage proprietor came out hot-foot to make the necessary repairs and soon Garnett was in the air again, but the delay had lost him all chance of the record. Garnett would, therefore, never have been heard of by the public on his arrival at Croydon three days later had it not been for an unexpected event.

Garnett landed, taxied up to the tarmac and cleared Customs. Several airline pilots, with the chivalry of their kind, went up to the aeroplane to congratulate him on what had been a fine achievement in flying, even if it had brought him no laurels.

Garnett was quite cheerful, they said afterwards, though naturally the strain of continuous flying showed itself on his face. When a ground engineer came up to manoeuvre his plane into the hangars, he said he would taxi it in himself—a matter easy enough, for the airport hangars have an enormous span of door.

With a grin and a wave, he opened the throttle again and the little plane lolloped into the far hangar. They heard what was apparently the backfire of an engine, but, when a ground engineer went in later, Garnett's head was leaning over the side of the cockpit, a bullet through his temple and a slightly surprised

---

* On 30 September 1966, the British protectorate of Bechuanaland became the independent republic of Botswana.

expression on his face. Green oil dripped on him in patches from the oil tank above.

The hangar was deserted . . .

Charles Venables, Crime reporter of the *Mercury*, was drinking a modest bitter in the bar of the aerodrome hotel, having called in there for refreshment on the way back from a holiday at Brighton. With him was Murgatroyd, a reporter on the same paper.

Captain Mainwaring, of Planet Airways, came into the bar looking a little pale, ordered a brandy quickly and then stared at Venables with an expression of startled incredulity.

The recognition was mutual, for Mainwaring was Planet Airways' private charter pilot and had often flown Venables on *Mercury* assignments.

'How on earth,' began Mainwaring, 'did you get here so soon? Damn it, it's not possible. It only happened three minutes ago!'

A faintly wolfish look came into Murgatroyd's eyes. Venables gazed blandly at his glass.

'You know what we newshounds are. We know a man's going to bite a dog before it happens. Tell us your version, Duggie.'

Mainwaring shrugged his shoulders.

'There's not much to tell you. Garnett landed and we said the kind word. Then he taxied out of sight. There was a bang and there he was.'

'There he was,' repeated Venables. 'Er—dead?'

'Of course. I say, though, how *did* you know?'

'We didn't, to tell you the sober and honest truth. We just butted in. What luck! But what are you doing in the public bar, Duggie, instead of being in the pilots' room?'

Mainwaring looked a trifle confused. 'Oh, I rather liked Garnett,' he said jerkily. 'I didn't somehow want to discuss—you know what it is—he's not popular here—stunt merchant, you know—still, a good lad—'

Mainwaring broke off abruptly and gulped down his brandy. Venables and Murgatroyd hurried off to the aerodrome.

At the entrance a uniformed attendant stopped them.

'That's all right, my man,' said Venables haughtily. 'We're from the Department of Works and Buildings.'

The attendant stepped aside respectfully.

'We've come to count the partridges on the aerodrome,' added Murgatroyd, who could never let a joke alone. 'We understand these airliners have been disturbing them, which is serious, as they are all the perquisites of His Majesty's Master of Buckhounds.'

By this time, however, Venables was halfway towards the hangars and no harm was done.

'Self-inflicted?' asked Venables gently of the doctor, who was wiping the drying blood from the wound.

The doctor was non-committal.

'That's for the coroner. Here's the revolver that fired the shot, clasped in his hand.'

'And could the wound have been self-inflicted?'

'It could,' admitted the doctor.

It was, decided the jury, after listening to the coroner's brief summing-up.

'You have heard evidence to the effect that Garnett was deeply in debt,' the coroner had said, 'and was relying on the successful outcome of this flight to get him out of his difficulties. You have heard the evidence of friends who tell you of his depression before he left for Cape Town. One of them admits that, before Garnett left, he said that if he didn't make a success of this last attempt, he would blow his brains out.

'He may not have been serious, of course, but we cannot overlook it. He deliberately refused the help of a ground engineer when taking his plane to the hangar, as if he had some purpose to accomplish which could only be done in secret.

'The doctor has told you that there is scorching on the skin, showing that the muzzle of the revolver was held almost in contact with the temple. In these circumstances it is difficult to see how the action could have failed to be deliberate, although we have no trustworthy evidence of his state of mind. I hope the example of this gifted but unstable young airman will dissuade other youngsters from rash and hazardous attempts to get rich quick.'

'Yes, yes, yes,' grumbled Venables to Mainwaring that evening, 'but why wasn't anything said about the oil tank? There it was, with a great rent in it big enough to put your hand in, oil splashed all over the machine, and over Garnett, too; and yet no one says a word about it at the inquest! It's not fair and it's not right, Duggie.'

'But what could they have said about it?' asked Mainwaring, reasonably enough.

'Nothing! Therefore all the more reason to mention it. I don't like it at all. Things like that *ought* to be explained.'

'He had oil leakage on his trip over South West Africa,' Mainwaring reminded him.

'Be reasonable, Duggie, please be reasonable! And you an airman and all. Garnett's trouble then was a leaky connection, with the oil seeping out gradually. But, good-night, *every* pint of oil in the tank would drop out of the hole we found! It isn't as if the oil tank were under the cowling, where he couldn't see it, as it usually is.'

'Ah—ha,' said Mainwaring, 'we've been studying our aviation, have we? So you think there's something serious, eh?'

'I will not deny,' answered Venables, 'that I do. As I was saying, the oil tank is in the centre section above the pilot, and he couldn't help noticing a leak. Besides, the hole has obviously been made with some kind of tin-opener. '

'Well, Venables,' answered Mainwaring more seriously, 'I won't deny that Garnett was the last person I should have imagined would take the coward's way out. He had a pretty tough streak in him. I could imagine him getting into any kind of trouble; in fact I had to caution him before this last show about the company he was keeping. But as to killing himself, no, that's not Garnett!'

'Pity you couldn't have told me all this before, Mainwaring,' said Venables, turning a pair of keen eyes on the other's cheerful, ruddy face. 'What sort of company, eh?'

Mainwaring looked uneasy. 'Keep it under your hat, Venables. It's like this. There's a certain crowd who've got an ancient "Moth" which they've been using for smuggling in saccharine from Germany. A risky job. I saw Garnett hanging round with the little German who runs the show; and I stopped it.'

'Stopped it?'

'Yes. I told the German that if he tried to get Garnett mixed up in his game I'd blow the gaff to the police. I haven't done it before because I believe in keeping my nose out of other people's business. Of course, as a result Garnett quarrelled with me and we weren't on speaking terms when he left; but I do know that he wasn't mixed up in that game.'

'There's a fishy smell about this, Mainwaring! I wish I'd gone into things closer. Can't you think of some reason for that confounded oil tank?'

Mainwaring scratched his head thoughtfully. 'Dashed if I can, Charles.'

Suddenly his face brightened. 'Here's an idea. Supposing the revolver were fastened inside it, so that when Garnett switched off the engine, the gadget automatically fired it?'

'And automatically thrust the revolver into his hand, at the same time blowing sky-high all traces of the remarkable apparatus. My poor dear Duggie, what have you been reading?' Venables laughed. 'Well, don't look so depressed. Tell me, do you know anything about Africa?'

"Fraid I don't. But Fawcett, who's on our Cape service, is in London now. He's South African born.'

Venables had a long conversation with Fawcett and promptly went on to see Detective-Inspector Bray, an old friend of his.

'Bernard, do you remember a neat little suicide at Croydon aerodrome?'

'I do,' said Bray, looking at him suspiciously.

'Quite sure it *was* suicide?'

'Oh, so you've got your nose on the trail, have you, you old devil!'

'I'm just asking; are you sure?'

'Well, the coroner was satisfied.'

'Bernard, don't be so damned diplomatic. Cough it up.'

Bray laughed. ' Ask our Press Bureau.'

Venables gave a groan. 'Look here, Bernard, I promise not to breathe a word. And if you tell me anything that's of any use, I'll turn in my information later before publishing it. That's fair enough!'

Bray considered. 'I can't tell you anything. But you ask and I'll answer.'

' Fingerprints on the revolver?'

'No smears of any kind. Wiped beautifully clean. Except the murdered man's.'

'No fingerprints! Very suspicious. Of course, Scotland Yard didn't think of examining the cartridges.' Venables dug Bray in the ribs.

'Got it in one!' said that gentleman. 'You're a sharp little cuss, aren't you? Yes, there were nice fingerprints on the cartridges.'

'Which perhaps matched the ones on the oil tank?' suggested Venables casually.

'Yes, confound you, they did. Has anyone here been gossiping?'

'Not a soul. All Charles' own deduction. Well, give us a print. I swear I won't let it go out of my sight.'

After a moment's hesitation, Bray agreed. 'Now what do you make of it?'

'It's what I'm going to make of it. Watch my dust!'

A little later, Mainwaring was surprised at the earnestness with which Venables pressed upon him a whisky and soda. He would have been even more surprised had he seen the sleight by which Venables replaced the used glass with another.

'Well, it's not Mainwaring, thank Heavens,' said Venables later, comparing the prints. 'A pity one has to be so suspicious in this game.'

Nathan Marcovicz, merchant of Hatton Garden, looked up with a smile of welcome on his face.

'Why, Venables, this is delightful!'

He had often pressed Venables to come in and look him up, ever since Venables had traced the missing Borridge diamond, which had disappeared while under Marcovicz's care.

Venables had refused to accept any reward from him, 'But one day I'll come down on you for help like a ton of bricks.'

Marcovicz, nervous, dark, with the slow stare of the short-sighted, had renewed his protestations of gratitude.

'Marcovicz, old boy, I'm in the market for diamonds! Lots of them.'

Marcovicz did not blink. 'Certainly. What weight and water? And how do you want them cut?'

'In the raw, if you please. Any size or shape, and so forth. But lots of them.'

Marcovicz frowned. 'But if you would tell me what you want them for—'

'I don't want them, see? You'll have to get them in on appro. in sackloads. Then when I've found out what I want, find some excuse to return them. I leave that to you.'

The diamond merchant was silent for a long time.

'You put me in a difficult position, Venables. I suppose the diamonds you want have been stolen. Well, I can get in touch with what we call the black diamond market here. I've kept clear of it before, of course, but I'll do it for you. But if the diamonds are stolen, I shall first be asked to give my word that I won't let anything out to the police. Naturally, in the ordinary way I should have nothing to do with such a promise. But if I had to give it for you—'

'You won't,' said Charles. 'The diamonds I want are the lawful property of the owner. He may even tell you where he got them from, if you ask him. And look here, I'm making you a present of a pretty little set of Woolworth's lighters. See that any likely client uses one, will you, and don't get them mixed up.'

Venables called in a few days later and found Marcovicz jubilant. 'I've got the bloke you want, I think. A fellow with pretty nearly a pint of large diamonds, won't say where he got them but swears they are his property. They're all uncut and I can't place them for the moment. They're not from the Kimberley deposits.'

'No, they're not,' said Venables. 'Let's have a squint at the lighter.' He compared the fingerprints. 'Yes, he's the man I want. Name and address? Sydney Jones, Marshalsea Hotel! Right! Send Jones a message to say that your client will come round to deal with him personally and send back the diamonds at the same time.'

'Right-ho!'

Venables fingered the dull-looking pebbles. Then he sniffed them. 'Do diamonds generally smell of petrol?'

'Good Lord, no!'

'Very interesting!' said Venables thoughtfully.

Humming gently to himself, Venables put several large rings on his fingers.

'What an invaluable place Woolworth's is!' he murmured, as

he adorned his tie with a large emerald pin. 'I think I look like the sort of person who would buy diamonds in quantity.'

With a silk hat on the back of his head and a large cigar in the corner of his mouth, Venables took a taxi to the Marshalsea Hotel and called on Mr Jones.

Mr Jones was a small man, looking rather like a prematurely bald monkey and dressed in violet plus-fours. Venables, who for the occasion talked in a loud American accent, began to discuss the diamonds expertly, having been instructed by Marcovicz.

Suddenly, in the middle of the conversation, he rose with a groan, clutched at his breast and, with contorted face, sank writhing on the carpet.

'Heart!' he muttered and then doubled up with pain again. 'I'll be all right in a moment,' he went on hoarsely. 'Do you mind popping out to the chemist and getting some sal volatile? I'll be right as rain when this attack's over.'

As soon as Jones had left, Venables recovered miraculously. He had already noted that the nearest chemist was some distance away. This gave him time to search Jones' luggage. He soon found what he wanted: a badly oil-stained shirt and coat sleeve thrust at the bottom of a trunk.

Carefully placing them in the briefcase he had brought with him, Venables equably awaited the arrival of Jones. Jones held out his purchase and, as Venables' hand came out to meet it, the little man suddenly found his arm seized in a grip of iron.

'Don't struggle, my dear soul,' said Venables chillingly, all trace of American accent gone. Otherwise there'll be a nasty wrenching sound. You're in quite the most effective grip, as taught at Peel House.'

'What is this outrage? Are you a thief?'

'Quite the opposite,' said Venables unblushingly. 'I happen to be a police detective.'

'You don't sound like a nark to me,' said the other suspiciously. 'Not the way you speak now.'

'I'm one of the police college products, dear old boy. Would you like to see the school colours on the underwear?'

The little man's eyes were wary now. He had gone pale, or rather his tan had become unappetisingly mottled. 'What's the charge?' he said in a low voice.

'Being in unlawful possession of stolen goods!' said Venables.

A feeling of immense relief crossed the other's face. 'What utter nonsense! I have every right to those diamonds.'

'Can you prove it?'

'I can, but I don't choose to.'

'Then I'm afraid the charge must go on. And we shall make a few enquiries about you. Searches and so forth.'

The little man hesitated. Venables absent-mindedly tightened his grip and he yowled with pain.

'All right,' he said at last, 'I'll tell you. You know in Bechuanaland there are deposits of diamonds in exposed places? You can go and fill your pockets with them. But you aren't allowed to dispose of them: or take them out of the province. Otherwise the diamond market would fall to pieces. Almost every native knows he can get a reward for information about diamond smuggling. But we got a few out of the country: and those are the diamonds.'

'Oh, Mr Jones! What a story! Diamonds you can pick up!'

'I swear it's true! Ask any South African.'

'Even if it is true you've been a bad boy. You smuggled them.'

'Yes, but it isn't an extraditable offence. I can make a good delivery of the diamonds here. You ask any lawyer. You can't touch me.'

'Got anyone who can back your story up?'

'Sure I have. Two friends here in London now!'

'Well, Jones, old boy, I like your frankness. You write down your piece in my little book, with the names and addresses of your friends, and I'll try to get the chief to believe it. I'm afraid I'll have to hang on to your left arm a bit longer, till you've done the writing.'

'Now can I go?' said Jones, when he had written down his story.

'By no means, no!' said Venables, bringing his wrists together and expertly clicking a pair of handcuffs in place.

'I shall have to verify your story,' he went on, as he gagged the pale and trembling Jones. 'Tell me if I hurt you, as the dentist always says when one can't speak.'

He marched his captive into the bedroom.

'Up on the bed, please, and we'll tie up your legs and make a job of it.'

Venables returned to the house 'phone. 'Is there a Captain Mainwaring waiting down there? There is? Please ask him to come to Room 28.'

'I've got the fellow, Mainwaring,' he told that airman. 'Just have a squint at him, will you? He calls himself Jones, but if that's a Welsh accent he's got, I'm a Dutchman.'

'Muller, the little swine!' exclaimed Mainwaring, as Venables ripped off the prisoner's gag. 'Our saccharine-smuggling friend. He's German, not Welsh.'

'German South African, I fancy. Had he a pal?'

'Yes, a yellow-faced bloke with a glass eye.'

'He'll be one of the two whose names I have here, so thoughtfully provided by our friend. What an unpleasant green colour Jones has gone! I fancy he guesses the charge is murder.'

Venables went back to the sitting-room and called up the Yard.

'Hello, Bernard! I say, I've worked out the Garnett business! Listen. Garnett got in with some German South Africans over here. They were smuggling saccharine. When it got too hot for them, they had the bright idea of smuggling diamonds from Bechuanaland. No, not I.D.B.*, but a similar kind of thing. They had a real brainwave. They reckoned no one would suspect a

---

* Illegal diamond buying.

record-breaking flier of smuggling, even if he forced-landed in the diamond area.

'An accomplice in Lichtenberg, who is running a garage there, rushed up to Garnett with the diamonds concealed in an oil can. The oil and the diamonds were poured into Garnett's plane, perhaps under the nose of a policeman! Mainwaring says the diamonds would have to be done up in some sort of bag so as not to get into the oil filter.

'Well, it was arranged for Garnett to meet Muller secretly at Croydon and to hand over the diamonds directly he'd passed Customs. But Muller wasn't going to split the proceeds four ways. He wasn't going to take the risk either of Garnett's having a fit of conscience and giving the show away, so he shot him directly he'd got the diamonds out of the tank, wiped the revolver, put it in the corpse's hand and beat it.

'When he got home, all he had to do was clean the diamonds in petrol, shove his oil-stained clothes out of sight and wait for the coroner's verdict.

'What proof have I? Only the diamonds *and* the oil-stained clothes *and* the owner of the fingerprints neatly trussed up next door, *and* the names and addresses of the accessories before and after, *and* a confession of smuggling all written out in murderer's own hand, *and* a witness ready to swear Muller was a notorious smuggler who'd been seen talking to Garnett. That's *all* I've got, Bernard!'

Venables replaced the 'phone. The smile faded off his face; the light of battle shone in his eyes. He picked up the 'phone again.

'Central 99000. *Mercury* News Editor, please. Venables speaking, and oh, boy, have I got a story!'

CHRISTOPHER ST JOHN SPRIGG

Born in England in 1907, Christopher St John Sprigg was educated at a school in West London, now known as St Benedict's. Aged fifteen, he left school to work on the *Yorkshire Observer*, where his father was literary editor, before joining a specialist aviation publisher, which had been founded by his brother Theodore.

Other than journalism, Sprigg's first published work was a poem, 'Once I Did Think', which appeared in March 1927 in *The Dial*, an American literary magazine; it was the only example of his poetry published in his lifetime. Around this time Sprigg also decided to try his hand at detective fiction. The first of eight crime novels was the surprisingly gruesome *Crime in Kensington* (1933) in which amateur detective Charles Venables investigates the murder and dismemberment of the owner of a small hotel. Another, *Fatality in Fleet Street* (1933), deals with the killing of an anti-Soviet newspaper proprietor, while *Death of a Queen* (1935) concerns a Ruritanian case of regicide. Sprigg also wrote various non-fiction titles such as *The Airship* (1931), *British Airways* (1933) and *Great Flights* (1935) as well as an instruction manual for pilots, *Fly with Me* (1933), one of two books he co-authored with Captain Duncan Davis, director of the Brooklands School where Sprigg had himself learned to fly.

In 1934, Sprigg discovered Marxism and joined the Communist Party of Great Britain. According to his brother it was to protect his reputation as a writer of thrillers that he did this under a pseudonym, 'Christopher Caudwell', taken from their mother's maiden name. As Caudwell, Sprigg wrote widely on the application of Marxist principles to a range of subjects including literature and philosophy, and he became involved in campaigning and fundraising for the Party, moving to Poplar in the East End of London.

In June 1936, Sprigg was one of a group of men arrested for disrupting a demonstration by Sir Oswald Mosley's British Union of Fascists; he was found guilty and fined for assaulting a police officer. On the outbreak of the Spanish Civil War, Sprigg's branch of the Party raised funds for an ambulance, which Sprigg then drove to Spain where he enlisted in the British battalion of the International Brigade. On 12 February 1937 Sprigg died in the battle of Jarama near Madrid 'when he stayed behind with his machine gun' to cover his battalion's withdrawal.

Sprigg's final detective mystery, *Six Queer Things* (1937), was published posthumously and his many essays were collected in volumes including *Studies in a Dying Culture* (1938) and *The Crisis in Physics* (1939), a collection compiled by Professor Hyman Levy, a communist academic. As an indication of how highly Caudwell was regarded by many of his contemporaries, not long after his death the writers J. B. Priestley, Ethel Mannin and Storm Jameson, together with the poet W. H. Auden and several Labour Party politicians, established a memorial fund for the purchase of an ambulance.

'The Case of the Unlucky Airman' was first published in *Everywoman's Magazine* in September 1935.

THE RIDDLE OF THE BLACK SPADE

Stuart Palmer

Uninvited and unannounced, a determined feminine figure marched into the sacrosanct precincts of the New York Homicide Bureau, with an afternoon paper under one arm.

Inspector Oscar Piper looked up from the little mountain of official memoranda which covered his scarred oak desk, and leaned back wearily in his chair. 'Oh, it's you!' was his greeting.

But Miss Withers was undaunted. 'Busy or not busy, Oscar Piper, you ought to be out on Long Island this afternoon instead of sitting here befouling the air with cigar smoke.'

She opened the paper with a snap. A two-column headline topped a box in the middle of page one, evidently the result of a last-minute change in make-up.

'"STATESMAN DIES IN FREAK ACCIDENT"', she read. Then—'"David E. Farling, former state senator and present Manhattan attorney, was struck by a golf ball and instantly killed at about ten o'clock this morning. The accident happened at the small public course known as Meadowland, located near Forestlawn in Queensborough.

'"Farling was discovered by fellow golfers lying face down near a large pool which forms one of the water hazards of the course. Beside him lay the golf ball which had struck his skull with a terrific impact, although the person who inadvertently drove it has not yet been identified . . ."!'

'Yes, Hildegarde,' the Inspector broke in testily. 'I know all that.'

'Well, do you know this?' she continued caustically. 'The newspaper story goes on to remark that while there have been records of six or seven such accidents every year in the New York area, this is the first time that it resulted in a fatality!' She tossed the paper to him. 'Now do you see what I'm talking about? Do you?'

'There has to be a first time for everything,' Piper reminded her. 'But if it makes you any happier, Hildegarde, you might as well know that I sent one of our best men out to help the Queensborough boys on the case. Dave Farling is too prominent a man to pass over easily, and there are too many people whose toes he has stepped on. But all the same—'

'All the same, you don't believe this could be murder?' Miss Withers sniffed. 'There's something fishy about this business, Oscar. Just because it happened out in the bright October sunshine instead of in a locked room, and just because the weapon was a golf ball instead of a pistol, you leap to conclusions.'

She drew a long breath. 'Oscar, who was the person who found Farling's body?'

'Person? There was a whole raft of 'em. He was playing with Sam Firth, his partner, John T. Sullivan, 'the golden-tongued orator', and his son, young Ronald Farling. They missed Farling when he didn't show up at the green, and after waiting for him a while to give him time to find a lost ball or get out of a sand trap, they started back to look for him. They got the Swiss who runs the place to help, and the whole party found Farling lying face down in the mud at the edge of the pool.'

'Giving each other a perfect alibi, or something,' put in Miss Withers. 'Go on.'

'That's all I know, so far,' said the Inspector. 'I'm only a cop, not a crystal-gazer.'

Miss Withers stood up. 'Well, what are we waiting for? Let's go out there.'

'Donovan knows his business,' opposed the Inspector. 'And the precinct boys out in Queens aren't likely to welcome too much meddling. Besides, there's no use to try to make anything except a freak accident out of this case unless—'

His telephone shrilled, and he barked an answer. 'Well, Donovan? What? Listen, is the body still there? Well, leave it. Hang on to the guy—wait for me at the course.'

He put down the phone, and his voice was full of amazement. 'Hildegarde, you're right. It's murder—and they've nabbed the dead man's son!'

She went through the door ahead of him, jamming her Queen Maryish hat a bit lower on her head. The thrill of the chase widened her nostrils, but as they sped through Manhattan's traffic in a long black squad car, heading toward the Queensboro Bridge, she grasped the Inspector's arm and shook her head.

'I don't believe it,' she announced. 'I don't believe it was the son that did it.'

'Such things have happened, and worse,' Piper reminded her. 'And don't think that Donovan doesn't know what he's doing. If he's made a pinch he's sure of his ground.'

Miss Withers had a retort ready, but the sudden screaming of the siren drowned her out. They cut through red light after red light, raced over the bridge, and then on a long straightaway past mile upon mile of used-car lots, garages, hot-dog stands, grocery stores . . . far into the vastness of Queens, which enjoys the reputation of being the largest and most unlovely borough of New York.

The day had been warm for October, but now as the sun set behind the towers of Manhattan to the westward, a chill wind began to sweep down from the Sound. Miss Withers could not help shivering as the fast car swung off the boulevard and shot south over a narrow macadam road. There was a faded sign: 'Meadowland Golf Club—Greens Fee 50c' . . .

On the right they could see a rolling green expanse of what had once been a succulent cow pasture. Now it bore signs of a sketchy landscaping and here and there a rain-streaked flag fluttered over a clipped green square of grass.

Far ahead of them they saw a small white building surrounded by autos, but at that moment their precipitous course was interrupted by a blue-clad figure which stepped out into the road ahead of them, waving its arms.

Brakes screamed. 'The Sergeant says I was to tell you that if you cut across the fence right here you'll find him where the body is . . .'

'Okay,' said Piper. He helped Miss Withers out of the car, which was simple, and over the barbed wire fence, which was fraught with difficulty and peril.

'Right straight toward the trees,' their guide advised. They went onward over a little hill, and came down upon another fairway. Ahead of them, from the depths of a narrow ravine which cut across the open fairway in a wide diagonal, rose the tops of a cluster of elms. But there was no sign of human presence.

'Under the trees, Inspector,' their guide insisted.

They came suddenly above the ravine, looking down upon a wide, leaf-choked pool near the elms. Smaller trees and bushes filled the canyon-like cut at the left, but ahead of them it lay open around the pool. Here were gathered an official little circle around a body which still lay face downward near the water's edge.

Photographers were taking their last shots in the fading light. Sergeant Donovan, red-faced and perspiring, came up the slope to greet his chief.

'Open and shut,' he announced. 'I washed it up pronto, Inspector. But you may as well have a look around.' He noticed

Miss Withers, and greeted her without enthusiasm. 'Afternoon, ma'am.'

'Open and shut,' she repeated blankly. 'Hmmmm.'

They looked at the body—a sprawled, plumpish man of fifty dressed in plus-fours and bright yellow sweater and stockings, and with a small circular indentation in the back of the skull. Then a tarpaulin was drawn over the grim exhibit.

'Right here was where they found the golf ball that did it,' the Sergeant was saying. 'About two feet from the corpse.'

From his pocket he took a wadded handkerchief, in the centre of which reposed a bright new golf ball, bearing on one side a tiny trademark consisting of a black spade—and on the other a dull reddish smear. 'Exhibit A, Inspector!'

Piper nodded. 'Seems to be clear enough. We may as well go on to the clubhouse, eh, Hildegarde?'

Miss Withers had discovered a dead branch nearby, with which she was poking dubiously at the deep leaf-choked pool. Its murky waters were reflecting the last glow of the sunset.

'But we've found the body, Hildegarde!' he said jokingly. 'Or do you think the murderer is lurking under water?'

She sniffed, and tossed aside the branch.

It was a good stiff walk back to the clubhouse, a small building of rattletrap structure. In the rear was a three-room apartment sacred to the gnarled Swiss who leased the land and operated the course. In the front was an office furnished with a cash register, a counter displaying sun hats, golf balls, patent tees and the like, and a screened porch boasting half a dozen tables with chairs and a dispensing machine for soda pop.

It was on this porch that young Ronald Farling waited, with a plainclothes detective on either side and a burly captain in charge. That worthy hurried down to meet the Inspector on the lawn.

'Greetings.' said Piper. 'Miss Withers—Captain Mike Platt, Queens Division. Congratulations, Captain.'

The captain grinned. 'Glad you agree that we've broken the case so early, sir. Just the same, I kept the young rat here so you could talk to him on the ground, so to speak . . .'

'Give us the picture, quick,' ordered Piper.

'Well,' said Platt slowly, 'it's not a nice picture at all. Farling and his son Ronald, together with Mister Sullivan and Mister Firth all came out early this morning for a round of golf. They often come to this little course because it's never crowded and because it's ten miles closer to the city than the nearest full-size course.

'Or so they say. We got statements from Firth and Sullivan and let them go. It seems that on the seventh tee each one of the four drove his ball into trouble—except for young Farling, who's an expert. He drove right over the tops of those elm trees, almost to the green. Sullivan landed in the woods at the left, Firth saw his ball roll into the rough ground near the hill, and Dave Farling topped his a measly twenty feet or so.

'The others left him there and went on, for he was an unlucky golfer usually. From there to the green, where they knock the ball into the little hole, Inspector, each man was separate and busy with his own affairs. But though nobody saw him—excepting the murderer—Dave Farling must have knocked his second shot into the pool. And while he was down trying to find his ball, somebody knocked a ball into the back of his head, smashing his skull . . .'

Miss Withers could see on the porch the drawn, handsome face of young Ronald Farling, between the two cops. 'Somebody, you say, but—'

'But how do we know it was him?' Platt laughed. 'Because he had a whale of a fight with his father yesterday in the office, over something his father wouldn't let him do. "Not while I live!" said the old man. Firth, the partner, overheard it. And he told us. Moreover, the young lad is what they call a "scratch" golfer. He likes to give exhibitions of driving a ball off a watch, or taking what they call a mashie and chipping balls twenty feet into a tin pail. He's probably one of the few men in these parts who could be perfectly sure of hitting just what he aimed at!'

The captain was beaming. 'Well, when Farling didn't show up at the green, the others figured he was looking for a lost ball. But then he didn't come and he kept a didn't coming, as the saying goes, and finally the three of them started back. They saw old Chris Thorr on the other fairway raking away at the autumn leaves, and called him to help. So the four of them came over the edge of the gully and saw Farling lying there, dead as a herring.'

'And the boy admits the crime?' asked Miss Withers.

Platt shook his head. 'Not him. He's a smooth one. But we'll make him talk before he sleeps or—'

'All right, Captain,' said Piper quickly. 'Medical examiner gone?'

Platt nodded. 'Doc Farnsworth it was—and he didn't like the looks of things. It was him refused us a certificate of death by misadventure. Wouldn't give his final opinion until the autopsy. But Donovan and I figured we didn't need to wait for that before getting young Farling safe behind bars.'

'Okay,' said Piper. 'Let's have a look at the lad.'

They went up the steps and through a screen door. The young man was very pale, and seemed chilled through in his light blue sports shirt and dark flannels. He leaped to his feet impulsively.

'How long are you going to hold me here? I tell you, I had nothing to do with what happened. Do you think I'd kill my own father?'

'Father—by adoption, wasn't it?' Miss Withers put in softly. 'Didn't I read something about it, some years back?'

Ronald Farling stopped short. His eyes clouded for a moment. Then— 'Yes, by adoption. David Farling and his wife adopted me nine years ago, when I was twelve. It was just after my own father . . .'

'Yes? Go on!' Piper pressed forward.

The boy gulped. 'Just after my real father was—was executed for murder! Dan Farling as his lawyer couldn't get him off, though it happened in a pitched battle between union men and company scabs. So he promised to take me, and bring me up as his own son. And he did . . .'

The boy stopped short, realizing too late what he had said. His fists clenched, and then opened helplessly. 'Like father like son, eh? I suppose that's what you're saying?'

'You had a fight with your foster-father in his office yesterday?'

Ronald nodded. 'Well, an argument. But not—'

'What was it about?'

'He didn't want me to get married.' confessed Ronald Farling simply. He drew a deep breath. 'And if you want the name of the girl you can rot in hell before I'll tell you and drag her through this!'

He subsided sullenly into his chair. During the latter course of the questioning Miss Hildegarde Withers had been doing a little quiet snooping nearby. She reappeared with a leather golf bag full of sticks in one hand. The initials on the bag were 'R.F.'

'This is yours?' she asked the prisoner.

He nodded. Miss Withers opened the zipper pocket and brought out half a dozen golf balls. Three were old and battered. The other three were almost new, showing only a few nicks. Each bore a tiny red heart as a trademark,

'Could I see the one you have?' she asked the Sergeant. She took it gingerly. 'Just as I thought. They don't match.' On an impulse she showed Ronald Farling the ball with the smear of blood. 'Recognize this ball. young man?'

He stared and frowned. Then his eyes widened. 'Why, that's my father's!'

The cops gathered instantly. 'What?'

'It is! You see, when we started out this morning each member of the foursome bought three new balls. Ask the girl inside at the counter—and of course we each got a different colour and mark so we could tell them apart easily. Most makes of balls are designed in sets of four that way. Firth chose clubs, Sullivan diamonds, my father—I mean my foster-father—chose spades, so that left me hearts. They were kidding me about it . . .'

'So David Farling was killed with one of his own golf balls!' said Miss Withers slowly. 'Can we prove that by comparing this with other balls in his bag?'

But the dead man's bag was empty of balls.

'This isn't getting us anywheres,' Captain Platt finally objected. 'Okay for me to take young Farling away, Inspector?'

Piper looked at Miss Withers, rubbed his jaw, and nodded. 'Keep him safe and sound,' he said. 'And don't yell at him all night,' he added firmly.

The young man was half-led, half-dragged, to a waiting police runabout, and Miss Withers had a last glimpse of his white, drawn, frightened face.

There was a brief interlude during which a grey ambulance lumbered out into the gathering darkness of the little golf course, its lights shining like two glaring tiger-eyes . . . at last David Farling was to be removed from the edge of the muddy pool. It was high time, thought Miss Withers.

The Inspector had left her to make a telephone call, and she wandered out through the littered yard in the rear. Here were old car tyres, sand boxes, broken greens-flags, and an ancient piano box—souvenirs of dead days. For the first time in her life she wished that she had taken up music and games and golf in her youth. A knowledge of what the Inspector called 'pasture pool' would be a great help to her now. She had a feeling that an essential clue was eluding her—and the police. Perhaps it was a clue that would cry out like a trumpet to a more experienced devotee of golf.

She sank down on a convenient bench overlooking the fairway, and rested her chin in her hand. Far ahead she could see the lights of the morgue wagon swing across the sky and then beam back towards the club house, its silent passenger safely aboard.

'A ride that each of us must take—and some before our time,' she was musing to herself.

At that moment a guttural torrent broke out almost in her ear. She turned suddenly, and realized that the speaker did not see her on the bench. He stood not far from the doorway of the living quarters, a gnarled, bitter figure leaning upon a long rake.

'*Ach, der Schwein . . .*'

Miss Withers had a vague knowledge of German and of French left over from her schooldays, and after a moment she realized that this endless torrent was a combination of both, which must be Swiss. Yet most of the words were, luckily, unfamiliar to her. Here and there she caught one which made the back of her neck turn bright red.

She made ready. There was always something to be said for the power of a surprise attack. She jumped up like a jack-in-the-box.

'Who are you?' she demanded, raising her umbrella threateningly.

'Who am I? She asks me, who am *I*?' The harsh voice rose shrill and high. 'Me, I'm poor Chris Thorr. Me, I'm the slave who must work week in and week out to make all smooth the grass where those *verdammte* pigs go joyriding with their unspeakable ambulance . . .'

His voice was full of great sobs. Suddenly Miss Withers felt a certain sympathy for him, especially now that the ambulance came lurching back towards the club house, leaving dark deep furrows in the soft turf, wheels spinning erratically right and left . . .

She tried to make some properly sympathetic remark. But Chris Thorr turned back towards his lighted doorway, shoulders slumped despondently. '*Es ist nicht der Mühe Wert!*' was his parting shot.

Miss Withers turned to see the Inspector beside her. 'I don't like that old buzzard,' he observed. 'What was that last crack?'

'Something about life being a bowl of cherries,' Miss Withers translated freely. 'I'm afraid Thorr is a pessimist.'

'Maybe,' said Piper, as they walked back towards the shack. 'From what I hear he's got reasons. This place barely pays expenses, next spring they're going to condemn most of it for the new Parkway, and his wife ran off with a travelling man or somebody last August.'

'But didn't I see a girl in the office?' Miss Withers asked.

Piper nodded. 'That's Molly Gargan, a neighbourhood girl that he hires to take care of the office and sell tickets to the players. Which reminds me, I'd better tell the boys it's okay to let her go home. We've been holding everybody . . .'

'Hold her a while longer,' Miss Withers decided. 'I want to see Molly.'

Molly Gargan was something to see, beyond a doubt. Miss Hildegarde Withers was prone to attach more importance to feminine brains than to beauty, but the black-haired girl with the bright blue eyes and full sculptured body was positively breathtaking.

She sat at a stool behind the counter, staring out of the window at the darkness of the golf course. Oddly enough, her blue eyes were raining tears down an utterly calm and lovely face. She wore a modest pink dress that was obviously homemade, and as Miss Withers came through the doorway she noticed that Molly Gargan had torn that dress in five or six places along the collar. Now, as if no part of herself, her long fingers were busily tearing yet another place . . .

Miss Withers cleared her throat. 'Whatever happened out on the course, it can't affect you, young woman, can it?'

Molly started, and then her lips tightened. 'Of course not . . .'

Miss Withers tried a rather mean trick. 'The young man whom

they arrested,' she said casually, 'insists that this morning, when the foursome started to play, they all purchased balls here.'

Molly nodded her lovely dark head.

'And he claims that all four of them bought balls with a red diamond on them—is that true?'

'Why, no! They—' Suddenly Molly stopped short. 'Yes, that's right,' she said evenly. 'I remember now.'

'Like fun you do,' Miss Withers said under her breath. 'Where do you live, Molly?'

Through the window Molly Gargan pointed to a white house perhaps a mile away, where the lights of the boulevard were glaring. 'My father runs a filling station,' she confessed.

'Very well, Molly,' Miss Withers advised. 'The police asked me to tell you that you may go home now.'

'Thanks!' said Molly Gargan fervently. With one quick motion she pulled a sweater over her dress, slapped a tam-o-shanter over her dark hair, and was out of the door.

Miss Withers watched the girl as she took a short cut across the darkened golf course in the direction of that dim white blotch in the distance which was home. Then she was aware that someone watched beside her.

It was Chris Thorr, shaking his head. 'They are all alike,' he observed gutturally. 'Women!'

He crossed to the cash register, pressed the 'no sale' key and scooped out the day's takings, a sorry morsel. Then he ostentatiously locked the display case, as if Miss Withers would have been likely to go in for shoplifting golf balls and wooden tees.

'You can't blame her for hurrying away on a day like this,' Miss Withers reminded him. 'What if she did forget to close up? She's a very pretty girl.'

Chris Thorr didn't seem interested in pretty girls. 'Bah!' said he. 'The prettier they are the less they know. I hope soon she gets married, and I hire a good sober girl, homely as a mud fence, *ja!*'

He moved around, turning out electric lights. 'You go home now—everybody go home, *ja?* I go to bed.'

Everybody went home—except for one chilled and unhappy cop who was assigned, according to regulations, to cover the scene of the crime. Patrolman Walter Fogle spread out a newspaper on the damp grass under the elms, and prepared for a long and lonely vigil above the dark and leaf-choked pool . . .

The wind howled eerily in the tree-tops that night, and the pale October moon was hidden behind ragged wisps of cloud. Patrolman Fogle realized that it lacked but a night or two of being All Hallows Eve, and towards morning he dozed off into a nightmare of witches and goblins and howling, dancing wraiths . . .

He awoke with a jerk to see a spectral white figure moving near the edge of the pond. Fogle blinked, pinched himself, and blinked again. But the figure remained.

'Hey!' he mouthed, through dry and trembling lips.

The white figure became a statue. 'What the hell are you doing there?' demanded the patrolman. 'Stop or I'll fire!'

The apparition dissolved in the direction of the clump of trees and brush further down the gully.

'Stop!' yelled Fogle. His gun came out, and he blazed away furiously. But to no avail.

Next morning, shame-faced, he made his report. 'Maybe it was a dead ghost and maybe it wasn't,' he insisted to Captain Platt. 'But I know for one thing that it could run like a rabbit. And it wasn't old Chris Thorr nosing around, because I went back to the club-house and dragged him out of bed.'

'Look at his shoes?' asked the captain. 'Heavy dew, wasn't there?'

The cop nodded. 'His shoes were dry, and he was sound asleep.'

'Okay,' said his chief. 'Go home and grab some sleep. We may want you this afternoon.'

At that moment Miss Withers and the Inspector were in deep conference. 'It's funny about the medical examiner's report,' Piper was saying. 'The doc insists that Farling's skull was of normal thickness and that a golf ball would have to be travelling with the speed of a bullet to make such a wound.'

'Oscar,' suggested the school-teacher, 'isn't that an idea? I mean, couldn't you shoot a golf ball out of a gun?'

He shrugged. 'Certainly not without leaving powder marks, even if you could get a gun barrel improvised out of a pipe or something. And as for that, Max Van Donnen just reported to me that while that golf ball bears traces of blood which check with Farling's, it has never been struck with a golf club! The waxy covering is intact, under the microscope! So there goes your gun theory.'

Miss Withers nodded. 'I suggested the gun because, you see, Oscar, I spent two hours this morning taking a golf lesson from a professional at the Lakewood Country Club. He's a better golfer than even young Farling, and he can drive a ball four hundred yards or lift one neatly into a tin pail twenty feet away. But not both at the same time, Oscar! By that I mean you can't combine speed with absolute accuracy in golf!'

'Which means that we're right back where we started,' said Piper.

She shook her head. 'We know that Ronald Farling didn't kill his foster father—at least not by driving a ball at him. Oscar, I think we're making this case too complicated. Did you get the report from the telephone company?'

He shook his head. 'Takes them time to trace those calls,' he pointed out. 'But I don't see why you think we'd learn anything if we knew how many phone calls, if any, have been made from the club house to Farling's office on Broadway, and vice versa. You don't think—'

She nodded. 'When there's a girl as startlingly beautiful as Molly Gargan in a case, you can take it for granted that she is somehow a part of the picture. Suppose the dead man had been playing regularly on that little course just to see the fair Molly, had become involved with her somehow, and then cast her adrift? And suppose the odd little Mr Thorr secretly nursed a love for his pretty clerk, and wanted to avenge the slight?'

She stopped, and shook her head. 'Thorr doesn't love the girl. On the contrary. And besides, Farling would not have brought his friends and son to play golf at the course after he was through with the girl . . .' She sank into a chair. 'I'm afraid we've drawn another blank . . .'

Just then the telephone rang, and Piper listened eagerly. He made notes on a piece of paper. 'Well!' he said. 'In the past three months there have been fourteen phone calls from the golf course office to Farling's office—twenty-three from Farling's office to the course, and seven from the Farling home on Fifth Avenue to the course!'

'Which means that your case against young Farling is blown higher than a kite,' Miss Withers reminded him. 'Besides, he couldn't have been the midnight prowler who frightened Patrolman Fogle out of his alleged wits last night.' She frowned. 'Oscar, you ought to drain that pool!'

Piper laughed. 'So you are looking for another body!'

'Another body—or another golf ball,' she reminded him. 'A golf ball with specks of powder burns on the cover, and a trademark which might be anything but a black spade.'

'Draining that pool seems like something of an engineering problem,' Piper objected. 'Besides—'

'And I think you ought to turn Ronald Farling loose,' she went on. 'There may be more to discover from him if he's free than if he's in the lockup.'

'The more we discover the worse off we are,' Piper objected. 'I naturally have had the other two members of that foursome investigated. Sullivan has been talking over the radio in behalf of the Citizens Committee, and naturally has been panning some of Farling's friends in politics. But the two men were personal pals. As for the partner, Sam Firth, he didn't gain anything from Farling's death, and he's probably lost a good share of his law business. Neither of them—'

'Business!' Miss Withers snapped. 'We're missing the whole key to this affair. I wish I knew more about pretty Molly Gargan. I still believe that she's the catalytic agent—'

Piper shook his head. 'Doesn't look like she'd throw a fit, to me.'

'I said catalytic, not epileptic,' Miss Withers snapped. 'Don't you remember your chemistry? Well, with a girl as beautiful as she around, anything that happens involves her somehow. Oscar, I'm going to telephone her, and arrange for a quiet little talk—'

She asked for Information, and then was connected with Gargan's Gas Station on Queens Boulevard. It was a worried Irish voice which answered her.

'Molly? This is her father speakin'. No, she's not here. She went out early this mornin', without giving me my breakfast. What? No, she didn't pack a suitcase. She was wearing a pink dress, I suppose.'

Miss Withers put down the phone. 'Oscar, doesn't pink look white at night?'

She gave him no time to answer. 'Come on!' she insisted. 'I think we're on the trail of something, and I don't like the scent.'

'Now listen!' objected her old crony. 'Good heavens, woman, I've got a Bureau to run . . .'

'It'll run by itself,' she came back. And the Inspector followed, for he knew her of old.

'We'll first have a talk with young Farling,' she decided. 'Tell the man to drive us to the Queens lockup.'

But when they had reached that outlying station they found that the talk with young Ronald Farling would have to be postponed indefinitely.

'He's flew the coop!' was the way Captain Platt put it. 'About half an hour ago Sam Firth, his father's partner, came out here with a writ of habeas corpus. They'd got wind of the medical examiner's report which cast doubt on the golf ball angle, so it was up to me to book the kid for murder or let him go. And we didn't have enough on him—'

'We can get him again if we need him,' said Piper. 'Well, Hildegarde?'

'We need him now,' she said shortly. 'Find out for me just what is the situation out at the golf course, will you? Anybody there?'

Captain Platt reported that Fogle was due to go back on duty at the course within the next few minutes, having had a short relief. 'We always keep a cop around the scene of the crime for a couple of days,' he informed her. 'Otherwise the place is closed up.'

Miss Withers then realized that Molly Gargan couldn't possibly be on duty. There would be no need to have her sitting on the stool behind that counter in the club house . . . yet where was she?

'Oscar,' she insisted, 'will you take me over to the course? But for heaven's sake let's have no blaring of sirens this time.'

They approached Meadowland very quietly indeed, and at Miss Withers' instigation the squad car was parked far down the macadam road.

Then, leaving the uniformed driver at the wheel, the Inspector followed Miss Withers over the wire fence and across the turf. 'Good Lord, woman, are you still harping on that pool?'

She sniffed, and led the way. 'I want a description from Patrolman Fogle of that ghost he saw,' she admitted.

But Fogle was not on duty above the pool. Another uniformed man approached after a moment, crashing through the under-brush down the gully. He snapped to salute.

'Where's Fogle?' asked Piper sharply.

'Hasn't relieved me yet, sir. I guess last night was too much for him, because he was due at two o'clock and it's nearly half past.'

'What were you doing off your post? Looking for him?'

The cop reddened. 'No, sir. I—I thought I seen something moving down there . . . '

Piper shook his head. 'I guess all you men out here believe in fairies,' he growled. 'Was it a grinning skull or a snake with wings?'

'No, sir,' said the patrolman seriously. 'It was a young guy in golf clothes, and he could run like a deer.'

'Yeah!' said Piper.

But Miss Withers, who had climbed back to the edge of the gully, was staring out over the course. 'He still is,' she remarked. 'Running like a deer, I mean. And if he doesn't look out . . .'

Piper and the cop joined her in time to get a clear, if distant, view of a young man who looked very much like Ronald Farling, as he vaulted the wire fence into the road and was immediately clasped in the brawny arms of the uniformed man who drove Piper's car.

When the others came up he was arguing furiously with his captor. 'Let him go!' ordered Piper.

Ronald Farling, looking a little wild and dishevelled from his night in jail, faced them. 'I suppose you want to know why I'm here?' he demanded.

Miss Withers shook her head. 'You're looking for the same thing we are,' she advised him. 'Come with us, if you wish. In the words of the popular song, we're heading for the last roundup.'

They crept towards the club house in silence, keeping always behind the rolling little hills, following gullies and the shadows of scattered trees. 'Hildegarde, what are you up to?' Piper begged.

'I haven't the slightest idea!' she admitted. 'But I'm going to learn something.'

The wind still blew gustily from the north, driving dead leaves into their faces, and bringing the sound of loud voices from somewhere behind the club house. They crept steadily on, and finally reached the vantage point of a hedge.

From here they could get a good view of the club house, and of the littered yard in the rear where Chris Thorr stood, raking at the refuse. Beside him was Patrolman Fogle.

'Say!' broke out Piper. 'There's something—'

But Miss Withers hushed him. 'Listen.'

'Well, then—I bet you twenty dollars against five that you can't hit it in one out of three tries!'

Thorr's voice came clearly, and it bore an undercurrent of masked excitement . . .

Fogle scratched the back of his neck, and drew out his service gun. 'You talk too loud, fella,' he said. 'I hate to do it, but I'm going to take your money.'

They were standing perhaps twenty feet from the broken-down piano case which Miss Withers had noticed last night. Now she saw with a gasp of surprise that a homemade target of black and white circles had been tacked on the side of the box.

'Okay,' Fogle said doggedly. 'I've got three tries to put a slug in the centre of that target, and if I do it you pay me twenty bucks.' He raised his gun . . .

Miss Withers tried to scream, and found that no sound issued from her throat. She grabbed the Inspector. 'Stop him!' she gasped.

'Illegal target practice within city limits of New York, illegal firing of service gun . . .' mumbled the Inspector. He stood up quickly.

'Hey, there! What the hell do you think you're doing?'

The two in the yard whirled to face them. Miss Withers tottered on after the Inspector, who glared at the patrolman.

Fogle was in a spot, and he knew it. 'I—sorry, sir. But he was razzing me about police marksmanship, sir. On account of my firing last night at the ghost or whatever it was. Claimed I couldn't hit the piano box, much less the target. So we made a bet—'

Piper was grinning. 'Oh, he thinks cops can't shoot, eh?'

Chris Thorr nodded. 'Couldn't hit a barn if you were inside with the doors shut. Not like the police in Switzerland, let me tell you. Say—'

Piper rubbed his chin. 'Fogle, how come you're stalling around here? Don't you go back on duty?'

'At two p.m., yes sir. But I just looked at the clock inside and it's only one forty-five.' He grinned. 'So I thought I had time to show this guy . . .'

'Go ahead and show him,' Piper ordered. 'Just this once we'll forget regulations . . .'

Miss Withers could hold herself no longer. 'Forget regulations and forget the common sense you were born with,' she screamed. 'But first me let get in that piano box . . .'

She attacked it furiously with tooth and nail, but it was stouter than it seemed. Young Ronald Farling came forward to help her, while Thorr and the cops looked blankly on. Then at last a board was pried away, and another . . .

'Oh, God!' cried Ronald Farling. 'Molly!'

It was Molly Gargan—her soft young body wound with cruel ropes, her red mouth gagged with a twisted rag. Tenderly they took her down from the hook which had held her there, with her heart beating just behind the bull's-eye of the target . . .

Only a half inch of soft pine lay between Molly Gargan and the leaden death which had hung poised above her . . .

It all happened in a split second. 'Get that man!' screamed Miss Withers.

Gnarled, dried-up Chris Thorr suddenly had come alive. He flung Fogle head over heels, knocked the Inspector to his knees with the ever-present rake which he had snatched from behind him, and was running amok towards the two women.

His mouth was open and frothing, and a shrill endless scream of antic insanity filled the air . . .

Then Ronald Farling stepped in, dodged the swinging iron

teeth of the rake, and brought his fist smartly into the madman's groin. Again—and then a right across to the chin that sent him backwards—

He did not rise. When things had calmed a bit, they found out why. He had fallen upon the tines of his own rusty rake, and three of the iron spikes had pierced his brain.

Farling and the girl leaned against the piano box, touching each other gently, wonderingly . . . they had no eyes or ears for anything else.

But the Inspector fairly gnawed at his cigar.

'Hildegarde! It's a madhouse!'

'Not quite,' she said. 'Thorr wanted to get Molly put out of the way, and chose this means. Fogle was to have shot her as she stood bound and gagged in the piano box. Then later Thorr would have hidden the body out on the course somewhere—and with one or more bullets from Fogle's gun in the body, he would be the one to be suspected, particularly since he shot wildly at a phantom last night . . .'

'Yeah, but what phantom?'

'I imagine it was Thorr, in his night-shirt and barefoot,' Miss Withers went on. 'He didn't know that there'd be a guard at the pool, or at least he wasn't sure. He had some unfinished business there—'

'So you say!' objected Piper. But why would Thorr want to kill Molly here?'

'Ask her,' said Miss Withers. 'She knows.'

Molly did know. It was because she had feared and suspected Thorr for some time, and therefore when her sweetheart was arrested for the murder of his foster-father she had started scouting around . . .

'And you found what?' Miss Withers asked.

'I found that there were some brown stains on the end of Thorr's rake handle,' said Molly Gargan. And suddenly the whole thing was clear to Miss Withers.

'That's why he tied you up when he found you examining his rake! It was the murder weapon—not the golf ball.'

Piper shook his head. 'You're still crazy. What possible motive would there be—'

'For Thorr to kill Farling? A very good one. Enter the pool once more, Oscar. You see, Farling must have been looking for his lost ball, and have poked at the water with that dead stick, just as I did. And Thorr, lurking nearby, saw him probing the pool and rushed up to hurl his rake like a javelin. The rake handle is just the diameter of a golf ball, Oscar. He thought of that when he had finished the deed, so he took the one remaining ball from his victim's bag, touched it to the wound, and dropped it nearby. He wanted it to appear like an accident, Oscar.'

'But why, in the name of heaven, should Thorr object to having Farling poke around in that pool?'

'Your guess is as good as mine,' said Miss Hildegarde Withers. 'We won't know for sure until you drag the pool, as I've begged you to do, again and again. But I've got a pretty good idea that you'll find the sunken body of the wife who is supposed to have left Chris Thorr last August and run away with a travelling man.'

'Well, who'd have suspected that?' exclaimed Piper.

'Who indeed—but I?' Miss Withers flashed back.

STUART PALMER

Charles Stuart Palmer, one of the great writers of comic detective fiction, was born on 21 June 1905 in a farmhouse on the Baraboo side of the Butterfield Bridge on the outskirts of Portage, Wisconsin. A lively child, Palmer played an active role in the junior branch of the Lower Narrows Farmers' Club in Portage, participating in social events like ice cream suppers and musical evenings, singing along to music played on a Grafonola. At Baraboo High School he demonstrated an aptitude for poetry and his first published work was a poem, 'The Saner Memory', which appeared in the *Chicago Tribune* under the pen name 'The Dauber'. That pseudonym reflected an equally precocious talent for drawing, which led to Palmer's studying at the Chicago Art Institute and then at the State University where he began writing in earnest. Various articles were published in the university's literary magazine and in *The Daily Cardinal*, whose popular Skyrockets column was edited by Palmer; he also contributed cartoons and skits to *The Octopus*, a campus humour magazine of which he also eventually became editor.

In later years, Palmer would claim to have had all sorts of jobs after he graduated, even a spell with the Ringling Brothers' famous circus. And perhaps he did. What *is* certain is that he wrote, a lot, with cartoons and short pieces appearing in *College Humor*, *Life*, *The New Yorker* and *Judge*, and he also edited several magazines including *Dance* and *Ghost Stories* which published Palmer's enduring hoax about the mysterious disappearance of David Lang, an entirely fictitious Tennessee farmer. *Ghost Stories* also published Palmer's first novel, *The Gargoyle's Throat* (1930), as well as several stories under the pseudonym 'Theodore Orchards'. While working as a journalist, Palmer also retained strong links with his university, editing a selection of undergraduates' work, *Wisconsin Writings 1931*. The anthology was published by the Mohawk Press which also published Palmer's second novel, *Ace of Jades* (1931), in which precocious teenager 'Bubbles' Deagan becomes embroiled with a bootlegger.

Ace of Jades drew Palmer to the attention of a larger publisher, Brentano's, where his editor suggested he next write a detective story and set it in the New York Aquarium. The result was *The Penguin Pool Murder* (1931) in which Palmer introduced a police inspector, Oscar Piper, and a 'horse-faced' Iowa schoolteacher, Miss Hildegarde Withers. Although it has been suggested that Palmer was influenced by Anna Katharine Green's tales of spinster Amelia Butterworth and police detective Ebenezer Gryce, Palmer often said that he conceived Withers only as 'a minor character, for comedy relief' but had found her 'taking over'. Withers was based on Miss Fern Hackett, Palmer's high school Head of English, whom he claimed had made his life miserable for two years but started him off as a writer.

The film rights to *The Penguin Pool Murder* were sold quickly and James Gleason and Edna May Oliver cast as Piper and Miss Withers. As Willis Goldbeck worked on the script Palmer fell in with the publicity drive, announcing his intention to travel to the Galápagos Islands to bring back the required penguins and suggesting that, if the expedition failed, 'a couple of trained ducks [be made up] as penguins'; he also arranged for the film to have its premiere at the Al Ringling Theater in his home town of Baraboo. *The Penguin Pool Murder* (1932) was an immediate success and two more films followed quickly: *Murder on the Blackboard* (1934), scripted again by Goldbeck, and *Murder on a Honeymoon* (1935), adapted from Palmer's novel *The Puzzle of the Pepper Tree* (1933) by Seton Miller and the humorist Robert Benchley. Unfortunately, Edna May Oliver left the series after the third film and neither of the actresses that followed—Helen Broderick and ZaSu Pitts—was a success.

In 1933 Palmer moved to New York and from there he relocated to Laguna Beach, California, where he later claimed to have built up an extensive collection of penguin statuettes—'second only to Roland Young'—while his pets apparently included a Wodehousian cat called PSmith and a wire-haired puppy called PJones. Although he would move house several times, Palmer remained in California for the rest of his life, gradually being joined there by others in his family.

After sharing credits on scripts for films like *Hollywood Stadium Mystery* (1938), co-written with Dorrell McGowan and Stuart McGowan, and *Yellowstone* (1936), the 'great geyser murder mystery' with Jefferson Parker, Palmer began writing scripts on his own for mysteries and comedies such as *Who Killed Aunt Maggie?* (1940) and *Pardon My Stripes* (1942). With the entry of the United States into the Second World War, Palmer spent six years with the army, attaining the rank of major, making training films and later serving in Washington DC as liaison officer between the army and the film industry. A few years later, writing as 'Jay Stewart', a name inspired by his father, Palmer drew on his wartime experiences for *Before It's Too Late* (1950), a murder mystery set in and around the Pentagon.

Palmer was discharged in 1946 and on returning to southern California resumed writing scripts, now mainly for television. He also continued to write novels and short mystery, science fiction and fantasy stories, as well as Sherlockian pastiches. In 1950 Palmer and his great friend, the crime writer Craig Rice (Georgiana Ann Randolph Craig), won first prize for 'Once upon a Train (The Loco Motive)' in a short story competition run by *Ellery Queen's Mystery Magazine*. As well as fiction, Palmer also wrote from time to time about real-life crime, including the 1932 Wanderwell mystery, and his life story of 'Bloody Babs' Graham was widely syndicated in the press in 1954, the year in which Palmer served as President of the Mystery Writers of America.

In the 1950s and '60s, Palmer made several radio and television appearances on shows like *You Bet Your Life*, hosted by Groucho Marx (whom, incidentally, Palmer later cast in a short story named for the show). In 1961 he wrote a romantic radio play, *Three-Dimensional Valentine*, for a marathon charity broadcast, and in the same year, as 'poet laureate' for the Society of Friends of Lizzie Borden—the alleged perpetrator of the Fall River axe murders—Palmer led an unsuccessful campaign to have a statue erected in her memory. He was active in the Baker Street Irregulars, where he had been ennobled as 'The Remarkable Worm', and he regularly gave talks at the Long Beach Writers' Club and elsewhere on 'How to be a Writer—and Keep on Living'. He even occasionally opened his home in Van Nuys, California, to host workshops for freshmen and sophomore writers whom he advised 'if you seek immortality you will find it in writing books . . . you never die when someone reads a page you have written'.

A ladies' man, Stuart Palmer was married five times, including to Winifred E. Wise, the writer of non-fiction for children whom he had met at university decades earlier. He died on 4 May 1968. His final novel, *Rook Takes Knight* (1968), was published posthumously, and after his death his widow created a scholarship in his name at Glendale College, California

The earliest of around a dozen uncollected Miss Withers stories, 'The Riddle of the Black Spade' was first published in *Mystery* in October 1934.

A TORCH AT THE WINDOW

Josephine Bell

It was a dark night in late autumn when the trouble started. There was no moon, and the large irregular bulk of St Stephen's Hospital loomed black behind the bright lights at the entrance gates and in the main porters' lodge. Beyond the first two blocks and the Out-Patient department the lamp-posts on either side of the main drive ended. They gave most light round the sweep of the Casualty entrance. Beyond that a car needed headlights to follow the winding macadam between the other blocks of the main building and the grounds behind them to the new Annexe block and the hospital boundary. It might have been a narrow country lane, and since the hospital stood on the outskirts of the market town it served, and in daylight there was a fine view over fields and distant hills, the night air there was always clean and sharp and smelled of the country.

In Brodie Ward in the Annexe most of the patients slept. It was after eleven, and they had been settled down some three hours earlier. Brodie was an orthopaedic ward for men, a surgical ward dealing with operations on bones and joints, with a never-ending turnover of road accidents and fractures sustained in factory or home. Because surgical patients of this type are seldom chronically ill people, most of them were sleeping peacefully in darkness. A few blue-shaded lights hung over the beds of those freshly operated upon, or over new accident arrivals, critically ill from shock or injury.

Out of the darkness and the silence a firm young voice called softly, 'Nurse!'

There was a rustle near the entrance end of the ward. A slim figure in uniform came out from the curtained cubicle where a blue light shone, and passed quickly down the ward. 'What is it, Barry?'

Nurse Farrer leaned over the young man's bed. She could barely see his square snub-nosed face in the dim light. He was lying back on his pillow, looking up at her with a half-smile. His dark eyes glinted in the light of her pocket torch as she switched it on. Immediately he covered the torch with a strong hand, extinguishing its beam.

'Douse that light!' he whispered, urgently. 'Look out the window!'

She moved a little from the bed to do so. Outside, the blackness was complete. She could not even see the boundary hedge of the hospital, ten yards away.

'I don't see anything,' she went back to tell him. 'You been having nightmares?'

The boy chuckled.

'No fear!'

'What was it, then?'

'Light. Someone came along all the windows this side, shining it in. Midnight snooper.'

'Sure it wasn't a car moving in and out of the car park?'

'It was a torch, I tell you. An ordinary hand torch, like this.'

With a smile she could not see behind the light, he switched on and handed her back her torch. She gave a little gasp.

'Barry! You're the limit! I never noticed.'

He raised himself on one elbow now to point at the window on the other side of the bed.

'Whoever it was came right down this side, flicking his torch into each window. Disappointing for him, wasn't it?'

He laughed again, a little louder, so that Nurse Farrer had to reprove him in her crisp, rather hard voice. But Barry was irrepressible. He caught at her hand to draw her closer.

'All that trouble and he only sees a lot of men. It was Treves Ward he was after, I don't mind betting.'

Nurse Farrer pulled away her hand.

'You go to sleep,' she said. 'And none of your nasty ideas in my ward. If you're not off by the time I'm back I'll have to give you one of your pink pills.'

He put up both hands in a mock gesture of self-protection, then pulled the bedclothes over his head and gave an artificial snore. Nurse Farrer went back to the concussion case in the blue-lighted cubicle.

But Barry's report had disturbed her. Twice before during her training, they had had this snooper trouble at the Annexe. The block consisted of six wards, a radium unit and operating theatres: all low, bungalow-type buildings, on either side of a central covered way, into which their entrance doors opened. Other doors led into the corridor at the lower end and at three places in the sides between the wards.

The boundary hedge behind the Annexe was the original one, now much broken down with age and very inadequately wired over its worst gaps. A proper wall or even fence would have given some protection. The present arrangement was almost an invitation to intruders.

Nurse Farrer determined to satisfy her own curiosity about Barry's report. The boy was a bit inclined to practical joking. He must not be encouraged. He had been in six weeks now, after a motor-bike accident in which his right leg had been cracked in two places below the knee. At first he had been exaggeratedly depressed, irritable and difficult. Now he was just the reverse, and the older men in the ward, some of whom were easily offended, were beginning to dislike his new high spirits.

So Nurse Farrer decided to check with the other wards in the Annexe. She called the probationer to watch the serious case, and went across the covered way to the door of Treves, a surgical ward for women.

As soon as she was inside its outer door she knew that something was wrong. There were several lights on in the ward, but the outer rooms, ward kitchen, sluice room, Sister's office, were all deserted. She pushed open the inner door and went in.

A babble of indignant voices rose in her ears as she did so. She saw her opposite number at the far end of the left-hand row of beds, trying to restrain an hysterical patient who was calling out and attempting to leave her bed. Farrer hurried down the ward.

The staff nurse looked up as she drew near. Though she resented Farrer's arrival as a typical piece of high-handed interference, in the circumstances she could not refuse her proffered help. Together the two nurses succeeded in calming the distraught woman in the bed, to the extent of persuading her to lie back and tell them what had upset her.

'Don't talk if you'd rather not, Mrs Holmes,' said the Treves Ward nurse, soothingly.

But Mrs Holmes was eager now to begin. Controlling her sobs she managed to say, 'I was having such a lovely sleep and then the light shone in my eyes, and woke me up. I thought it was you, nurse, at first. Then the light moved away on to Mrs Brook, and I glimpsed an awful face at the window, sort of glaring in. Like a horror film on the telly, it was. My heart seemed to stop and then Mrs Brook gave a scream and the lights went on down the ward and we were all starting up and calling out and I suppose I lost my head a bit. I'm ever so sorry, nurse.'

She was crying freely now. Nurse Farrer patted her shoulder briskly.

'We saw the light in Brodie, too, across the way,' she said. 'Someone thinks it fun to do a Peeping Tom, I expect. I hope he's disappointed. We'll report it to Sister, of course.'

'I have reported it,' said the nurse in Treves, coldly. She wished Farrer would go. Interfering, as usual. The only one who knew what to do, of course, and told others to do it. Bossy wasn't the word!

Nurse Farrer, realising at last that her presence in another ward would not look too good if Sister found her there, turned away abruptly, and hurried back to her own territory, where she immediately rang up Night Sister to tell her of Barry Williams's experience. She did not mention the later commotion in Treves. It was the deputy she spoke to. Night Sister had already left to go to the Annexe, she learned. So, determined to go one better than Treves, she rang up the porters' lodge at the main gates of the hospital.

Here she was answered by Bates, the senior night porter. He and his colleague, Holford, shared the work between them, Bates remaining at the telephone exchange, and Holford carrying out such jobs as wheeling an emergency case from a ward to an operating theatre and back again later, or taking a dead body from a ward to the mortuary, or directing and assisting an ambulance to park and discharge its occupants. If no such work turned up, Holford's duty was to patrol the grounds once or twice during the night.

When Nurse Farrer's call came through, Holford was sitting in the lodge, relaxing with a cigarette and an evening paper. He was not at all pleased, and for some minutes made no attempt to move.

'Better see if you can locate the perisher,' suggested Bates. 'He only seems to have been at those two wards nearest the hedge. Scarpered when the women started their hullabaloo, I reckon. But you better have a look round.'

'I'll give him another minute or two,' answered Holford, who had no desire to meet the intruder on a pitch black narrow path in the wilds, as he called the undeveloped part of the hospital grounds between the Annexe and the main block. 'I'm not risking my life with a lunatic. And that's what he must be. Nasty-minded beggar at that. Why don't they get on with this plan for a new laboratory? Then it would all join up, so you could walk right through the place without crossing the open.'

'That wouldn't stop a snooper,' answered Bates, reasonably. 'Good high wall with wire on top. That's what we need.'

Holford put his head out of the lodge, cursed the darkness of the night, and withdrew to take up his torch. It was a powerful one, rubber-covered to protect it from rain. He wrapped a scarf round his neck, put on an overcoat, and set off towards the Annexe, shining a long beam from side to side, but not venturing from the middle of the path as he moved along.

Arriving at the Annexe covered way, he found Night Sister and the two staff nurses standing there. The unwanted visitor had not been seen at any other windows in the block. Evidently the disturbance he had caused in Treves had scared him away. Holford reported that he had seen no one on his way from the porters' lodge, and they all agreed there was nothing more to be done. Night Sister left, accompanied by Holford, and before they parted at the main building she asked him to go back again, to escort the nurses across the grounds to the main dining room where they had their midnight meal. Rather reluctantly, for the night was cold, Holford set off once more.

Meanwhile, in the corridor at the Annexe, Nurse Farrer and Judy, the staff nurse from Treves, were on the point of returning to their respective wards, when they heard a tapping at one of the doors farther up the corridor. Both girls started, but Farrer recovered first and hurried towards the door. When she had peered through the glass upper part, she unlocked it quickly, and Dr Guy Stevens came through.

'What's the big idea, locking me out?'

She told him. Night Sister had ordered all three of the side doors into the covered way to be locked at night until further notice. The main entrance was open, and well lit outside and in. No sinister person would be likely to go near it.

Guy Stevens was inclined to make light of the matter. He was a house officer of only two years' standing, working on the surgical side. His experience was limited. Nurse Farrer, a couple of years his senior, did not hesitate to tell him so.

'And you're always right, Betty, aren't you?' said Guy, still refusing to be serious.

She hustled him into Brodie Ward. He had taken her out once or twice, and she was really rather attracted, except when he behaved as he did now. For his part, Guy was beginning to feel she was more of a liability than an asset. But it was not going to be easy to shake her off.

He did his night round in Brodie, and Nurse Farrer went to the door of the ward with him. In the dim light of the corridor she looked appealing. He caught her hand to pull her to him, but she had been offended by his earlier attitude, and was not going to give in now.

Judy, just inside the door of Treves, heard the ensuing scuffle, and caught sight of Dr Stevens's furious scarlet face as he was flung out of the Annexe. Quarrelling again, she thought. Honestly, some people don't know when they're well off.

A fortnight passed, with no further alarms. Night Sister had reported the occurrence to Matron, who told the Hospital Secretary, who telephoned the Chairman of St Stephen's House Committee, who mentioned the matter to the Chairman of the Hospital Group Management Committee. The matter was placed on the agenda for the next cycle of committees in two months' time. Recommendations would be made and passed on, until they reached the Regional Board, which would inevitably turn down any project so costly as a wall or an extra member of the staff.

The Matron, however, did manage to arrange for Holford to act as a permanent escort for the Annexe night nurses on their way to and from the main dining room.

This worked smoothly until a night when Holford's services were required in the operating theatre at the Annexe. He was still on duty there at midnight, and the nurses decided that they would go together in a body rather than wait for him. By this time they had forgotten the former panic, which after all had affected the patients much more than the staff. The girls gathered in the covered way, pulling their cloaks round them.

'Where's Betty?'

'Go and tell her, Judy.'

The girl was back in a few seconds.

'She says go without her. One of her patients has gone along to the toilet and not come out. She must wait for him, she says.'

'Typical!'

'She'll catch us up.'

They trooped off in a body, leaving the wards in charge of the probationers, whose turn for a meal came after their seniors got back.

Nurse Farrer did not catch them up. She did not appear while they ate their meal. When they got back to the Annexe she was not there. Night Sister and Holford, now free to help, searched the grounds between the main block and the Annexe, and at three in the morning they found her, lying outside the Hospital Secretary's office, dead.

The Senior Registrar was called, and Matron, and the police. There was nothing the doctor could do, except confirm Night Sister's finding. Before long Detective-Superintendent Coleridge was on the scene and the investigation was under way.

The Hospital Secretary's office formed one half of a one-storey concrete building, situated near the boundary, not far from the Annexe. The other half held the engineer's stores and had its own entrance. At the office end a wide door was set back between the two walls of a short porch. Nurse Farrer was lying face downwards in a corner of this porch. Her forehead was grazed, her neck was broken. On the back of her head was a fairly large bruise.

'Looks as if she was hit from behind,' said the police doctor, who had arrived soon after Superintendent Coleridge. 'She fell against the corner of the wall, I think, and broke her neck. Otherwise she'd be alive now. This blow wasn't enough to kill her, only concuss. She's been dead about three hours, I imagine.'

There had been no struggle, no assault. Simply that one blow from behind, and the unlucky fact that she was near the door when it was delivered.

'Why was she here at all?' Coleridge asked aloud.

'She shouldn't have come this way,' Matron explained. 'She ought to have been with the others.'

She explained the circumstances and Coleridge nodded. He had seen the hospital report about the snooper two weeks ago.

'She may have seen or heard someone on the path, and gone out of her way to avoid him,' he suggested.

Matron shook her head.

'Nurse Farrer wasn't the sort to run away. If she heard anyone behind her she'd turn to face him, and get the better of him, too. She had a sharp tongue in her head, and was rather too fond of using it, poor girl.'

Superintendent Coleridge did not seem to be listening. The Hospital Secretary, roused from his bed, had just arrived with the keys to the office.

'Sorry to get you up, but we need your help.' Coleridge explained. 'Looks as if she noticed something wrong near your office, while she was going, alone, towards the main block. Perhaps a light on inside, or a figure moving. Open up, please.'

Mr Walters, considerably shocked and still only half awake, did as he was told. When he had opened the door he stood back, expecting Coleridge to go in.

But the Superintendent merely pushed the door wide open and shone his torch into the darkness. He saw a short passage with closed doors at either side, and an open door ahead. He turned to Walters.

'Take my torch,' he said, 'and go into the room at the end. That's the main office, I take it?'

'That's right.'

Walters again did as he was told, and stood in the office turning the torch slowly from side to side. He was plainly visible from the doorway and beyond. Also clearly to be seen was a large safe.

Superintendent Coleridge walked in and switched on all the lights.

'Right,' he said, briskly. 'No disturbance here, but you never can tell. I'll leave you with Detective-Sergeant Jones, Mr Walters. He'll go through everything with you. Try the safe for a start. You keep a certain amount of money there, I suppose?'

'Wages, yes. And deceased patients' property until it's claimed by the relatives. And petty cash.'

'Just so.'

Leaving Sergeant Jones to supervise this move, and the taking of fingerprints and photographs on the spot, he went away to the main block to pursue his inquiries with the hospital staff.

Night Sister, convinced that the crime had been committed by the unknown intruder who had so startled the Annexe a fortnight before, explained her views with much emphasis.

'Nurse Farrer was an excellent worker,' she said, 'but a bit too self-reliant. Tonight's behaviour was typical. First she thinks she ought to make sure all her patients are in bed before she leaves. Quite unnecessary. There is always someone in charge. Then it was very silly to think she could order a grown man out of a lavatory.'

'Was that what she did?'

'So I hear. It meant Nurse Farrer had to start out alone. The others were tired of waiting for her, quite naturally. Even so, it was very officious to go out of her proper way to find out what was happening at the office, if anything was.'

Superintendent Coleridge pursed his lips.

'You don't think she had a date?' he asked, drily.

Sister's face grew scarlet.

'Our nurses don't behave like that,' she said.

'Don't they have boyfriends?'

'Of course they do. But they keep their private affairs for their off-duty periods.'

'I see.'

The Superintendent did not look convinced.

'It has been suggested to me that Nurse Farrer was interested in one of the resident doctors. And that they had quarrelled recently.'

'You mean Dr Stevens? Well, I know for a fact he was in the operating theatre tonight. An emergency appendix. That was why Holford was not able to escort the girls over.'

'I see,' said the Superintendent again. 'I wonder if I might have a word with Dr Stevens?'

'Must you get him out of bed again tonight?'

'I'm afraid so. And its nearly morning, after all. I'd like to see him here in about half an hour from now.'

Guy Stevens did not appear at his best with the Superintendent. He was half asleep and very tired after his exertions of the day before, and his work in the theatre only five hours ago. The added shock of Nurse Farrer's violent death only made his confusion and resentment worse. Coleridge was ready to believe he was lying, and rather poorly at that.

'Do you deny you were interested in this girl?'

'In Betty Farrer? Well, yes, up to a point.'

'Up to what point?'

Guy flushed.

'She threw her weight about too much,' he said, ungallantly.

'She was so efficient,' he amended, not wishing to slander the dead, and rather horrified at his own complete lack of any sense of grief or loss. The Superintendent had also remarked this.

'You don't seem much upset,' he said.

'Of course I'm upset. It's terrible. But there was never anything serious between us. I've hardly spoken to her for the last couple of weeks. We quarrelled, actually.'

'Sure you didn't make a date tonight?'

'Why should I?'

'To make it up. Sure you didn't meet her and quarrel again?'

Guy's sleepy confusion parted, and a cold sinister light shone through at these words. There was no mistaking the Superintendent's meaning.

'I was in the theatre,' he said.

'But the operation was over and the theatre cleared quite five minutes before Nurse Farrer left Brodie Ward.'

When Coleridge rejoined Sergeant Jones he found that considerable progress had been made. Though the office had shown no signs of disturbance, a large sum of money was, in fact, missing from the safe. The latter had not been forced, however—merely opened. An inside job, obviously. The laborious work of identifying fingerprints began.

In the late afternoon of the same day, the Superintendent went to Brodie Ward. It seemed to him now that his first suspicions of Dr Stevens had very little foundation. Nurse Farrer must have been attracted to the office by a noise or a light. Perhaps she had seen and recognised the thief; this inside thief who could well be known to her. And who more likely than the staff, particularly the cleaners, whom she knew? On the other hand, she had been struck from behind, perhaps while all her attention was focused on the thief. That suggested an accomplice, and the fact that the blow had not been hard enough to kill, might mean a female accomplice. He entered the ward with an open mind.

The Day Sister and her staff were prepared to help, but they knew nothing. Coleridge tackled the patients instead. Some swore they had slept through the night; one or two road accident cases were suspicious and tongue-tied. He gained most from an elderly man whose broken leg was fixed to an elaborate pulley system.

'Poor kid!' he said, referring to Nurse Farrer. 'It was her own fault. She'd no business to go chasing up young Barry.'

Coleridge had heard the story twice. He looked round the ward.

'You won't find him,' the old man went on. 'He was discharged this morning. Been due to go out for a day or two.'

'Fit?'

'Good as new.'

'Which was his bed?'

The old man pointed to the drawn curtains round the bed next to his own.

'He liked joking with the nurses. He wouldn't move while she was badgering him, but he was back from the toilet in his bed inside three minutes after she left.'

'Is that so?'

'Practical jokes. That was his line. I've not said this to Sister, but it's my belief that snooper, as they call him, was Barry himself.' The old man caught at Coleridge's sleeve. 'Suppose he pretended he'd seen a face at the window. We were all asleep but him. When nurse had gone back behind the curtains of that bad case they had that night he could nip out to the toilet and climb out and frighten the women in Treves, just before she went across to see what they were doing there. Then he'd be back when she got back, see?'

Coleridge looked at the old man with surprise, which he managed to suppress.

'You have a new patient in his bed?' he asked, changing the subject.

'Yes. Barry'd not been gone an hour when they brought this chap in. Fell off some scaffolding, they say.'

The Superintendent nodded, and went away down the ward to the bathrooms. As the old man had said, anyone normally agile could climb through a lavatory window, only a few feet from the ground, and return the same way. He hurried back to find Sister.

'That young Barry Williams? Did be discharge himself? '

'Oh, no. He's been fit to leave for days now. But his people hadn't brought his clothes.'

'Why not?'

'Londoners. No sense of time or dates. I sent them the usual notice of his discharge. We sent again yesterday and a friend turned up this morning.'

'Only a friend?'

'In a car.'

Coleridge nodded and got to work, rather against Sister's will, on the cubicle so recently vacated by Barry Williams. As he pointed out, the new patient, being unconscious, would never know about it, and valuable evidence must not be lost.

The results of this, taken with the investigation in the office, were revealing. In the office all the fingerprints taken matched with members of the hospital staff. Those from the cubicle, besides the staff, were identified as belonging to a certain Bernard Grant, who had already two convictions for robbery with violence.

Grant, alias Barry Williams, was soon picked up by the London police and questioned. Most of the money from the safe at St Stephen's Hospital was still with him. He agreed that he had used an alias on admission there after his road accident. Since this had been due to a skid and involved no one else, there had been no police inquiry when it happened.

'What were you doing at the time?' Coleridge asked.

'Just having a run in the country.'

'Planning a job?'

'Certainly not.'

They got nothing from him but the money, less a deposit he had made on a new car. The old man's suggestion that he had been the snooper he dismissed with a light laugh, though they thought they detected an uneasy note in it. He refused to say how he had opened the safe, and he swore he'd had nothing to do with Nurse Farrer's death. His mother, when approached, was more revealing.

Superintendent Coleridge, again accompanied by Sergeant Jones, went up to St Stephen's Hospital and asked for Holford.

'Up at the theatre,' Bates told them, and went outside the lodge to point the nearest way to the Annexe.

They were just passing the Hospital Office building when they met Holford, coming down the path towards them. He stopped at once, and stayed quite still as they went up to him.

'James Holford?' asked the Superintendent.

'Yes. That's me.'

'Have you a sister called Amelia Grant?'

'Yes.'

'And a nephew called Bernard Grant, alias Barry Williams?'

Holford's face had gone very white. His eyes wavered from side to side before fixing again on the two police officers.

'I'm warning you,' went on Coleridge. 'Understand?'

'Yes.'

'When you left the operating theatre on the night of Nurse Farrer's death, did you use this path, passing the office?'

'Always do.' The voice was hoarse, reluctant.

'It would be dark. Did you have your torch with you?'

Holford made a convulsive move off the path on to the grass, but Sergeant Jones side-stepped also, and he stopped, breathing heavily.

'Well, did you?'

'Always do,' he repeated, in the same tone.

'And you saw Nurse Farrer looking into the office?'

'The nurses had gone down on their own. I was too late to go with them.'

'Not Nurse Farrer. You expected her to be gone but you saw her. You knew she had discovered Grant in the act of burgling the safe, so you went up behind and struck her with that big rubber-covered torch of yours, and you killed her.'

Holford gave a cry, covering his face with his hands.

'I never meant it,' he groaned. 'Only to give her a mild concussion, so she'd forget seeing Bernie. I could've passed it off, she'd tripped and hit her head on the step or something. Then I found she was dead. I've been out of my mind since.'

He took his hands away, staring at the Superintendent.

'I'd nothing to do with the job,' he pleaded. 'The boy thought that up. Must have. He's been getting about all over the hospital the last fortnight. He's bad all through. I did it for Mellie's sake. My sister. I only wanted Nurse to forget. I didn't strike her hard.'

Coleridge looked at him with contempt.

'Family likeness,' he said. 'The boy swears he only stole. You say you only killed by accident. You're both as guilty as hell. Robbery and murder. A capital offence. How did Grant get into that office and into that safe if you didn't manage to get keys for him? He wouldn't have had the time or the means. He was back in the ward, going through the toilet window, as he'd been practising, inside three minutes after Nurse Farrer left. I've got a solid witness for that. You'll have to come with us, Holford, and I warn you again, anything you say . . .'

JOSEPHINE BELL

'Josephine Bell' was the pseudonym of Doris Bell Collier. She was born on 8 December 1897 in Chorlton-on-Medlock, Manchester, the daughter of Maud Tessimond Windsor and Joseph Collier, a surgeon. From 1910 she studied at Godolphin School, Salisbury, and in 1916, at the age of eighteen, she went up to Cambridge University to study Natural Sciences at Newnham College, taking time out to work on the land towards the end of the First World War.

Collier graduated in 1919, the same year that her elder brother Jack was killed in a flying accident in Spain, devastating her mother and her other brother Donald. In 1922, following in the footsteps of her father and great-grandfather, she decided to become a doctor and enrolled as a student at University College Hospital, London. She was diligent, even working in the emergency department of Hampstead General Hospital as a casualty officer. But she also had time for extramural matters and, on 6 January 1923 married Norman Dyer Ball, a pathologist at UCH who had lost an eye in the Great War. The following year, which included a spell as house physician, she gained the customary double degree of Bachelor of Medicine and Bachelor of Surgery.

The couple moved to Croom's Hill in Greenwich where Dyer Ball set up in general practice, working alongside his wife until 1935 when ill health forced him to sell up. They moved to Walden in Headley, Hampshire, to stay with Collier's mother, whose second husband Jean Éstradie had died three years earlier. Dyer Ball's health began slowly to improve and the couple decided that the following summer they would make a long sea voyage. However, on the day after their thirteenth wedding anniversary and not long after he had been involved in a minor car accident, Dyer Ball drove up to London to do some shopping. He bumped into the wife of one of his neighbours at Croom's Hill and offered to give her a lift home. However, their journey ended in tragedy when the car mounted the kerb, rolled over twice and collided with a lorry. His passenger died almost immediately while Dyer Ball died in hospital a little time later.

Not even forty years old and widowed with four young children, Collier moved to Bordon in East Hampshire. She secured a position as a Clinical Assistant at the Royal Surrey County Hospital in Guildford and to supplement her income turned to writing. Her first novel, *Murder in Hospital* (1937), dedicated to her late husband, was written under a pseudonym that some have suggested was an homage to the original of Sherlock Holmes, Dr Joseph Bell. However, the truth is much simpler: in coining the name 'Josephine Bell', Collier simply combined her own middle name with the first name of her father, who had died in 1905 before she was ten. Any connection to Joseph Bell was at most a happy coincidence.

Murder in Hospital was praised for its clever plot and even more so as a study of hospital mores. However, there are moments that jar for modern readers not least the portrayal of some characters that, while they might simply reflect the attitudes prevailing in the 1930s, are variously antisemitic and racist. For the novel, Bell introduced Dr David Wintringham, who would appear in eleven more novels including *From Natural Causes* (1941), which features an unusual method of murder, *Death by Clairvoyance* (1949), in which one of six identically dressed clowns is murdered at a buffet, and the horrific *Bones in the Barrow* (1953). Wintringham also appears in numerous short stories, many of which were published in the *London Evening Standard*.

As well as the Wintringham series, Collier wrote many other crime novels, often with a medical background and some with novel settings such as *The House by the River* (1959), set in Brittany, *New People at the Hollies* (1961), set in an old peoples' home, and *A Hole in the Ground* (1971) in which a doctor returns to Cornwall to investigate an accident that he had witnessed twenty years earlier.

Collier also wrote historical romances and serial thrillers for magazines, such as *The Dark Tide* (1951). Her numerous straight novels include the possibly autobiographical *Compassionate Adventure* (1946) and *The Bottom of the Well* (1940) about a mismatched couple, but the best of her non-crime output are *Total War at Haverington* (1947), set during the air raids and chaos of war-torn London, and *Wonderful Mrs Marriott* (1948), about a domineering woman and the damage she wreaks on her family. There was also a non-criminous radio drama about a typhoid outbreak entitled *Hidden Death* (1949).

All the time Collier was writing, she continued to work, not least because she had four children to raise on her own. In 1941, she moved to the Royal Surrey's gynaecology department until in 1944, a year after her mother's death, she set up in general practice at 'Willoughby', 13 Albury Road, Guildford, still also pursuing her hobbies—gardening and sailing her five-ton sloop.

After retiring in 1954, Collier joined the management committee of St Luke's Hospital in Guildford, a position she held until 1962. Perhaps more significantly, 1954 was also the year that she was elected a member of the Detection Club, the dining society for crime writers. A year later, Collier was among the founder members of the Crime Writers' Association, later serving as the chair for 1959–1960. In this role, she spoke widely on crime fiction, including in 1959 a talk on the history and future of the crime novel to the literary society in Cranleigh, East Sussex. In 1960 she contributed to a series of radio plays by CWA members and in 1961 a series of short stories written by CWA members for newspaper syndication. After her term as chair ended, Collier remained on its main committee taking part in one of its most unusual meetings, held in the Chamber of Horrors at Madame Tussaud's and broadcast by the BBC in July 1967.

Writing almost up until the end of her life, Doris Bell Collier died in 1987. 'A Torch at the Window' was originally published in *She*, January 1960.

Grand Guignol

John Dickson Carr

A Mystery in Ten Parts. The performance staged under the direction of M. Henri Bencolin, prefect of police of Paris.

The Cast of Characters:
M. HENRI BENCOLIN.
M. ALEXANDRE LAURENT, *scholar, former husband of—*
LOUISE DE SALIGNY, *the wife of—*
RAOUL, *fourth Duc de Saligny, eminent sportsman.*
M. EDOUARD VAUTRELLE.
SIGNOR LUIGI FENELLI, *maestro of several enterprises.*
JACQUES GIRARD, *jockey.*
MR SID GOLTON, *late of Lincoln, Nebraska, USA.*
FRANÇOIS DILLSART, *operative of the prefecture.*
M. LE COMTE DE VILLON, *juge d'instruction,*
and others.

The Place: Paris.
The Time: 1927.
The action covers a period of twenty-four hours.

I
THE OVERTURE: *Danse Macabre*

'*Le jeu est fait, 'sieurs et dames; rien ne va plus.*'

The voices stopped. It was so quiet that from anywhere in the room you could hear the ball ticking about in the wheel. Then the shrill, bored voice chanted:

'*Vingt-deux noir, 'sieurs et dames . . .*'

One man got up from the table stiffly, with an impassive face. He made a defiant gesture at lighting a cigarette, but the flame of the briquet wobbled in his hand; he smiled in a sickly way, and his face glistened when he looked from side to side. A woman laughed. There was the booming of an English voice, swearing triumphantly.

Paris has many such miniature casinos, which attract the most mixed throng of any places in that mixed city. This was a long red room, in a walled house of a discreet neighborhood at Passy. A harsh colour scheme of red and crystal; a harsh sound of voices, and bad ventilation; a harsh jazz orchestra downstairs mangling tunes already execrable; poor cocktails supplied by the house, and a clientèle at once fashionable and dowdy—above everything, a gloomy tensity of thousands being played across the table. The hard light showed worn places on faces and furniture. The women used too much perfume; men took an enormous delight in shaking out two-thousand-franc notes like tablecloths.

At a lounge near one of the windows, from which you could see the Citroën advertisement spraying coloured lights up the side of the Eiffel Tower, I sat with my friend Bencolin. He idly twirled the stem of a cocktail glass; with the points of his hair whisked up, and his black beard clipped to a sharp point, he looked even more Mephistophelian than usual. The wrinkles round his eyelids contracted in amusement, and he smiled sideways when he pointed out each newcomer round the clicking wheel.

They were interesting. There was Madame That and the

Marquise This, octogenarian crones whose faces were masks of enamel and rouge, dyed hair piled like a scaffolding; they smirked and ogled at their gigolos, smooth-haired pomandered young men whose gestures were like a woman's, but with manners and evening dress flawless. A crone's hand would shoot out like a claw after a new pile of banknotes; then the gigolo applauded politely, and smiled in a glittering way at the leering woman. There was a Russian lady with a Japanese face and a pearl collar—not beautiful, flourishing skinny arms like wings—but several men were eager to back all her bets. There were loud Argentines, the deepest plungers, and an American too drunk to follow the play, but falling over everybody's chair and demanding to know who wanted to start a poker game. An attendant led him suavely away to the bar . . . Gestures were shriller, bolder; the hard light drew lines and wrinkles, and showed up splotches of powder on bare backs; no fog of smoke could eliminate the wet odour of the bar, or any amount of music blat down that insistent song of the wheel.

'They are fools,' said Bencolin idly, 'to play against a double zero.' He glanced over as another burst of laughter came from the tables. 'And the foreigners will play nothing else. Baccarat, chemin-de-fer—never. It must be quick, like a drink of whisky, *voilà!*' He snapped his fingers. 'Their only system is the martin-gale, doubles or quits, and they do not last long. '

'Is the game straight?' I asked.

'Oh, yes. Cheating is quite unnecessary, and too dangerous . . . Well,' he added, smiling, 'am I not showing you Paris, my friend Jack?'

'And much obliged. Except that I had hoped to go slumming. This is as dull and decorous as the Latin Quarter.'

'Yes, but wait,' Bencolin remarked softly. 'I seldom go anywhere for pleasure. I think you will find that this is no exception.'

'A case?'

He shrugged his shoulders. For a time he sat staring with

blank eyes at the crowd; then he took out a black cigar, and rolled it about in his fingers. Absently he continued:

'It has been in the past my good or bad fortune to be concerned only in cases of an outlandish nature; cases whose very impossible character admitted of just one solution. Cast your mind back. There was one way, and only one, in which the smuggler Mercier could have been strangled*; there was one way for La Garde to have been shot†, and one way for Cyril Merton to have accomplished his "disappearance"‡. Is a person, then, to evolve a philosophy that there is but one way for any crime to be committed? Hardly; and yet—' He scowled across the room.

'The Duc de Saligny,' he went on abruptly, 'is good-looking, wealthy, and still young. He was married at noon today to a charming young woman. There, you will say, is a perfect cinema romance. The bride and groom are both here tonight.'

'Indeed? Aren't they going on a wedding-trip?'

'To the modern marriage,' mused Bencolin, 'there seems to be something slightly indecent about privacy. You must act in public as though you had been married twenty years, and in private as though you had not been married at all. That, however, is not my affair. There is a deeper reason for it.'

'They don't love each other, then?'

'On the contrary, they seem to be violently in love . . . Have you ever heard of the bride?'

I shook my head.

'She was Madame Louise Laurent. Three years ago she was married to a certain man named Alexandre Laurent. Shortly afterwards, her husband was committed to an asylum for the criminally insane.' He was silent a moment, thoughtfully blowing smoke at the ceiling.

---

*   Carr's short story 'The Murder in Number Four'.

†   'The Fourth Suspect'.

‡   'The Shadow of the Goat'.

'Laurent was examined in a psychopathic ward. I was present at the time, and I give you my word that Cesare Lombroso would have been delighted with the case. He was a mild-appearing young man, soft-spoken and pleasant. The black spot on his brain was sadism. Usually lucid, he would have intervals in which the temptation to kill and mutilate became overpowering; and none of his crimes ever became known until after his marriage. Of course, such a neurosis could have no normal marriage, and culminated in what is known as "lust-murder". He attacked his wife, with a razor. She contrived to lock him in his room, for she is strong, and summoned help. By that time the frenzy had spent itself, but his secret was out.'

Bencolin spread out his hands.

'A genius, Laurent, a scholar, a prodigy in the languages. He spent his days in the asylum very quietly, at study. The marriage, naturally, was annulled.' Bencolin paused, and then said slowly, 'Six months ago, he escaped from the asylum. He is at large today, and the confinement seems only to have unbalanced him more completely.

'What did he do? He set out to find a perfect disguise. In these days, my friend, they are childish who seek to disguise themselves with any stage-trappings: paint, or false hair, or anything of the kind. Even an unpractised eye, such as your own, could penetrate such subterfuges without difficulty . . . No, Laurent did the only perfect thing. He put himself under the care of Dr Grafenstein, of Vienna, the greatest master of plastic surgery. He had himself remade entirely, even to his fingerprints. When this had been done, he quite coolly killed Dr Grafenstein—the only person who had ever seen his new face. Even the nurse had never laid eyes on the patient: in the first stages, he was swathed in bandages; when he began to heal, he concealed himself in his own room. Yes, he killed Grafenstein. He is now in Paris. Two days ago, he wrote a letter to the young Duc de Saligny. It said simply, "If you marry her, I will kill you." And I very much fear, my friend, that he will.'

I do not believe that I was ever in my life struck with so much horror as at this unemotional recital. Bencolin had never raised his voice. He smoked meditatively, watching the crowd; out of his words there grew in my mind a distorted picture of a lunatic, a Grand Guignol madman stepping through green dusk. Bencolin turned his sardonic face, shook his head, and remarked as though in response:

'No, we are not dealing with the conventional killer or the blood-curdler, who betrays himself in public. Have I not said that Laurent is mild-mannered and pleasant?—only with that clot on his brain. And what does he look like? The good God knows. He may be that fat banker over at the roulette table; he may be the young American, or the croupier, or any of them, or he may not be (and probably is not) here at all. But I shall not forget the Duc de Saligny's face when he brought that letter to me. A tall swaggerer with bloodshot eyes and an excitable manner: he kept biting his lips, and looking round until you could see the whites of his eyes. He was frightened, but he refused to admit it. Yes, he would go through with the wedding, and so would Louise. But you will see that he longs for public places now, until my men can step out and lay their hands on Laurent.'

That was the beginning of the nightmare drama. It seemed to me that the voices had grown more shrill, the gestures more elaborate; and that some force of Bencolin's words had penetrated to everybody in the room. It was not possible for them to have heard him, and yet you would have said that everyone was conscious of it, and was looking over towards us, furtively.

'Is he always dangerous?' I asked.

'Any man who has committed one murder is always dangerous. And Laurent especially, for our pathological case has discovered how pleasant it can be.'

'How does madame—*madame la duchesse* take all this?'

Bencolin was regarding a very oily and effusive gambler, who proclaimed his losses at the top of his voice; then the detective laid his hand on my arm.

'You will see for yourself. Here she comes now . . . You notice? No emotion or agitation; she looks as though she were in a drug-fog.'

A woman was crossing the room towards us; she moved in a rather vague way, with expressionless eyes and a slight smile. She was beautiful, but she was more than this. Even her hair had a cloudy look. The eyes were heavy-lidded and black, with not too much mascara, the lips of a sensual fullness which just escaped being coarse. In dress she was perfect, the black gown accentuating the invitation of shoulder and breast. She twisted her pearls vaguely. There was a little silver anklet under the grey stocking . . . She came straight up to Bencolin. When he bent over her hand she was negligent, but, closer, you could see a vein pulsing in her throat.

Bencolin introduced me, and added, 'A friend of mine. You may speak freely.' She looked towards me, and I had a sense of veils being drawn away. It was a look of scrutiny, not unmixed with suspicion.

'You are affiliated with the police, monsieur?' she asked me.

'Yes,' said Bencolin unexpectedly.

She sat down, refused one of my cigarettes, and took her own from a little wrist-bag. Leaning back, she inhaled deeply; her hand trembled, and her lips stained the tip of the cigarette as though with blood. She wore some kind of exquisite perfume; one was conscious of her nearness.

'*Monsieur le Duc* is here?' asked Bencolin.

'Raoul? Yes. Raoul is getting nervous,' she answered, and laughed shrilly. 'I don't blame him, though. It is not a pleasant thing to think about. If you had ever seen Laurent's eyes—'

Bencolin raised his hand gently. She shivered a little, looked slowly over at me, and then said. 'There goes Raoul now, into the card-room.' She nodded towards a broad back disappearing through a door at the far end of the room. I saw no more than that, for I happened to be looking at my wristwatch. I looked at it twice, absently, before I noticed that the hour was eleven-thirty.

'Orange blossoms!' she said, and laughed again. 'Orange blossoms, lace veils. A lovely wedding, lovely bride, with even the clergyman staring at us and wondering if there were a madman in the church. Orange blossoms, "till death do you part"—death! Very possibly!'

This was sheer hysteria. The sights and sounds of the casino blended in with it; the banging of the jazz band became nearly unbearable. That voice of the croupier rose singing over it, like the bawling of the man who announces trains. Louise, Duchesse de Saligny, said abruptly,

'I want a cocktail. Don't mind me if I seem upset. I keep thinking of Laurent crawling about . . . M. Bencolin, you're here to see that no harm comes to Raoul, do you hear? "Till death do you part"—' She shivered again.

There was silence while Bencolin looked round for the boy with the cocktail tray, a silence, and none of us intruded on each other's thoughts. A man and woman walked past us, almost stumbling over madame's feet; and I recall that the man was saying heatedly in English, 'Five hundred francs is entirely too damn much!—' The voices trailed away.

Somebody had come up in front of us, and coughed discreetly. It was a tall man; dapper, blond, with an eyeglass and an almost imperceptible moustache.

'Your pardon if I'm intruding,' he remarked. 'Louise, I don't believe I know—' He took out his handkerchief unnecessarily, wiped his lips, and stood fidgeting.

'Oh . . . yes,' she murmured; 'these are gentlemen from the police, Edouard. Allow me to present M. Edouard Vautrelle.'

Vautrelle bowed. 'Very happy . . . Raoul's gone to the card-room, Louise; he's been drinking too much. Won't you play?'

'That music—' she suddenly snapped; 'damn that music. I can't stand it! I won't stand it. Tell them to stop!'

'*Doucement, doucement!*' Vautrelle urged, looking round in a nervous way. With an apologetic nod at us he took her arm and led her towards the table; she seemed to have forgotten our existence.

Bencolin picked up the cigarette-stub she had left in the ashtray. He was juggling it in his palm, when suddenly he looked up. Madame and Vautrelle were in the centre of the room directly under one of the large chandeliers; they stopped. We all heard the crash of breaking glass, and saw the white-coated servant leaning against the door of the cardroom. He had let fall the tray of cocktails, and was staring stupidly at the wreckage.

Everyone turned to look. With the cessation of voices, the jazz band had stopped too. The manager, his fat stomach wobbling, was hurrying across the room. But most distinctly emerged the drawn, shiny face of the servant—who had seen something, and was desperately afraid.

Bencolin did not seem to hurry, but he was across the room immediately. I was directly behind him; he extended in his palm, for the manager's gaze, the little card with the circle, the eagle, and the three words, 'prefecture of police'. Together we went through the door of the cardroom.

My sensations were the same as those I had experienced once at a sideshow when I had seen some mountebank swallow a snake. The room was not well lit; its leprous red walls were hung with weapons, and a red-shaded lamp burned beside a divan at the far end. A man had fallen forward before the divan, as though in the act of kneeling—but the man had no head. Instead there was a bloody stump propped on the floor. The head itself stood in the centre of the room, upright on its neck; it showed white eyeballs, and grinned at us in the low red light. A breeze through an open window blew at us a heavy, sweet smell.

II
RED FOOTLIGHTS

With the utmost coolness, Bencolin turned to the manager.

'Two of my men,' he said, 'are on guard at your door. Summon them; all the doors are to be locked, and nobody must leave. Keep them playing, if it is possible. In the meantime, come in yourself and lock this door.'

The manager stammered something to an attendant, and added, 'Nobody is to know about this, understand?' He was a fat man, who looked as though he were melting; a monstrous moustache curled up to his eyes, which bulged like a frog's. Tumbling against the door, he stood and pulled idiotically at his moustache. Bencolin, twisting a handkerchief over his fingers, turned the key in the lock.

There was another door in the wall to our right, at the left side of the dead man as he lay before the divan. Bencolin went over to it; it was ajar, and he peered outside.

'This is the main hall, monsieur?' he asked.

'Yes,' said the manager. 'It—it—'

'Here is one of my men.' Bencolin beckoned from the door, and held a short consultation with the man outside. 'Nobody has come out *there*,' he observed, closing the door. 'François was watching. Now!'

All of us were looking about the room. I tried to keep my eyes off the head, which appeared to be gazing at me sideways; the wind blew on my face, and it felt very cold. Bencolin walked over to the body, where he stood and peered down, smoothing his moustache. Beside the neck-stump I could see projecting from the shadow a part of a heavy sword—it had come, apparently, from a group on the wall, and though the edge was mostly dulled with blood, a part near the handle emerged in a sharp, glittering line.

'Butchers' work,' said Bencolin, twitching his shoulders. 'See, it has been recently sharpened.' He stepped daintily over the red soaking against the lighter red of the carpet, and went to the window at our left. 'Forty feet from the street . . . inaccessible.'

He turned, and stood against the blowing curtains. The black eyes were bright and sunken; in them you could see rage at himself, nervousness, indecision. He beat his hands softly together, made a gesture, and returned to the body, where he avoided the blood by kneeling over the divan.

'Jack,' he said suddenly, looking up, 'pick up the head and bring it over here.'

No doubt about it, I was growing ill.

'Pick up—the *head*, did you say?' .

'Certainly; bring it here. Watch out, now; don't get the blood on your trousers . . .'

In a daze, I approached the thing, shut my eyes, and picked it up by the hair. The hair felt cold and greasy, the head much heavier than I had thought. While I was going towards Bencolin, I recall that the jazz band started playing again downstairs, dinning over and over, '*Whe-en ca-res pur-suoo-yah, sing hal-le-looo-jah—*'

'I shouldn't tamper with this,' Bencolin observed, 'but nobody can give me orders; and I don't think we need a coroner's report about the manner of his death.' He fitted the head against the trunk and stood back, frowning. I sat down heavily on the divan.

'Come here, monsieur,' said Bencolin to the proprietor. 'This sword: it comes from the room here?'

The manager began talking excitedly. His syllables exploded like a string of little firecrackers popping over the room; the almost unintelligible clipped speech of the *Midi*. Yes, the sword belonged here. It had hung with another, like itself, crossed over a Frankish shield on the wall near the divan. It was an imitation antique. Oh, yes, it was razor-sharp; this lent such a semblance of reality, and the patrons like reality.

'The handle,' remarked the detective, 'is studded with round brass nail-heads; we shall get no clear fingerprints from it, I fear . . . Do you ever use this room, monsieur?'

'Oh, yes; frequently. But we haven't used it tonight. See, the card tables are folded against the wall. Nobody wanted to play. It was all that roulette.' Volubly eager, the manager waggled his fat hands. 'Do you think it can be hushed up, monsieur? My trade—'

'Do you know this dead man?'

'Yes, monsieur; it is M. le Duc de Saligny. He often comes here.'

'Did you see him go in here tonight?'

'No, monsieur. The last I saw him was early in the evening.'

'Was he with anybody then?'

'With M. Edouard Vautrelle. The two were great friends—'

'Very good, then. You may go out now and inform *madame la duchesse*; be as quiet about it as possible—better take her out in the hall, in case she makes a scene. Tell M. Vautrelle to step in here.'

He went out by the hall door, leering over his shoulder with tiny wrinkled eyes. Bencolin turned to me.

'Well, what do you make of it?'

I could not collect my thoughts, and blurted dully, 'They were fortunate to keep it from the crowd out there—'

'No, no: the murder?'

'It was a terrific blow. It must have taken a madman's strength.'

'I wonder!' said Bencolin, beginning to pace up and down. 'Not necessarily, my friend. It was a two-handed blow, but, as our manager says, that sword is razor-sharp. I do not think that such gigantic strength was essential. You could have done it yourself. Look at the position of the body; does it convey nothing to you?'

'Only that there seems to have been no struggle.'

'Obviously not. He was struck from behind. We may assume that he was sitting on the divan before he was struck; but he got to his feet. Mark that: he got to his feet also before he was killed—you note that he is some distance out from the divan . . .'

'Well?'

'Yes, there are a number of pillows on the divan.'

'Pillows?'

'Certainly. Great God! Where are your wits? Don't you understand?'

'It suggests nothing except—except an amorous implication.'

'Amorous the devil!' snapped Bencolin. 'There was nothing amorous about the situation here.' He laughed wryly, and added, 'Our madman is now in these gaming-rooms. Nobody has left, unless my agents were asleep.'

'By the hall door?—'

'François has been there since eleven-thirty. Do you know what time Saligny came in here?'

'I recall exactly, because when madame pointed him out I was looking at my watch. It was eleven-thirty.'

Bencolin looked at his own watch. 'Just twelve; it should be easy to check alibis . . . How do you account for the fact that the head lies at some distance from the body, standing up?'

'It certainly couldn't have rolled to that position.'

'Well, stranger things have happened, but it didn't—you can see that there is no blood trail between the head and the body. No, the murderer put it there.'

'Why?'

'You forget that this is no sane mind. Can't you imagine it? The murderer triumphantly holding up the head of his victim; mocking it, addressing words to it while he walked round shaking it by the hair—'

'What a cheerful imagination *you* have!'

'But it is necessary,' he murmured, shrugging. Then he bent down gingerly and started to go through Saligny's pockets. Presently he straightened up and indicated a pile of articles on the divan. There was a queer smile on his face.

'The crowning touch . . . his pockets are filled with pictures of himself. Yes. See?' He ran his hands through clippings and pasteboards. 'Newspaper pictures, and a few cabinet photographs. Photographs of himself, every conceivable sort; pictures where he looks handsome, pictures where he looks ghastly . . . here is one on horseback; another at the golf links . . . Hm. Nothing else except some banknotes, a watch, and a lighter. Why these photographs at all? And especially why are they carried in evening clothes?'

'Conceited ass!'

Bencolin shook his head. He was squatting by the divan, idly turning over the clippings. 'No, my friend, there may be another reason—which is the peak of all this odd business. Cabinet photographs. *Diable!*'

We were suddenly startled by a tearing, rattling sound. The door to the hall was pushed open despite a protesting officer in plain clothes; there lurched into the room a short, pudgy, wild-eyed young man with a paper hat stuck on the back of his head. He grinned foolishly, his clothes were awry, and the noise was being made by one of those wooden twirlers they give as favours at night-clubs. He gave that sort of drunken leer very popular at weddings, shook the rattler at us, and smirked at the silly sounds it emitted.

'Party here,' he said in English, ''scort couple home. Always do't 'scort to the home to, as it were. Let's have a drink. Got any liquor?' he demanded interestedly of the plain-clothes man.

'*Mais, monsieur, c'est défendu d'entrer—*'

'Cutta frog talk. No comprey. Got any liquor? Hey?'

'*Monsieur, je vous ai dit!—*'

'N'lissen! Gotta see m'friend Raool. He's married; hellva thingta do!—'

The young man was pleading and persistent. I went over hurriedly and spoke in English:

'Better go out, old top. You'll get to see him—'

'By God, you're m'friend!' crowed the young man, opening his eyes wide and thrusting out his hand. 'Got any liquor? I've been drinkin',' he confided in a low tone, 'but gotta see Raool. He's married. Let's have a drink.' Suddenly he sat down in a chair near the door and fell into a half-stupor, still twirling the rattle.

'*Monsieur!*'—cried the policeman.

'I'm gonna pop *you*,' said the newcomer, opening his eyes again and pointing his finger at the policeman with a curiously intense look, 'sure'z hell I'm gonna pop you 'fyou don't getaway! C'mon, get back, 'm gonna pop 'im!' He relapsed again.

'Who is this?' I asked Bencolin.

'I have seen him before, with Saligny,' the detective replied. 'His name is Golton, or something of the sort: an American, naturally.'

'We had better put him—'

Again there was an interruption. We heard a woman moaning, 'I can't stand it! I can't stand it!' and other feminine tones urging her to be quiet. It was Madame Louise's voice. The door to the hall opened, and Edouard Vautrelle entered. He was very pale, but supercilious; he polished the eyeglass on his handkerchief, and looked round coldly.

'Was this necessary?' he said.

Supported by a little wizened woman attendant, Madame Louise came after him. She glanced at the thing on the floor; then she stood stoically, upright and motionless, with the rouge glaring out on her cheeks. Her eyes were dry and hot.

There was a space of silence, so that we could hear the curtains rustling at the window. Suddenly Golton, the American, looked up from a glassy contemplation of the floor, and saw her. He emitted a crow of delight. Never noticing the body, he rose unsteadily, made a flamboyant bow, and seized madame's hand.

'My heartiest congratulations,' he said, 'on this, the happiest day of your whole life!—'

It was a ghastly moment. We all stood there frozen, except Golton, who was wabbling with hand extended in his bow. Golton's eyes travelled up to Vautrelle, and he added waggishly:

'Sorry you got the gate, Eddie; Raool's got more money'n you, anyhow . . .'

III
DEATH GUIDES THE CLOCKS

Vautrelle snarled, 'Get that drunken dog out of here!' and made a movement that was restrained by Bencolin.

'Take him out,' the detective whispered to me, and added under his breath: '*Learn what you can.*'

Golton was more easily led away by one of his nationality; besides, at that moment he gave signs of becoming unwell. The policeman passed us out into the hall, and I supported him down its length to the men's lounging room, which was equipped with deep chairs and many ashtrays. Stoutly denying the need of assistance, he disappeared for a time and presently emerged looking pale but considerably more sober.

'Sorry to be such an inconvenience,' he said, sinking into a chair. 'Can't hold it. All right now.' After a time of staring at the floor he said irritably: 'What's alla fuss about?'

'Your friend, Raoul.'

'Yeah; he's been married.'

I adopted the easy camaraderie of Americans in a strange country. 'Known him long?'

'Two'r three months. Met him when I was on a trip to Austria.'

'He and his wife have been engaged a long time, haven't they?'

'I'll say! Must be two years. I don't know what's been delaying 'em. Ever since I've been in France, I guess . . . Say, lemme introduce myself. Sid Golton's the name, from Nebraska. I think I could stand a drink.'

'You were an intimate of his, then?'

'Not exactly, but I knew him pretty well. Way I met him, I saw his picture in the papers—great horseman; so'm I. Walked up on the train and says, "I'm Sid Golton. I wanta shake your hand".'

'That was very tactful.'

'Sure. Well, he spoke English all right. But I never got a chance to go riding with him. Useta drop round to his house. It was a swell wedding they had . . .' It suddenly penetrated Golton's mind that something was wrong. His face was assuming normal lines after a squashed-clay appearance, and resolved into pudgy, reddish features under thinning hair. He demanded: 'What's all this about, anyhow?'

'Mr Golton, I am sorry to say that the Duc de Saligny has been murdered—'

Golton's eyes turned as glassy as marbles. He was halfway out of his chair when the door to the hall opened, and Bencolin entered with Edouard Vautrelle. The ensuing few minutes showed Golton, maudlin and fearful, grotesque with his scared features under the paper cap, insisting that he 'didn't know a damn thing about it, and if he wasn't let out of there right away there'd be trouble, because he was a sick man'.

'You are at liberty to go, of course,' Bencolin said. 'But please leave your address.'

Golton blundered out the door, loudly declaring that he was headed for Harry's New York bar. His address he gave as 324 Avenue Henri Martin.

'Sit down, please, M. Vautrelle,' Bencolin requested.

Vautrelle was the essence of coolness. His shirt-front did not bulge when he sat down, the wings of his white tie were exactly in line; even the colourless face had no wrinkles, but the movements of his eyes jarred it in quick darts. He crossed one leg over the other in a bored way

'A few questions, please, monsieur. You understand that this is necessary . . .' (Vautrelle inclined his head) . . . 'May I ask the last time you saw M. de Saligny alive?'

'I can't recall the exact hour. It may have been ten o'clock.'

'Where was he then?'

'He had just left Louise with some of her feminine friends. He was going towards the tables. He seemed in high spirits. "I'm going to play the red, Edouard," he cried; "red is my lucky colour tonight . . ."'

I could have sworn that there was a faint smile on Vautrelle's face.

'Then,' Vautrelle continued, 'he turned to me as though with an afterthought. "By the way," he said, "what was that cocktail you were describing to me: the one the man makes in the American Bar at the Ambassador?" I told him. "Well, then, do me a favour, will you?" he said. "Get hold of the bar steward here and tell him to mix me a shaker of them, will you? I'm expecting a man on something very important tonight. And, oh, yes! While you're there, you might tell him to bring it to the card-room when I ring. I expect the man about eleven-thirty o'clock. Thanks." I rejoined some friends—'

'One moment, please,' interposed Bencolin. He pulled the bell-cord at his elbow. Presently there entered the white-coated servant who had dropped the tray on entering the room of the murder. He was freckled and ill at ease and his huge hands tugged at the bottom of his jacket.

Bencolin, standing with one elbow on the mantelpiece, extended his hand.

'Steward, you were the person who discovered the dead man?' he asked

'Yes, monsieur. Monsieur there,' he nodded towards Vautrelle, 'had told me to expect a ring around eleven-thirty from the card-room and I took in the cocktails monsieur had ordered. I saw . . .' His eyes wrinkled up, and he protested: 'I could not help breaking those glasses, monsieur! Really, I could not! If you will speak on my behalf to—'

'Never mind the glasses. You heard the bell ring, then? At what time was this?'

'At about half-past eleven; I know, because I was watching the clock for it. M. de Saligny always tips—tipped—well.'

'Where were you at the time?'

'In the bar, monsieur.'

'Where is the bell-cord in the card-room?'

'By the door into the main hallway, monsieur. You may see for yourself.'

'You came immediately?'

'Not immediately. The bar-steward took his time about mixing the cocktails, and insisted that I wash some sherbet-glasses. It must have been ten minutes before I answered the ring.'

'By which door did you enter?'

'By the door into the hallway; it is closer to the smoking room on which the bar gives. The light in the card-room was bad, and when I entered (I got no reply to my knock)—' He began to speak very fast, and shift his glance from side to side, 'I did not at first perceive the—that anything was wrong. I . . . *mère de Dieu!* I walked across, and almost stumbled over the head. I cried out; I reached the door of the main salon, and I could hold my tray no longer. That is all, monsieur! I swear to you before all—'

He fidgeted, and backed towards the door. Abruptly, not at all muffled by the closed door, the orchestra downstairs commenced again on another ancient tune which had just come to Paris; a throaty voice warbled in English:

'*Pack up all my care and woe*
Here I go, singing low—'

Bencolin turned his back and stood for a time looking out of the window. Then he motioned the steward to go. He returned to the table beside which Vautrelle sat bolt upright with an amused smile.

'Here,' he said, sketching rapidly and tearing out a leaf of his notebook, 'is a rough plan of the floor. I have consulted the clocks in the smoking room and on the staircase. They agree with my watch that it is now . . . What hour have you, M. Vautrelle?'

Vautrelle turned over a thin silver watch in his palm. He consulted it with great deliberation, and announced: 'Exactly twenty-five minutes past twelve.'

'To the second,' agreed Bencolin. He turned to me. 'You have—?'

'Twenty-four and a half minutes, to the second.'

Bencolin scowled at the plan.

'Very well. To proceed, M. Vautrelle, can you tell me your whereabouts at half-past eleven, when M. de Saligny entered the card-room?'

'Within a few seconds, monsieur, I can.' Vautrelle hesitated; then, startlingly, he burst into a roar of laughter. 'I was speaking to your detective on guard at the end of the hall, and I stayed with him for over five minutes, when I walked into the main salon under his observation and was introduced to you.'

Bencolin nearly lost his temper. After an interval of silence, during which he stared at Vautrelle, he yanked the bell-cord. François, the plain clothes detective, came in with an air of importance, rubbing his large nose.

'Why, yes, monsieur, the gentleman there was with me,' he replied. 'I was sitting in a chair reading *La Sourire*, when he came up to me, and offered me a cigarette, and said, "Can you by any chance tell me the right time? My watch seems to be slow." "I am positive," said I, "that my watch is right—eleven-thirty—However, we can consult the clock on the staircase."'

François refreshed himself with a glance at all of us. He resumed:

'We walked to the head of the stairs, and, as I knew, the clock confirmed my watch. He set his own, and we stood there talking—'

'So,' interrupted Bencolin, 'that you were directly before the hall door into the card-room within a minute after M. de Saligny entered the room from the gaming-salon?'

'Yes. We stayed there over five minutes, and then monsieur there walked down the hall and entered the main salon. I remained at the head of the stairs . . . Incidentally, I saw the boy go in with the tray.'

'You are positive, then, that nobody left by the hall door.'

'Positive, monsieur.'

'That is all.'

Bencolin sat at the table with his chin in his hands. After a time Vautrelle remarked: 'Of course, you are at liberty to imagine that there has been tampering with clocks.'

'There has been no tampering with the clocks, nor with my friend's watch, nor with mine. I have made certain of that.'

'Then I suppose that I am at liberty to go? I dare say madame needs attention, and I shall be glad to take her home—'

'Where is madame now?'

'In the ladies' room, I believe, with an attendant.'

'I presume,' observed Bencolin, with a crooked smile, 'that you will not take her to the home of M. de Saligny?'

Vautrelle appeared to take the question seriously. He put the glass in his eye and answered: 'No, of course not; I shall take her to the apartments she occupied previously in the Avenue du Bois. In case you want my own address,' he extracted a card case, 'here is my card. I shall be pleased to present you with a duplicate at any time in the future you feel called on to be as insulting as you have tonight.'

He preened himself as he rose, and his manner said, There's no reply to *that!* Standing in the doorway, he called for his wraps. Bencolin, thoughtfully turning the card over in his fingers, looked up with wrinkled forehead.

'Saligny was a great swordsman, too, I take it,' he said softly. 'Tell me, M. Vautrelle: did he speak English?'

'Raoul? That is the most amusing question yet. Raoul was essentially a sportsman, and nothing else. Yes, he was a swordsman, and a spectacular tennis-player—he had a serve that nearly stopped Lacoste—and the best of steeplechase riders. Of course,' Vautrelle added smugly, 'he *did* sustain a fall that nearly paralysed his wrist and spine, and had to see a foreign specialist about it; but yes, he was a fine athlete. Books he never opened.

Tiens, Raoul speaking English! The only words he knew were "five o'clock tea".

A servant had brought in Vautrelle's coat—long and dark, with a great sable collar, and hooked with a silver chain, it was like a piece of stage-property. He pulled down on his head a soft black hat, and the monocle gleamed from its shadow. Then he produced a long ivory holder, into which he fitted a cigarette. Standing in the doorway, tall, theatrical, with the holder stuck at an angle in his mouth, he smiled.

'You will not forget my card, M. Bencolin?'

'Since you force me to it,' said Bencolin, shrugging, 'I must say that I would much prefer to see your identity card, monsieur.'

Vautrelle took the holder out of his mouth.

'Which is your way of saying that I am not a Frenchman?'

'You are a Russian, I believe.'

'That is quite correct. I came to Paris ten years ago. I have since taken out citizenship papers.'

'Oh! And you were?'

'Major, Feydorf battalion, ninth Cossack cavalry in the army of his imperial majesty the Czar.'

Mockingly Vautrelle clicked his heels together, bowed from the hips, and was gone.

IV
HASHISH AND OPIUM

Bencolin looked across at me and raised his eyebrows.

'Alibi Baby!' I said. 'I don't see how you're going to shake it, Bencolin.'

'For the present, it is not necessary that I should. Question: where does this species of fire-eater get the income to go about with a millionaire like Saligny?'

'You suspect that he is our madman?'

'Frankly, I don't. But I very much suspect that he has been in the habit of supplying *madame la duchesse* with drugs.'

'Drugs?'

'When she came over to us this evening,' went on Bencolin, hunching up in the chair, 'I remarked that she looked as though she were in a drug-fog. I did not know it at the time, but that was the literal truth. Did you see me pick up the cigarette she left in the ashtray near us?' He fished it out of his vest pocket. 'It is very thoroughly doctored; with what, I can't say until our chemists analyse it. It is either *marijuana*, the Indian hemp-plant—the Mexicans use its dried leaves as a cigarette-filler—or the Egyptian *hashish*. She is a confirmed user, or it would have made her violently ill. You noticed the expression of her eyes and the wildness of her conversation: she is no novice in its use. Some say it kills, you know, within five years. Somebody is most earnestly trying to do away with her.'

He was silent, tapping the pencil against the table; and because I was busy forming a theory I made no comment. He viewed the case with sardonic eyes, sour and unsurprised.

'Well, I want to speak to one other person,' he said at length. 'Then we shall have to go on a little errand I have in mind. François!—Send the proprietor in.'

The gentleman came in wild-eyed, his moustache drooping like a dog's ears. 'Monsieur,' he cried, before his stomach had preceded him through the door, 'I beg of you, you must countermand that order that nobody is to leave! Several have tried to go, and your men downstairs stopped them. They demanded to know why. I said it was a suicide. There are reporters—'

'Sit down, please. You need not worry; a suicide will enhance the reputation of your establishment. Is the medical examiner here?'

'He has just arrived.'

'Good. Now . . . Before coming here this evening, I consulted the files for some information about you—'

'It is a lie, of course.'

'Of course,' agreed Bencolin composedly. 'Chiefly I want to know if there are any patrons here tonight who are unknown to you?'

'None. One must have a card to enter, and I investigate them all: unless, of course, it is the police. I should be grateful if my compliment to you were returned.' He was drawn up in offended dignity, rather like a laundry bag attempting to resemble a gold-shipment.

Bencolin's pencil clicked regularly against the table.

'Your name, I am informed, is Luigi Fenelli; not a common patronymic in France. Is it true that some years ago the good Signor Mussolini objected to your running an establishment for the purpose of escorting weary people through the Gate of the Hundred Sorrows? Briefly, monsieur, were you ever arrested for selling opium?'

Fenelli lifted his arms to heaven and swore by the blood of the Madonna, the face of St Luke, and the bleeding feet of the apostles that such a charge was infamous.

'You give good authority,' said the detective thoughtfully. 'Nevertheless, I am inclined to be curious. Does it require a card, for example, to be admitted to the fourth floor of this establishment? Or is the soothing poppy dispensed, like the cocktails, by the courtesy of the house?'

Fenelli's voice raised to a shout; Bencolin's hand silenced him.

'Please!' said the detective. 'The information was mine before I came here. I give you twelve hours to throw into the Seine whatever shipment you have on hand. This leeway I grant you on one condition: that you answer me a question.'

'Even the illustrious Garibaldi,' said the other dramatically, 'was sometimes forced to compromise. I deny your charge, but as a good citizen I cannot refuse to assist the police with any information at my command.'

'How long has M. le Duc de Saligny been a user of opium? Don't deny it! He has been known to come here.'

'Well, then, within the last month, monsieur. I was shocked and grieved that such a fine young man—'

'No doubt, no doubt. Did the woman who is now his wife contract any charming habits here also?'

'Each,' replied the manager loftily, 'was very much concerned about concealing it from the other.'

'Ah, yes. Who instigated this?'

'You asked for one question, M. Bencolin, and I have answered you two. That is all I will tell you if they subject me to torture!'

'Such a contingency is hardly likely. At any rate, I advise you become busy turning your fourth floor into a bar or a bagnio or something equally harmless . . . That is all, Fenelli.'

When the manager had gone, I looked up from an ostentatious studying of the floor plan, and said: 'May I ask how much of your information you're concealing, Bencolin? This was the first mention of that angle: Saligny as a drug-taker.'

'Ah, but that's another pair of sleeves completely. I was not sure it had any bearing on the case. Now I am morally certain it has.'

'How did you learn about Fenelli's private parlour on the fourth floor?'

'Saligny told me about it.'

'*Saligny* told you about it?—You don't mean Saligny, do you?'

'Yes.' With an injured and virtuous air. 'Jack, find me a person in this whole affair who is acting rationally, and I'll make you chief of detectives! Now in a moment we shall be invaded by the whole horde—I hear screamings and protestings out there— and I want you to accompany me on an expedition I have in mind. But first let us argue the case a bit. I am curious to get a layman's reaction.'

He rose and began to pace about, hands clasped behind his back, head bent forward. Mephistopheles smoking a cigar, several of him reflected in the mirrors around the walls as he passed up and down; a queer and absurd little figure in motion, but Paris's avenger of broken laws.

'You want me to name the man I think is Laurent?' I inquired.

'Hm . . . that would be deducing from insufficient evidence, at this stage of the game. You have not seen everybody here, nor one-fifth of the people who might be Laurent. I imagine that all our characters have not yet appeared . . . But proceed. You think you know the man who killed Saligny?'

'The chances are I'm wrong, naturally. But I'll have a guess.'

'Well?'

'The American, Golton.'

Bencolin stopped abruptly and removed the cigar. '*Tiens*, this is interesting! Why? Do you have reasons, or are you guessing detective-story fashion?'

'I give them to you for what they're worth. Reason number one: Golton's behaviour. It doesn't ring true; it is overdone; it is a little *too* American. That byplay in the card-room, for example. It doesn't seem possible that any man, no matter how drunk, should fail to notice such a shambles directly before him.'

'An American should be the best judge of that, I confess. Still, the servant seems to have walked halfway across the room without . . . I wonder . . . No matter; go on.'

'His behaviour, then. He sobered up remarkably fast, too, after telling that bit about Vautrelle being cut out by Saligny in madame's affections. Reason number two: He says he met Saligny when he was returning from Austria. I may point out that it was from Vienna that Laurent escaped.'

'If he is Laurent, he would be a lunatic indeed to tell you that voluntarily. Austria, moreover, has several cities besides Vienna.'

'Reason number three: According to every bit of evidence we have, Saligny could not speak English. Yet according to what Golton told me, we have him speaking English quite well. More than that, we have Golton, who says *he* speaks no French, going about constantly with a man who speaks no English! How is that to be explained?'

'Touch!' said Bencolin, snapping his fingers. 'You score there, certainly. Golton seems to have slipped up in that respect. However, it is hardly an indication that he is the murderer.'

'You yourself have told me that Laurent is a genius as a linguist. Certainly, if Golton is Laurent, he is amazingly adept with the idiom.'

'Now let us carry this on. What is Golton's procedure? How has he contrived to kill Saligny?'

'Let me ask a question. Do you subscribe to the theory that Laurent, in whatever guise, killed Saligny?'

'Most emphatically yes . . . Proceed.'

'He might very well have been the man whom Saligny proposed to entertain.'

'He might, of course. Which way did he go into the card-room?'

'By either door. He might have been there early.'

'Yes. Now let me ask you,' Bencolin suddenly leaned across the table and pointed his cigar—'*which way did he go out?*'

During the silence, while the detective stood motionless, I realized the significance of that remark, and I swore at myself for dropping into the trap. But there was a chasm at our feet much wider than this.

'The murderer,' I said slowly, 'did not go out by the hall door—'

'Because my detective was standing directly before it a few seconds after Saligny entered the room from the salon-side, and he did not leave it until after the murder was committed!'

'And the murderer did not go out by the other door into the salon—'

'Because I myself was watching it from the time Saligny entered to the time we ourselves went in! In other words, we

have a locked-room situation worse than any I have ever encountered, since I myself can swear nobody came out one door, and
one of my most trusted men swears that nobody came out the
other!'

Still he did not move, but he looked as haggard as a man
crucified.

'I wondered,' he said in a low voice, 'how long it would
take you to see that situation. It doesn't seem to have occurred
to these people even now. I examined the window immediately, you remember: forty feet above the street, no other
windows within yards of it, the walls smooth stone. No
"human fly" in existence could have entered or left that way
. . . No place in the room for a cat to hide; I searched for
that, too. No possibility of false walls, for you can stand in
any door and see the entire partition of the next room. Tear
open floor or ceiling, and you find only the floor or ceiling
of another room; that way is blocked. Yet we know, in this
of all cases, that the dead man did not kill himself . . . It is
the master puzzle of them all.'

He turned round, and slouched across to the window, bent
shoulders silhouetted against a faint glow from the street. There
was a clamour of excited voices in the hall. Hands thudded at
the door.

I cried, 'Bencolin!' and leaped up. 'Bencolin, do you realize—
the boy who brought the cocktails! The only one who could have
been in the room—alone with Saligny—hired by Fenelli to kill
the informer!—'

I was so excited that I did not at first understand his wry
smile . . .

'Likewise impossible, Jack,' he answered softly. 'Did you not
hear him, how he protested that he could not help dropping the
tray? How he kept his hands along the bottom of his jacket; did
you not notice? The fingers of his right hand were amputated
long ago.'

V
THE TRUNK FROM VIENNA

It was two o'clock when Bencolin and I left the house. Sounds threw sharp, brittle echoes in the cul-de-sac of the rue des Eaux; there was a thin mist, and a wind blew from the river in the raw spring moonlight. The tops of apartment-houses were drawn against the sky as on glass, and a few windows were alight against their black walls. The rumble of a metro train swelled out of its tunnel and passed on the trestle over the rue Beethoven . . . distantly you could hear the motor of a cruising taxi.

Bencolin's car was parked not far from the Avenue de Tokyo. He had not spoken for some time, and when he climbed in at the wheel I asked:

'Incidentally, where are we going?'

'Put your hand down in the pocket of the door there,' he said. 'What do you find?'

'It appears to be the handle of a rather heavy pistol.'

'Precisely; put it in your pocket . . . Do you still want to go?'

'Delighted, if I can contrive to hit anything.'

'That was all I wanted to know; the thing isn't loaded. Put it back where you found it.' When he had got the engine started, he tapped his breast-pocket. 'This one,' he added absently, '*is* loaded.'

We turned into the Avenue de Tokyo, a vast plain, with the parapet-lamps of the river marching away in curved lines to the right. Beyond them the high fretwork of the tower was printed spider-black against the moonlit sky. The river-breeze smelled of rain. Bencolin's big *Voisin* roared past the Pont d'Iena, and one had a sensation as of wings.

At length he volunteered, 'We are going to the home of the Duc de Saligny.'

'Oh . . . then why the gun-parade? That isn't dangerous, is it?'

'I have reason to believe that there are things in his house which a certain somebody will be very anxious to remove—if that person doesn't get there before us. The address, by the way, is number 326 Avenue Henri Martin. Which means—' He looked sideways.

'That our friend Golton lives next door. But you have pretty well exploded my theory of the murder.'

'Pardon, I didn't say you were wrong. I said we must examine the evidence from all sides.'

He relapsed into silence. I sat back and closed my eyes. From Paris you can get no distant vibration, no far heavy rumble of traffic such as one hears in London. When the siren of the flying car screamed, horns picked it up and answered as from a gulf. There was the rattle of a late tram in the pale glitter of the Place de l'Alma. We swerved to the left up the hill, and presently the grey Arch dawned among hooting taxis. A few drops of rain blurred the windshield . . . and the head of Saligny floated against the dark . . .

The wan sheen of thoroughfares dwindled away; we were in a street of trees where the headlights showed flashes of budding green, but a black arch devoid of movement.

Before the gate of 326 we stopped. Twin globes of light burned yellow on either side, and shone on the dark windows of the concierge's lodge. Bencolin's fingers clicked a tattoo against the glass.

'*Sieur et dame!*' said a sleepy voice inside, 'my felicitations—'

When the iron gate swung back, we were looking into the sleepy face of a woman in curl-papers. The concierge was about to dart back in alarm when Bencolin intervened:

'Prefecture of police. I must ask you to admit us.'

He received the key from the babbling woman, and ordered her back into the lodge. We could hear her wailing, 'Murdered! Murdered! I knew it—wake up, Jules!—'

'Be silent!' Bencolin snarled over his shoulder.

Fitting the key into the lock of the house-door, he whispered:

'There are no servants here. If I find anybody prowling, it will be necessary to shoot.'

We entered a dark hallway which smelled of flowers. I could hear Bencolin's steady breathing. He guided my arm across towards the vast curve of a stairway, down whose railing moonlight shone from a window. A rug slipped under my foot on the hardwood floor . . . We reached the top of the staircase; Bencolin turned, cloaked and weird against the moonlight. He nodded towards a door at the other end of the second floor. There was a thread of light under the sill.

When he put his right hand softly on the knob of that door, his left was inside his breast-pocket. He threw the door back.

A man sprang round to face us. He was standing in the middle of a room fully lighted, though the shutters were up. There was a great canopied bed nearby, and you noticed at its head a woman's blue fur-trimmed slippers . . . The man was small, with thick red hair, and when his mouth opened in surprise it disclosed many missing teeth. He had the cut of an overweight athlete. Bencolin closed the door.

'Hello, Girard,' he said. 'I had hardly expected to find *you* here. Turn out those lights, and lower your voice—'

'M. Bencolin!'

'Quite; what are you doing here?'

'I am the *monseigneur's* most personal servant,' said the man called Girard. He wagged his head, and grinned proudly. 'I have been with him for over a month. I was preparing the bridal—' he leered and rubbed his hands.

Bencolin whistled. He gestured towards Girard. 'Formerly,' he explained, 'the hero of Auteuil; a jockey I have put my money on in preference to the horse . . . *Dame de Trefles*, three to one, Girard up . . .'

'But overweight, monsieur. I have been out of the game for some time. See . . .' He lifted a tawdry affair of red roses, shaped

like a horseshoe, and inscribed in white roses with the legend,
'*Bonne chance*' . . .

'My tribute; it brings good luck.'

Bencolin stared at him speculatively.

'You're up late, Girard.'

'Yes, but—monsieur, why are *you* here?'

'I want you to turn out those lights; then tell me about your
new position.'

The room went dark. The puzzled, suspicious Girard hung
the wreath around his neck and stood gesturing in a vague glow
from over the transom.

'Why—monsieur, I do not understand this. But whatever M.
Bencolin says, I will do without question. I used to know M. de
Saligny in the old days; once I rode his filly *Drapeau Bleu*. But
then, you know how it is, I could not make the weight; rubber
suits, blankets, diet, roadwork, still I could not make forty-six;
you know—no, no! . . . I went to Marseilles. At last, in that
despair, you know, I returned. I sought out M. de Saligny, but
of course he did not remember me. "A bit of work round the
stables, monsieur," I pleaded. "Ah, Girard," he said, "you speak
like a man of education, though not of intelligence. Can you use
a typewriter? And give my stable a workout if I am not able to
do so?" "But certainly, *monseigneur*," I say. "I have hurt myself,"
he explained, and I went into a frenzy of grief—*monseigneur*,
the great horseman! "I cannot use my hand well; therefore I
shall dictate my correspondence—" *Et puis voilà!*'

He drew a long breath. 'And this lady that he has married, I
would die for her! She is so lovely; if anyone sought to—'

The sentimental soul paused. Bencolin inquired:

'*Monseigneur* had much correspondence?'

'Oh, yes; he is very prominent. And he receives many things—
that trunk—you can see how everyone likes him—'

'What trunk?'

'Why, the trunk that arrived two days ago. It was comical,

you know. He had been in Vienna, and when he sent on his trunks one was misdirected. It wandered about from one address to another, and was returned to his hotel in Vienna. It had no name on it, but they recognized it, like that!' There came a snapping of Girard's fingers. 'And they sent it on to him—'

'Where is it now?'

'Why, in his study—'

Bencolin said very slowly, 'Is—it—possible? . . .' There was a silence, among the night-creakings of the house. The horror of an unknown thing jumped back to a vital force when we heard the tone of his next words.

'Girard, don't ask any questions. Do exactly as I tell you. Go to your room now, and whatever happens don't stir out of it! There is, or will be, somebody in this house—'

'Who, monsieur?'

'A killer,' said the detective. He opened the door softly. Against the faint moonlight I could see that he had a pistol in his hand.

VI
WHITE ROSES FOR MURDER

I felt a sickly empty sensation around my stomach when we went up another flight of stairs towards Saligny's study, whose location Bencolin seemed to know very well.

'Stand in the door,' he whispered; 'I want to see that the shutters are up . . .' There was a space when I stood with my back to the hallway and heard Bencolin lightly trying the windows. The study smelled stuffy, and there was another queer odour . . . He returned presently, took off his cloak, and when he closed the door behind him he laid the cloak along the bottom of the door.

'Now turn on that lamp at your elbow. Keep your hand on the button, and if you hear any movement anywhere, shut it off.'

It was a dull lamp, with a globed shade set in green glass, and its light made crooked shadows in a small room hung with pictures. Beside the door was a large trunk, on which I sat down to watch the detective.

'Hm,' he muttered, talking fast and in a low voice: 'Dozens of sports pictures—himself with silver cups—Ascot, Longchamps, Wimbledon—amateur fencing team—fine stag's head, that—yes, and big game—gun-case—Manchurian leopards—that racquet needs re-stringing—'

He was walking about, glancing at this and that, picking up articles and laying them down; powerful, imbued with terrific wiry energy. The table in the middle of the room claimed his attention.

'Typewriter . . . What's this? Books. Open here; drawers are filled with them. The works of Edgar Allan Poe. Barbey D'Aurevilly; *Diaboliques*. Odd fare for a sporting man . . . Baudelaire, Hoffmann; *La Vie de Gilles de Rais*—'

He closed one book with a snap. 'That settles it.'

The idea I had in mind seemed too outlandish and appalling; but I suddenly got up. We stood face to face, and by the expression of his eyes I could see we both knew . . .

'The man,' I said slowly, 'who for the past two months has been posing as the Duc de Saligny is in reality—'

'Laurent himself,' supplied Bencolin. 'Laurent, a master of irony! Laurent, with an eye to what he thinks is poetic justice. Over a year ago the engagement of the Duc de Saligny to Madame Louise was announced in every newspaper of Europe. There were a hundred pictures of Saligny to draw from. He had the plastic surgeon make him into such a perfect image of Saligny that Madame Louise herself does not even now know the difference. I have never encountered such an artistic cutthroat!—he planned and succeeded in marrying her a second time, and tonight, in that room downstairs, he would have avenged himself, if somebody had not discovered it—'

In one blinding glare every piece of contradiction showed up as one perfect whole. Bencolin, leaning across the desk, checked off the points on his fingers:

'First, we have Saligny taking a trip to Vienna two months or so ago. When he leaves, he is the master sportsman: rider, swordsman, hunter, tennis-player, but a not over-bright individual who rarely reads a printed line and speaks no language but his own. When he returns, he has unaccountably acquired an excellent knowledge of English, such that one of his closest companions is an American who speaks no French. His whole character changes. He does not ride, play tennis, or indulge in any sports whatever—even sports where his injury would not prevent him. He refuses: because he no longer knows how—he is another man. Instead, he takes to opium-smoking! He hires a jockey—whom he does not recognize, although that jockey formerly rode his best horse—to inspect his stables for him. He hires this man to take dictation, because otherwise his handwriting would be recognized as not that of the man he is impersonating. He cultivates a new circle of friends (witness Golton), and goes in for the life of the boulevards. Yet here, as the marked books of this man who "never reads", we have volumes in three languages and of a sort which shows an entire change of mind.'

The detective shrugged. 'Yes, that is the way I read it. He intended, of course, to come to Paris and do away with Saligny here; but by a circumstance fortunate for him Saligny *did* go to Vienna, where somehow Laurent got into his hotel—and I very much suspect that the trunk on which you are sitting contains the body of the real Saligny.'

I was no longer sitting on it. I had backed away, and in the weird green light the thing explained possibly that odour . . .

'Bencolin,' I said, and with a calm not very convincing, 'the trunk is unlocked.'

'Chance tripped him up . . . Yes, you see what he did?' the detective was rambling on. 'He sent the trunk to a false address; to be rid of it, he thought, and make another "trunk murder" to baffle the police. But the trunk came back, and the manager of the hotel recognizing it, shipped it on to—'

'The trunk is unlocked,' I repeated monotonously. And then I reached down and threw open the lid.

Bencolin came over swiftly. It was nearly full of sawdust, sawdust tossed about as though something very heavy had been removed from its packings. There were brown stains streaked through the mass.

'Laurent removed the body before he was married!' I said, 'but . . . what are you doing?'

The detective's head was bent down into the trunk.

'No, Jack. This sawdust on top is damp and fresh; it came from the bottom of the trunk. The body was disturbed more recently than that. Probably—tonight.'

For a moment he let the sawdust run through his fingers. 'Don't you see? We are dealing with a man much more dangerous than Laurent himself, whom this man killed. We have found out about Laurent, but we are still at the beginning of the riddle. It is even less explicable now than it was before, for we have no madman on which to saddle a motiveless crime.'

'Who is the man, then? You seem to—'

'*Turn off that light!*'

I reached over, fumbling, and switched it off. For a time there was absolute silence; then a faint creak as Bencolin eased open the door. Against the lesser darkness I could see his dim shape, motionless in the aperture. From the chasm below I thought I could hear a faint rasping noise, as of a shovel scraped over stone . . .

Bencolin's figure moved forward, soundlessly. I edged out beside him, planting my steps to avoid creaky boards. Again he stopped; somewhere, a person was treading on stairs. There was the pale oblong of the window at the stairhead, and dull moonlight on the pattern of a carpet. So slowly we edged towards those stairs that the window grew on one's vision, like a scene viewed through shortening opera glasses. He bent down when we reached the window, bent down and peered around the newel post, and I through the balustrades. Darkness . . . But the footsteps were coming up the second flight of stairs. They hesitated on the second floor, and crept round to the third. Suddenly switched into our faces was the glare of a flashlight.

'*Haut les mains!*'

Bencolin fired two shots, very deliberately, into the beam of light. Their flat bang was like the burst of an explosion. The light vanished, and the footsteps thudded in leaps down the other flight of stairs. I stumbled, brought my hand in numbing contact with the stair-wall, and blundered down into the dark. Down to the first floor . . . there was a crash as a door was flung open, and other running footsteps joined the first. We heard a blubbering cry.

Somehow I found myself, trembling, unable to speak, leaning on a table in the lower hall. When the lights came on I blinked; the lights swam, and came into slow focus. Bencolin stood near the switch, the fingers of his hand crooked before his face, breathing heavily . . . In the centre of the Aubusson carpet, Girard lay on his back with a knife driven through his side. His oyster-eyeballs rolled, and he gurgled through brimming lips when he tried to move his head. His arms were thrown wide, fingers picking at the carpet, and one leg was drawn up as though in an attempt to rise. Around his neck was still a crumpled horseshoe of red roses, and framed his head with the white inscription, 'Good luck . . .'

VII
'ALL THROUGH THE NIGHT—'

At four o'clock a.m. the events of this amazing night were over, at least so far as the butcheries were concerned. But for Bencolin the work was just beginning. I never saw him so upset as at this latest development, the murder of Girard by the prowler; his hand shook when he telephoned the prefecture, he cursed himself in a low bitter monotone, like a man praying, and he cursed Girard for not following his advice. As nearly as it could be reconstructed, Girard had retired to his room on the ground floor. When he heard the shots he came from the back of the house, saw the intruder running down the stairs, and interfered at the cost of his life. Bencolin's bullets had apparently taken no effect. Both were buried in the floor, one having shattered the flashlight and the other nicking the newel post about three feet from the floor. From the remnants of the flashlight, a long Tungsten with a head much broader than the barrel, it was clear that the bullet had pierced the reflector without even grazing the hand of the man who had held it . . . In the cellar we found the reason for the sound we had heard. Fresh mortar between the bricks behind a pile of debris, and a trowel concealed under some straw, led to the discovery of a hollow. Inside a body was doubled up, horribly decomposed but recognizable as that of Saligny; Laurent, it seemed, was not the only person in the case who had read well in the works of Poe. The knife with which Girard had been stabbed had first been used to pry out the loose bricks; bits of dust and mortar still clung to the underside of the haft. After the murder, the assassin had gone out of the cellar door by which he had entered . . . To this day I can see Bencolin, holding up a lantern as he looked into the ghastly hollow behind the bricks. The chill damp of the cellar, the wind banging the open door, the rat that scurried past my foot: they are details indelible.

When we left the house at four o'clock in possession of the police, Bencolin gave his last instructions: 'Above all, give nothing out to the press. I do not think you will find fingerprints, for the handle of the knife is dusty and has prints of what seem to be gloves—but make the test. I will 'phone in an hour.' And then he said to me:

'We will go to my rooms and get coffee. Do you mind driving? I want to study this . . . Avenue George V; if you're not sure of the way, get back to the Champs Elysées and then you can't miss it.'

On the return drive he sat strained forward, head between his hands, staring at nothingness.

'We know hardly more than before—' I murmured. He turned savagely.

'Yes? You say that to *me*? I tell you I know the whole devilish plan. I know the height of the murderer, and that he wore evening clothes; I know when he came and why he came; I know the reason he tried to come upstairs, and what his connection was with Saligny; in short, I can draw you a picture of Girard's assassin. But—well, that is to be seen. Our organisation is a devil-fish, which can extend a thousand arms—'

'And, according to natural history, it can throw out from itself a quantity of dense black liquid to obscure the view—'

'*Peste*, you needn't snap! And your hands are trembling on that wheel; well, it's an ordeal to turn anyone's stomach. We shall both need brandy . . . Turn to the right here.'

Between weariness and the horror of recollection, we exchanged no more words. Bencolin's rooms were in an apartment-building not far from the American church. He kept such irregular hours that he had his own key, and we did not rouse the concierge at the front door. The automatic elevator made a slow ascent to the sixth floor.

'My servant,' Bencolin explained, 'never knows when I shall be here; there is always coffee on the stove, and a fire in the study.'

It was a formal apartment, stiff and luxurious in a stereotyped fashion, with the customary mirrors and Louis Quinze furniture—all except the study . . . A tiny balcony, books to the ceiling, and a fire. Certainly the most untidy room I have ever seen. There were great padded chairs with inclined backs before the fireplace. A letter had been thrown down carelessly on the hearth, beside a tabouret with brandies and cigars; and the first sentence of the letter caught my eye, '*De la part de sa majesté, le roi d'Angleterre—*'

'Clean off that chair and sit down,' said Bencolin. He began to sweep a pile of debris from the neighbourhood of the hearth; a flutter of red fell from it, and I said,

'My Lord, man, be careful! That's the ribbon of the Legion of Honour.'

'I know it,' he returned irritably. 'Make yourself comfortable . . .'

Presently I fell into a doze, and vaguely heard him fuming at something in the kitchen. The prospect of the evening danced in my brain; became linked with a crazy jingle, 'Heads and knives, swords and wives, how many are going to St —' and there swam across it the vision of Vautrelle polishing his monocle, of the flashlight in our faces . . . I stirred, and opened my eyes. Bencolin was sitting across the hearth in one of the great chairs, with the firelight on his sardonic face. He pointed to a cup of coffee at my elbow.

'In a moment,' he said, 'you are going to hear the prefecture in action. This,' he tapped a telephone beside him, 'is my private wire. There is another 'phone on that table at your left—push the books away—there. Listen to them, now.'

Both of us picked up the 'phones. 'Hello!' he said. '*Bureau centrale*. Bencolin speaking.'

There was a prolonged clicking. '*Bureau centrale*,' a voice answered.

'Dulure's laboratory, please . . . I want the reports on the Saligny case. Have they finished?'

'Two-eleven speaking,' said another voice. 'Report as follows: There are no clear fingerprints, due to the brass nail-heads on the handle of the sword; an identification is impossible. There are several prints on the glass of the window, but they do not correspond to any in our files. The dust of the carpet and that of the cover on the divan has been swept up; the glass here sifts out nothing but cigarette ashes, mud-traces, and a few grains of candy.'

'Have these been analysed?'

'Not yet. There will be a report by morning as to whether the ashes are of the same quality as those of the cigarette submitted. This cigarette contains hashish.'

'Very good. Shift me to the general office; one-thirteen . . . One-thirteen speaking? You followed the American, Golton, from Passy?'

'Yes. He took a taxi to Harry's New York Bar, Boulevard des Italiens. He remained there half an hour; on emerging, spoke to two women but went with none; walked to the opera and there took another taxi. He returned to his home, 324 Avenue Henri Martin, arriving there at one forty-five.'

'You looked him up in the files?'

'Resident of Paris for two years, no occupation, reputable account at Lloyd's bank. I have a list of his associates.'

'It will keep. I will speak to one-eleven now . . . One-eleven?'

'Edouard Vautrelle,' said still another voice, 'left the house in Passy at twenty minutes to one. In his own car he escorted Madame de Saligny to her home, 144 Avenue du Bois. He left there in five minutes, returned to his car, and drove downtown to Maxim's, rue Royale. I lost him, monsieur; he apparently left through a door into a neighbouring shop. I questioned the proprietor, but he will say nothing. Very sorry.'

'No matter . . . His antecedents?'

'Came to Paris in 1917, during the Russian revolution. Enlisted for military service; army of occupation until 1922. Gives his occupation as that of playwright—'

'Questions to the theatres?'

'The managers of all theatres in Paris are being sent a blank form asking if any plays by a person of that name have been submitted.'

'Good. Now forty-six, please . . . Luigi Fenelli? What of him?'

'To the best of my knowledge, he has not left his establishment tonight. Seventy-one is still at the corner; no 'phone message yet. Fenelli came to Paris a year ago, and sent circulars of his new house to prominent people. Twice arrested in Italy, but never imprisoned. Charges: peddling opium in Naples; aggravated assault and battery.'

'That is all . . . Head central! 'Phone me if any report comes from the laboratory. Instruct them to examine Saligny's fingernails. I want fingerprint samples from all these people. Post a man at the concierge's box in the Fenelli house.'

'Any further instructions?'

'None until tomorrow. Make me an appointment with the *juge d'instruction*.'

Slowly Bencolin replaced the 'phone.

'You see,' he remarked, 'the octopus reaching. It is a gigantic system. I can, at this hour, ascertain the whereabouts of any man in Paris. And you also note how it fails!' He slapped the chair-arm; his eyes were bright, and he knocked over a glass with a nervous arm when he reached for a cigar. 'They do not sleep, these men. I have my hands on all Paris as on a map; a finger moves across streets, up squares, and pauses at a house—a few words into this 'phone, and the police trap snaps like a deadfall. But the brain of one man opposing us renders all this organization useless. You can fight him only with the brain.' He brooded, head in his hands. Then he growled: 'Drink your coffee. It's getting cold.'

This was another person from Bencolin the suave and mocking, the Voltaire of detectives and the Petronius of the boulevards: the man himself, in carpet slippers. I sipped the coffee, but it gave only a whirling sensation to my drowsiness. He sat there in the chair, motionless, with the smoke thickening about him and the ash sliding down his shirt-front. As though slow curtains were drawn, it faded—the gaunt face with its pointed beard, staring blindly into the red firelight. Somewhere a clock chimed. The glow of the fire played on the ceiling, made deep shadows round his chair, glimmered on the nickelled telephone . . .

When I roused out of confused dreams, dawn was creeping up the opposite wall. The whole room had turned to grey and shadows, and it was deadly cold, coloured like ashes, the whole litter, and shivered with the rattling of the window. The fire was out. Dimly I could see Bencolin's figure detach itself from the gloom of the tall chair across the hearth. He had not altered his position, though the hearth was strewn with cigar-stumps and an empty bottle of brandy hung from his hand. He still sat, chin in his fist, staring into the empty fireplace.

VIII
WHEREIN THE DOUBLE-DOORS ARE OPENED

Others have written of the finale to this case; my own account can have no virtue except that of an eyewitness. There were wild accounts in most of the papers, and what irritated us all most was *Le Figaro's* smug assertion that 'it is amazing that the only person to see the truth was M. Bencolin, since all the details were before the eyes of the witnesses from the first.' Whatever the general public may think of that, it will probably agree with me that the reason why Bencolin staged his dénouement in the fashion he employed was rather for a psychological vengeance on his adversary than any real desire to extract a confession. You shall judge.

Around eight in the morning, I went to my rooms in the Square Rapp for a bath and a change of clothes. My charitable landlady drew her own conclusions, and solicitously inquired after the health of 'my little girl'. Then she found a couple of blood-spots when I sent my dinner clothes out to be pressed, and became sympathetic to such an extent that I hesitated to tell her they had been caused by a severed head. Madame Hirondelle is prone to hysterics.

Unquestionably, I thought when I was drinking chocolate by my own fire, it had been a Night. In retrospect, which is the best way to enjoy excitement anyhow, I contemplated it with entire satisfaction. I had had my murder. 'We will forget the matter until this evening. I am going to have you all as my guests at the central office,' Bencolin had said. 'In the meantime, I suggest you call up some girl and go to an afternoon dance as an antidote against the future.'

When I did use the telephone to suggest this—it is a hall-phone, and Madame Hirondelle's door is always open—my astonished landlady inquired after this and that, and fell to dietary suggestions of more theoretical than real usefulness.

Paris was preening its finery that day; the gigolos were all a-cackle on the Champs Elysées, there was a warm wine-like air made luminous around the green of the Tuileries, whose aisles were in bloom with the early-spring crop of artists painting the vista towards the Arc de Triomphe. It was all highlights and watercolour, with the grey face of the Madeleine peering down her street at the obelisk from the Nile. I very nearly forgot the black business of last night in mingling with the whirligig life in the company of my friend Marguérite (she was a *demi*, which is the word customarily used with *tasse*), until we entered one of those dancing-places where the extra charge is put on the champagne instead of the cover, and the cover is therefore permitted to be dirty. There the inspired orchestra played 'Hallelujah', and followed it up with 'Bye, Bye, Blackbird' . . . then, over in a corner, I saw Mr Sid Golton. He had just neared that mild state of happiness wherein flipping water in a spoon seems highly humorous, and this he was doing to calculate his range when he should begin in earnest. I saw him look at me, seem puzzled, and then he waved in recognition. His shiny cheeks were freshly shaven and blooming as a baby's; his thin hair was plastered down, and the blue eyes far less bloodshot. A smile dawned. He waddled over, after an appraising glance at the lady beside me.

It was the stage for an experiment. I rose, and thrust out my hand deliberately. He responded.

Now I have normally anything but a strong grip, yet under the pressure when he shook hands Mr Golton perceptibly winced.

'Geez, go easy!' he protested. 'Got a sore hand; fell on it last night—it's no fun.'

'Nor is the sensation pleasant,' said I, 'when a bullet hits a flashlight.'

'You're drunk,' observed Mr Golton casually. 'Wouldn't have thought it, but you are. Well, order 'em up. Hey, garsong, oon Marteeni, see?'

The afternoon passed somehow. I was a bit preoccupied, and Golton took care of the amusement of my companion, reciting droll stories of his adventures as a ranger in Yellowstone until somebody had discovered on his property an oil gusher spouting—he illustrated the spouting of the gusher with appropriate pantomime—and delivered to him what he described as bokoo dough. Various parlour-tricks served to keep the company at the nearby tables interested in life.

We separated at six-thirty, and Marguérite, being philosophical, was content to regard one's mood and one's friends as just another of those things. Golton said that he had got a message from Bencolin to 'be on hand, pronto, at nine o'clock, at the police station.' Undoubtedly there hung over us the shadow of that night . . .

When I returned to my rooms, I found Madame Hirondelle in possession of the afternoon paper; she had even violated an ancient French custom and bought two. All such ladies being embryo tabloid-sheets, there is no reason for the tabloid in French life. She brought me in a special tray of tea and croissants in order to dilate on broken romances, which particularly reminded her of the case of her cousin by marriage, who had blue eyes and lived in Bordeaux, and was (figure to yourself, monsieur!) only the bride of a night when, etc. . . . I pondered the etiquette of wearing evening clothes to Bencolin's party, which seemed rather like debating the correctness of a morning coat to attend a guillotining. Then, upstairs, somebody's insufferable gramophone started to scratch through 'Hallelujah' . . .

Everything made a person's thoughts all out of proportion. I gagged at the thought of food, but something was necessary to take one's mind off a killer. A taxi took me to the grand boulevards, already flowering with pink lights, and I dropped into a cinema. The player-piano rang with a flat stereotyped sound, like a newspaper editorial, and the peanut shells . . . then the picture leaped out at me, and I was struck with the extraordinary resemblance of the star to Bencolin. Except for the latter's beard, the likeness was perfect. Nor could I imagine Bencolin plunged in the amorous intrigue whose chief purpose seemed to lead the hero as many times as possible into the wrong bedroom. But there was no getting away from that likeness. The piece was called 'La Blonde ou la Brune?' and featured Mr Adolphe Menjou. Presently, in one of the feminine leads, who bore the flamboyant name of Miss Arlette Marchal, I began to see a resemblance to Madame Louise de Saligny. This is a state called nerves, and is not at all pleasant.

It was eight-thirty when I arrived at the vast Palais de Justice. You cannot imagine the size of this Palace, which resembles a pictureless Louvre; so I naturally wandered into the department whose purpose, I learned, was inquiring into the whereabouts of lost dogs. This was laudable but uninteresting. I penetrated three or four corridors before I was found at last by a clever detective and escorted through a maze of rooms to the office of Bencolin.

It was a small room panelled in dark wood and lighted by green-shaded lamps. Bencolin stood behind the desk in no way like the man I had seen the night before. His suavity was a mask, his voice low and clear, his beard freshly barbered. In a chair beside his desk sat a great lump of a man, like a bald Buddha, with flabby hands folded in his lap; his eyes blinked slowly, automaton fashion, and his jaw was buried in his collar.

'M. le Comte de Villon, the *juge d'instruction*', Bencolin introduced.

The judge looked me over craftily, so that I had an uncomfortable idea he would ask for my fingerprints. He grunted, and closed his eyes. Bencolin indicated a pair of closed folding doors behind him.

'The room of my entertainment,' he said.

That was all, except for a faint glittery smile. I sat down, and for many minutes there was no sound except a deep humming from somewhere in the building. A watch on the table ticked audibly.

'M. Luigi Fenelli,' a voice suddenly announced. I jumped around and saw Fenelli being escorted in. He was very haughty; he fingered his curled moustache, and his hair positively bubbled with oil, so that some of the oil seemed to be spread over his fat face. Tiny eyes darted round.

'Me, I am here,' he proclaimed, and thrust his hand under the breast of his coat. Cloak and hat he offered to the escorting detective.

'Sit down, please,' requested Bencolin.

Again that silence, and the ticking of the watch . . . Presently Golton came in like a landslide, exuding geniality. But the atmosphere of the room awed him before long. He demanded to know 'why they didn't have magazines here, like any good dentist's office', but his facetiousness trickled away; he sat down and shifted his feet nervously. François, the detective who had been on duty in the hall the night before, entered and stood in one corner.

Bencolin began to click a pencil against the table, just as he had the night before when he was questioning . . .

'Madame Louise de Saligny and M. Edouard Vautrelle.'

The circle was complete. Madame wore a black wrap with a collar of ermine. From this collar she looked out lazily, and her face was like a lovely photograph slightly out of focus. But her black hair was bound back to a knot tonight, which seemed to make the countenance thinner, and her mouth slashed with lipstick. Only the dark speculative eyes were the same. She greeted Bencolin without the slightest semblance of interest . . . Vautrelle, ostentatiously cool, ran the tip of his finger along the thin line of his moustache. His colourless eyebrows were raised.

'We are all present,' Bencolin said. 'M. Vautrelle, will you be so good as to tell me the time?'

'Your questions seldom vary, do they, monsieur?' asked the other. 'Again subject to confirmation it is five minutes past nine.'

Bencolin contemplated the watch on his desk.

'Yes. But for the purpose of this meeting,' he remarked softly, 'I prefer that the hour be *fifteen minutes to eleven*. François, will you be so good as to open those double doors?'

The distant humming died away. The demonstration had begun.

IX
THE LAST ACT

Bencolin asked us all to enter the room disclosed when the double-doors were opened. It was very large, the walls and floor covered with white tile, so that it resembled an operating-room in a hospital. Four lamps with green shades hung from the ceiling, immediately above six chairs ranged in two lines in such a way that the chairs of the second row were in the open spaces between those of the first, all of them three feet apart. The first row was about fifteen feet from the opposite end of the room. There were no windows.

'We have often been asked,' Bencolin continued, 'why the

prefecture has no psychological laboratory such as that suggested many years ago by Professor Münsterberg of Harvard. I wish to show you now that we have our own conception of a psychological laboratory. It is eminently a practical one, and, so far as I know, there is no duplicate of it in the world. I am going to ask you to assist me in a parlour game which has often caused much amusement. I am going to ask you all,' he continued after a silence, 'to be secured firmly in these chairs, and also gagged, for all the world as though you had been kidnapped by a cinema-inspired villain. I promise that the fastenings will not chafe you, and that you will suffer no annoyance from the gag. I should prefer that everyone accede in this, including you,' he turned to me, 'François, and Madame de Saligny—although madame will be excepted, if she prefers.'

I looked round at the group. Vautrelle laughed.

'It is obvious,' he remarked, 'that children's games are not confined to the nursery. Well, I have no objection, if you don't mean to rob us while we are helpless. Hein, Louise? I—'

'This is an outrage!' bellowed Fenelli. His coat rose on his back like feathers. 'To such proceedings—'

'You are, of course, at liberty to refuse,' said Bencolin carelessly. Fenelli worked his mouth a moment, and added, 'But if the others agree—' Bowing, Bencolin turned to Golton and rapidly translated his words into English.

'Sure, it's all right with me. But no funny business, mind!' Golton amended. He stared at the detective, and whispered to me, 'Wise guy, that one!'

Madame de Saligny showed no more agreement or disagreement than before. She simply shrugged, 'I do not care.'

Manacles, felt-lined, were on the arms and legs of the chairs. Bencolin left us all to the selection of our chairs, standing before the group like a professor before his class. There was hesitation; we all glanced at each other, and it was madame who first sat down in the end chair of the first row to our left. Vautrelle took the one beside her, then Fenelli. Golton took the end chair to the right in the second row; then François, finally myself. Two attendants appeared out of a door I had not previously seen, and went about fastening the manacles on our wrists and legs with snap-locks. They produced half a dozen gags, like moustache-smoothers, with cotton for the covering of the mouth.

'Before these are fastened,' said Bencolin, 'I should like to ask one question . . . M. Fenelli, how should you describe the late Saligny?'

I could see Fenelli's profile partly turned in astonishment.

'Why—why, monsieur—he was tall, and good-looking, and blond; he was—' the manager hesitated, and chewed at his moustache. 'I don't know that I can make it clearer—he was—'

'Can *you* make it any clearer; describe Saligny?' Golton was asked next.

'Why—sure—big fellow, always wore mighty fine clothes . . .'

'M. Vautrelle?'

'Precisely six feet tall,' responded Vautrelle amusedly, 'weight, 70 kilos; eyes, brown; nose, convex; teeth, perfect; mole on right eyebrow . . . is this detailed enough for you?'

'You may apply the gags, messieurs.'

The gags did not make one uncomfortable, but the helpless feeling these and the manacles engendered caused uneasiness. It was final; no matter what happened, you stayed; a murderer could . . . Suddenly the lights went out, all except a drop-lamp over Bencolin's head where he stood immediately at our left, causing us all to turn our eyes. He stood weird and inscrutable in that spot of light, which showed the hollows in his face. The face became Satanic; he smiled, and for some reason I felt a shiver of nervousness. Darkness, tied and gagged in one's chair. There was not a sound in that vast building until Bencolin spoke.

'The last light. Please . . .'

We were in total darkness now. My heart was beating heavily . . . Fully ten minutes passed . . .

'The first thing which enters one's mind,' Bencolin continued in a low monotone which drifted from another corner as though he were no longer there, 'is the idea of a church . . .'

Was somebody talking? A mass of people? I heard a deep but very faint humming of voices, broken with tinny laughter; the sounds of people shuffling. An auto horn honked; two of them. Distinctly I could smell the scent of banked flowers, hear a rustling. The blackness whirled before one's eyes, resolved into shapes and twistings; those tiny voices made a laughing, rising blur. Suddenly, there crashed through the room the sweep of an organ swelling the Wedding March from Lohengrin . . .

The organ died away. There was a faint, rasping sob. The darkness assumed gigantic and horrible shapes, wove and broke like foam on water. After a silence Bencolin's voice drifted dully:

'Certain people have discovered that this man who stands as bridegroom at the altar is not the true Saligny. No, the true Saligny—'

That sound, far away in the dark; the bumping of a trunk being hauled upstairs. *Thump . . . thump . . .* the wheeze of panting breath.

'It was six months ago, in another city, that something came to that trunk—'

At first it seemed an illusion, and yet the darkness changed colour, shifted with a weird green light as against gauze; the sound of lapping water . . . violins in the waltz of the Blue Danube . . . a shadow shot across this light before our eyes, the monstrous shadow of a man upreared in profile. Something sprang at it, and there lashed down a *knife*; a thud from sudden darkness again, and a faint groan. Then I no longer heard lapping water but a slow drip, as of thick fluid. The violins pulsed, were joined by other instruments . . .

'The people have discovered all this before the marriage. But the marriage takes place . . . Night comes to Paris—'

Now that distant muted music blew faster, a hysterical note

that swung to 'Hallelujah'. The song beat against one's ears in tinny resonance. Over it drifted a hum of conversation, the high laughter, the shrill chant of a croupier, the clicking dance of the ball in the wheel. The air was overpoweringly hot, and dense with a smell of powder; and the orchestra-beat shook against it like a madman on a cage.

'It is not loud,' said Bencolin's far voice, 'because you are in the card-room. The clock—'

Yes, the clock was striking. It tinkled with eerie chimes; then it sounded clear notes. One. Two. Three. Four. Five. Six. Seven. Eight. Nine. Ten. Eleven, with maddening deliberation.

'Already,' Bencolin's voice was becoming more swift, 'the assassin is preparing. The sword has been taken down from the wall, and hidden beneath a row of pillows on the divan for use later. *Look! The assassin is closing the door!*'

It had been so vivid that I had a mental picture of the card-room before me. Then it was that I realised it was no mental picture at all. Staring into the dark, eyes growing used to it, I could *see* the inside of the card-room. I looked at it from the side on which the window would be. There were the leprous red walls. There was the door to the salon at my right; in the wall directly ahead the door to the hall. There at the left was the divan, dull old rose with its pillows, and the red-shaded lamp on the table throwing a subdued light over it. But I saw that scene as through a faint mist, hazy and unreal, a stage for ghosts, and yet with those sounds and that human laughter pulsing around . . . Yes, and the door into the hall was being softly closed, so softly that it hardly swayed the bell-rope beside it; the knob turned, the latch clicked, and was still. Just a few minutes after eleven. The murderer had planted his sword, and left the room . . .

Faint music in a long interval. The knob was turning again! I could feel that the gag against my mouth was drily rubbing my teeth; the scene whirled. *The dead man walked into the room*; Saligny—or, rather, Laurent posing as Saligny—vital, alive, carrying on his shoulders that head I had seen grinning from the floor. Behind him came the woman who was his wife, Louise, languorous, feverish-eyed. Not a word was spoken. The two moved like phantoms. They stopped in the middle of the room, and the horrible marionettes kissed.

Kissed . . . he seemed to be speaking inaudible words, and she was replying. She lighted a cigarette, inhaled deeply a few moments, and laughed soundlessly; you could see him smirking sideways at you now. She ground out the cigarette against an ashtray. Her eyes moved towards the place where the window should be, and I stared into them. Then she pointed to the button of her slipper, which had become unfastened; she advanced almost to the divan, and put out her left foot. While he knelt over the slipper, she threw her weight to the right, as though leaning against the divan . . . Catlike, she leaped aside. In her hands the great sword flashed aloft and fell.

His head seemed to leap like a grisly toy, springing out on wires . . . The scene went dark. Somewhere the orchestra banged into the last bar of 'Hallelujah!'

'It is not yet eleven-fifteen,' Bencolin's voice snapped. 'See, she looks around. She shakes the head aloft in triumph. She picks up the head and gestures like Salomé—this man, who would have killed her, *she* has killed. Then she becomes tense, ready, watchful. She has left a cigarette; that must be destroyed. She drops it into her wrist-bag. There are some ashes on the rug; she grinds them into the nap with her heel. Then she leaves again by the hall door, having raised the window to let the smoke out.

'And why has she done this? Why has she not denounced this man, whom she knows to be an impostor, to the police? So that the world will never know he is not the real Saligny; so that she, having married him, will inherit his fortune—which she can enjoy with her confederate . . . Vautrelle! Now, the murder committed, Vautrelle, who planned all this, must supply her with an alibi . . .

'She knows that the detective Bencolin is sitting in the main salon, down at its far end. Very soon she joins him. To all outward appearances, Saligny (or Laurent) is not yet dead; she talks of him. At precisely eleven-thirty, according to a prearranged signal, a man walks through the door of the card-room from the salon. His back is turned, and he is thirty feet away from the people she has joined, but he is tall and blond. She says, "There goes Raoul now . . ." But that man was Vautrelle.'

(As one puzzles at a cryptogram, and slowly sees the letters click into place, one by one, fewer gaps and fewer) . . .

'Vautrelle simply walked through the card-room, pulling the bell-cord deliberately as he went, walked out into the hall. *But* he turned to his left and entered the smoking room by the door in the projection of the wall which conceals the card-room door from the eyes of the detective seated at the end of the hall. Vautrelle walks out the door of the smoking room into the hall, and speaks to the detective. The whole process, by time-tests, consumes just twelve and one-half seconds. His own alibi was now complete, as well as that of his colleague. He has summoned the boy with the cocktails, by pulling the bell, so that the body may be discovered and he can possess this alibi.

'Ladies and gentlemen,' Bencolin cried out of the dark, 'there will be no more pictures, no more stage-effects. You see now that these two were working together to gain control of Saligny's fortune; Mr Golton blurted out the truth about their affair. That was why it was necessary to go through with the marriage.

'But the body of the real Saligny must be disposed of. This body was then in a trunk at the home of Saligny, and Vautrelle must have known of it. He left the gambling-house, took madame home, and then (knowing that he was followed) he eluded my shadower at Maxim's and drove to the back door of Saligny's house, arriving there around one-thirty. He carried the body downstairs, having wrapped it in a blanket; then he walled it up in the cellar. By that time my companion and I had arrived. He did not know of our presence, and tried to come upstairs—probably to get rid of the bloodstained sawdust or dispose of the trunk by carrying it away. The intervention of Girard led him to murder. He escaped by the cellar door, having stolen a bunch of keys on a previous visit to Saligny. Just when he learned that Saligny was the madman Laurent we shall have to ask him to tell us himself . . .'

The single drop-light appeared over Bencolin's head, but the rest of us were in shadow. I leaned back limply, and I was exhausted.

'And now,' said Bencolin, 'before turning on the lights over you, I may tell you the purpose of this experiment. I venture to predict that M. Vautrelle's chair is empty. If you will examine your manacles, you will see that with a little easy manipulation you could have slid them off without difficulty. None of you has tried to slip them off, I venture to assert; this was because you were innocent. The crux of our practical psychology, and the reason why this test was tried, is that *the guilty person always does*.'

The room appeared in a flood of light. There was a nervous, exhausted calm, and a strained silence. The sweated hair clung to Golton's forehead and I could hear him wheezing behind his gag. Fenelli seemed about to melt. Madame lay back in her chair, head lolling, one wrist free. Vautrelle's chair was empty.

Bencolin walked to the middle of the room, but he did not speak. The tile walls lent that room the chill semblance of a morgue. Laboriously madame worked herself free. She rose, swayed a little; tried to untie the gag, and finally ripped it off. Her ermine collar lay back from her throat, and she was panting. The face was sunken, a Madonna out of which peeped a vulture, and the dry lipstick cracked on her mouth. Her eyes, as she turned her head from side to side, were empty and frightening; a ruin.

Hard, harsh light . . . then the sound of steps on the tile floor. Two gendarmes appeared, escorting Vautrelle between them. He carried his coat over his arm, and he had casually lighted a cigarette.

'You weak-knees!' Louise de Saligny said, with sudden shrill-ness. 'You left, did you?—Damn you.' She leaned crookedly against the chair. The beauty and languor peeled away from her. 'Well, tell them—go on—frightened at a lot of stage-traps—tell them!—'

Vautrelle was breaking. He tried to keep his mouth straight, but his forehead was a glitter of sweat; he tried to be contemp-tuous, but the ivory cigarette-holder trembled.

'You fixed up that story about ordering the cocktails,' madame said, giggling. 'I knew it—wouldn't go. *You* wanted me to kill him; *you* hadn't the nerve . . . in a public place where we could prove an alibi . . . if you'd listened to me,' she smirked. 'Yes. I'll tell them! Do you think *I* care about my precious neck? Or do you want to kiss my neck now—as you used to? "Ah, that divine neck"—you goat of a Russian!—well, go on; it will be your last chance before the guillotine hits it.' She drew her hand across her throat, and her laugh echoed against the walls.

Vautrelle's face was ghastly. The coat slid from his arm, and the cigarette spilled fire down his chin. With a terrific gritting of his nerves, he drew himself up. In a clear, defiant voice he sneered at Bencolin:

'Why, yes, I left your performance. I thought I would go up and see the Grand Guignol. If your men hadn't interfered, I should have been just in time for the second act.'

He essayed a bow towards the detective; then he lurched, and slid down in a dead faint. High and shrill against the tiles rang the laughter of Louise de Saligny.

X
BENCOLIN TAKES A CURTAIN-CALL

'You will want some explanations, I take it,' said Bencolin. 'Well, there were certain features of the case which were clear from the moment I entered the room of the murder, and others which baffled me for the extraordinary time of nearly twelve hours.'

Again we were sitting in his littered study, before a fire which looked a great deal more cheerful than that of the night before. He had mellowed under the influence of an appalling quantity of *Veuve Cliquot*, and I was far from taciturn myself. He lighted a cigar luxuriously, and leaned back to blow thoughtful rings at the firelight.

'Let us take it from the beginning. Before Madame Louise was supposed to know about the murder, when we were all sitting there in the salon, you remember that I salvaged her cigarette, as I told you. Possibly the implication of much hashish has not occurred to you. It is the killer's drug. If you doubt it, look up the origin of the word "assassin", which is a direct derivation. A confirmed user is at any time liable to go amuck—we get that phrase from the drug, too. It makes them nearly as insane as our first trouble-maker, Laurent.

'Then we were called into the room of the murder. You probably noted that heavy, sweet odour; if you ever dabble with this case in fiction, be sure to include it. It suggested hashish. She smoked before us, in the other room, but the overpowering collection of other smells made it confused with powder and perfume. Now that room was perfectly clear, and it appeared quite distinctly. The window was up, which might or might not have been an indication that it was raised to drive out the odour. At any rate, it created a strong suspicion that madame had been there *a short time before*. A short time, or the odour would have been entirely dissipated.

'Next we examined the position of the body. It was in a

grotesque *kneeling* position; showed no sign of a struggle, and indicated that he had been hit from behind, as I pointed out. The body of a decapitated man, as we discover at the guillotine, has a habit of freezing into its position. Now imagine to yourself the only way in the world it would have been possible to *get* him into that position, so that he could be struck from behind! Why, attending to the fastening of a lady's slipper! It is not normally necessary to demand masculine attention to the stocking or the garter—well, or the roll, if you insist. My comment about pillows, which seems to have puzzled you, was perfectly simple. It might surprise the victim to see a sharp sword lying in full view on the divan, and pillows in a line would very effectually conceal it.

'Thus far, it was a woman's crime; and I thought I could name the woman. Strength? Remember that once before Madame Louise had overpowered a madman, as I told you; and so it was no very far stretch of the imagination to conceive of her wielding that sword.

'Was it possible, I thought, that the time of the crime might have been *before* half-past eleven? I would pigeonhole the idea with the question, Who was the man who actually entered, and why?

'Before I came there, I already had a suspicion that the man posing as Saligny was Laurent. When we found the pictures of himself in his pockets, it suggested not so much conceit as an endless studying of his prototype; especially since some of the pictures were not at all flattering. Find me the beau who preserves pictures that make him look hideous! Then that question of a weapon in his pockets—it was curious—'

'But we found no weapon in his pocket!' I protested.

'Ah, that was the curious thing. Put yourself in the place of a man who fears for his life from an unknown assailant. Would you go around entirely unarmed, particularly if you were one of the finest pistol-shots in Europe? Now, I thought to myself, is it possible that Madame Louise knew this too? Might she have killed him because of it? If so, why in the devil's name does she not speak and exonerate herself? Hold that idea in mind, please. Remember that Laurent is a cunning villain, who sends notes to himself and, when he knows he is being shadowed at the opium-house, voluntarily tells the police so that we shall believe he has merely been collecting evidence.

'Then came the crux: that outlandish business of the bell being rung. The question is, Who rang it; the false Saligny or the murderer? If Saligny rang it, the murderer certainly was insane, for, after his victim has rung a bell which will summon a witness quite soon, he coolly kills Saligny anyhow! If the murderer rang it, the same rule applies: he blithely rang for a witness to see him commit the murder, since he could not have known that the boy would be delayed in answering the bell. The only tenable hypothesis, however, is that the man whom we saw enter the room rang the bell. If it was not Saligny, who was it; and (here is the locked room) where did that man go?

'I now switch back to the idea that when the bell was rung the victim had already been killed, and the evidence points to Louise de Saligny. Who could have been the man who entered the room? By his size and the colour of his hair, only Vautrelle! Well, then, Vautrelle knew about the crime; and madame knew it was he who entered, if she had just left her husband without a head. It was pretty evidence of collusion, when coupled with Golton's drunken assertion about a possible affair there.

'Collusion, *why*? The answer is obvious. They know about the false Saligny, but they must keep the world thinking it was Saligny, or there would be no fortune. But how could they have known this? The probability was that the false Saligny's refusal to indulge in sports had aroused Vautrelle's suspicions, and he investigated Saligny's house—indicated by the fact that he stole the cellar keys.

'When he learned about the trunk we shall not know until

the *juge d'instruction* gets his confession, but clearly he had to hurry to Saligny's house and destroy that damning evidence that an impostor was about. The house would have been gone over by the attorneys and the appraisers of the estate, and a conspicuous trunk in the study would assuredly have been opened.

'Having already proved an alibi for madame and for himself, Vautrelle would return to Saligny's home as soon as he could. I did not, naturally, know about the trunk until we ourselves reached the premises; but it seemed probable that there was in that house some evidence of a false Saligny which Vautrelle would wish destroyed. I shall be very much surprised if the executors do not unearth a diary, some letters in Laurent's hand-writing, or other suspicious material. That Vautrelle had visited Saligny's home on the day before the murder is fairly clear since he knew about and suspected the trunk. This was probably when he stole the keys of the cellar door . . . So after the killing of Laurent he gave my shadower the slip (recall the operative's report over the telephone), and went back to hide the body of the real Saligny. Fresh mortar does not ordinarily lie about loose in cellars, and presents another indication that not only was the prowler familiar with the house, but that he had prepared for his work on that or the preceding day.

'The intruder was, then, a close friend of Saligny—'

'But why didn't Golton fit in as well? He lived next door, too.'

'*Zut alors!* That Golton hypothesis of yours is an *idée fixe!*'

I narrated the experiment of the handshake in the café, and added, 'That was why I suspected him to the very last minute—'

Bencolin chuckled. 'Well, some of our evidence hinges round the flashlight; let us take that into consideration. Golton's bad hand was no evidence at all that he was guilty. Have you ever had anything knocked out of your own hand by a pistol bullet?'

I confessed to no such charming experience.

'A light object would cause no more disastrous result than a momentary jar. Something very heavy, of course, might numb one's hand; but certainly not an electric torch. Did you think for a moment that I was trying to hit the intruder with my shots?'

'Since you fired point-blank at him, it seemed highly probable.'

'Why? I knew who the intruder was and I also was morally certain he carried no pistol—why should he? He expected to find the house deserted. But remember above all that we ourselves were fully as guilty of house-breaking as he. I hardly wanted to complicate matters by unnecessary shooting. Had I known that Girard was in danger I would have dropped him, but I cannot lay claim to omniscience. What I was doing—sound as it may like the master detective of fiction—was estimating his height . . . How? Well, if you are holding an electric torch, what is the natural position of your hand? Try it. You see—waist-high. Now I took good aim—I couldn't have had a better target—and put two bullets through the flashlight firing from the stairs. One of the bullets nicked the newel post at the precise height of the electric torch, and then entered the floor. Calculating from my own position on the stairs, and estimating the mark on the newel post as indicating the man's waist, it was not too difficult to estimate his height at about six feet.'

'It is without doubt a unique, if somewhat too spectacular, method of taking a man's measurements. But it seems to this hard-headed person that it would have been much simpler neatly to put those bullets through both legs—'

'My dear fellow, you are saturated with traditions of American gunplay! In France the police shoot only as a last resort. Besides, a sense of drama prevented me from pouncing too soon on my victim.'

'And thereby cost a man's life. But proceed.'

'So the height of the murderer,' went on Bencolin expansively, 'excludes definitely your candidate, M. Golton. Your last remarks indicate why I did not give you a loaded pistol. Had you been in my place, you would have felt an overwhelming urge to clutter up the premises with bullets on the slightest provocation. You would have caught the machine-gun urge of New York and Chicago—in which cities, I am told, under the beneficent American government, a man has no personal liberties except the full and free right to commit murder.'

'Thereby,' I said, 'causing French detectives to talk like United States senators . . .'

'It is true!' he protested. 'That is the philosophy of your great country. It is even so bad that every time I see in the newsreels a picture of your president M. Coolidge, he is either wearing a cowboy suit or indulging in rifle-practice. *Diable!* The crime-situation must be terrible.'

'It is certainly a branch of crime,' I said, 'sponsored by the W.C.T.U.* and kindred producers of nausea . . . You were saying?'

'About the murder. When you add the evidence of the cigarette ashes in the card-room containing hashish, the fingerprints on the window being those of madame, you add a couple of details which never interested me, but which would be highly valuable in a court of law. A search of Vautrelle's house tonight produced the gloves he had worn to bury Saligny and kill Girard—'

'What is the evidence in a pair of soiled gloves? I have a pair myself.'

'I would warn you never to discount the efforts of our tireless laboratory. Did you know that the fibres of certain fabrics, impressed on a receptive surface, will print their individual weave exactly like fingerprints? And that no two weaves, even on a machine-made article, are precisely similar under a microscope? No, Jack, it is no longer safe even to use gloves. The fibreprints on the dust of the knife that stabbed Girard correspond with the soiled gloves Vautrelle had neglected to throw away.'

'Is there any more of this scientific evidence?'

'All the evidence which will convict those two is scientific. You recall my request to examine the false Saligny's fingernails. Clinging

* Women's Christian Temperance Union

to the inside of the nail on the first finger of his right hand was a bit of silk, about a sixteenth of an inch long, scratched from madame's stocking when he fell. Of course, I could not see it; I did not know it was there. But I trusted to the laboratory to discover anything that *might* be there. The octopus has eyes, too . . .'

'You neglect nothing, do you? . . . Then all that mummery of reproducing the crime was unnecessary!'

'Oh, well, I had to have a little personal satisfaction,' he explained, somewhat apologetically. 'I am inherently a mountebank. It is our national weakness as constant gunplay is yours. When I can be aided by dummy tile walls, pleasing musical effects, shadowgraphs, and certain actors expertly made up (one with a wax head, which will fall at the application of a tin sword), I cannot resist the temptation to become a disciple of Hollywood. Besides, I am fond of sticking pins in my fellow-mortals to see how they will react . . . I studied Vautrelle, and I fancied he would break before madame. It was a test . . .' He sat a long while silent in the firelight, so motionless that the ash did not fall from his cigar. 'Examine closely, my friend,' he said at last, 'the extremely contained person who never cuts loose; who never indulges in a good, healthy, plebeian brawl; who affects indifference and boredom— that man is the extreme in self-consciousness. He is never sure of himself, and at the climax he will crack. Madame, on the other hand, was the opposite; you recall how she was willing to speak so freely and personally before you, a stranger. I rather imagined she would outlast him. And I was curious about both Golton and Fenelli.' He chuckled. 'Again I guessed correctly. The American had nothing on his mind; it scared him to a shadow, and thus he enjoyed it thoroughly. And, at least, it will furnish a better subject for conversation than Yellowstone Park. As for Fenelli, it was almost necessary to escort him home in an ambulance . . .

'And now,' he concluded, reaching over to take the champagne bottle from its cooler, 'we have finished. I give you a wish, the conclusion of all cases—'

The broad glasses clicked together in the firelight. Then, at Bencolin's elbow, the telephone rang. The pieces of his overturned glass lay shattered on the hearth, and, as he picked up the 'phone eagerly, the spilled champagne crawled and sizzled about the burning logs.

JOHN DICKSON CARR

John Dickson Carr was born in Uniontown, Pennsylvania, on 30 November 1906. As a child, he attended Uniontown High School where he took part in several theatre productions. Fired up by his father's extensive library and inspired by ghost stories he had been told as a boy, Carr's first short story was published in the school magazine. More stories appeared and, despite being written by a teenager, all are immensely enjoyable. After school and in the holidays he hung around the offices of the *Uniontown Daily Herald*, which his father had at one time edited. He managed to secure ad hoc employment reviewing sporting events and theatre as well as what would now be styled an op-ed, in which he expressed sometimes controversial opinions on anything from politics to spiritualism, even the Darwinian theory of evolution.

Journalism and the pressure to meet deadlines gave Carr invaluable experience but his real love was storytelling. From Uniontown High School he went to the Hill, where he wrote detective stories and ghost stories, an adventure serial and essays on political themes like the value of supranational leadership through the League of Nations. On leaving the Hill, Carr went up to Haverford College in Pennsylvania, where unsurprisingly he quickly began writing for the college magazine—mysteries, historical romances, ghost stories, poetry and humorous stories, including one that advocated raising babies on a diet of beer. He was soon appointed editor of *The*

Haverfordian and sat on the board of *Snooze*, the college humour magazine.

In the autumn of 1926, Carr created the character of Henri Bencolin—a French investigator who owes something to Aristide Valentin, the anti-companion of G. K. Chesterton's Father Brown— who would appear in several novels and short stories. In the early 1930s, Carr created his best-known character, Dr Gideon Fell, whose intellect and physique were inspired by Chesterton himself. Over the next thirty-five years Fell would appear in short stories, radio plays and twenty-three novels confronting Carr's hallmark mystery, the impossible crime: murder behind locked doors, in the middle of a snowy street or in plain view of spectators when no murderer can be seen; death in the centre of an unmarked tennis court, on top of an inaccessible tower or during a séance when everyone in the room is holding hands. Carr's ingenuity was boundless.

Carr also started writing under other names. As 'Carter Dickson', the best known of his pseudonyms, he created the ebullient and eccentric British peer Sir Henry Merrivale, known to one and all as 'H.M.', who was based on Carr's father but also has something in common with Sherlock Holmes' brother, the intelligent if indolent Mycroft Holmes. The Merrivale mysteries are also concerned with impossible crimes, although the problems are, if anything, even more incredible than those encountered by Dr Fell: in one book someone disappears after diving into a swimming pool; in another, a man is apparently ejected from a roof by invisible hands; victims are shot or stabbed within locked rooms or found clubbed to death within a building that is surrounded by unbroken snow. 'H.M.' appears in twenty novels and a few Merrivale short stories.

As well as several standalone novels, Carr collaborated on one mystery with his friend John Street, who wrote as 'John Rhode', whom Carr used as the basis for another detective, Colonel March of *The Department of Queer Complaints* (1940). Carr was passionate about history, which led to *The Murder of Sir Edmund Godfrey* (1936) in which he investigated a crime that had taken place almost

300 years earlier, the mysterious stabbing of a magistrate close to Carr's London home.

In 1939, Carr joined the British Broadcasting Corporation, primarily to write morale-boosting propaganda plays for the radio like *Britain Shall Not Burn* and *Gun-site Girl*, to highlight bad behaviour at home in docu-dramas such as *Black Market* or to expose Nazi atrocities in thrilling dramas like *Starvation in Greece*. Of course he also wrote mysteries, including one with an extraordinary 'least likely suspect' solution that Agatha Christie herself would have envied. Carr *loved* writing for radio and he has a good claim to be the most important author of Golden Age radio mysteries. He is certainly the only person to do so on both sides of the Atlantic, with plays in two major, long-running series— *Suspense* in the US and *Appointment with Fear* in the UK. Carr also created the series *Cabin B-13*, scripts from which are to be published by Crippen and Landru. While working for the BBC, as well as writing original plays and adapting his own short stories, Carr adapted the work of some of the writers who had most influenced him, including that of Sir Arthur Conan Doyle (whose biography he wrote in later years), along with a series of pastiche adventures, *The Exploits of Sherlock Holmes* (1954), co-authored with Conan Doyle's son Adrian.

After the Second World War, Carr turned to historical mysteries as a means of escaping post-war austerity, including the excellent *The Devil in Velvet* (1951) and *Fire, Burn!* (1957). In 1958 Carr and his wife left Britain for America, where they set up home near Fred Dannay—half of the 'Ellery Queen' partnership—and the magician Clayton Rawson. Both were luminaries of the Mystery Writers of America, of which Carr had been made President in 1949 and was the only person to hold that position as well as Secretary of the Detection Club in Britain. Carr continued to write and he also undertook a lecture tour, but his health was beginning to decline and in the spring of 1963 he suffered a stroke, which paralysed his left side. Even after this he did not stop writing, now using only one hand, although his later novels do not compare well to the superbly plotted mysteries he produced in the 1930s, '40s and '50s. For several years Carr also reviewed books for *Harper's* and *Ellery Queen's Mystery Magazine*. He died of lung cancer on 27 February 1977.

Grand Guignol, the only uncollected novella to feature Henri Bencolin, was first published in *The Haverfordian* in March and April 1929. It was expanded by Carr into his first novel *It Walks by Night* (1930).

A KNOTTY PROBLEM

Ngaio Marsh

CHARACTERS

DR BURNLEY . . . President of the Auckland Society of Arts.

HAROLD TILLET . . . businessman and philanthropist.

LADY RUBY KERR-BATES . . . an art lover.

BEATRICE PAGE . . . an art teacher.

BOB HEMMINGS . . . an artist.

DENNIS RAYBURN . . . an artist.

VIOLET CROSS . . . an art lover.

BRADLEY CREWES . . . Director of the Harold Tillet Gallery.

BIDDY THORNTON . . . secretary to Mr Crewes.

JILL WALKER . . . an art student.

MRS BURNLEY . . . the president's wife.

NZBC TELEVISION PRESENTER.

NZBC TELEVISION INTERVIEWER.

A BARMAN.

A WAITER.

Police:

SUPERINTENDENT RODERICK ALLEYN . . . Scotland Yard.

SUPERINTENDENT DAWSON . . . Auckland Police.

INSPECTOR FRAMPTON . . . Auckland Police.

OTHER POLICE OFFICERS.

PART ONE

TEASER: THE GALLERY

(*In this preview of Scene 14, the opening of the exhibition at the Harold Tillet Gallery is underway. The gallery is orderly. All the pictures are in place and a crowd of 25 people is listening to DR BURNLEY's speech. During his speech we see HAROLD TILLET, a big aggressive businessman, looking very tense; RUBY, an infinitely well-dressed social lady, looking worried; BEATRICE PAGE, cool middle-aged and rather antiseptic; BOB HEMMINGS with long hair and a dour air of uncooperation; DENNIS RAYBURN, the artist on show, nervous, and JILL WALKER, concerned about Dennis; VIOLET CROSS, over-dressed and vacantly pixilated is listening with a rapt attention. During the speech we cut to a female hand that slips into a masculine hand and squeezes it, then the masculine hand withdraws and we pan up to see that it was Dennis who did not respond and Jill who made the gesture.*)

DR BURNLEY: This building will be a magnificent addition to the Auckland art world and the man behind it deserves nothing but praise for his foresight, understanding and generosity. Mr Tillet, we are all extremely indebted to you.

(*Applause*)

I know only a little about the artist whose work has been chosen to open this gallery. But a glance has shown that he—er—has a talent worthy of careful study. Mr Rayburn, young as he is, is a painter of great promise.

(*Applause*)

He has in fact completed a portrait of Mr Tillet which will hang in the foyer of this gallery as a reminder of the man who made it all possible and which I have much pleasure in unveiling.

(*Applause. He takes the string and pulls. It doesn't work. He pulls again. There is an awkward laugh and giggle. Bradley bounds forward and tries to pull the string*)

Oh dear, what do you do at a launching when the champagne bottle doesn't break?

(*General light laughter. Bradley takes out a knife and cuts the string leaving the knot intact. Burnley takes hold of the cut strings*)

BRADLEY: I can't understand it. It worked perfectly last night. It's most embarrassing.

BURNLEY: Our thanks to Mr Tillet and best wishes for the gallery's success.

(*Burnley lets the cloth drop. We do not see the picture but we see the horrified reactions of Dennis, Jill, Ruby, Violet, Bradley, the 'set' look of Beatrice, Bob's laughter, climaxing in:*)

HAROLD: My God!

(*Fade to black. Main credits.*)

SCENE 1: FILMED INSERT

(*On a TV screen, Alleyn is being interviewed at Mangere Airport, Auckland. for 'Town and Around'**)

INTERVIEWER: This is not the first time you've been to New Zealand is it, Mr Alleyn?

ALLEYN: No. I've been here twice before.

INTERVIEWER: And on each occasion you were caught up in cases?

ALLEYN: As it happened—yes.

INTERVIEWER: And this time?

ALLEYN: This time it's strictly a holiday. I'm staying with friends and am hoping for a little fishing at Taupo. That's all.

FRONTMAN: That was my colleague talking to Detective-Superintendent Roderick Alleyn at Mangere Airport this morning.

(*Pull back from the screen to reveal:*)

---

* 'Town and Around' was a nightly magazine programme shown on New Zealand television in the late 1960s. For the broadcast, presenters from the programme played the interviewer and the front man.

SCENE 2: DRAWING-ROOM

> (*Lady Ruby Kerr-Bates' house, evening. Ruby turns off the TV set. Her drawing-room is expensively designed, vogue, modern, with elegant furniture, mostly reproductions. The pictures on the wall are 'acceptable'—representational. Alleyn, Dr Burnley, his wife and Harold Tillet are having pre-dinner drinks. Ruby has a 'Bloody Mary'*)

RUBY: Isn't it exciting having a celebrity to dinner?

DR BURNLEY: I thought you'd enjoy meeting Mr Alleyn, Ruby.

RUBY: Indeed, yes. Do you often go on television, Mr Alleyn?

ALLEYN: Thank the Lord, no. A terrifying experience.

RUBY: Oh, but you were so good—so natural. You'll have to give Harold a few tips.

HAROLD: Me! Why?

RUBY: I'm sure they'll want to interview you. It's not every day somebody builds a new art gallery.

HAROLD: I'd break the cameras.

RUBY: (*laughing*) Oh, go on. (*To Alleyn*) It's quite a new departure for Harold. There was an article in the paper the other day—'Christmas Card King Turns Art Patron'. Harold didn't like it at all, did you dear?

HAROLD: Young reporter with hair like seaweed wanted to know what I thought about pop art and spatial conflicts, for God's sake. I told him straight—I might have built an art gallery but that didn't mean I was going Bohemian. Not that it means much. Everybody knows Ruby bullied me into it.

RUBY: Bullied indeed. You make me sound like an ogre—or is it ogress?

HAROLD: Would you believe witch?

RUBY: (*uncertain how to interpret Harold's remark*) Oh dear. (*To Alleyn*) The opening's tomorrow. You must come. Everybody will be there. Doctor Burnley's doing the honours.

DR BURNLEY: Yes, and I haven't prepared a word. I hope it'll come as a nice surprise—to all of us!

RUBY: I'm sure you'll do it beautifully. And you'll have plenty to talk about. It's a lovely gallery. Harold never does anything by halves. He's even brought a director over from Sydney to run it.

SCENE 3: THE GALLERY

(The Harold Tillet Gallery is new, fresh, well designed, with attractive textured walls and a number of wooden 'sculptures' designed to be permanent features. Quite a lot of bustle—pictures being hung, piles of packing, etc. There are two or three young people working who don't interest us personally. The main people are the director, BRADLEY CREWES, a neat young man, precise to the point of being finicky. At the moment his striped shirt-sleeves are rolled up and he is wearing a patterned waistcoat and well-pressed suit trousers. We also see his neat, efficient young secretary, BIDDY THORNTON, and BOB HEMMINGS who is wearing jeans and a scruffy jersey and has his hair long. Bob and Biddy are helping to hang the pictures. Bradley is sorting through a small pile of canvasses. The work is almost finished)

BRADLEY: *(looking at a very ordinary landscape)* What the hell's this? It's not even numbered.

BOB: It's new. I brought it from the flat. Dennis wants it hung.

BRADLEY: Where, for God's sake?

BIDDY: With the other landscapes?

BRADLEY: What the hell does he think he's doing? A new gallery—the full opening champagne jazz and what are we offering? A first exhibition by an unknown artist who doesn't know the difference between pale puce and clockwork orange. He's got something, I'll give him that, but can you see it for the junk?

BOB: Could you say he's changed his style?

BRADLEY: Changed his style! Bob, look at that. It's fine—a first class piece of work. When I saw it I took it for granted they'd all be at that level. But look at that! It's not even Kandy Krunch! This is not an exhibition—it's a rag bag.

BOB: Yeah. Ruby Kerr-Bates can be very persuasive. As I well know.

BRADLEY: You mean she's behind the Pretty Peep?

BOB: Well, Dennis didn't do any pop stuff until Ruby started raving on about exhibitions.

BRADLEY: My God! The critics'll crucify us.

BIDDY: I don't know. They could say it's promising.

BRADLEY: And they could say it's crap. What possessed me to take this job? Don't answer—money! Why is my life so full of wrong decisions? (*He looks back at the landscape*) And now this: It's too much! I give up! He can supervise his own hanging. (*Realises*) What a delicious thought! Bob, where the hell *is* Dennis? You'd think an artist would take some interest in his first exhibition.

SCENE 4: THE STUDIO

(*Dennis Rayburn lives in a scruffy old house converted to flats. A large window makes the room useful as a studio. The furniture is pretty threadbare and the wall is littered with unframed sketches and paintings. A major picture—the portrait—is propped on an easel. The door opens. Jill Walker comes in. She is young, attractive, an art student. She is surprised to see Dennis*)

JILL: Hullo.

DENNIS: Jill! How marvellous!

JILL: (*still at doorway holding up a wrapped bottle with a card on it*) It's a good luck present. I was going to leave it. I thought you'd be at the gallery.

DENNIS: No. Leave it to the experts. (*He kisses her, takes the bottle*) Thanks. Come in.

JILL: Why the glad rags? (*They move into the room*)

DENNIS: Going to Ruby's for dinner. I'm late already.

JILL: I don't think I've ever seen you in a dinner suit.

DENNIS: Ruby's always been one to put business on a firm social footing. You know, I was beginning to wonder if I had leprosy or something. I haven't seen any of the gang for weeks.

JILL: Perhaps we're all a bit jealous.

DENNIS: And I haven't seen *you* for ages.

JILL: I wasn't sure you wanted to see me.

DENNIS: Of course I wanted to see you. What on earth makes you say that?

JILL: Well, whenever I call you're out, if I ring you're busy—it gets embarrassing.

DENNIS: Nonsense. It's just that I've been so tied up. There's a hell of a lot of work involved in an exhibition like this.

JILL: You mean Ruby and The Christmas Card King don't leave much time for your friends?

DENNIS: That's unfair: If it wasn't for Ruby and Harold where would I be now? I owe everything to them. I've got to make some sacrifices.

JILL: At whose expense—mine?

DENNIS: That's ridiculous.

JILL: Dennis, I don't enjoy being turned on and off like a tap when you happen to need sympathy. You've got to make up your mind—you can't always have the best of both worlds.

SCENE 5: THE GALLERY

(*Bob, Bradley and Biddy are still working*)

BRADLEY: Where's the portrait of Tillet? Bob, where's the portrait?

BOB: At the flat. Or it was when I left.

BRADLEY: Hell's teeth. Bloody portrait of bloody philanthropist to be unveiled to-bloody-morrow and we don't know where it is. Isn't it marvellous? Give him a ring will you?

BOB: He won't be there.

BRADLEY: Why not?

BOB: He's going to Ruby's.

BRADLEY: What?

BOB: Dinner. 'We dayne at nayne', or used to in my day.

BRADLEY: I didn't know Madam was having a dinner party.

BOB: Weren't you asked, then?

BRADLEY: Good grief. It's got nothing to do with me. She can invite whoever she likes to her mad tea parties. I don't care. (*Beatrice Page enters. She is tall, middle-aged, antiseptic. Bradley sees her*)

BRADLEY: I'm sorry, we're not open yet.

BEATRICE: I know. But do you mind if I have a glance? I shan't get in the way. Hullo, Bob.

BOB: (*mumbling*) Hi.

BRADLEY: Oh, but you're Beatrice Page. You're the wonderful influence I've heard so much about.

BEATRICE: How do you do?

BRADLEY: (*to Bob*) Why couldn't you say so?

BOB: Influence? I wouldn't mind sixpence for every time Beatrice's bawled us out. Dennis never got away with second best when she was around.

BRADLEY: (*laying on the charm*) Do look, by all means. I'm afraid we'll be closing soon. In fact all we're waiting for is Mr Tillet's portrait.

(*During the following exchange Beatrice looks around the pictures with a cool eye*)

Bob, do you think you could get it?

BOB: Won't tomorrow do?

BRADLEY: How about now? We'll be here for another half hour or so and even if we lock up, the key is behind that brick nonsense by the door. Take a taxi.

BOB: We're not all rich and famous.

BRADLEY: (*handing over a note to Bob*) Here you are. Get a receipt.

BEATRICE: Could I come with you, Bob? Do you mind?

BOB: Okay by me.

(*Beatrice and Bob start to go*)

BRADLEY: (*looking round*) I dread to think what the portrait's like.

SCENE 6: THE STUDIO

(*The portrait of Harold Tillet is on the easel. Dennis is looking at it. He pours himself yet another glass of wine and looks back at the portrait*)

SCENE 7: DRAWING-ROOM

(*The dinner guests from Scene 2 are chatting*)

RUBY: I've seen it. It's wonderful. Such a sensitive piece of work and so like you, Harold. It's quite uncanny.

HAROLD: He wouldn't let me look at it, which seemed damn' funny. I like to see what I'm paying for. Well, at least it's a relief to know he hasn't given me four eyes or two heads.

MRS BURNLEY: They do say two heads are better than one.

HAROLD: Yes, and better two-headed than two-faced. (*They laugh*)

SCENE 8: THE STUDIO

(*Dennis, Beatrice and Bob are looking at the portrait*)

DENNIS: Beatrice, it's a map of his face. That's the sort of thing he wants and that's the sort of thing he's getting. I did what I was paid for.

BEATRICE: And that's enough?

DENNIS: Alright, alright, so you don't like it.

BEATRICE: What do you think, Bob?

BOB: Leave me out of it, please. I have to live here.

BEATRICE: No, tell me, Bob, honestly. What do you think?

BOB: We all have to earn a crust.

DENNIS: (*to Beatrice*) There you are! That's what I mean!

BEATRICE: Has *he* seen it?

DENNIS: No. I wouldn't let him look.

BEATRICE: Don't worry, he'll eat it up. (*Bob grunts*) And the other work? (*Dennis looks at Beatrice questioningly*) I've been to the gallery.

DENNIS: Oh.

BEATRICE: Some of those things are fine, Dennis. The stuff you painted before—before Ruby Kerr-Bates got her hands on you—is first class. But this new stuff? Is this what all the midnight oil was burned for? All those arguments about honesty and artistic arrogance?

DENNIS: A lot of people are going to see that exhibition, Beatrice—a lot of different people—

BEATRICE: And you're going to please them all?

DENNIS: If I can. An exhibition has got to have a wide appeal. It must have variety. To concentrate on one style, it's artistically self—self-indulgent.

BEATRICE: Who said that? Ruby Kerr-Bates?

DENNIS: It doesn't matter who said it.

BOB: Excuse me. I hate to break up a row but can I take it? Bradley's waiting to close up.

DENNIS: Why not? It doesn't seem to have found much favour here. (*Bob picks up the portrait and goes*) Beatrice, I'm a painter. I have to sell pictures to live. I have a certain talent. Some of that stuff is pop. Okay, but it's well done, it couldn't have been done by anybody else. What's wrong with that?

BEATRICE: I'll tell you what's wrong. Your talent is not yours, Dennis. It's other people's, too. All the people who've worked with you, who've encouraged you, who've given you their time and their experience. People like me, Dennis. And when you prostitute your talent with that sort of muck you not only betray yourself, you betray me. That's what I mean.

SCENE 9: THE GALLERY
(*Bradley is placing the portrait on an easel in a prominent position and arranging a cover which will fall away when a slip knot is pulled*)

BIDDY: I've checked the catalogue. Everything seems to be right—

BRADLEY: Don't worry about tidying up. We can do that tomorrow. As long as the main junk is in the stack-room. The important thing at the moment is—will it work? (*He pulls the string, the cover drops away*) It does.

BOB: (*clapping slowly*) And what do you do for an encore?

BRADLEY: Very funny (*He re-ties the string*) Well, that's it.

(*Jill enters*)

JILL: Hullo, who's hungry?

BOB: Me for a start.

BRADLEY: Come on, let's get out of here.

(*We hold on Jill who looks round at the pictures with growing anxiety*)

SCENE 10: DINING-ROOM

(*At Lady Kerr-Bates' house, Harold, Ruby, the Burnleys, Alleyn and Dennis are now at table in the dining-room. Soup is being served*)

RUBY: We'd given you up for lost.

DENNIS: I'm terribly sorry. I was held up.

RUBY: Well, this time we'll forgive you. After all, you're the guest of honour.

HAROLD: You're lucky you're not in business, young man. You wouldn't last long if this is how you keep appointments.

RUBY: Now, now, he said he was sorry.

DR BURNLEY: You're sure you won't have some wine, Ruby? It's very good.

RUBY: No thank you. It's an awful social sin, I know, but I just don't like wine. One of my little quirks I suppose. I'm perfectly happy with my 'Bloody Mary'.

HAROLD: How does the gallery look? Everything in the right place?

DENNIS: Yes, I think so.

HAROLD: Think so? What do you mean, 'think so'?

DENNIS: Well—

RUBY: I'm sure it's perfect. Now don't worry the poor boy.

HAROLD: And what about *this* poor boy? It's my gallery, after all.

RUBY: Well, if you're so worried let's go down after dinner and have a look.

DENNIS: I'd rather you didn't.

RUBY: Why not? A sneak preview?

DENNIS: No, please. Anyway, they'll have locked up by now.

RUBY: That doesn't matter. We can always get in. The key'll be behind that brick wall thing. It always is.

SCENE 11: THE FOYER
(*Outside the gallery door a hand comes into view and finds the key behind a nook in the brick wall. It unlocks the door and an unrecognisable figure goes in*)

SCENE 12: DINING-ROOM
(*Same as in Scene 10*)

HAROLD: You know this is going to be quite an eye-opener for Auckland. A new gallery and not one piece of four-eyed rubbish.

DR BURNLEY: Come now, that's hardly fair. There's a lot of fine work being exhibited in Auckland.

HAROLD: Don't try to sell me that. When Ruby first got this bee in her bonnet about a gallery, I did a tour. Squiggles and lines and splurges. You call that art?!

RUBY: Oh, Harold, it's only a phase. Dennis went through it too. He was painting all sorts of horrible pictures. But now he's doing lovely work. And I might say I had a wee bit of influence in that—didn't I, dear?

DENNIS: (*bitterly*) But an exhibition can't be all Christmas cards.

HAROLD: And what's that supposed to mean? You're not putting rubbish up in my gallery, boy. You'll get short shrift if you do.

RUBY: Now, Harold—

HAROLD: I'm holding you responsible Ruby, you know that.

RUBY: Harold—

HAROLD: My gallery is going to offer a real service—strike a blow for public taste. What do you say, Alleyn?

ALLEYN: I'm afraid only the usual things. A painter must be allowed a certain freedom. He has the right, even the responsibility, to express himself in his own way. Unless he does, how can art develop those sorts of things?

DR BURNLEY: I agree. An artist must—

HAROLD: So you'd give every beatnik with a brush the right to paint whatever cockeyed idea enters his head?

ALLEYN: Finally—yes.

HAROLD: Oh, for God's sake!

ALLEYN: Anything else, to coin a phrase, is artistic prostitution. (*To Dennis*) What do you think?

(*During this exchange we have been watching the growing tension in Dennis. At this point he breaks. He stands up, scraping his chair back. He grabs the table for a moment, sways, then turns and staggers from the room*)

HAROLD: Good God.

ALLEYN: I'm sorry. I seem to have upset him.

RUBY: Not at all. It's the exhibition tomorrow. He's a very nervous boy. Very sensitive.

HAROLD: He's been drinking too much!

RUBY: I'd better see what's the matter. Will you excuse me? (*She leaves the room*)

HAROLD: God preserve me from sensitive artists.

SCENE 13: DRAWING-ROOM

(*After dinner at Ruby's house. Dennis is standing, tight and tense. He flops on to a sofa. Ruby enters*)

RUBY: I understand, dear boy, I know what you're going through.

DENNIS: Do you?

RUBY: Of course I do. I know how deeply you feel things. I do too.

DENNIS: Why can't I be left alone? Everybody thinks they own me. God, I wish I was back six months ago.

RUBY: (*a little hurt*) That's not very flattering to me, darling. (*No reply*) Is it? (*Still no reply*) You're upset. Heavens, tomorrow you'll wonder what all the fuss was about. (*She sits beside him*) Now don't worry, I'll be there to look after you. (*She takes his head in her lap*) To protect you from all those awful people who don't understand. (*She kisses him, then starts gently rocking him*) We're a team, remember. Just the two of us—a team. Darling . . . darling.

(*As she rocks him, Harold comes in*)

HAROLD: Is everything alright? (*He sees them*)

RUBY: Shsh.

(*Harold looks at them as Ruby rocks on*)

SCENE 14: THE GALLERY

(*The opening is under way. Groups of people, much chatter. Wine is being served by waiters in jackets. We see Violet Cross peering through her opera glasses, Beatrice talking to Bob, Bradley Crewes on tenterhooks, Jill looking for Dennis who is trying to make himself as unobtrusive as possible*)

BRADLEY: What are you doing here? (*with urgency*) Come on. The new man from the *Herald* wants to talk to you. (*Bradley notices Violet Cross. He turns to his secretary*) Who's that?

BIDDY: Violet Cross. She was very upset that we didn't send her an invitation. She goes to all the exhibitions, she says.

BRADLEY: Really? Come on, Dennis.

(*Shot of Beatrice and Bob together*)

BEATRICE: Tell me, Bob, if someone offered you money and all this, would you paint a thing like that?

BOB: That's the $64,000 dollar question—and for $64,000—(*he shrugs*) Everybody's got a price, I suppose.

(*Bradley spots Ruby and Harold and bounds forward to meet them in the foyer*)

RUBY: Oh, it's all so exciting. Is everybody here?

BRADLEY: Yes, dear lady, now you've arrived.

RUBY: (*laughing*) Any reactions?

BRADLEY: I don't know about the pictures, but the champagne's having its calculated effect.

HAROLD: (*seeing one of the wooden sculptures in the foyer*) And what's that?

BRADLEY: Just a decorative piece.

HAROLD: Chi-chi nonsense.

(*A waiter brings tray of champagne glasses*)

WAITER: (*to Ruby*) Champagne?

HAROLD: 'Bloody Mary'.

WAITER: I beg your pardon, sir?

BRADLEY: Lady Kerr-Bates doesn't drink wine. Allow me.

RUBY: Thank you. (*Bradley moves off*) I can hardly believe it's really happening at last!

HAROLD: Ruby, before we go in, will you tell me something. What took your fancy first, the gallery—or the artist?

RUBY: (*as if about to say* 'what?' *and somewhat incredulous*) —

HAROLD: (*stares at her for a second*) Think about it. (*He strides off. Ruby follows*)

(*We thread through the crowd seeing all the main characters, picking up Bradley who is explaining a bottle of vodka and a jug of tomato juice to barman. He pours a glass and points out Ruby to second waiter who takes the glass and we follow him past Beatrice, Bob, Violet Cross, Alleyn, Dennis and Jill to Ruby who takes the glass automatically, her mind on the pictures, surprised by the abstracts and worried what Harold will say. Harold appears—furious*)

HAROLD: Is this your idea of a joke?

RUBY: Harold, please! People are—

HAROLD: Look at it! Just look at it!

RUBY: Harold, I honestly didn't realise.

HAROLD: A new artist you said! New artist—huh! I blame you for this Ruby.

RUBY: Be fair, Harold. I honestly didn't know about these pictures.

HAROLD: Nobody makes a fool of me and gets away with it. (*Bob comes up to them*)

BOB: (*stirring it*) Enjoying the show?

RUBY: Oh, hullo Bob. Harold this is a young artist friend of Dennis's—Bob Hemmings.

HAROLD: Do you do this sort of muck too? (*Bob looks at the picture Harold is indicating, then back at him*)

BOB: Yes, but I only wish I could do it as well.

HAROLD: Hah! (*He moves off*)

BOB: What's biting him then?

RUBY: Bob, will you do me a favour? Will you keep an eye on Harold. I'm scared he might do something foolish.

BOB: Like what? String up Dennis among the artwork?

RUBY: Bob, I'm serious, Please, for my sake.

BOB: Ruby my love, I stopped being your errand boy a long time ago: Ask Dennis. He's the obliging one—remember? (*Bob goes off. Ruby moves towards Harold, who we see is at the bar. She brushes past Beatrice*) Excuse me.

BEATRICE: Certainly: (*We hold on Beatrice watching Ruby. Dennis is with Jill as Ruby comes up to them*)

RUBY: Dennis, how could you do this to me? (*Dennis gives an inimical look at her*) Don't I matter any more? You promised not to include those horrible old—you promised, and now look what you've done. You've ruined everything! (*She moves on to the bar and rejoins Harold, also there. Her glass is empty. Bradley is hovering during the exchange between them. Ruby's glass is taken by barman and refilled.*)

RUBY: Harold?

HAROLD: What?

RUBY: There are some people I'd like you to meet.

HAROLD: So that they can laugh in my face instead of behind my back?

RUBY: (*brightly, trying to wave off his bad mood*) Harold, please.

HAROLD: Have you thought about the fun the newspapers will have—'Christmas Card King Patronises Modern Bilge'.

RUBY! But darling, think of all the publicity.

(*Bradley comes upon them, interrupting*)

BRADLEY: It's time for speeches. Stand by. (*He moves off again*)

VIOLET: (*coming up and addressing herself to Harold*) What a fine job you're doing, Mr Tillet—and you too, Lady Kerr-Bates. It's a lovely gallery, isn't it?

HAROLD: Is it?

BRADLEY: (*ringing a small bell*) Ladies and gentlemen, could I have your attention, please. (*We see him by the portrait with the doctor*) As Director of the Tillet Gallery I have the honour to introduce Dr Burnley, the President of the Auckland Society of Arts.

(*Applause. Dr Burnley clears his throat*)

BURNLEY: Ladies and Gentlemen, what a great pleasure and privilege it is to be chosen to open this new and exciting gallery.

(*Among the crowd are Alleyn, Jill, Dennis and Beatrice, who is looking at Dennis*)

The art world here in Auckland never ceases to amaze me. The variety of fine work is really astonishing. These last 10 or 15 years have seen the rise of a new generation of artists who have richly contributed to the culture of this community. And equally important we have seen the development of a genuine interest from the public—the people who make it possible for artists to pay the rent. (*Light laughter from crowd*) This building will be a magnificent addition to the Auckland art world and the man behind it deserves nothing but praise for his foresight, understanding and generosity.

Mr Tillet, we are all extremely indebted to you. (*Applause*) I know only a little about the artist whose work has been chosen to open this gallery. (*Dennis takes Jill's hand but she pulls away*) But a glance has shown that he—er—has a talent worthy of careful study. Mr Rayburn, young as he is, is a painter of great promise. (*Applause*) He has in fact completed a portrait of Mr Tillet which will hang in the foyer of this gallery as a reminder of the man who made it all possible, and which I now have much pleasure in unveiling.

(*Applause. He takes the string and pulls. It doesn't work. he pulls again. There is an awkward laugh and giggle. Bradley bounds forward and tries to pull the string*)

BURNLEY: Oh dear, what do you do at a launching when the champagne bottle doesn't break? (*General light laughter. Bradley takes out a knife and cuts the string leaving the knot intact. Burnley takes hold of the cut strings*)

BRADLEY: I can't understand it. It worked perfectly last night. It's most embarrassing.

BURNLEY: Our thanks to Mr Tillet and best wishes for the gallery's success.

(*Burnley lets the cloth drop. Instead of the portrait, a revolting cartoon of Tillet is revealed. It is clever but vicious. It has 'A Happy Xmas To All Our Viewers' scrawled on it. There is a stunned hush. The first reaction comes from Bob, who lets forth a peal of loud laughter*)

HAROLD: My God.

RUBY: Harold!

BRADLEY: I didn't put that there!

VIOLET: (*quizzing cartoon through her glasses*) Good heavens!

DENNIS: That's not mine! I didn't paint that! (*The hubbub builds up. There is a startled cry and we see Ruby sink to the floor.*

Violet utters a little shriek. Dr Burnley hurries across and Alleyn also moves over. Burnley kneels beside Ruby, quickly examining her. Bradley kneels by him)

BRADLEY: Should we take her through to the office?

(Burnley looks up at Alleyn and shakes his head to signify she's dead. From his attitude we realise the face is not a pretty sight. Alleyn looks at the body, then the glass that Ruby has dropped, then he looks at the group of people and we superimpose 'END OF PART 1' caption)

PART TWO

SCENE 15: THE GALLERY

(A few seconds later. Bradley has gone to the phone. Alleyn moves to kneel beside Dr Burnley)

ALLEYN: Did you happen to notice her before she fell?

BURNLEY: No, I didn't.

ALLEYN: Neither did I. *(Alleyn rises and moves towards the office. Bradley is in the office ending his request to the police. Dr Burnley's wife intercepts Alleyn)*

MRS BURNLEY: Is there nothing you can do, Mr Alleyn?

ALLEYN: Not at the moment, Mrs Burnley.

BRADLEY: *(hanging up and coming to Alleyn)* The police are on their way. They asked if you'd hold the fort.

MRS BURNLEY: There you are!

ALLEYN: Mr Crewes, make sure that nobody leaves, will you?

(Bradley moves to the centre of the gallery)

BRADLEY: Ladies and gentlemen, could I have your attention, please? This is Superintendent Roderick Alleyn of Scotland Yard. The police are on their way and until they arrive I suggest we do exactly as he asks.

ALLEYN: If you will remain precisely where you are for a few moments, ladies and gentlemen, it would be a great help.

VIOLET: The police? Why the police?

(*During this time we see Bob move away from the scene of the crime. He stops when instructed by Alleyn. Dennis is ashen. The doctor has moved to the portrait and picked up the cover. He is about to spread it over the body*)

ALLEYN: I'd rather you left that, Dr Burnley, if you would.

(*The doctor moves off to get a tablecloth. Alleyn takes out a notebook and starts to make a plan of the positions that people are standing in. Dennis is white, Beatrice fixed, Harold staring, Bradley doesn't know what to do, Jill is cool, Violet is gazing vacantly elsewhere. Alleyn moves to the bar*)

ALLEYN: (*to barman*) Don't touch anything, please, until the police arrive. (*A uniformed policeman enters. He has a walkie-talkie. Alleyn sees him and goes to him*) Ah.

POLICEMAN: Mr Alleyn?

ALLEYN: That's right. Sergeant, if I ask everyone to move into the foyer, would you take names and addresses?

POLICEMAN: Of course, sir.

ALLEYN: Ladies and gentlemen, would you all move into the foyer, please? This officer will take names and addresses. Mr Crewes, would you and the barman stay behind? (*As the crowd moves off, Alleyn threads his way to the bar, passing Dennis and Harold on the way. Both are still. They don't seem to have heard Alleyn's request*) I'm sorry about this, Mr Rayburn. Mr Rayburn—? (*Dennis responds*) Would you mind waiting in the foyer? (*Dennis moves off in a daze. Alleyn carries on to Harold*) Mr Tillet, would you mind?

HAROLD: What's this mean? Murder?

ALLEYN: The police will be here soon.

(*Harold moves off. Alleyn approaches Bradley: he is still sketching his plan*)

BRADLEY: (*standing by the cartoon*) Mr Alleyn, that string worked perfectly last night. I checked it.

ALLEYN: Have you an invitation list?

BRADLEY: Yes, in the office.

ALLEYN: Do you know how many of these people were intimately connected with Lady Kerr-Bates?

BRADLEY: I'm afraid I don't. I only flew over from Sydney a few days ago—to take over the gallery. But a number of them, I guess. Dennis Rayburn, Bob Hemmings, Mr Tillet, of course. I wouldn't know.

ALLEYN: Mr Crewes, I wonder, could you mark the names of people on the invitation list who you think have a special relationship with Lady Kerr-Bates? Perhaps your secretary could help you. Then give it to the police officer outside.

BRADLEY: Yes, of course. (*He moves to the office*) What a fine way to open a gallery.

(*Alleyn moves to the barman*)

ALLEYN: Did you serve Lady Kerr-Bates?

BARMAN: Yes, I did.

ALLEYN: A 'Bloody Mary'?

BARMAN: Yes.

ALLEYN: Was it her first?

BARMAN: No. Mr Crewes mixed one and the waiter took it to her. I mixed the second. She was standing quite close to the bar. I passed it to her.

(*Alleyn sniffs the vodka bottle and the jug of tomato juice*)

ALLEYN: Did you leave the bar at any time?

BARMAN: No, not really. I stood over there for the speeches.

ALLEYN: Did anyone touch the bottle or the jug—besides Mr Crewes and yourself?

BARMAN: I didn't notice. I don't know.

ALLEYN: Would you join the others in the foyer, please?

(*As the barman moves off, Alleyn turns to the cartoon. He picks up the cover and looks at the knot*)

SCENE 16: THE FOYER

(*In the gallery's foyer, the uniformed policeman is taking names. There is a tense atmosphere*)

POLICEMAN: (*checking*) Miss Violet Cross, 56b Harcourt Road,
   Grafton.

VIOLET: That's right. Will we be long, do you think?

POLICEMAN: I can't say. (*He goes on to the next*) Your name,
   sir? (*A plain-clothes policeman, Dawson, his number two,
   Frampton, and two others bustle into the foyer. The policeman
   sees them*) Superintendent Alleyn is in there, sir. (*The plain-
   clothes men hurry through*)

SCENE 17: THE GALLERY

   (*Alleyn is looking at the cartoon. The plain-clothes men hurry
   to him*)

DAWSON: My name is Dawson. Detective-Superintendent.

ALLEYN: Alleyn. How do you do?

DAWSON: What happened, Mr Alleyn?

ALLEYN: Lady Kerr-Bates is dead. The climax to a very eventful
   few minutes, one way and another.

DAWSON: You were here, were you?

ALLEYN: Yes.

DAWSON: Any ideas?

ALLEYN: Well, to begin with I'd say that jug on the bar was
   worth looking at.

   (*Dawson glances at his number two, who goes to the bar with
   the other assistants*)

DAWSON: I don't have to say it's a privilege to have you on the
   spot, Mr Alleyn.

ALLEYN: Oh, my dear chap—I didn't see much, I'm afraid. At
   least, not till after the event.

DAWSON: I'd be very grateful if you'd co-operate.

ALLEYN: I'm supposed to be on holiday.

DAWSON: Make it a busman's holiday?

ALLEYN: Alright. I'll do what I can. But please tell me if I get
   in the way.

SCENE 18: THE FOYER

(*In the assembled group, Dr Burnley and Bradley are giving the invitation list to a policeman. The taking of names and addresses progresses*)

HAROLD: (*looking hard at Dennis*) Why, boy? Revenge? (*Dennis just looks at him, dazed*) Is that what you call it? (*Beatrice is listening*)

HAROLD: (*carefully placing each word*) Is it?

BEATRICE: What are you trying to say, Mr Tillet?

HAROLD: Ask our little gigolo. He knows—don't you, boy? (*Alleyn is on the edge of the group, listening*)

BEATRICE: Accusations at this time are rather pointless, Mr Tillet.

HAROLD: You've got a real talent for twisting people round your little finger, haven't you, my lad? But not this time. Mr Alleyn, can I have a word with you?

ALLEYN: No, Mr Tillet, I think you'd better wait for Superintendent Dawson—he's handling the enquiries.

HAROLD: So it's all going to be done according to the regulation red-tape, is that it?

ALLEYN: More or less. Yes.

HAROLD: Tell me one thing. Is any of this likely to get into the papers? I mean, before it's all sorted out?

BEATRICE: What worries you most, Mr Tillet—the death of Lady Kerr-Bates or the cartoon? (*Harold looks at her, starts laughing without mirth*) May I set your mind at rest on one point? Dennis didn't do that cartoon.

HAROLD: Oh?

BEATRICE: He wouldn't be capable. I know him very well, very well indeed,

HAROLD: What's your attraction, boy? You look ordinary enough to me.

BOB: My God. What a lovely mind you've got.

HAROLD: You involved in this, too?

(*Bob hates him. Alleyn, listening, turns to have a word with the uniformed policeman*)

SCENE 19: THE GALLERY

(*Police at work. Alleyn joins them*)

ALLEYN: I think your officer has completed the list of names and addresses.

DAWSON: I'd better start taking statements. Any ideas, Mr Alleyn?

ALLEYN: Not really, I'm afraid. But here's a plan of the people who were nearby when Lady Kerr-Bates collapsed. It mightn't be a bad idea to start there. Mr Crewes is the Director of the gallery. (*Indicating*) I'm sure he'd put his office at your disposal.

DAWSON: Will you join us?

ALLEYN: I *think* I'd rather nose around here, if it's alright with you.

DAWSON: Just as you like. We'll begin by taking preliminary statements at this stage. We can fill in the details later.

ALLEYN: Good idea. (*Dawson moves off. Alleyn looks at the cartoon*) I wonder who did you? And more important still—why?

SCENE 20: THE FOYER

(*Harold is still arguing*)

HAROLD: A cartoon, you call it. I didn't think it was very funny.

BOB: Depends on your sense of humour, doesn't it? I thought it was hysterical.

JILL: Yes, it would appeal to you.

(*Harold looks at her*)

BOB: Don't look at me. I didn't do it. I wish I had. But—sorry—

JILL: (*unconvinced*) Ever since this exhibition came up you've been sniping at Dennis.

BOB: Darling, I don't give a damn. Do you think I envy Dennis his rot-gut? You must be joking.

JILL: Am I?

DENNIS: No, Jill. Bob wouldn't—

(*Alleyn of course is listening*)

ALLEYN: Mr—er?

BOB: Try Hemmings.

ALLEYN: Mr Hemmings, do you think I could have a page of your sketch block? I want to take a note or two. I've a filthy memory. Do you mind? (*Before Bob can reply, Alleyn has taken the block, cut the string to preserve the knot, and turned to a blank page*)

BOB: Be my guest.

HAROLD: I'd say you had an interesting little conspiracy on your hands, Alleyn.

ALLEYN: Really?

HAROLD: There's more than one person involved in this affair.

BEATRICE: Attack is not always the best defence, Mr Tillet. (*Harold laughs*) As a rich man, you must know that money can destroy as well as create.

HAROLD: Destroy? That's a bloody funny sort of word, isn't it? What d'you mean—*destroy*?

SCENE 21: THE GALLERY

(*Alleyn approaches the portrait, compares the knot on the cover with the knot on the sketchbook*)

ALLEYN: Interested in art?

POLICEMAN 2ND-IN-CHARGE: Not really, sir. Seems a strange picture to hang in a place like this, though.

ALLEYN: You're right—it's a mistake.

POLICEMAN 2ND-IN-CHARGE: Mistake. Substituted for the real thing?

ALLEYN: Yes. But when? And by whom?

POLICEMAN 2ND-IN-CHARGE: Do you think there's a connection between the murder and that picture, Mr Alleyn?

ALLEYN: I don't know. Do you? (*He turns over pages in sketchbook*)

SCENE 22: STACK-ROOM

(*The gallery's storeroom is dark, with stacks of pictures on all sides. The light thrown on the wall shows a door has been opened. We follow a pair of feet along and see a pair of hands sorting quickly through some canvasses. A noise off is heard. The feet, in distinctive shoes, hide. A second pair of feet comes into view. The first pair of feet advances quietly. There is a crunch, a moan, and Bradley drops into view. Hands are seen to take the wrapping off a canvas and clean the frame with a handkerchief. The figure then goes*)

SCENE 23: THE GALLERY

(*Alleyn has the cover of the portrait propped up and is sketching on Bob's sketchbook the intertwining of the strings. Dawson approaches him*)

DAWSON: Mr Alleyn, did you by any chance let Crewes go?

ALLEYN: No. I think I made it clear that nobody was to leave until you'd finished with them.

DAWSON: That's odd. (*He moves back into the foyer and crosses to the policeman who is still taking names. He presumably asks him Bradley's whereabouts. Policeman shakes his head. Dawson then crosses to the secretary*)

DAWSON: Have you seen Mr Crewes?

SECRETARY: Not in the last few minutes, Mr Dawson.

(*Violet Cross is standing nearby and overhears them*)

VIOLET: Did I hear you say you've lost Mr Crewes?

DAWSON: That's right, madam. Have you seen him?

VIOLET: Yes. Only a few minutes ago. He went through there.

SECRETARY: That's the stack-room.

SCENE 24: STACK-ROOM

(*Dawson and Alleyn find Bradley Crewes just as he is starting to come round*)

BRADLEY: Ooh! Does anybody want a head?

DAWSON: What happened, Mr Crewes?

BRADLEY: I don't know. I came in here to look for the portrait.

DAWSON: And—?

BRADLEY: (*indicating his head*) Boom!

ALLEYN: You didn't find it?

BRADLEY: The portrait? No. (*Alleyn starts hunting round as Dawson helps Bradley up*)

DAWSON: Easy now. That was a silly thing to do, Mr Crewes. Leave police work to the police.

BRADLEY: From now on I'm twice shy. I promise—I promise—I promise!

ALLEYN: (*holding up portrait*) Is that what you were looking for?

BRADLEY: That's it! Where was it?

ALLEYN: Down here.

BRADLEY: So I nearly had it.

ALLEYN: I wonder why you didn't?

BRADLEY: Search me—but gently!

SCENE 25: THE FOYER

(*Dawson helps Bradley out of the stack-room and seats him. Alleyn follows with the portrait*)

SECRETARY: Mr Crewes, are you alright?

BRADLEY: If I can just sit down.

HAROLD: Is that it—the portrait?

ALLEYN: I should imagine so.

HAROLD: Can I see? (*Alleyn holds it up for his inspection*) Yeah, but that's good—very good. (*Turning to Dennis*) You're a funny kind of joker, aren't you?

(*Cut to close up of Dennis, then pull back to reveal Jill and Bob, all three of them now in the studio*)

SCENE 26: THE STUDIO

(*Jill is just bringing in a tray of coffee mugs*)

JILL: (*to Dennis*) How do you feel?

DENNIS: I'm alright.

JILL: Sure? (*Dennis nods*) What a revolting character Harold Tillet is. That cartoon didn't do him justice.

BOB: (*collecting his coffee*) He nearly burst a gasket when he saw the exhibition. Did you know he blamed it all on Ruby?

DENNIS: Ruby? Why?

BOB: I suppose for allowing you to sully his precious new gallery with your mucky daubs. Ruby was quite cut up.

DENNIS: Bob, you didn't do that sketch, did you?

BOB: Me? Well, you know my warped sense of humour.

JILL: I'm sorry, Bob. I didn't mean to sound off at you. It was just that everybody seemed to be getting at Dennis—and I remembered all those capping gags of yours.

BOB: Such is fame. (*Jill and Bob laugh lightly*)

JILL: I realised straight away that you couldn't have—or at least that you couldn't have put it there.

DENNIS: How?

JILL: I met Bob at the gallery last night after I left here. They were closing up. We went for a meal.

BOB: But I could have gone back later.

JILL: No, you couldn't. It was locked up.

BOB: The key was outside. I could easily have let myself in.

JILL: Bob, let me go to the police. I'll tell them I made a mistake and apologise.

BOB: (*rather violently*) You'll do no such bloody thing!

(*Dennis and Jill react to his outburst*)

JILL: (*surprised*) Why not?

BOB: (*modifying his tone a little*) Because I say so. You keep away from the police. Let them do their own dirty work.

JILL: But, Bob—

BOB: Look, why get involved? With a bit of luck they'll get so snarled up they won't know who did what and to who. (*Rather vehemently again*) And that's just the way I want it! (*He kicks off his shoes as he stretches out on the sofa—the shoes we saw*

in the stack-room, and we realise that he was the one who
knocked out Bradley Crewes)

SCENE 27: THE GALLERY
(Dawson, Frampton, 2nd-in-charge, Alleyn, portrait, cartoon.
Everything is still set up as previously)

DAWSON: Now, where are we? (*He refers to his notes*) Lady
Kerr-Bates had the first 'Bloody Mary' poured by Crewes and
handed to her by the waiter. Five minutes later—at the most—
she has a second, mixed and delivered by the barman. That
means the poison must have been placed in the jug during
those five minutes. Cyanide, I would think by the smell.

ALLEYN: (*thinking*) Cyanide . . .

FRAMPTON: Just as well they weren't all drinking 'Bloody Mary's.

ALLEYN: I suppose we can take for granted that Lady Kerr-Bates
was the intended victim.

DAWSON: According to a number of witnesses her dedication
to 'Bloody Mary's was well known.

ALLEYN: So the murderer must have had everything lined up
before the unveiling.

DAWSON: Do you think there's a connection? Between the
murder and the portrait business?

FRAMPTON: I asked that.

ALLEYN: And the answer's still the same. I don't know.

DAWSON: (*continuing with his report*) Well . . . next, everyone goes
out to the foyer. Bradley goes picture hunting—gets clobbered.

ALLEYN: And nobody sees anybody but Bradley go into the
stack-room.

DAWSON: Somebody couldn't have been in there all the time,
could they? I mean prior to the unveiling—hiding perhaps?

ALLEYN: It's worth following up. See if you can get a minute-
to-minute cross reference of people's whereabouts in the foyer
after the murder.

DAWSON: Thirty-odd people!

ALLEYN: (*dryly*) Yes, too bad.

(*A policeman enters*)

POLICEMAN: Message for you, sir. No dabs on the picture frame so far, sir.

DAWSON: Wiped clean?

POLICEMAN: Looks like it, Mr Dawson. And Mr Tillet is here, sir.

DAWSON: Oh, good. Show him in, will you? (*Policeman exits*) Will you, Mr Alleyn?

ALLEYN: No, no, no, please. Carry on. But if anything occurs to me, you won't mind my chipping in?

DAWSON: Not at all.

(*Policeman ushers in Tillet*)

HAROLD: What's all this about? I've told you everything I know.

DAWSON: That was only preliminary, Mr Tillet. Now we want to shape a more solid pattern if we can.

HAROLD: Look here, I'm a very busy man.

DAWSON: We appreciate that, Mr Tillet, but I'm sure you must be as anxious as we are to trace Lady Kerr-Bates' murderer.

HAROLD: Yes, of course, of course, fire ahead. But I still say we're both wasting our time.

DAWSON: You're quite convinced that it was Mr Rayburn.

HAROLD: You saw him last night, Alleyn. He was in a terrible state. And he was even worse this morning.

DAWSON: Wouldn't that suggest a rather less premeditated form of murder?

HAROLD: I don't understand.

DAWSON: From what you say I can see Rayburn lashing out in fury perhaps—but poisoning? Now that's something that requires a cool head—careful planning.

HAROLD: Yeah—and he's got just the right devious and twisted mind. Look! (*He indicates the pictures about them*)

ALLEYN: And you think he also did the sketch of you, Mr Tillet?

HAROLD: I'm not so sure about that. But if he didn't, then that mate of his certainly did.

ALLEYN: Mr Hemmings?

HAROLD: That's right.

DAWSON: Mr Tillet, was there any change in the grouping of people in the foyer while you were waiting for the police? That is, prior to the discovery of the real portrait and Mr Crewes being knocked out?

HAROLD: No, not as far as I can remember. Alleyn, of course, was in and out all the time. The boy himself, Rayburn, was there, his girlfriend, the tall woman, Beatrice something-or-other, that other oaf, Hemmings—Wait a minute, Hemmings wasn't there all the time!

DAWSON: Please think carefully, Mr Tillet. You're sure that Mr Hemmings disappeared at some stage during the time in question?

HAROLD There was a lot of milling about—you know, people going in and out—but I seem to remember turning to ask Hemmings if he knew Ruby and he wasn't there. Then later, when I saw the portrait, he was back again.

DAWSON: Thank you, Mr Tillet. You've been a great help.

ALLEYN: Had you known Lady Kerr-Bates long?

HAROLD: Yes, we were old friends.

ALLEYN: More than just a business acquaintance?

HAROLD: Yes. She persuaded me to open this place, God help me.

ALLEYN: And she exerted personal rather than business pressure?

HAROLD: You could say that.

ALLEYN: So there was quite a deep relationship between you?

HAROLD: Why not? She'd been a widow for years. She was a very attractive woman.

ALLEYN: Indeed she was. What happened, Mr Tillet, when you left the dinner table last night—after Mr Rayburn and Lady Kerr-Bates left the room? (*Dawson isn't following conversation*)

HAROLD: I went into the living room and they were—(*suddenly remembers and stops short*) And they were talking.

ALLEYN: Yes? Do you remember what they were talking about?

HAROLD: (*starting to get annoyed*) They were talking! Just talking!

ALLEYN: Nothing occurred that might have upset you?

HAROLD: (*very upset*) Why the hell should I be upset? What is this?

ALLEYN: I was only wondering if Mr Rayburn or Lady Kerr-Bates did or said anything that might have upset you.

HAROLD: Upset me? That pipsqueak! (*Pause*) I think that's all I can tell you. Unless you want to ask any sensible questions, Dawson? (*Dawson glances at Alleyn, who shakes his head*)

DAWSON: No, that'll be all for now, thank you, Mr Tillet. We'll get in touch with you later if necessary.

HAROLD: Right. You know where to contact me. Though I'd appreciate it if you kept to the point. (*He exits*)

DAWSON: What was that all about?

ALLEYN: He's a very clever man. He saw what I was up to. It seems to be pretty common gossip that Lady Kerr-Bates and our Mr Tillet were more than friends, and equally common gossip that the same Lady Kerr-Bates was addicted to attractive young men. Bring those three into a triangle—

FRAMPTON: And you have a pretty furious Mr Tillet.

ALLEYN: Exactly. I don't think he's the sort of man who'd give up happily to younger competition.

DAWSON: That opens up a new field.

FRAMPTON: What about Hemmings? From what Mr Tillet said, he could quite easily have slipped into the stack-room.

ALLEYN: But why?

FRAMPTON: To stop anybody from getting the portrait?

ALLEYN: Crewes, for instance, who gets a tuppenny one for his pains. But the portrait itself wasn't lifted. That suggests that whoever clobbered Crewes was after something else. Let's go and have another look. (*Alleyn strides off to the stack-room. Dawson and Frampton follow, rather bewildered*)

SCENE 28: STACK-ROOM

(*Alleyn moves through the stack-room, Dawson and Frampton following*)

FRAMPTON: What are we looking for?

DAWSON: I'm not sure.

ALLEYN: (*discovering the corrugated cardboard and string that Bob removed from the portrait and dropped*) This, for instance?

FRAMPTON: What is it?

ALLEYN: Come along. (*Alleyn strides back to the gallery. The others follow*)

SCENE 29: THE GALLERY

(*Alleyn, still with the cardboard and string, goes to the portrait and drops the cardboard over it. The bends fit*)

DAWSON: Why on earth would anyone risk going into the stack-room at a time like that just to take the wrapping off a picture?

ALLEYN: To clean off the fingerprints?

DAWSON: You mean the murderer didn't think about the finger-prints till later?

ALLEYN: (*is not sure*) Now, according to Crewes the portrait was in position when he locked up last night. Everything appeared normal this morning and from the time the gallery was open there were always people about. That means the switch probably happened overnight. Not a very valuable piece of information, since even I knew where the key was. (*He looks at the string, then takes two other pieces of string out of his pocket*) And now we have three knots.

DAWSON: Knots?

ALLEYN: I don't know if it's of any importance, but this is the string from the portrait cover (*he hangs it over the portrait*), this from Hemmings' sketch block (*he drapes that one too*), and this from the stack-room. And *only one of them* slips.

DAWSON: Which one's that?

ALLEYN: The one from the sketch block.

DAWSON: Pity. That suggests it wasn't Hemmings who retied the cover and wrapped up the portrait.

ALLEYN: Pretty flimsy evidence, I admit. Even so, I don't think another word with Mr Hemmings would be entirely out of place.

SCENE 30: THE STUDIO

(*Beatrice and Dennis. Beatrice is turning over a portfolio of sketches. She is very sympathetic. Dennis is still tense*)

BEATRICE: I was wondering how you were getting on.

DENNIS: Fine, thanks, Beatrice.

BEATRICE: You were taking it so hard I was worried.

DENNIS: Beatrice, I'm very grateful to you. I only wish I'd listened to you earlier.

BEATRICE: Perhaps. Hullo, here's that drawing of me you did last year. I'd forgotten how good it is. It's superb.

DENNIS: Have it if you like. Have the lot.

BEATRICE: Do you mean that? I'd love to. Are you sure?

DENNIS: Of course—like old times—I'm sorry I lost my temper.

BEATRICE: Never mind. Where's Bob?

DENNIS: At the gallery. The police called him back.

SCENE 31: THE GALLERY

(*Alleyn, Dawson and Frampton are interviewing Bob Hemmings*)

BOB: Once and for all, I've got nothing to say.

DAWSON: Does that mean you were in the stack-room?

BOB: It means I've got nothing to say.

DAWSON: Mr Hemmings, you must realise that this attitude only proves that you're hiding something.

BOB: No, it just proves that I'm not a very good co-operator. I don't like team sports and I don't like policemen.

DAWSON: That doesn't mean you're not incapable of inflicting grievous bodily harm.

BOB: You'll have to do better than that. I read books, you know.

ALLEYN: That sketch block of yours I borrowed. Did you tie it up yourself?

BOB: Yes, I think so. Why?

ALLEYN: Miss Beatrice Page called into the gallery last night, I understand?

BOB: That's right. She came with me in the taxi when I went to collect the portrait.

ALLEYN: Which you brought back before Crewes locked up.

BOB: That's right.

ALLEYN: Not that it would have mattered—you knew where the key was. (*No reply from Bob*) Mr Hemmings, how did you feel when Mr Rayburn was offered the exhibition? (*Bob shrugs in reply*) Did it produce any sort of tension between the two of you?

BOB: Mr Alleyn, I'm a painter. Quite good, but I'm not in Dennis's class. That's not something to bitch about—it's just fact.

ALLEYN: So there was no friction between you?

BOB: Not on my side.

ALLEYN: On his?

BOB: Maybe. I think he felt guilty—playing the success game. He had a hell of a time one way or another.

DAWSON: And Lady Kerr-Bates?

BOB: Huh. She wouldn't notice if the sun set in the east—unless it was to the greater social glory of Ruby.

DAWSON: You knew her well at one time, I understand.

BOB: So-so. She thought I had an 'interesting talent'.

DAWSON: Till Mr Rayburn came along and elbowed you out?

BOB: You're a real copper, aren't you? I've got nothing to say.

DAWSON: Get out then. But you can be sure of one thing, Hemmings. We'll be calling on you again.

BOB: Good dog. Keep to it, boy. (*He exits*)

ALLEYN: I have a feeling he's not really as odious as that.

DAWSON: You mean he's protecting someone?

ALLEYN: Perhaps.

DAWSON: Looking at your plan, Mr Alleyn, there were nine people near enough to the bar to have placed the cyanide in the jug during those critical five minutes: Crewes, the barman, the waiter, Tillet, Rayburn, the girl Jill Walker, Miss Page, Miss Cross and Hemmings.

FRAMPTON: Lady Kerr-Bates herself?

DAWSON: Hardly likely.

ALLEYN: Nor is the barman or the waiter, I suppose. So what does that leave us with? Let's recap. Start with Dennis Rayburn—now what have we got there? Personable young man, promising artist. Taken under the victim's protective wing. What motive would he have for killing the golden goose? Nerves? Prostitution of his talent? No, not a very likely suspect. Hemmings?

DAWSON: Rejected, would-be protégé? Jealous of his friend's success? The portrait could easily have been his handiwork.

ALLEYN: I don't know about that.

DAWSON: Killing Lady Kerr-Bates could be an oblique way of revenging himself on Tillet—or even Rayburn. Too subtle?

ALLEYN: I don't know . . . there's something there . . . something odd.

DAWSON: What about the girl? Jill Walker?

ALLEYN: Not a serious contender I'd say but she might be more deeply involved with Rayburn than we think.

DAWSON: What about Tillet?

ALLEYN: He was furious when he arrived at the gallery. But I doubt if he's the sort of person who would carry poison on the off-chance that he wouldn't like an exhibition he was sponsoring.

DAWSON: But there's also your triangle theory. He must have known about Lady Kerr-Bates' tastes and habits. Rayburn could have been the last straw.

ALLEYN: That's reasonable. And Beatrice Page?

DAWSON: There's an odd one. Can't see how she fits in.

ALLEYN: She was Rayburn's guiding light for many years before Lady Kerr-Bates came on the scene. And Hemmings' for that matter. Obviously a very dedicated woman with strong feelings.

DAWSON: Then there's Bradley Crewes. But I can't see why he should bite the hand that feeds.

ALLEYN: He does feel the exhibition is below his artistic dignity, but it's not a very strong motive for murder. Not very convincing reasons all round really. I wonder if there's something we've overlooked. And not one of these motives tied up with Bradley Crewes' little escapade.

FRAMPTON: Who was it who saw Crewes go into the stack-room? That eccentric woman with the opera glasses, wasn't it?

DAWSON: Miss Violet Cross.

ALLEYN: Yes, what about her?

FRAMPTON: She was standing beside Lady Kerr-Bates at the crucial moment. And I've suddenly remembered something— her name wasn't on the official invitation list. I wonder if she saw more than she's admitted to.

SCENE 32: STUDIO FLAT

(*Alleyn is interviewing Violet Cross in her own studio*)

VIOLET: No, no, I don't think so—I told the police everything I could remember. Mr Tillet just standing there, the barman with the drink, the speeches, poor Ruby collapsing—I told them all about that.

ALLEYN: Do you know Mr Tillet?

VIOLET: Not really. I usually design my own Christmas cards.

ALLEYN: Oh, you also paint?

VIOLET: I dabble a little—in watercolours—but very rarely now. My eyes are not the best.

ALLEYN: Is that why you carry the opera glasses?

VIOLET: Yes—I find sculpting more satisfying—there's so much you can do by touch, you see—I don't have to rely so much on my eyes.

ALLEYN: But from what you've told us, very little seems to have escaped you.

VIOLET: Oh, do you think so?

ALLEYN: Perhaps the artist's eye for detail?

VIOLET: Perhaps.

ALLEYN: Do you know Mr Hemmings?

VIOLET: Slightly. I meet most of Beatrice's fledglings—that's what I call them at her place—we were at art school together, years ago now—don't ask how many. Beatrice's dedicated her life to young artists, you know—the helping hand, the encouraging word—she's very little money of her own. And of course she chooses very carefully—she doesn't suffer fools gladly. Oh no.

ALLEYN: You mean she has enemies?

VIOLET: Enemies?—that's a strong word. I will say this. If you're a young artist, you're either in the Beatrice Page group or you're out of it—no half measures with Beatrice.

SCENE 33: LIVING-ROOM

(*Alleyn is with Beatrice Page in her living-room*)

ALLEYN: Do you paint, Miss Page?

BEATRICE: No.

ALLEYN: Oh. Perhaps you have some recent work of one of your protégés here?

BEATRICE: I don't think so.

ALLEYN: But you used to paint.

BEATRICE: I beg your pardon?

ALLEYN: Miss Cross told me you were at art school together.

BEATRICE: That was 20 years ago, Mr Alleyn.

ALLEYN: Oh.

BEATRICE: Some are born actors, Mr Alleyn, and some are

born critics. My work didn't satisfy me and so I stopped. I've never been one to accept second best.

ALLEYN: That was when you decided to work through other painters?

BEATRICE: I suppose so. I didn't think of it in those terms at the time.

ALLEYN: And you haven't touched a brush in those 20 years?

BEATRICE: No.

(*Alleyn indicates packet of sketches*)

ALLEYN: So those are not yours?

BEATRICE: No. They're Dennis's. He gave them to me.

ALLEYN: When?

BEATRICE: This afternoon.

ALLEYN: May I?

BEATRICE: Of course.

(*He pulls the string. It is not a slip knot*)

ALLEYN: Oh no—Ladies' knots, or am I wrong?

BEATRICE: I'm afraid you're quite right. Why not cut it?

ALLEYN: Not yet. Basically he's good, isn't he? A good painter?

BEATRICE: Yes. And he'll be better now.

ALLEYN: Your star pupil? (*Beatrice smiles in reply*) It must have been disappointing for you when Lady Kerr-Bates adopted him.

BEATRICE: I don't think you can destroy real talent, Mr Alleyn.

ALLEYN: No, I suppose not. Especially when there's someone like you behind him. A woman of character, of judgement, of great determination. A woman who, once she's taken hold, doesn't let go?

BEATRICE: You're quite a judge of character.

ALLEYN: And on top of all this, a woman who is—or was—herself an artist?

BEATRICE: 'Is' is right. I still do a bit.

ALLEYN: Ah, I thought I smelt paint when I came in.

BEATRICE: (*abruptly*) In fact, Mr Alleyn, I should like to try my hand on you now, do you mind? Are you sure?

ALLEYN: By all means. (*She takes paper and pen feverishly*)
(*Bob Hemmings enters*)

BOB: (*to Alleyn*) What are you doing here?

ALLEYN: Oh, gathering information—and you?

BEATRICE: Bob often drops in, Mr Alleyn. This is open house to my friends.

BOB: (*seeing Beatrice sketching*) What the hell do you think you're doing, Beatrice?

BEATRICE: A police portrait.

BOB: For God's sake! Look, I want to have a word with you. Dennis told me you'd been at the flat.

ALLEYN: You hadn't seen Miss Page since the opening this morning?

BOB: So what?

ALLEYN: Nothing at all.

BOB: Beatrice's a wonderful woman, Mr Alleyn. She's done a hell of a lot for Dennis—and for me—

ALLEYN: Yes, that sort of debt is hard to repay.

BOB: Debt? What do you mean 'debt'?

BEATRICE: Bob!

BOB: What does he mean, 'debt'? Bloody policemen and their double talk. You'd better be careful, Alleyn. Making accusations like that.

BEATRICE: Bob . . . !

BOB: Okay. Okay. But you be careful what you say to him, Beatrice. I don't trust policemen.

BEATRICE: (*to Alleyn*) He's very loyal.

ALLEYN: Loyal enough to cover up a crime, Miss Page? Loyal enough to wipe the fingerprints off an important piece of evidence, do you think? Loyal enough to knock somebody senseless in the process?

BOB: Shut up.

ALLEYN: Somebody he knew very well—somebody he admired and loved?

BOB: No, that's not true!

BEATRICE: Is he so sensitive? Yes, perhaps he is.

ALLEYN: Yes, Miss Page, I think perhaps he is. (*Bob sits, putting his head in his hands*) As for the murder, it must have been quite easy to get into the gallery. Everyone seemed to know where the key was.

BEATRICE: Behind the bricks near the door.

ALLEYN: Slip in, wrap up the portrait, put it in the stack-room, substitute the cartoon, slip out again . . .

BEATRICE: Yes.

BOB: Beatrice, please—please—

ALLEYN: But where would the murderer get cyanide from?

BEATRICE: Rat poison would be quite appropriate, don't you think? Shall we go, Mr Alleyn?

ALLEYN: Mr Dawson will be here soon. (*He collects sketches*)

BEATRICE: (*looking at Dennis's packet*) I never was very good with knots. But I've no regrets, Mr Alleyn. A bitch like Ruby has a lot to offer a boy like Dennis. But she forgot me, Mr Alleyn. As you say, once I've taken hold I don't easily let go. Your portrait, Mr Alleyn. There's no need for me to sign it, is there?

(*We see the portrait in close up—its style is identical with the Tillet caricature. Under the end credits we mix to the Tillet cartoon to endorse the parallel*)

NGAIO MARSH

Edith Ngaio Marsh is one of the Crime Queens of the Golden Age, the others acknowledged to be Margery Allingham, Agatha Christie and Dorothy L. Sayers.

Born in New Zealand in 1895, Ngaio Marsh was a precocious child with a love of drama and history nurtured by her mother. She was educated at St Margaret's College, Christchurch, where she excelled in the arts and academic subjects and began to develop her lifelong interest in the theatre. Her first play, *Noel*, was performed at the College in 1912 and others—*The Moon Princess* and *Mrs 'Obson*—were staged at a nearby school in 1913. After leaving St Margaret's, she studied painting at the Canterbury College School of Art and in 1919 joined the Allan Wilkie Shakespeare Company on a tour of New Zealand, an experience she would draw on some time later for a crime novel. In 1920 she joined the Rosemary Rees English Comedy Company and, as well as acting, she continued to write plays, including *So Much for Nothing* (1921) and the curiously titled harlequinade *Little House Bound* (1924).

In 1928, Marsh moved to London where she and a friend, Helen Rhodes, ran an interior decorating business in Knightsbridge. She stayed for four years and while there decided to write a crime novel. For this, her main inspiration was naturally enough something she had read—'a Christie or a Sayers, I think'—but she was also influenced by the Murder Game, then a dinner party staple. The result,

A Man Lay Dead (1934), introduced ''andsome Alleyn' of Scotland Yard who would go on to appear in a total of thirty-two novels and some plays that Marsh adapted or co-adapted from them. Alleyn— pronounced 'Allen', like the English school—also investigates in five short stories, one of which remains unpublished. Another, 'which would explain why he left the Diplomatic Service for the Police Force', was never written.

Whereas many mystery writers plan stories around plots or situations, Ngaio Marsh always began with characters. Like her great contemporary Agatha Christie, she was very much influenced by the theatre, but whereas Christie drew on her knowledge of theatrical tropes to deceive her readers, Marsh simply wrote like a playwright, structuring and pacing her novels like a play: the scene is set, the cast of characters introduced, and the plot is unravelled as carefully and methodically as it was constructed. Just as the audience at a play sees the plot unfold through the eyes of a protag- onist, in a Ngaio Marsh novel the reader is guided for the most part by the investigator, seeing what he sees and hearing what he hears. Thus Marsh's work adheres very strongly to the fair-play principle and the reader has every chance of beating the detective to the explanation of the crime.

While she would write crime fiction for the rest of her life, Ngaio Marsh's first love was always the theatre. Between 1943 and 1969, she produced more than half of Shakespeare's plays and created the British Commonwealth Theatre Company, which toured in the early 1950s. Her understanding of Shakespeare's works and technique led to appearances at numerous international conferences and, in 1966, she was appointed a Dame Commander of the Order of the British Empire. Through the 1970s, while Marsh's energy and appe- tite for new challenges remained undimmed, her health was beginning to decline. Her final novel was the supremely theatrical *Light Thickens* (1982), which centres on a production of *Macbeth*, a play that Marsh had herself directed in 1946 and 1962.

Ngaio Marsh died on 18 February 1982 at her home in the

Cashmere Hills near Christchurch. Despite the passage of nearly forty years, her novels remain extremely popular, and in 2018 her many admirers were treated to a new Alleyn mystery: *Money in the Morgue* was written by Stella Duffy working from little more than three initial chapters by Marsh and, while many of the most famous characters of the Golden Age have been reincarnated in new continuation novels, *Money in the Morgue* is among the very best.

'A Knotty Problem' was first broadcast under the title 'Slipknot' on 19 September 1967 as part of the New Zealand Broadcasting Corporation's 'Television Workshop' season. Sadly there are no extant recordings and this is its first publication.

THE ORANGE PLOT
MYSTERIES

In the mid-1930s, many national newspapers in Britain published short stories and serials, with mysteries proving to be particularly fruitful. One of the most popular weeklies was the *Sunday Dispatch* which, in 1938, commissioned two series of stories from the Crime Club, a publishing imprint created by the publishers William Collins. In his definitive and lavishly illustrated history of Collins Crime Club, *The Hooded Gunman* (2019), John Curran recounts how it evolved out of the publishers' earlier initiative, the Detective Story Club, to become the best-known and longest-lived brand in crime and mystery fiction. Between 1930 and 1994, a total of 2,012 Crime Club books were published, including titles by Agatha Christie, Ngaio Marsh and many of the biggest names of the genre.

The first tranche of stories commissioned by the *Sunday Dispatch*, all six of which are included here, appeared weekly between 6 March and 10 April 1938. Each of the six writers, including the series 'compère' Peter Cheyney, who also wrote the first story, and William Collins himself, who wrote the last, was challenged to write a short story around the following plot:

'One night a man picked up an orange in the street. This saved his life.'

THE ORANGE KID

Peter Cheyney

Snevelski, Third Assistant in the District Attorney's office, who trebled his official salary by 'fixing' for Parelli, the local big-shot, walked out of the elevator and along the passage. He had his coat collar turned up but he couldn't disguise his bow legs, his thin shoulders, his peculiar walk.

Lounging outside Parelli's main door, Scanci and Fannigan, the mobster's two gorillas, quickly recognised him.

Scanci grinned.

'Hey-hey, lookit,' he mouthed. 'Here comes the law. Howya, Snev? Haveya come for a cut or are you pinchin' somebody today?'

Fannigan raspberried. Both gorillas laughed.

The Third Assistant D.A. shot them a venomous look. Pushed past, went through the first door along the passage, through the second into Moxy Parelli's room.

Parelli pushed the girl he was kissing back into her chair. He straightened up. His wide mouth eased into a grin when he saw Snevelsky.

'Hey, where's the fire?' he said cheerfully. 'What's eatin' you, Snev? Have they got wise to you around at the D.A.'s office an' handed you a kick in the pants or have you come around here to say that you're thinkin' of raisin' the ante? If so, come again. There's nothing doin'. Not a thing.'

Snevelski turned down his coat collar. There were beads of sweat across his forehead.

'Send that moll outa here,' he said. 'This is business.'

Parelli nodded at the girl. She got up and went out. She pulled a face at Snevelsky as she went. She was twenty-three, plump in the right places, with good legs and an impudent expression. She was expensively and somewhat flashily dressed with a skirt that was too tight round the hips. Snevelsky found himself thinking that he liked molls in tight skirts.

'So what?' said Parelli. He did not offer a drink. He didn't like the Third Assistant. He despised him.

'It's bad, Moxy,' said Snevelsky. 'Here's the set-up. We can't cover up any longer for you on that downtown warehouse shootin'. The Feds are on the job. They got some tie-up that the shootin' was connected with a Treasury bond grab. They're makin' it a Federal job, see? O.K. The D.A. had me in today an' gave me a nasty one off the ice.

'He says we gotta pull somebody in for that killin'. He don't care who, but it's gotta be somebody an' it's gotta be quick. If we don't, that lousy "G" crowd will be around here puttin' the heat on the town generally an' we'll all be sugared. Got that?'

Parelli sat down. He ran a finger between a fat neck and a silk collar. He thought.

'I got it,' he said at last.

He began to grin. He leaned forward as far as his gross stomach would let him. Then:

'Get this, Snevelsky,' he said, 'an' get it right. I'm goin' to throw a party tomorrow out at the Grapevine Inn. O.K. The place will be full up an' they'll all be my boys, see? There won't be strangers around.

'Right. At eleven forty-five you concentrate a police cruiser out there. They can hide in among the trees on the other side of the highway. O.K. They just stick around, see? They wait there.

'At ten minutes to twelve I'm goin' to send a certain guy out of the inn by the front doorway. This guy will have an orange in his hand—you got that? That's good enough for you. Directly the cruiser squad see this guy come out with the orange in his hand they let him have it plenty. They don't arrest him. They just let him have it good in the guts an' they're goin' to be justified, see? The reason they shoot right away like that is becos he's got an orange in his hand, see?'

Snevelsky looked across at Parelli with wide eyes.

'You mean . . .' he said. 'You mean . . .'

'I mean the guy with the orange will be the Orange Kid,' said the mobster. 'Ain't that good enough?' He grinned. 'Everybody knows that when that bozo chucks a bomb it's always inside an orange skin. So all the cops have gotta say is that he was just about to chuck one of his usual egg-bombs inside the usual orangeskin an' they hadta shoot first.'

'I got it,' says Snevelsky. 'But why the Kid? Why . . .?'

'Don't get curious,' said Parelli. 'You keep your nose clean an' shut your trap. I got reasons.' He grinned. 'That was the Orange Kid's doll in here just now,' he went on. 'See?'

'I see,' said Snevelsky. 'O.K. I got it. We give it to the Kid for resistin' arrest an' attemptin' to throw a bomb, an' we discover afterwards that he was the guy who pulled the warehouse killin''

'Correct,' said Parelli. 'Now scram becos you make me feel sick in the stomach.'

It was eleven-thirty. The party at the Grapevine was tops. Everybody who was anybody was there. Most of them very high. When Parelli threw a party he threw one.

Irma, who was dancing with the Kid downstairs, stopped when she saw Scanci giving her the eye-sign. She told the Kid she had broken a suspender, that she'd be back in a minute.

Upstairs in the bedroom corridor Parelli was waiting for her. He gave her a big hug.

'Now listen, kiddo,' he said. 'Here it is. In five minutes I'm goin' to send for the Kid. I'm goin' to send him out to pick up a guy on the other side of the highway.

'Just as he's goin' outa my bedroom here you come along the passage an' ask him to bring you back an orange with him.

'I've fixed that the only place where there's an orange is on the stand just inside the front entrance, an' there'll only be one orange there, see?

'So the Kid will grab it off the fruit girl pronto becos it's the only one an' he'll take it out at the front entrance with him so's nobody else gets it, becos he loves you so much.'

He grinned.

'After which we'll buy him a nice wreath of roses with "He was our dear pal" in silver wordin' on it, an' you can move over to me. Got that?'

'I got it,' she said. She put up her lips. 'Gee, have you got brains, Moxy!' she gurgled.

Fannigan found the Orange Kid in the bar. 'Hey, Kid,' he said, 'the Big Boy wants you—he's up in his room—it's business.'

The Kid nodded. Finished his rye. Turned round and made for the stairs. He was five feet ten, slim, an elegant dresser. He'd got style. He moved like a professional dancer and he could twist a four-inch nail between his fingers. He had big blue eyes and an innocent expression. Women went for him.

The Kid had played along with Parelli for five years. He knew where he was with Parelli. To him the mobster was the Big Boy—the real thing. To an East-Side wop kid, brought up to pinchin' off barrows from the age of four, snatching bags in the street, and acting as look-out for 'the Boys' from the age of ten, and every sort of mayhem from the age of fifteen, Parelli looked like the real business.

Parelli had made him what he was. And he was the finest shop-front blaster in the business. From the time the bombs were made down in McGarrow's warehouse basement to the time when the Kid threw them concealed in the usual orange skin with unerring aim into the shops, offices, even bathrooms of such folk as were foolish enough not to consent to pay for 'protection'.

The Orange Kid saw the business through coolly and smilingly. And even if the blasting business was not so profitable since repeal, he was also a very good and useful guy with a gun.

Life was O.K. The Orange Kid thought he was big-time in the mob, thought that Irma was the cutest doll ever. Everything was okey doke. So what the hell?

He pushed open the door of the bedroom and sauntered in. Parelli was sitting at a desk in the corner. Scanci grinned at the Kid and handed him a highball.

'Sit down, Kid,' said Parelli. 'Here's the way it is. Windy Pereira is coming down tonight from Wisconsin. He's due to show up here right now. O.K. Well, I don't want him to come in here.

'I just come to the conclusion that it wouldn't be so good. There's too many wise guys around here tonight who might put the wrong sorta construction on me havin' a meetin' with Pereira, see?

'Scram downstairs, Kid, an' go over the other side of the highway. Flag Pereira when you see that light blue sedan of his an' tell him to lay off comin' in here. Tell him to ease right along to the Honeysuckle Inn an' that I'll come along there an' talk business to him at twelve o'clock. You got that?'

'O.K.' said the Kid.

He swallowed the drink and went out of the room whistling. Outside down the passage he met Irma coming out of a bedroom.

'You wanna dance, Kid?' she said.

He smiled at her.

'Nope. I'm doin' a little job. I'll be seein' you.'

'I'm stayin' right up here till you come back, Kid,' she said. 'I don't want them monkeys downstairs man-handlin' me on the dance floor. I'll wait.'

He lit a cigarette.

'Sweet baby,' he said.

He gave her a hug.

'An' bring me back an orange, Kid, when you come,' she said. 'There's some at the entrance. You better grab one as you go out becos they all got dry mouths downstairs an' they'll be fightin' for 'em later on.'

'O.K., honey,' said the Kid.

He walked towards the stairs.

The orange basket in the front hall was empty.

'I'm sorry,' said the fruit girl. 'Some drunk grabbed the last one before I could stop him. I told the sap that Mr Parelli said it wasn't to be touched, but he wouldn't listen.'

'Where'd he go?' asked the Kid.

'He went outa the side entrance,' said the girl. 'He was high all right!'

The Kid walked back along the passage and out by the side entrance. Away across the lawn, leading to the side road, he could see the drunk lurching along precariously. The Kid went after him.

Out on the side road he stopped with a grin. The drunk had evidently dropped the orange. It was lying in the gutter. The Kid picked it up and polished it with his handkerchief.

As he stood in the shadow of the hedgerow that surrounded the Grapevine he stiffened suddenly. Two cars slid along the side road, pulled up on the waste ground in the shadow of the trees.

The Kid watched them. Saw four men get out of each. Two with Tommy-guns, two with sawn-off shot-guns. Moonlight flashed on a Sam Browne belt buckle. The law!

The Kid stood there thinking. There flashed back into his

mind the remark of the fruit girl—'I told the sap that Mr Parelli said it wasn't to be touched . . .'

Why should Parelli want that orange left there, and why did Irma suddenly want an orange? And why was he sent out to meet Windy Pereira and his exit timed with the arrival of a couple of police gun-squads?

The Kid got it. So he was to be the sucker!

He walked quickly back across the lawn, around to the back of the Grapevine, into the garage. He found his roadster, started it up, backed it out on the gravel path at the back of the inn rear wall. He got out and left the engine running.

He opened the tool box in the rear carrier and took out what he wanted. He put it inside the breast of his jacket. Then he eased quietly around to the side entrance, went in and up the stairs.

Irma was waiting in the corridor. She looked a trifle surprised when he appeared.

'Hello, kid,' he said. 'Come along here. I got something funny to tell you.'

They walked along to Parelli's room. The Kid kicked the door open, pushed the girl in and stepped in after her. He had a flat, snub-nosed automatic in his left hand.

Inside Parelli, Scanci and Fannigan looked at him. Nobody said anything.

'O.K.,' said the Orange Kid. 'Here we go!'

He put his right hand inside his coat, brought it out with something that looked like an orange in it. He threw it into the room, stepped back, shut the door. As he ran for the stairway the bomb detonated. The roar shook the inn. Downstairs a woman shrieked.

The Orange Kid put his foot down on the accelerator and headed for the State line. He didn't expect to get far, but it was worth trying.

He was doing 70. He took his right hand off the wheel and felt about on the floor. After a second he found the orange he was feeling for.

He changed it over to his left hand and drove with his right. He bit hard through the orange skin and appreciated the tang of the juice.

Somewhere behind him a police siren shrieked.

PETER CHEYNEY

Reginald Evelyn Peter Southouse Cheyney was born in 1896 in Whitechapel, London, the youngest of five children. At the age of fifteen, his parents removed him from Hounslow College, where the only subject for which he had shown any aptitude was mathematics. After a spell in a solicitor's office he embarked on a career in the theatre, appearing in plays such as *Break down the Walls* and *The Butterfly on the Wheel*. He enlisted on the outbreak of war in 1914 but was invalided home after being wounded by a bomb in the second battle of the Somme two years later. Despite his experiences in the First World War, during the Second World War, at the height of his fame, Cheyney joined the Home Guard and commanded its sole armoured unit.

After the Great War, Cheyney had returned to theatre, writing character sketches and songs for music hall artists such as Nellie Wallace and Albert Whelan. He also took to the stage himself and in 1923 performed monologues and songs on 2LO, which became the British Broadcasting Company. Cheyney also produced several plays but the rewards were low so he got a job as a journalist, reviewing new films, writing special features and working as a crime reporter. Around this time, while going through a protracted divorce from his first wife, Cheyney decided to try his hand at fiction. Published as newspaper serials, these early efforts had Rohmeresque titles like *The Gold Kimono* (1930), *The Vengeance of Hop Fi* (1931),

Death Chair (1931) and *Deadly Fresco* (1932). A friend then bet Cheyney that he couldn't write a thriller 'in the American gangster vernacular' . . . The result, *This Man Is Dangerous* (1936), was the first novel to feature Lemmy Caution, a character whose language and mannerisms are almost laughable today but in the 1930s and '40s was so popular that one newspaper would later estimate that Cheyney had earned the equivalent of more than ten million pounds from his many books. Ironically, none of them was published by the Crime Club.

Peter Cheyney died in a London hospital on 26 June 1951 with his third wife at his bedside. He had been suffering from bronchitis and heart trouble.

'The Orange Kid' was published by the *Sunday Dispatch* on 6 March 1938.

AND THE ANSWER WAS . . .

Ethel Lina White

'Before you go home, Jones,' said Timothy Rolls, 'bring me in a cup of tea and three ham sandwiches.'

Casually he rattled off the order, which was to be of vital importance to his destiny.

'Are you working late, Boss?' asked his staff—a youth of seventeen.

'Yes, Jones, I'm not so lucky as you. I've a darn bad employer. But he won't sack me, and I can't give him notice.'

His staff grinned dutifully at his joke, which expressed his pride and wonder at being his own master.

As he sat at his sewing-machine in the window of his shop, the light glared down on him. He was a little man with a plucky smile and pale from a constant steam atmosphere.

His large eyes held a wistful expression which was the result of muddled thinking about War, unemployment, and Eternity; but that evening their gravity sprang from a different cause.

He was concerned about the recent murders in the town. Two women had been killed and the criminal was still at large. As long as he lurked hidden—like the shadow quivering in deep sea-water, which alone betrays the presence of the shark—there was menace to every unprotected girl.

In particular, Rolls feared for his fellow-boarder—Miss Loretta Smith—who was employed in the bureau of the Bear Hotel and

kept late hours. She was an attractive blonde, with a smart line
of repartee and sound sense which would make her an ideal
life-partner to a young man starting in business.

Because of her possible peril, Rolls scowled at the pair of
trousers he was repairing, while his staff came back with his tea.
The youth had left a few minutes when the door-bell jangled
violently to announce a customer of municipal importance—the
Mayor of Millbrook.

He was a prosperous and popular auctioneer—sandy and
burly—who modelled himself on John Bull and thereby did the
National Character grave injustice. At first, Rolls did not recognise him, for his normally florid face was pale and his light
overcoat splashed with mud.

'Been bowled over by a blasted bike,' he panted. 'Chap
scorched off before I could take his number. Here—take my
coat and clean it up. Can't go through the town looking like a
tramp.'

Rolls carried the coat over to the board, and, conscious that
he was watched, tried to make a sponging-record, before placing
the garment between the steam-rollers.

When the Mayor recovered his breath, he began to chat.

'How do you like the provinces after London, Rolls?'

'Fine, sir. This town's more friendly than London . . . Only—
it's not safe for ladies until they catch this murderer.'

'Hum. He seems too smart for the police.'

'Not quite, sir. I lodge with Mrs Bull, and her husband's been
in the force, so I get the inside dope. He says these mystery
cases are usually the work of a sort of Jekyll and Hyde—like
the film.

'The police may know who he is, but they can't convict him
without direct evidence. And the people who know, won't tell
. . . I would.'

'More fool you. Suppose you got something on some big man.
Who's going to believe *you*? They'd think you potty. And if there's

the least shadow of doubt, you might as well put up your shutters. You'd be finished here.'

Rolls shuddered at the thought as he turned the coat inside out, to examine the lining. Arrested by the sight of a dark smear around the pocket, he made a closer examination.

'I'm afraid, sir,' he suggested diffidently, 'this coat ought to be sent to the cleaners. I couldn't get out the blood.'

'*Blood?*'

The Mayor's voice was that of a stranger. Their eyes met . . . In that moment, Rolls felt transported to a dark unfamiliar place where he was locked in a stranglehold of horror.

'It's *him*,' he thought. 'I'm holding the evidence. Here—in my hands . . . If he won't leave the coat, I'll *know*. I must ring the police. He can't kill me here, with people passing the window . . . But I must *keep* the coat.'

Suddenly he returned to his own brightly lit shop at the sound of the Mayor's laugh.

'Good show. That's the other chap's claret—not mine. Glad he got what was coming to him . . . Well, Rolls, send the coat to be properly cleaned. When do you knock off?'

'I'll be late tonight, sir. Good-night, sir.'

Directly he was alone, Rolls locked the garment in his press. Although the Mayor had vindicated himself, he felt vaguely upset by the incident. He went back to his machine, gulping down his tea and sandwiches as he worked.

It was after nine when he finished, which was too late to go back to the boarding-house, and too early to meet Miss Loretta. He decided therefore to go to the pictures, although he had to pay more than his usual price for a seat, since the cinema was crowded.

He enjoyed the first film, because he could imagine Loretta as the blonde, wise-cracking heroine, but the second was disquieting. It was about a girl who witnessed a murder and, consequently, became a fugitive from gangsters.

To increase his discomfort, he grew extremely thirsty—the penalty for eating lean ham, plastered with mustard—so that he could only think of ways of getting something to drink.

All the public houses would be closed and also the cafés. Eventually, however, he remembered a coffee-stall which was open all night for the benefit of motor-traffic.

While he was at the cinema his boarding-house was honoured by a personal visit from the Mayor.

'I want to see young Rolls,' he said pompously to the overworked slattern who answered his ring. 'I'll go up and wait for him if he's not in. Where's his room?'

'Top. First door,' replied the woman.

'Right. I'll find my way up. Don't wait. I'll let myself out.'

Apparently he was doomed to a long vigil, for it was after eleven when Rolls left the cinema and began to trudge towards the Gloucester Road. Presently he left the shops behind him and reached a bleak indeterminate region where town and country fused in a desolate road.

As he caught sight of the cheery glow from the coffee-stall, he hurried towards it eagerly, fishing the while for the last coin in his pocket. When he held it to the light he found, to his keen disappointment, that instead of being sixpence it was a farthing.

Too late, he remembered that he had paid extra for his seat at the cinema. As he lingered on the muddy footpath—too diffident to borrow from strangers—he was cheered by another recollection.

The room below his own at the boarding-house was occupied by a genial married couple—the Mitchells. The man was conductor of the Bear Hotel orchestra and came home late, when his wife always made coffee for him in their room.

Rolls was sure that they would not grudge him a cup. He turned to hurry back, when his attention was caught by something a man at the stall was saying.

'She put up a good fight, but she was all in when my Alf heard her holler. Bleeding like a stuck pig, she was, but they say at the hospital as she'll pull through.'

'What's that?' asked Rolls.

'Not heard?' The man was delighted to get a new listener. 'Major Blake's daughter was attacked by a chap with a knife, on her way home from hockey. Young Alf chased him, but he got away. The girl says his face was covered with a dark handkerchief, but he was a big chap and wore a light fawn overcoat.'

'W-what time?' quavered Rolls.

'Round about six-thirty.'

Rolls grew cold as he made a rapid calculation. At that time, he had sent his staff home and the Mayor had burst into his shop a few minutes later.

He hurried back to the town—a prey to conflicting emotions. A bomb seemed to have exploded inside his brain, spattering blazing thoughts.

'*Me*. A little repairing-tailor—against His Worship the Mayor. He'll stick to his tale about the blood coming from the cyclist and the police won't have it tested, to compare it with the young lady's . . . And suppose he doesn't want any talk? *I'm* the only one that knows.'

Suddenly he realised the loneliness of his surroundings. On one side was a cemetery—on the other a football-ground. The dim light revealed a cinderpath, a thorn hedge and a hoarding where torn posters hung forlornly. Every shadow was a crouching form, poised to spring—every corner a test for quivering nerves.

When—at long last—Rolls reached the security of the High Street, he was exhausted and out of breath. Released from fear, he grew conscious again of his thirst. By this time it had increased to a pitch of near-torture, when every shred of ham turned to a little Red Devil goading his baked tongue.

Suddenly, he saw lying upon the pavement an orange, which had evidently rolled from a shuttered fruiterer's shop.

In that parched moment, it seemed a wish fulfilled; but although his eyes gleamed, he did not pick it up. He was very particular about food and shrank from eating an orange that had been lying in the dirt of the street.

As he passed it the town hall clock began to strike. To his dismay he counted three chimes . . . By a quarter to twelve the Mitchells would be in bed. No coffee for him from them.

Water, then? That too was denied him. He could not grope down into the basement without disturbing the Bull family who slept there; and he dared not risk drinking from his dingy carafe, which, in spite of his complaints, always smelt stale.

Turning back, he picked up the orange. By the time he reached Madeira Terrace, he had wiped it clean and scooped out a bit of peel. As he let himself into the stuffy gloom of the hall, he began to suck the juicy pulp greedily—noisily. Treading softly, he felt his way upstairs. When he reached the Mitchells' room no light shone through the transom, so he began to creep up the last flight.

Suddenly the darkness above him seemed to shake slightly, as though someone had moved. Aware that something was wrong, he dropped his orange and made an instinctive dart forward towards the light-switch. In the same moment, he felt a dull crash upon his skull, as though the roof had fallen, and then he knew no more.

Before he could fall, a man, who bore some resemblance to the Mayor, caught him and tugged him inside his room. This person was worked up to a state of dangerous excitement when the veins in his temples beat like tiny gongs and a red mist obscured his sight.

Dragging his victim over to the gas fire, he draped an eiderdown over him and the stove and then turned on the tap.

There was a frozen grin of ferocity upon his lips as he pocketed his weapon—a length of lead piping wrapped in a woollen sock—before he laid a letter upon the table. It was in his own handwriting and bore his signature, but was, by implication, Timothy Rolls's suicide letter.

Dear Rolls

Re the matter we discussed in your shop this evening. I regret I can advance no capital to finance your business. My feeling is youth should have the guts to succeed without help, as I did myself.

Shutting the door carefully behind him, the Mayor prepared to steal from the house. His foot had barely touched the first step when he trod on the slippery remains of the orange. Instantly his heel shot out and he crashed heavily down the stairs.

As he lay at the bottom, half-stunned, the landing light was switched on and the huge band conductor, looking like Hercules in pyjamas, rushed out.

'Why, Mr Mayor,' he shouted. 'What's up, sir?'

It was then that the shock of his fall proved the Mayor's undoing, since it had re-started the old mental trouble, previously released by a recent accident to his head. Dazed and unaware of his action, he drew out his cosh and tried to attack the conductor.

While the two men struggled together Mitchell bellowed an order to his wife.

'Little Rolls. See if he's all right.'

As the two young gentlemen from the drapery rushed out of their rooms to assist her husband, Mrs Mitchell nipped up the stairs for she could smell gas. The bedroom was far from being lethal, but Rolls, who had monopolised most of the output from the stove, was already passing into a nice long sleep.

She opened the window, turned the tap of the gas, and then dropped on her knees beside the unconscious man. Rolling him over and over, she got him outside the room.

An hour later he was still on the landing, lying on a pile of rugs, while his room was being aired. He had already surrendered his keys to the police, who had the bloodstained coat in their possession, besides the person of the Mayor. All around him were the other boarders and drinks were in circulation as each person shouted against the other.

Presently Rolls spoke to Loretta alone.

'I keep thinking how queer things work out. Are they planned? Why did I have to pick up an orange at 11.45 to save my life?'

'Orange?' repeated Loretta smartly, snapping at her chance. 'Then the answer is not a lemon.'

ETHEL LINA WHITE

Ethel Lina White (1876–1944) was born in Wales and, together with several of her siblings, worked for her father's construction materials business. After their mother died and the family lost all their money, White and two sisters moved to London where she got a job with the Ministry of Pensions. She had been writing for many years and had had several short stories published. In the mid-1920s she completed her first novel, *The Wish-Bone* (1927), and the modest success of this and two other early titles—including the futuristic fantasy *The Eternal Journey* (1930)—prompted her to take up writing as a career. Her first novel-length mystery, *Put Out the Light* (1931), is a brilliantly structured puzzle. It is especially noteworthy for the focus on the psychology of the characters, something that became a hallmark of her work.

White's many novels include *Some Must Watch* (1935), filmed as *The Spiral Staircase* (1946), and *The Wheel Spins* (1936), filmed as *The Lady Vanishes* (1939). Both films have been remade and her work remains popular with anthologists.

Even at the height of her success, White shunned publicity and would not talk about herself. As Peter Cheyney wrote in introduction to this story: 'She says in answer to my queries: "I was not born. I have never been educated and have no tastes or hobbies. This is my story and I'm sticking to it."' 'And the Answer Was . . .' was published by the *Sunday Dispatch* on 13 March 1938.

HE STOOPED TO LIVE

David Hume

The man enjoying his Christmas Eve by arranging a couple of violent deaths lit another cigarette and smiled at the three men facing him.

They did not smile. Their boss, Steve Kelly, might take it the wrong way. And if he did, startling things might happen.

'Charlie Ross ain't going to reach Christmas Day,' said Kelly, 'and Sammy Prince won't get far into the New Year. Everything's in the bag.'

'Blimey, Steve,' said the man on his left, 'you aren't going to see both of 'em out of the party, are you?'

'You guess well, mate. When I fix things they stay fixed. So that goes for both of 'em. Think l was going to take any more rough stuff from blokes like them, and sit back twiddling my fingers? Forget it!'

'Well, we know you're a smart Alec, boss, but our own crowd is pretty hot, and we don't want the cops putting the skids under us.'

'You're shouting hot air. Ever know me arrange things so that they went wrong? That wasn't how I came to sit on top of the dump, was it? I reckon I've stacked this deck of cards so that they just can't come unstuck.

'I've got everything that opens and shuts. But what the hell are you blokes screaming about? Don't you reckon they've done enough to ask for all that's coming to 'em?'

'They've certainly given us a real basin of trouble. But still . . .'

'Stow it,' snapped Kelly. 'We cased that Walworth warehouse, didn't we? Had everything set, hadn't we? And Charlie and Sammy dive into the dump under our noses and clean the lot up. Think I'd stand tor that?

'We worked that Bruton-street smash. And what happened? Charlie and Sammy stuck up our lads, knew we couldn't squeal, and got away with the whole issue. Now they've got to pay for it—and pay plenty.'

'You reckon you've worked out a really fast stroke, eh?'

'I could laugh about it. I reckon I've struck a new joke. Know what I've fixed? You'd never guess. You can leave little Steve to hit the high-spots. We're going to murder Charlie Ross, and Sammy Prince is going to take the long drop for it! Can you beat that, mates? Murder the one, and get the other swung. I call that a bit arty.'

Kelly smiled again. The other men gaped incredulously.

'Thought that would tickle you,' he said. 'I'll tell you the whole lay, and then you'll see the certainty we're backing.

'In half an hour's time Charlie Ross will be heading along Landor Road for home. I've fixed that. He's at the Stockwell Casual Club now.

'So is one of my boys, and he's escorting Charlie from the club to see that he arrives where we want him about half-past eleven. He'll leave Charlie at the corner, and we put him all set for the mortuary slab. But that's only the beginning.

'Sammy and Charlie have had some trouble. Seems they couldn't quite agree about their last split. It wasn't fifty-fifty.

'Sammy has been shouting the dome off his head, telling the world that he's been crossed and double-crossed, mentioning just a few of the things likely to happen to Charlie when they meet.

'A dozen boys have heard his squeals. I know 'em, and I can

slam them into the box at the Old Bailey to start the gallows march. But even that's nothing.

'You blokes know I hold my ears pinned to the floor when the boys start talking. Right. I've got the best information in the world that Sammy is pulling a single-handed stroke tonight.

'So he's sunk when the splits collect him, and he starts thinking about an alibi. There's plenty more yet.

'Sammy left his place two hours ago. He didn't take his car. I've got it tucked away round the corner now.

'We're going to use that bus when we crease Charlie. And I don't mind if a few folks get a good look at it! I don't mind if they remember the registration number.

'As soon as we've done the rubbing-out we're going to head towards Crouch End and abandon the car some distance from Sammy's hang-out.

'And in the leatherwork I'm going to slide the gun I used on Charlie. There won't be any prints on it. The splits wouldn't expect a cute bloke like Sammy to leave any.

'Then, to complete the picture, I'll see that the cops receive a mysterious message—just a nice, homely little story about the row between the pair of 'em.

'They know that Sammy has got a record that'd stretch from here to Dartmoor. Believe me, they'll collect him before he can fill the kids' Christmas stockings. Now what d'you say?'

The three men nodded appreciatively. They certainly had to hand it to Steve Kelly. He knew everything it needed to fix things.

The boss rose slowly to his feet, pulled a pair of gloves over his hands, smiled again as he slid an automatic from his pocket, examined it and replaced it. Then he grabbed a hat and headed for the door.

'Then we're all set. Come along. I want you three to drop off the car at odd places when I tell you. I'm going to dump the car myself. But the bunch had better start in on the party in case anything slips up.'

The men filed out of the room. A minute later they were on their way. It was exactly twenty-five minutes before midnight when Charlie Ross lurched to the pavement in Landor Road with a bullet in his brain.

The man staggering about the pavement along East End Road, East Finchley, showed every sign that his Christmas Eve had been celebrated with more enthusiasm than discretion.

In his right hand he carried a heaped basket of mixed fruit.

The task of balancing the fruity pile at moments caused him extreme difficulty.

Twice an orange from the summit of the stack bounced to the pavement. And both times the reveller laid down his basket, cursed, bent down as though likely to arrive on the sidewalk for the full count and recovered the fruit.

A few yards behind him a little man was watching the performance with a smile. Then, for the third time, the orange arrived on the pavement.

For an instant the inebriate hesitated, swaying like a reed in a gale. At last he reached a decision, kicked at the fruit, missed it, and continued with staggering progress.

The man following in his wake picked up the orange, started to hurry after the reveller, changed his mind, and slipped it into his pocket.

A local church clock chimed quarter to midnight.

Anxious to arrive at home, Sammy Prince kept his hand on the orange, hastened his step along Archway Road, cut off along a side street soon after passing through Highgate. His wife was waiting for him in their unpretentious house.

Before he had time to slide out of his overcoat a double rap sounded on the door. Sammy opened it—and gasped. He knew detectives quite well when he met them!

'I thought you hadn't had time to get out of your gear,' said one of the officers. 'We're taking you along with us. Are you ready?'

'Why, mister, what've I done? You can't grab folks like this.'

'Maybe at the station you'll be telling us what you've done tonight.'

Sammy winced, cursed softly. What a start to Christmas Day. He knew argument was useless. So he waved to his wife, and vanished into the night.

For hours at the police station Sammy faced a battery of questions. He shook his head over and over again, asked why he was wanted. Finally, a divisional inspector shot the simple remark:

'Charlie Ross was murdered tonight. And you can tell us plenty.'

The little man shook his head emphatically. Now he knew that he could maintain silence no longer.

So with a shrug of his shoulders he gave them the news—he had made an unsuccessful attempt to break into a house near St. Marylebone Cemetery.

He was never out of North London. Had anyone seen him? No. Could anyone swear to an alibi? No.

So the Inspector talked for five minutes, reciting the abundant evidence in their hands to prove that Sammy shot his friend, that he was in South London.

Prince spent two days in gaol, pacing the cell helplessly. He was in a jam, couldn't see a way out. The police had searched him, laughed when they found the orange, handed it back to him.

Without thinking, he took a bite at the fruit. Then the gaoler dashed through the cell door. For Sammy had raised a vicious curse and spat the piece of orange on the cell floor.

'What on earth's wrong? Can't you even eat an orange? You must be mad.'

'Mad be damned, man. I've never in all my life . . .'

Sammy ceased speaking with dramatic suddenness, stared at

the orange, remembered the queer antics of the Christmas Eve reveller. Then he shouted hurriedly:

'Get me a lawyer immediately. And I want a good one. Hurry up.'

Half an hour later a solicitor left the police station with the orange in his pocket. He had just heard a queer story. It fascinated him. Sammy waited patiently for the time for his court appearance. He felt better.

Prince's appearance before the court was weird and wonderful. Counsel representing him decided to save time by making a statement. He had already consulted with Crown counsel. His opening was startling:

'The defence in this case is an unbreakable alibi. A gentleman named West won a prize in the Christmas draw at the East Finchley Bachelor Club. He was presented with a basket of fruit. At the top of the pile was an orange.

'Some fellow members of the club decided to play a practical joke on Mr West, who admits quite candidly that he was intoxicated.

'Using a fountain-pen filler, they pierced a hole in the orange, injected into the fruit a considerable quantity of olive oil and an amount of ink.

'Eight members of that club are in court today to testify that Mr West left the club at half-past eleven. His father is here to swear that his son arrived home at midnight. The odds would be ten million to one against there being any other such orange in the world.

'On his way home Mr West lost that orange. The accused will tell you the circumstances in which he picked it up in East End Road, East Finchley.

'The fruit was in his possession when he was taken into custody. He will tell you that he picked up that orange at exactly a quarter to twelve.

'While in custody the accused took a bite at the orange, discovered the appalling taste, realised the significance of it, and arranged for the fruit to be analysed.

'As the result of that analysis his legal advisers appealed through the Press for assistance in tracing the orange. The task was not difficult. The club members came forward immediately with their story.

'There is little more to state. Charlie Ross, the deceased, was shot in Landor Road, Clapham, at about 11.35. In East Finchley, some twelve miles from the scene of the murder, the accused, who had no car with him, picked up the orange that must have been lost by Mr West at some time between half-past eleven and before midnight.

'For the accused to have committed this crime is a complete impossibility.

'Reflect that he was arrested at his home shortly after midnight, and that, having picked up the orange in East Finchley, he was moving towards Clapham and not away from it.

'That fact alone demonstrates the accuracy of his statement when he placed the time of the incident at 11.45. I will call the witnesses as soon as it is convenient . . .'

Two hours later Sammy Prince was discharged. An orange he had stooped to collect had saved his life!

DAVID HUME

'David Hume' was one of the pen names used by John Victor Turner (1900–1945), who was known to his family as Jack. He also wrote crime fiction as J. V. Turner and as 'Nicholas Brady', whose series character was the Reverend Ebenezer Buckle.

Born in Manchester in 1900, Jack Turner left school at sixteen to work on the *Warwick Advertiser*, and later moved to Walton in Staffordshire where he worked on a Leicestershire newspaper before joining the law courts staff of the national newspaper, the *Daily Mail*. After his wife committed suicide, the result of severe post-natal depression, Turner became crime reporter on the *Daily Herald* where he claimed to have a network of contacts in the London underworld. Drawing on his experience, he began writing fiction and his first novel, *Bullets Bite Deep*, was published in 1932. Its success led Hume to give up his career as a journalist and he went on to write dozens of fast-moving thrillers, many of which feature Mick Cardby, the 'quick-decisioned, hard-slogging, amazingly intrepid younger partner in [a] famous firm of private detectives'.

Several of Turner's books were made into films and, badged by his publisher as 'the new Edgar Wallace', he claimed at one time to be writing 'a novel a fortnight'. Although none of his Hume or Brady novels were published by the Crime Club, it did publish two of the seven mysteries written as by J. V. Turner—*Homicide Haven* (1935) and *Below the Clock* (1936).

On 3 February 1945, Turner died at his home in Eastern Road, Haywards Heath, apparently after contracting tuberculosis. A few days later, he was cremated at Brighton crematorium, mourned by his children and his second wife, to whom he left only £300, equivalent to about £13,000 today.

'He Stooped to Live' was published by the *Sunday Dispatch* on 20 March 1938.

MR PRENDERGAST AND
THE ORANGE

Nicholas Blake

There were five of us in the room that afternoon, listening to the carol service from King's College Chapel.

Nigel Strangeways, as usual, had his ear right up against the radio; he liked his music hot and strong, he said.

Prendergast, the nice little man he had brought along with him, was sitting bolt upright in an armchair; he looked worried and attentive, like a clerk being interviewed for a job; one expected to see the bowler hat and the pair of shabby kid gloves on his knee.

Hailes, Aston, and myself made up the party.

The last refrain of 'The Holly and the Ivy' died away, with that long, beautifully controlled diminuendo in which the King's College choir excels.

. . . The playing on the merry organ,
Sweet singing in the choir.

Nigel turned the knob, and the room was silent for a few moments. Then Hailes launched forth:

'Yes, it's all very fine. But it's artificial. Nowadays there's nothing at Christmas but the professional sort of stuff we've been listening to and those dismal gangs of brats who go around caterwauling 'Good King Wenceslas', out of tune, all

December. All the joy, the spontaneity, is gone, Now, in the good old days—'

'In the good old days you had a gang of drunks going around, blaring out 'Good King Wenceslas' equally out of tune, no doubt.'

Aston can never resist pulling the leg of Hailes' hobby-horse. Soon they were at it, hammer and tongs, and the atmosphere got quite heated. Nigel interposed, changing the subject tactfully:

'You ought to tell them about that Christmas you were arrested for murder, Joe.'

We all gazed at the little man with interest . . .

Mr Prendergast fidgeted, looking bashful, sulky, and deeply gratified in turn, like a boy asked to recite in a Victorian draw-ing-room. Then, rather breathlessly, he began.

'It was the orange, really. I mean, if it hadn't been for the orange I shouldn't be here to tell the tale. The orange—and Mr Strangeways, of course'—bobbing his head in Nigel's direction.

'Five years ago it was. About the middle of December. I'd lost my job; and the wife and kiddies—well, you know how it is. So I decided to go down to Cheltenham and make a last appeal to my aunt, Eliza Metcalfe.

'She'd never answered my letters—my mother married beneath her, she thought, and she'd said none of us should ever cross her threshold. A very hard woman was Eliza Metcalfe, gentlemen.'

Eliza Metcalfe! Now I remembered. RICH RECLUSE FOUND MURDERED. A man had been arrested, and—

'So I thought, well, perhaps if I go to see her myself, she might lend me enough to tide us over. So I took a ticket to Cheltenham—cleaned me out, it did—and went to her house.

'I can see her now, with her lace mittens and ivory stick—an old-fashioned lady, you know, but hard as nails.

'She pitched into me, too. My word! What did I mean by forcing my way into her house? My mother'd been no better than a you-know-what. She'd see the pack of us dead before she gave us any help.

'Well, I was desperate; and I told her so. And after a while she sort of relented. 'Young man,' she said, a bit gruffly, 'it's against my principles to lend money. I'll give you £10. And don't let me see your face again.'

'I reckon she felt a bit guilty, you know; it was like conscience-money. At any rate, she went into the next room, and I heard her rummaging about.

'When she returned, she was sucking her finger; she'd pricked it on a needle in the drawer where the money was kept, I suppose. There was a stain of blood on one of the pound notes she handed me. Nearly did for me, that bloodstain.'

Mr Prendergast paused, a look of consternation creeping into his eyes as he remembered that dreadful night five years ago.

'What about the orange?' said Aston gently.

'I'm coming to that. Well, gentlemen, I dare say £10 doesn't mean much to any of you. But when you're on your uppers it's as good as a million.

'I walked out of the house and had a cup of coffee at a stall; the chap who kept the stall noticed I was all excited—"agitated" was the word the police used afterwards.

'You see, I was thinking that the kiddies'd be able to have their Christmas presents after all.

'That was just 10.30 p.m. A lovely night, stars and frost twinkling, and that ten quid in my pocket.

'So I thought I'd take a bit of a walk. I'd no idea where l was going. In the end I found myself walking up a long hill right out of the town—the Cirencester road, they told me it was later.

'I was so elated, I didn't particularly notice anyone I passed or what roads I took; and, believe it or not, I'd been walking for three-quarters of an hour before I realised I'd left my stick behind at Aunt Liz's.

'It was a nice stick—an ash-plant with a silver band and my initials on it; the wife'd given it me for my birthday. So I thought I'd call in at Aunt Liz's and pick it up before I found a place to sleep the night.

'Well, I'd got to the end of the street where her house was—and that's when I saw it, in the street, in the lamplight. The orange.'

'A nice, big, juicy orange,' said Nigel dreamily.

'Now, I'm an inquisitive chap, and I couldn't help asking myself whoever could it be that went about so late at night dropping oranges. I could have sworn it wasn't there when I'd come along this street before. I bent down to pick it up.

'Funny, you know, for a moment I thought it might be some sort of practical joke, like leaving red-hot pennies on the pavement.'

Mr Prendergast blushed and giggled. Somehow it made us all feel very warm-hearted towards him.

'I bent down to pick it up; and just then it struck a quarter to twelve.'

'And what happened?' asked Hailes excitedly.

'Nothing. Not at the moment. I put the orange in my pocket—I noticed there were tooth-marks in the skin—and went along to Aunt Liz's.

'There were lights in the windows still. I thought I'd best go round to the back and ask the maid to give me my stick. I didn't want to knock up against Aunt Liz again that night.

'So I went quietly down the side-passage—and walked straight into a policeman. "What's your business here?" he said. "I'm Miss Metcalfe's nephew," I said.

'He took me inside. I was told my aunt had been found murdered. It knocked me over, I can tell you. I remember saying, in a dazed sort of way, "I came back to get my stick."

'And at that very moment the maid came in. "Why, that's the gentleman who was here two hours ago—him I was telling you about," she said. Two days later I was arrested.'

Mr Prendergast paused tantalisingly.

'You'd better ask Mr Strangeways to tell you the rest of the story,' he said at last.

'I became interested in the case through Inspector Blount, a friend of mine,' Nigel began crisply. 'The case against Joe Prendergast was based on the following pieces of circumstantial evidence.

'(1) The maid overheard a scene between him and her mistress, in the course of which he exclaimed, "I'm desperate. I'd do anything to get it!"

'(2) After this they had lowered their voices, and the maid, losing interest, had slipped out to post some letters, met her young man, and not returned till nearly eleven o'clock.

'(3) On her return, the maid found Miss Metcalfe in the hall, her head battered in.

'(4) The drawers in Miss Metcalfe's boudoir had been rifled; there were eight £5 notes and ten £1 notes missing.

'(5) The £1 notes were discovered in Joe's pocket-book; there was blood on one of them, of the same blood-group as the deceased's.

'(6) The bundle of £5 notes was found later hidden in a hedge beside the Cirencester road.

'(7) The coffee-stall owner recognised the prisoner as the man who had come to his stall in a "highly agitated" condition on the night of the crime.

'(8) The prisoner had endeavoured to get into the back garden, and in this garden the police found his walking-stick, blood-stained, with strands of the deceased's hair clinging to it.

'The theory was, of course, that Miss Metcalfe had refused Joe any assistance, that he had struck her down, stolen the money, and in his panic, flung away the stick as he left the house: that he had then gone for a walk to steady his nerves, realised that the £5 notes were traceable, and hidden them in the hedge, and returned to get the stick—the most damning evidence against him.

'Well, it seemed a water-tight case. But there were things in it that puzzled me. I got permission to interview Joe, and he convinced me that his version of the story was the right one.

'But it wasn't till he told me about the orange that I saw any hope of proving it.

'I'll put it to you like this: Who would throw away a perfectly good orange, in which he had set his teeth, late at night, in the middle of December?'

'We racked our brains. A number of theories were evolved, some flippant, all more or less fantastic.

'I imagined a murderer, creeping out of Miss Metcalfe's house with an orange he had stolen, starting to eat it, then flinging it down in revulsion.

'But he wouldn't do murder for an orange unless he was starving,' said Nigel patiently, 'and if he was starving, he wouldn't throw it away. No, the whole point is that he'd had a surfeit of oranges.'

'A murderer who'd had a surfeit of oranges?' I repeated, gazing owlishly at Nigel.

'No, you ass. Not a murderer, a carol singer—one of Hailes' "caterwauling brats".'

Gradually it dawned upon us. So simple. So obvious.

'Yes,' said Nigel, 'those boys who go round singing carols—people don't like sending them empty away; they give them an apple or an orange. You see, if Joe was right in saying that orange hadn't been there when he left the house, there was a fair chance that some carol singers had been down the street *after* he'd left.

'There was just a chance that they'd called at Miss Metcalfe's house and, as the maid was out, she'd have to go to the door. Which would prove that she'd been alive after Joe had left her.

'Of course, he might have come back later and killed her. But at least it gave us a loophole. Well, to cut a long story short, I found those two boys.

'After the murder had come out, they'd been afraid to tell

anyone they'd been to Miss Metcalfe's house. But they had, and she'd come to the door and given them a proper ticking-off; and that was at half-past ten, when Joe was at the coffee stall.

'They'd been given oranges at the next house, but they were so stuffed with dessert already that they couldn't eat one of the oranges, and threw it away after one of them had set his teeth in it.

'This made the police think again. They got the right man in the end—a burglar. He'd got into Miss Metcalfe's house over the back garden wall just after the carol singers left. He was surprised by the old lady in the hall, and hit out at her with the first object that came to his hand—Joe's stick.

'Then he started rifling the drawers, but he was in such a state by then that he couldn't go through with it properly; he just seized the bundle of notes and fled out by the back door again, throwing the stick away in the garden.

'He walked out of the town—it was one of those coincidences that you lawyers hate to admit, Aston—by the same road that Joe had taken.

'He found that the notes were £5 ones and traceable, so he hid them away. Then he jumped a lorry that was going to Swindon. That's how Joe saved his life by picking up an orange.'

'Well,' said Hailes after a long silence, 'I hope this will be a lesson to our lawyer friend about the dangers of circumstantial evidence.'

But Aston, as usual, had the last word:

'And a lesson to our mediaevalist friend,' he replied, 'that there's something to be said for his "dismal gangs of brats who go around caterwauling *Good King Wenceslas*".'

NICHOLAS BLAKE

'Nicholas Blake' (1901–1972) was the pen name of the Irish writer and poet Cecil Day Lewis, who was educated at Sherborne and Wadham College, Oxford. As Blake, Day Lewis wrote twenty novels, a handful of short stories and a couple of plays; he also reviewed crime fiction. Some of his novels are pure detective stories with clues to find and alibis to unravel—novels like *There's Trouble Brewing* (1937) and *Malice in Wonderland* (1940)—but he also wrote psychological crime novels, the foremost being *A Tangled Web* (1956), which incidentally was the only one of his titles not published by the Crime Club.

The Nicholas Blake books were immensely popular, not least for the strictly fair-play approach to the detection of the criminal that he takes in the sixteen novels that feature Nigel Strangeways, an amateur sleuth in the classic mould. Arguably the best of the Strangeways canon is *The Beast Must Die* (1938), in which a man sets out to commit murder but events do not go entirely as planned, and the suitably tongue-in-cheek *End of Chapter* (1957), in which Strangeways investigates murder at a publishing house.

'Mr Prendergast and the Orange' was published by the *Sunday Dispatch* on 27 March 1938.

THE YELLOW SPHERE

John Rhode

Noiselessly the young man crept up the alley until he reached the window of the back parlour of the Black Swan.

Since it was now eleven o'clock at night, the doors of that excellent hostelry had been closed—officially—an hour before.

But a light shone through a chink of the curtains drawn across the window, and a sound of murmuring voices reached the sharp-set ears of the young man without.

Inch by inch he crept forward until he could see through the chink. One swift glance at the four people seated round the card-table in the centre of the room was enough.

Carrying his suitcase in his hand, he glided out of the alley into the old-fashioned and at that hour practically deserted High Street of the little port of Sandhaven.

After a swift glance in both directions, he set off at a rapid pace towards the quay, little more than a quarter of a mile distant.

It was a fine night in early spring: dark, for the moon had not yet risen. The young man, in his anxiety to avoid observation, kept as closely as possible under the shadow of the houses.

As he passed the closed door of a greengrocer's shop, his foot came into contact with something that rolled away from him and came to rest in the centre of the pavement.

He appeared not to notice the incident, for his eyes were fixed upon the open space ahead of him. A minute later he had reached the quay.

It was even darker here than it had been in the High Street, for the waterside was illuminated only by feeble gas lamps, set at wide intervals. But the young man did not hesitate. He struck diagonally across the quay until he could see the thin pencil of a mast outlined against the skyline.

He increased his pace, reached the edge of the wharf, and stared down at the deck of the motor-cruiser *Amelia*, a couple of feet below the level of the quay.

At this time of year very few of the yachts belonging to the port had yet been fitted out, and the *Amelia* was the only craft tied up alongside the quay.

Her owner, Mr Peter Underwood, was a well-known local character. A childless widower, he was a rich man, as wealth was estimated in Sandhaven.

He lived in a rather pretentious house in the newer part of the town, where his material wants were faithfully attended by an elderly housekeeper.

But every now and then an urge for more cheerful companionship would seize him, and he would spend a convivial evening at the Black Swan or one of the other taverns in the old town.

On such occasions, if the *Amelia* was in commission, he preferred to spend the night on board her rather than return home. The motor-cruiser had no censorious eyes. For Tom, her one-man crew, slept ashore.

The young man seemed to be well aware that the *Amelia* was untenanted, for after a sharp look up and down the quay to make sure that he was unobserved, he caught hold of a shroud and swung himself lightly down upon the motor-cruiser's deck.

He ran forward, slid back the forecastle hatch, and dropped into the darkness beneath.

The forecastle contained nothing but a bunk along one side

and a lot of gear stowed in lockers on the other. The young man took an electric torch from his pocket, and balanced it so that its rays shone on the floor.

He lifted one of the floor boards revealing the ribs of the craft and the strakes of planking beneath them.

Then he opened his suitcase and took from it a two-inch auger, with which he rapidly bored a hole in the strake nearest the keel.

As he withdrew the auger, a jet of water followed it, and he surveyed this with grim satisfaction.

'That'll do the trick,' he muttered. 'She'll fill gradually by the head in two or three hours, and Uncle Peter, damn him, asleep in the cabin aft, won't know anything about it until she dives head-first into the harbour. And if he can manage to get to the surface after that—well, I lose, that's all.'

He replaced the auger in the suit-case, switched off the torch, and swung himself on deck. Then, having closed the hatch, he vaulted on to the quay and disappeared.

It was roughly half an hour later that the card game in the back parlour of the Black Swan came to an end. Mr Peter Underwood drained his glass and stood up, rather unsteadily.

'Well, I must thank you and the ladies for a very jolly evening,' he said to Mr George Blickfield, the landlord. "Time for me to turn in now.'

'You're not going to sleep on board the *Amelia*, surely, Mr Underwood?' Mrs Blickfield asked, a trifle anxiously.

'Ah, but I am.' Mr Underwood replied, with an inebriated leer. 'And if you or that good-looking daughter of yours likes to come with me, I shan't raise any objection.'

'How you do go on, to be sure!' exclaimed Mrs Blickfield. 'George'll show you to the door. And mind the two steps outside, they're treacherous.'

After repeated good-nights, Mr Underwood was safely escorted out of the side door of the Black Swan. Mrs Blickfield listened to the irregular sound of his footsteps receding down the alley.

'Do you think he's all right, George?' she asked her husband. 'I shouldn't like him to fall into the harbour or anything like that.'

'Oh, you needn't worry about him,' Mr Blickfield replied. 'He's gone on board dozens of times when he was much worse than he is now. Come along, let's go to bed. It's just on a quarter to midnight."

Mr Underwood reached the end of the alley, and turned down the High Street towards the quay.

His progress, though perhaps not in an undeviatingly straight line, was stately and dignified. Damn good chap, Blickfield. Keeps a decent drop of whisky, too. And his wife and daughter. Good sports, both of them.

Hullo, what's that?

Mr Underwood had caught sight of an object lying in the middle of the pavement, right at his feet. He stopped and surveyed it suspiciously.

By this time the moon had risen, and by the soft light that filtered into the High Street he discovered the object to be an orange.

'Well, I'm blest!' he muttered. 'Fancy leaving a thing like that where anyone might tread on it. Damn carelessness, I call it. Might break a fellow's neck. Lucky I spotted it before . . .'

He bent down to pick it up, but his sense of position was none too accurate, and the orange rolled away a few inches, eluding his grasp. He made a second grab at it, which was successful.

'Aha, got you this time!' he chuckled as he straightened himself triumphantly. 'Old Peter isn't so drunk as you might think.'

And as he went on towards the quay, he absentmindedly put the orange in his jacket pocket. As he did so, the town hall clock chimed the quarter before twelve.

When Mr Underwood reached the quayside, the tide had risen, so that the deck of the *Amelia* was almost level with the wharf.

He stepped on board with an air of easy confidence, and stood for a moment looking over the unruffled waters of the harbour, shining like silver under the bright moon.

'Fine night, and not a breath of wind,' he muttered. Then he stepped into the cockpit and, opening the folding doors, entered the cabin which occupied the stern of the motor-cruiser.

The cabin was arranged with a centre table and a bunk on either side, at the forward end of each of which was a capacious locker. Mr Underwood made his way to the starboard locker, took from it a bottle and a glass, and poured himself out a generous tot of whisky.

'Must have a nightcap,' he muttered as he seated himself heavily on the nearest bunk. 'Best thing to clear away the cobwebs. How much have I had to drink this evening, I wonder?

'That confounded chap Blickfield would keep filling up my glass as we were playing. Well, must drown one's sorrows sometimes. Damn that young rascal! He's quite upset me.'

As Mr Underwood reached for his glass he became aware of the bulge in his jacket pocket. He withdrew the orange and stared at it owlishly. It was almost perfectly round, smooth-skinned and yellow.

'Well I'm blessed!' he exclaimed to himself softly. 'Whatever possessed me to bring a thing like that on board now? Never mind, it'll do for some kid or other in the morning.'

He put the orange on the cabin table in front of him and drained his glass to the last drop. Then, not without difficulty, he began to undress. He found it an unduly lengthy process for his fingers seemed to have lost their aptitude for undoing buttons and studs.

By the time he had removed his outer garments, further effort seemed hardly worthwhile. Still clad in his shirt and pants, he lay down on the bunk and rolled himself in his blankets.

But sleep refused to come to him. He could not drive from his mind the memory of the interview with his nephew that morning.

Hateful business driving out one's own kith and kin like that. Having no children of his own, Mr Underwood had always looked upon his sister's only son as his natural heir.

But Victor had been a ne'er-do-well ever since the time he had left school.

Time and again his uncle's money and influence had got him out of nasty scrapes. But when it came to giving stumer cheques in Mr Underwood's own native town . . . !

Oh, he'd been fair enough to the young rascal, nobody could deny that. He had sent for him that morning and told him exactly what he meant to do.

He would meet the cheques, and buy him a ticket for any part of the Dominions he might care to select. But, at the same time, he would write to his lawyer and instruct him to draw up a will in which Victor's name should not appear.

What else could he have been expected to do? Fair? Of course he had been quite fair . . .

At last Mr Underwood dozed off, for how long he could not tell. Then, still more than three parts asleep, he shifted lazily into a more comfortable position, and, as he did so, half opened his eyes.

His glance fell upon the orange, conspicuous on the table in the bright moonbeams that poured through the cabin skylight.

And it seemed to Mr Underwood's senses, clogged with sleep, that the orange was moving, rolling slowly towards the forward end of the table.

Ridiculous! Must be the effect of the whisky. If he opened his eyes wider, he would see the orange standing perfectly stationary where he had put it.

But no. The orange continued to move, increasing the speed of its rolling until it reached the end of the table then fell, with a splash, not a thud, on the cabin floor.

Mr Underwood sprang out of his bunk and stood for an instant on the floor, ankle-deep in water.

The *Amelia* was tilting, ever more rapidly: the water surged past his feet like a mill race. He must get out quick, before . . .

Somehow he tore open the folding doors, struggled into the cockpit, and thence on deck. The motor cruiser's bow was already beneath the surface of the water.

Mr Underwood leapt for the quayside, slipped back. His groping hands clutched a mooring-ring, and with a supreme effort he dragged himself to safety.

As he picked himself up the *Amelia*'s stern rose vertically into the air. Mr Underwood held his breath as she remained in that position for a couple of long-drawn seconds.

Then, with a prodigious gurgling, she plunged bow-first to the bottom of the harbour, leaving behind her a swirl of oily water.

Mr Underwood's mind was so enthralled by the miracle of his escape that for the moment he could spare no thought for the cause of the foundering.

'Talk about a bit of luck!' he exclaimed. 'If it hadn't been for that blessed orange . . .'

JOHN RHODE

The writer best known as 'John Rhode' was born Cecil John Charles Street (1884–1964). He is one of the most prolific writers of the Golden Age, responsible for around 150 novels, published under four pseudonyms. As well as crime fiction, which he took up only after an impressive career as a military propagandist, he wrote short stories and plays, and also translated from the French biographies of Sébastien Le Prestre de Vauban, a military engineer of the seventeenth century, and the explorer Captain Cook. Street was awarded the Military Cross and the Order of the British Empire for his war work, but is today best known for his crime fiction and the extraordinarily diverse and creative means of murder he devised. While some find John Street's fiction humdrum, others delight in his ingenuity and the gentle pace with which the mysteries are carefully unravelled. His major series are those published as by 'John Rhode', the majority of which feature the sleuth Lancelot Priestley, and as by 'Miles Burton', all but six of which feature Desmond Merrion. In a third series, published under the pen name 'Cecil Waye', the detectives are siblings, Christopher and Vivienne Perrin.

As well as writing extensively, Street also played a major role in the life of the Detection Club, the dining club for crime writers established by Anthony Berkeley at the end of the 1920s. Most notably, he was responsible for wiring up the eyes of Eric the

Skull, the gruesome artefact on which all new members are required to take the Club's light-hearted oath of allegiance.

'The Yellow Sphere' was published by the *Sunday Dispatch* on 3 April 1938.

THE 'EAT MORE FRUIT' MURDER

William A. R. Collins

Let us consider Mr Hildegard Silvercat, who stood leaning precariously against the sharp corner of a shop window in the region of Berkeley Square on a winter's night.

And, while we are about it, let us face the fact that Hildegard had dined both wisely and too well.

Wisely because his prolonged dinner with his partner, Mr Anthony Gallery, had resulted in a nasty hatchet being buried; too well because Hildegard—a very simple soul really—was not so used to champagne and brandy as the more alcoholic Anthony, and the night air was a little too strong for his already tremulous mind.

Hildegard gazed, wide-eyed, across the square with that peculiarly wise expression that denotes the second stage of intoxication.

Hildegard was happy. He realised that life could still be worth-while, that Anthony, in spite of his bad tempers, his drinking, and his suspicions, was an extraordinarily nice feller, dammit, and that Venetia Gallery, his wife, was a definitely nice feller too—and a wise one.

Say what you like, Hildegard told himself, giving a manly push against the window and thereby obtaining sufficient momentum to begin to negotiate the square—say what you like, there were moments when a woman's intuition was definitely the thing.

If it hadn't been for Venetia's intuition, if she hadn't guessed somehow that Anthony had got the ridiculous idea into his head that there was something going on between herself and Hildegard, there might have been the devil to pay.

But she had. She had somehow guessed that the tortuous and odd mind of Anthony was filled with vague suspicions about his wife and his partner. She had observed his growing ill-tempers, his hatred for the inoffensive Hildegard.

What had put such a fatuous idea into Anthony's head in the first place?

Hildegard attempted to shrug his shoulders. He failed dismally, merely succeeding in hiccoughing with such energy that he nearly ricked his neck.

By Jove, sir, it was clever of Venetia to have found it out, to have shown her husband what a fool he had been, to have convinced him of the idiocy of his baseless suspicions, and then, as a supreme gesture, persuaded him to ask Hildegard to dinner, to open his heart and to apologise for all the nastiness, the bitter remarks, the quarrels of the last six months.

Ten minutes ago Anthony had left him. Somebody had telephoned, and Anthony, staggering back from the call, had informed Hildegard that he was leaving, that he had to go home.

He was careful to instruct Hildegard that he was to follow, in ten minutes' time. Anthony had ordered a final brandy for Hildegard before he had gone off. Anthony was a good feller, dammit.

Hildegard crossed the road and stood swaying gracefully in Davies Street, gazing at a poster that exhorted the world to 'Eat More Fruit.'

Eating more fruit, ruminated Hildegard, was a national necessity. The poster was right.

He, Hildegard, believed in eating more fruit, dammit, and if he could get some fruit at that moment he'd just show you something—a nice juicy orange, for instance.

The very idea made him run a somewhat furry tongue over dry lips.

And at that very moment it happened. In answer to his prayer, a fruit barrow came out of a mews half way down Davies Street.

Hildegard, thanking a kindly fate for hearing his prayer, endeavoured to hasten after it. But it was of no avail. The barrow moved faster than he. No matter how he might try he could not catch up. His legs just wouldn't work properly.

Fate intervened again. As the pusher of the barrow swung it across the road an orange fell off, rolled, unobserved by its rightful owner, into the gutter.

Using a first-class Red Indian technique, Hildegard stalked that orange. He approached it as a cat approaches a mouse. He sprang upon it eventually with joy.

It was a very good orange. Hildegard, having laid his overcoat in the gutter, examined it with pride, then, with great difficulty, he pushed it into the inner breast pocket of his evening tail coat. He would eat it with triumph just before he went to bed.

He looked about for a cab. He forgot that he was supposed to go along to the Gallery flat. Turning, he saw for the first time that evening Venetia, gracious, dark and mysterious as ever.

'Well . . . well . . . well, Hildegard,' she said softly. 'You are in a state, aren't you? But I can understand. I'm so glad that you two have talked all this nonsense out and that everything's all right.

'I was just going home when I saw your distinguished figure reeling in the distance. You'd better come in for a nightcap.'

Hildegard explained that that was what he was doing. That somebody had telephoned Anthony and that Anthony had instructed him to follow to the flat. Venetia smiled and took his arm.

'Come along, Hildegard,' she said. 'We'll go in by the side entrance. You wouldn't want the porter to see you like this, would you, Hildegard?'

The Chief Inspector looked at Detective-Sergeant McCaffey, with a raised eyebrow.

'Just where is Silvercat?' he asked.

'He's round at the office,' McCaffey said. 'He professes to know nothing about it at all. He says that he met Mrs Gallery on the way home, while he was walking down Davies Street. He says he was fearfully tight.

'His story is that somebody telephoned to Gallery while they were drinking liqueurs after an excellent dinner which had been going on since nine o'clock, and Gallery said that he had to go off home and asked Silvercat to follow on after him.

'When they got to the flat he says he threw his coat on to the hall table, that Mrs Gallery insisted that he had another drink— that she gave him a strong one, and that he sat in a chair and went off to sleep.

'He says he woke up at some time after midnight and went off quietly. He walked home.'

The Chief Inspector grunted.

'He did it all right,' he said. 'There's motive proved and everything. The woman's story is supported by statements taken from half a dozen people.'

He paused.

'But before we do anything serious,' he said, 'you might get around to his flat, McCaffey, and see if you can get hold of his evening clothes. Have a look at them and see if there are any bloodstains. We might as well get every bit of corroborative evidence we can.

'Pick up Silvercat on the way back. Ask him to come down here and make a statement. We can get the warrant while he's down here if necessary and arrest him here.

'I suppose Brown is keeping an eye on the office in case he decides to try and run out on us?'

McCaffey nodded.

'There's just one other thing,' he said. 'It's not important. Silvercat says that he met Mrs Gallery by accident.

'He says that he crossed the road to pick up an orange that fell off a fruit barrow. He says he was thirsty and thought he'd like an orange!'

The Chief Inspector grunted again.

'I bet he'll feel like eatin' one the day they hang him,' he said grimly. 'Go ahead, McCaffey,' he concluded, 'and on your way down ask them to send Mrs Gallery in again. I want to check her statement.'

'I don't think that there are any other points, Mrs Gallery,' said the Chief Inspector. 'The main points are these. Interrupt me, please, if everything isn't exactly right.

'For the last six months Silvercat had been making unpleasant advances to you. You told your husband about this, and there had been trouble between the two men.

'Your husband was keen on trying to put the matter right without having to dissolve the partnership.

'Last night Silvercat invited your husband to dinner. You were rather frightened of this because you thought that Silvercat had something in his mind. You asked your husband not to go. Your husband arrived home at eleven thirty, rather intoxicated.

'He told you that he had quarrelled with Silvercat, who had made one or two slighting remarks about you, that he had got up and walked out of the restaurant after telephoning you to say that he was coming home.

'Ten minutes afterwards Silvercat telephoned from a callbox. He said that your husband had walked out on him, and that he was coming along and going to give him a first-class hiding.

'Almost immediately after this call your husband arrived home.

'He was in a state of intoxication and went straight to his room to bed. Your one idea then was to prevent Silvercat from coming into the flat.

'So you went out and walked down the street to meet him and ask him to go away.

'He was perfectly sober. You talked him into a better frame of mind, and he said that he would go off quietly if you allowed him in for a final drink with you. You agreed.

'He went into the flat with you, threw his overcoat in the hall.

'You went into the kitchen for some soda water. While you were there you heard the sound which you describe as a bump, and you imagined that your husband had fallen over in his room.

'When you returned from the kitchen Silvercat was standing in the hallway outside your husband's door, laughing fiendishly. Instinctively, by his expression, you felt that something awful had happened.

'You dropped the glass and ran up to him. You seized him by the lapels of his coat and you saw, protruding from the inner breast pocket, the butt of an automatic pistol.

'Silvercat pushed you away, and you fell. You struck your head in falling against the flat side of the hall table. You became unconscious. When you came to he was gone.

'You remembered what had happened: you went into your husband's room and found him dead, shot through the chest. You immediately telephoned the police.'

The Chief Inspector looked up.

'Is that right, Mrs Gallery?' he said.

She nodded. She could not speak.

The policeman shook his head.

'It's a bad business, Mrs Gallery,' he said. 'But if it's any satisfaction to you to know it, his murderer won't get away with it. It's an obvious case. There isn't any possibility of doubt.'

She got up slowly as the telephone bell rang. The Chief Inspector answered it. He talked for some time. Then:

'Mrs Gallery,' he said. 'Just a minute. I've just heard that one of my people has been examining Silvercat's coat. There's an orange stuck in the breast coat pocket. It's stuck there so hard that it can't be moved without a great deal of force.

'The coat was lying on the floor where Silvercat evidently threw it last night. Tell me, Mrs Gallery,' said the Chief Inspector. 'Just how was the pistol butt protruding from the small inner breast pocket if an orange was jammed there?

'You can't carry a .32 automatic and a large orange in the inner breast pocket of an evening coat.

'The point's rather important,' said the Chief Inspector, 'because Silvercat told us something about an orange. We didn't believe him. We thought he was trying to make out he was drunk.

'But the detective sergeant who found the orange has made some enquiries in Davies Street.

'A street-hawker keeps his barrow in a mews there. This hawker says that he lost an orange somewhere in that district last night, that he was an orange short this morning.'

He folded his hands and looked at her seriously.

'Sit down, Mrs Gallery,' he said kindly. 'Perhaps you'd like to have a cup of tea and think things over.

'Perhaps you'd like to make another statement about what really happened last night, but,' he went on quietly, 'I must tell you that anything you say from now on may be used in evidence against you . . .'

WILLIAM A. R. COLLINS

William Alexander Ray Collins, known to all as Billy, was born in 1900. Educated at Harrow and Magdalen College, Oxford, he accepted his destiny and in the 1930s joined the family business, the publishing firm of Collins, which had been established in Glasgow by his ancestor William Collins in 1819. Collins was of course the publisher behind the Crime Club imprint.

'One's first impression is that he is *very* intellectual and possibly inclined to asceticism,' wrote Peter Cheyney. 'As usual, one's first impression is quite wrong. He rides to hounds twice a week, shoots, plays no mean game of tennis, and finds time to talk to verbose people like myself. He directs—with other members of the Collins family—a publishing business which, last year, published an average of two books a day!'

Billy Collins became the company's Chairman and Managing Director in 1945. His drive and abilities were the stuff of legend and, widely acclaimed as one of the greatest publishers there has ever been, he guided the firm through a period of significant growth, internationally as well as at home. He developed a particularly strong friendship with Agatha Christie, admittedly influenced by her significant value to the company, and was invited to deliver the eulogy at her memorial service in 1976, shortly before his own death. Outside publishing he was a keen ornithologist and cared passionately about wildlife conservation: like the actor David Niven, he accepted an invitation from the naturalist Gerald Durrell to be a trustee of the Jersey Wildlife Preservation Trust. In recognition of his many achievements, he was awarded many honours and knighted in 1970.

Sir William Collins OBE died on 21 September 1976. 'The "Eat More Fruit" Murder' was published by the *Sunday Dispatch* on 10 April 1938. Despite publishing detective fiction throughout his working life, this story appears to have been Collins' one and only attempt at writing it . . .

ACKNOWLEDGEMENTS

'Hot Steel' by Anthony Berkeley reprinted by permission of The Society of Authors as the Literary Representative of the Estate of Anthony Berkeley Cox.

'The Murder at Warbeck Hall' by Cyril Hare reprinted by permission of United Agents LLP on behalf of Sophia Jane Holroyd.

'The House of the Poplars' by Dorothy L. Sayers copyright © 2020 The Trustees of Anthony Fleming (deceased).

'The Hampstead Murder' by Christopher Bush copyright © Christopher Bush 1955, reprinted by permission of Giles Dalton.

'The Scarecrow Murders' by Joseph Commings copyright © the Catholic Diocese of St Petersburg, Florida, 1948.

'The Incident of the Dog's Ball' by Agatha Christie copyright © Christie Archive Trust 2009. All rights reserved. Agatha Christie and Poirot are registered trade marks of Agatha Christie Limited in the UK and elsewhere.

'The Riddle of the Black Spade' by Stuart Palmer reprinted by permission of the author's estate and the agents for the estate, JABberwocky Literary Agency, Inc., 49 W 45th St Ste. 12N, New York, NY 10036.

'The Torch at the Window' by Josephine Bell copyright © the estate of Josephine Bell, reprinted with permission of Curtis Brown Group Ltd, London.

'Grand Guignol' by John Dickson Carr copyright © John Dickson Carr 1929.

'A Knotty Problem' by Ngaio Marsh copyright © Estate of Ngaio Marsh 2020.

'The Orange Kid' by Peter Cheyney copyright © Peter Cheyney 1938.

'Mr Prendergast and the Orange' by Nicholas Blake reprinted by permission of Peters Fraser & Dunlop (www.petersfraser-dunlop.com) on behalf of the Estate of Nicholas Blake.

'The Yellow Sphere' by John Rhode copyright © Estate of John Rhode 1938.

'The "Eat More Fruit" Murder' by William A. R. Collins reprinted by permission of HarperCollins Publishers Ltd.

Every effort has been made to trace all owners of copyright. The editor and publishers apologise for any errors or omissions and would be grateful if notified of any corrections.

Crushing Avalanches

Heinemann
LIBRARY

Louise and Richard Spilsbury

www.heinemann.co.uk/library
Visit our website to find out more information about **Heinemann Library** books.

To order:
☎ Phone 44 (0) 1865 888066
▤ Send a fax to 44 (0) 1865 314091
▢ Visit the Heinemann Bookshop at www.heinemann.co.uk/library to browse our catalogue and order online.

First published in Great Britain by
Heinemann Library, Halley Court,
Jordan Hill, Oxford OX2 8EJ, part of
Harcourt Education.
Heinemann is a registered trademark of
Harcourt Education Ltd.

Editorial: Andrew Farrow and Dan Nunn
Design: David Poole and Paul Myerscough
Illustrations: Geoff Ward
Picture Research: Rebecca Sodergren and
Debra Weatherley
Production: Edward Moore

Originated by Dot Gradations Limited
Printed and bound in China by WKT

ISBN 0 431 17831 3 (hardback)
07 06 05 04 03
10 9 8 7 6 5 4 3 2 1

ISBN 0 431 17859 3 (paperback)
08 07 06 05 04
10 9 8 7 6 5 4 3 2 1

**British Library Cataloguing in
Publication Data**
Spilsbury, Richard, 1963 –
Crushing avalanches. – (Awesome Forces
of Nature)
1. Avalanches – Juvenile literature
I. Title II. Spilsbury, Louise
551.3'07
A full catalogue record for this book is
available from the British Library.

Acknowledgements
The publishers would like to thank the
following for permission to reproduce
photographs:

Alamy p. **12**; AP pp. **5** (Lechiner), **16** (Georg
Koechler), **17** (Douglas C. Pizac), **18** (Dietner
Endlicher), **19** (Rudi Blaha); Corbis pp. **11**,
13, **21**, **26**; Das Fotoarchive p. **22** (Marcus
Matzel), **27**; Eric Limon Photography p. **14**;
Rex Features pp. **15** (SIPA Press), **25** (Toby
Rankin); South American Pictures p. **10**; SPL
p. **7**; Still Pictures pp. **4** (Roberta Parkin), **24**
(Andreas Riedmiller); Trip pp. **23** (Mountain
Sport), **28** (Ask Images); Venture Pix p. **8**;
Yoram Porath p. **9**.

Cover photograph reproduced with
permission of Roberta Parkin/Still Pictures.

Every effort has been made to contact
copyright holders of any material reproduced
in this book. Any omissions will be rectified
in subsequent printings if notice is given to
the publishers.

Contents

*Any words appearing in the text in bold, **like this**, are explained in the Glossary.*

What is an avalanche?

When snow slides or slips down mountainsides we call it an avalanche. The word avalanche comes from a French word that means 'descent' or fall. As the snow slides down, it bashes into ice, rocks, soil and trees. If it hits them with enough force, they come hurtling down the mountain too.

When do avalanches happen?

There are many avalanches every year, usually at the same times of year. They can only happen after snow has fallen and collected on mountainsides during cold seasons. Most avalanches in Europe and North America happen between January and March. Some happen later in the year, when temperatures start to get warmer and the snow and ice start to thaw. In these conditions, big chunks of snow do not stick to the ground very well and may start to move.

An avalanche like this can come racing down a mountainside without any warning. Eyewitnesses say that a speeding mass of ice and snow like this sounds like a roaring thunderstorm.

4

Destructive forces

Avalanches vary in size and force. They can be slow movements of a few kilograms of snow over a few metres. They can also be massive shifts of hundreds of tonnes of snow and rock. These speed for several kilometres down a mountainside, like express trains.

Big avalanches can destroy anything that gets in their way. In some places big avalanches knock down trees and affect the lives of mountain animals. In other places they can crush whole towns and the people who live there. In these places, avalanches become terrible natural disasters.

An avalanche can bury cars, buildings, roads, animals and people under a heavy blanket of icy snow.

AVALANCHE ⚡ FACTS

! There are perhaps a million avalanches each year around the world; most cause very little damage to people.

! Avalanches can move at up to 300 kilometres per hour – that is the speed of a Formula One racing car. They usually move much faster than any person can run.

Where do avalanches happen?

Avalanches happen all over the world where snow falls and there are mountains. Many of the avalanches that take place go unnoticed by people because they happen in remote snowy places where nobody goes. Some avalanches affect people who live on or at the edge of mountain ranges. Mountain ranges where there are lots of avalanches include the Alps in Europe, the Himalayas in Nepal and Tibet (in Asia), the Andes in South America, and the Rocky Mountains in the USA.

Avalanches often happen in exactly the same locations within these mountain areas. This is because only certain slopes are steep enough for snow to settle and to slide down.

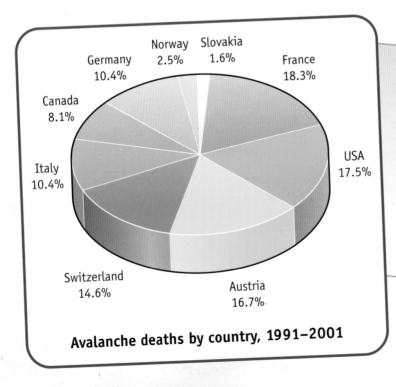

Avalanche deaths by country, 1991–2001

*Over 1300 people died in avalanches between 1991 and 2001. This **pie chart** shows that most deaths resulting from avalanches happened in France, Austria and the USA.*

What causes an avalanche?

Snow that has already fallen and built up on a slope is called **snow cover**. Most snow cover is stable, which means it stays where it is on a slope. But some snow cover is unstable and this may start an avalanche.

Types of snow cover

Snow falls from the sky as star-shaped flakes or as rounded granules, depending on the temperature. After snow lands it changes shape because of the weight of more snow landing on top of it and because of temperature changes. This is called settling. When flakes settle they form stable snow cover, but granules roll over each other, and settle as weak layers of snow. If a lot of snow falls quickly on top of a weak layer – for example in a **blizzard**, or when thick, heavy **snowdrifts** form in heavy winds – then it may form unstable snow cover. Avalanches are **triggered** by slight movements of unstable snow cover.

Snowflakes settle to form stable snow cover because their points lock together like pieces of a jigsaw puzzle.

Triggers

Sometimes small movements can trigger an avalanche, such as the movement of a wild animal or the melting of a layer of snow. Some avalanches are caused by the shaking force of a loud machine or even an earthquake. However, most fatal avalanches are triggered by people.

Are all avalanches the same?

Not all avalanches are the same. There are four main types, depending on snow cover: dry slab, wet slab, wind and ice.

Dry **slab avalanches** are most common. Layers of settled snow build up to form a thick, dry snow slab which can become as brittle as a pane of glass. When triggered, it can suddenly shatter and break into big chunks of ice that slide down mountainsides at high speeds.

Wet slab avalanches happen when rain and sun weaken large slabs of snow cover. They slip down the mountainside much more slowly than shattered hard slabs. As they are wet and heavy, they drag boulders, trees and soil along with them.

Dry slab avalanches slip like fast sledges over the weak snow layer underneath.

Wind avalanches are less common. Occasionally snow falls and settles as a mixture of flakes and granules, forming a loose, light powder. When an avalanche is triggered, the powder forms giant snowclouds. These snowclouds travel down slopes very quickly, creating a ferocious wind ahead of them.

Ice avalanches are rare, but they have caused some of the worst avalanche disasters. **Glaciers** are immense slabs of ice that form on shallow slopes after years of snowfall. They usually move really slowly because they are so heavy. Sometimes huge chunks of glacier can break off and start an ice avalanche. They may move fast, sweeping hundreds of tonnes of snow, rock, soil or water in front of them.

When ice avalanches fall into water, they can cause big, destructive waves.

Yungay, Peru, 1970

Yungay is a small town in the Andes mountains, in Peru. On the afternoon of 31 May 1970, many of the town's people were listening to the soccer World Cup on the radio. At 3.23 p.m. a huge earthquake shook most of Peru. Walls and houses crumpled and whole streets split open. But this destructive force was just the beginning – it also triggered an awesome **ice avalanche**.

Falling mountain

Mount Huascarán – the tallest mountain in Peru – is nearly 7 kilometres high. It is at one end of a high-sided valley containing Yungay and several villages. Before the earthquake, a **glacier**, high on Huascarán, had been weakened as it thawed during the spring. When the earthquake hit, it shook loose a piece of the glacier.

'At that time I heard a great roar coming from Huascarán. Looking up, I saw what appeared to be a cloud of dust and it looked as though a large mass of rock and ice was breaking loose from the north peak.' Mateo Casaverde, survivor

The centre of Yungay in 1968. These palm trees survived the avalanche in 1970.

Speeding wave

The ice avalanche was around 1 kilometre across and weighed millions of tonnes. It dropped nearly 4 kilometres before it hit the valley floor. It then hurtled down the valley towards Yungay, pushing an immense wave of snow, rock, soil and water in front of it.

'The crest of the wave had a curl, like a huge breaker coming in from the ocean. I estimated the wave to be at least 80 metres high. I reached the high ground of the cemetery a few seconds before the debris flow struck the base of the hill.' Mateo Casaverde

The wave took about 3 minutes to travel 15 kilometres to Yungay. The town was completely buried by the avalanche. Of the town's 25,000 inhabitants, only around 2000 survived. It was the world's worst recorded avalanche.

This photo, taken after the avalanche, shows the valley where Yungay once stood. The town has disappeared.

What happens in an avalanche?

When an avalanche happens people do not get any warning. Sometimes people report hearing a soft 'woosh' sound or a loud crack. Usually the first thing they know about it is being knocked over and carried fast down a mountainside.

'I heard a deep, muffled thunk as it fractured. Then it was like someone pulled the rug out from under me.' Bruce Tremper, dry **slab avalanche** survivor

Tumbling

Survivors of avalanches often describe being spun around so much they do not know which way is up. They say this is a bit like being in a tumble dryer full of snow and ice! The force of moving snow is so great that people cannot control the direction they are sliding. It is difficult to slow down because avalanches speed up as they move.

This snowboarder is trying to get safely out of the way of an avalanche that is moving down the slope.

Dangers

The biggest danger in an avalanche is not having enough air to breathe. When people are falling, the air is so full of snow that it is hard to breathe. If they get buried under snow, only a tiny amount of air is usually trapped with them. The danger is that it will run out before rescuers reach them.

Some people are injured when the avalanche throws chunks of ice, rocks and trees into them. Others suffer from **hypothermia** – they get so cold they become ill. Avalanches also bury buildings, cars, roads and tunnels under tonnes of snow, ice and soil.

Snowmobiles are heavy and can easily trigger slab avalanches.

What should people do in an avalanche?

These are a few things that people who get caught in an avalanche should do:

- Try to get off the moving slab of snow and ice.

- Try to grab a tree or boulder quickly before the avalanche builds up speed. This may help them to slow down their sliding.

- Keep moving, as if swimming hard, using their arms and legs. The greatest danger is to sink deeper into the snow.

- Try to clear a large space in front of their mouth before the avalanche stops. Then they will have a pocket of air to breathe.

- Before the snow settles, people should push a hand upward so that rescuers might see them. A good way of telling which way is up is to dribble some saliva (spit) – it always moves down towards the ground!

When big avalanches threaten towns amongst snowy mountains, the people who live there need to know what to do to remain safe.

Les Orres, France, 1998

On 23 January 1998, a group of students on a school trip set off for a walk on **snowshoes** in Les Orres in the French Alps. They had several guides with them and had just spent a week learning about snow sports and snow hazards. Heavy snowfall in the area meant there was risk of avalanches, but their guides still decided to go.

> *'One cannot criticize these people in such a tragic moment, but personally, I wouldn't have gone trekking today in these conditions.'* Gerard Bouchet, leader of one of the rescue teams

As the group walked up to a ridge above some woods, disaster struck. Their movements triggered a dry **slab avalanche** up to 300 metres wide, which swept the students down the slope. Rescue workers later found many of the survivors dazed and clinging to trees.

Out of the party of 42 that set out, 11 people were killed and 21 were injured in the avalanche at Les Orres. Over 150 rescue workers helped rescue survivors.

Who helps after an avalanche?

Avalanche victims have to be found fast because of the danger that they will run out of air. That is why trained, expert assistance is necessary in areas where avalanches are a problem.

Getting help

Rescue teams work in particular areas of the mountains. They have detailed knowledge of avalanche **terrain** – the areas where avalanches are more likely – and how to find buried victims there. They also watch for changes in the weather in mountains, and know when avalanches are more likely. When avalanches happen they organize teams of **volunteers** to help them find survivors. They work closely with emergency services such as the police.

AVALANCHE FACTS

! Only half of all avalanche victims survive after being trapped in snow for more than 30 minutes.

Rescue teams try to get to the avalanche site quickly, often using helicopters and snowmobiles.

Finding people

Rescuers look for avalanche clues such as broken trees and mounds of snow with rubble. They also look for signs of buried people such as scattered clothing and rucksacks. Most buried people are found if rescuers can see a part of their body, such as a hand, sticking out of the snow.

Many others are found using probe lines. These are made up of rescuers spread out in a line, walking slowly and quietly forward. They gently poke long, thin poles into the snow, every 50 centimetres, to find buried people.

Transceivers

If a person who is buried in the snow is wearing a **transceiver**, he or she is more likely to receive help quickly. The transceiver sends out regular signals so that rescuers, who have receivers, can pinpoint exactly where the signals are coming from. This leads them to the avalanche victim. Many people who live and work in avalanche areas carry transceivers.

These people have formed a probe line. If one of their poles touches something, rescuers use shovels to carefully but quickly dig the victim out.

Helping dogs

Rescuers also use working dogs to find avalanche victims. Most of the dogs are German Shepherds, but some are St Bernards and labradors.

Rescue dogs are specially trained by their owners. First the dogs are trained to recognize a human's smell. Then they are trained to smell this smell through deeper and deeper snow. Most rescue dogs can find people buried up to 4 metres, but a few have found survivors under 10 metres of snow. The usual reward for these dogs is to spend some time playing with their trainer!

Sensitive noses

People always give off a faint scent because of **bacteria** growing on their skin. Dogs can smell this scent thousands of times better than people can. If someone is caught in an avalanche, their scent spreads through the snow around them. Rescue dogs search for patches of snow where the smell is strongest.

One rescue dog with its trainer can search avalanche areas about eight times faster than 20 people in probe lines.

Medical care

Once avalanche victims have been found, many need immediate first aid. Rescue teams are trained to deal with injuries such as broken limbs, cuts and knocks. They also treat **hypothermia** by gently warming the victims using special heated vests and blankets. Victims with more serious injuries are taken by helicopter to specialist hospitals where experts can treat them.

Other dangers

When avalanches hit towns or cities, large numbers of people may face other dangers. The force of an avalanche can trap people under collapsed buildings or inside cars. It can pull down **powerlines** that may **electrocute** people. Powerlines can also make sparks that start fires.

Sometimes emergency services like the police work with national forces such as the army to rescue victims. Some poorer countries have fewer rescue workers and less rescue equipment. They may ask for help from richer countries after a major avalanche disaster.

After an avalanche – or any other natural disaster – more victims will survive if emergency services can find them and help them as quickly as possible.

Anchorage, Alaska, USA, 2000

The Seward Highway is the main road connecting the cities of Anchorage and Seward in Alaska, USA. It is the route that is used for the transportation of food and other goods to people living on the Kenai peninsula. It is also one of the most avalanche-threatened roads in North America because of the high cliffs and steep slopes on either side of it.

The winter of 1999–2000 was a bad one in Alaska. Very cold weather froze the snow that had fallen. Then temperatures rose and thawed the fallen snow, making a weak layer. In January, four times the usual amount of snow fell around Anchorage. This added thousands of tonnes to the **snow cover** on top of the weak layer.

Warmer weather, high winds and rainstorms **triggered** many dry **slab avalanches**. One of these avalanches flattened buildings in the city of Cordova, causing US$2.6 million in damage. On 2 February 2000, several avalanches up to a kilometre across covered the Seward Highway, cutting off around 2000 people in Kenai. Tens of thousands of people had no electricity for a week after **powerlines** were knocked down.

The Alaskan avalanches of 1999–2000 were a major disaster affecting thousands of people.

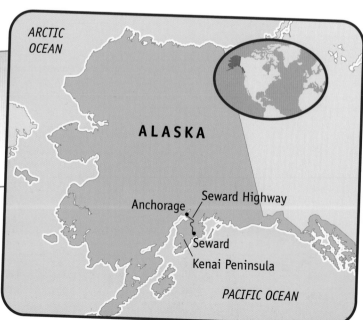

ARCTIC OCEAN

ALASKA

Anchorage

Seward Highway

Seward

Kenai Peninsula

PACIFIC OCEAN

Rescue and clear-up

National guards, police and other emergency services worked together to rescue stranded people quickly. Highway workers and **volunteers** cleared most of the Seward Highway using bulldozers and shovels.

Helicopters dropped **explosives** to clear patches of thick snow from slopes above the road. This was done to stop a big avalanche threatening the workers below. However, when three bulldozers started to clear the road of snow, strong winds above the slopes started a wind avalanche. The drivers had little warning before it hit them.

> *'I could hear the windows starting to crackle and shatter. Then one popped and so did the others.'* Larry Bushnell, bulldozer driver

Two of the bulldozer drivers were only slightly injured, but the third died. His 16-tonne machine was pushed 100 metres by the avalanche and rolled upside-down. Although they faced dangerous conditions, workers eventually managed to clear the road.

Rescue and repair workers clearing up after avalanches are often at high risk of further danger.

Can avalanches be predicted?

Many people who live in and around snowy mountains make their living from **tourism**. They provide food, hotels and lessons for winter visitors who want to ski, for example. To keep tourists safe they rely on the accurate prediction of avalanches.

Avalanche institutes

There are special avalanche **institutes** in many countries such as Japan and the USA where avalanches are a problem. Avalanche institute workers collect information about avalanche **terrain**, such as how steep mountain slopes or valleys are. They also record whether trees in woodland are close together or not. When trees are close together, they hold the fallen snow in place. When trees are far apart, avalanches can run between them. Avalanche institutes use all this information to draw avalanche hazard maps. These maps show which areas are more likely to have avalanches.

RISQUE D'AVALANCHE
PROMENADE INTERDITE

NO ENTRY
RISK OF AVALANCHE

LAWINENGEFAHR
FÜR FUSSGÄNGER VERBOTEN

STRADA VIETATA PER
RISCHIO DI VALANGA

When avalanche institutes have worked out which areas are at risk of avalanches, they can warn people about the danger.

Weather and snow cover

Avalanche institutes also collect information about the weather, and especially about snowfall. They measure how much snow falls each day, the direction the wind is blowing, and air temperature. Scientists **forecast** how the weather might change and **trigger** avalanches. They use information from photographs of clouds taken by **satellites** in space and from their knowledge of **climate**.

Scientists examine **snow cover** to see if it may avalanche. By looking at the thickness and type of snow in its layers, they can see whether it has settled tightly. Snow that has not settled tightly has air spaces in it, and sounds hollow when it is tapped.

Acid rain and avalanches

When **pollution** in the air mixes with rainwater, it makes acid rain. The acid rain then falls on trees and kills their leaves. If acid rain kills trees in avalanche areas, it means the trees cannot act like fences to stop or slow down avalanches.

Scientists look closely at snowcover in avalanche hazard areas by carefully digging holes called snow pits.

Can avalanches be prevented?

Avalanches are natural forces. People cannot stop avalanches once they are in motion, but they can prevent thick **snow cover** building up in the first place.

Looking after trees

Trees are an important way of making slopes stable. Trees are a natural barrier to avalanches and their roots also help to hold **topsoil** together. When people cut down trees for **timber** or **firewood**, the topsoil is exposed and may be washed away by rain or carried away by avalanches. Eventually this may leave a surface of bare rock. Snow cover is even less stable on bare rock.

Tree protection

Even six hundred years ago people knew that trees could stop avalanches. In forested avalanche areas of Switzerland, forest inspectors punished people for damaging trees – even for just picking their berries and cones. In the worst cases, the punishment was death.

People should only cut down a few trees from mountain slopes, so there are enough trees left to help stop avalanches.

Breaking up snow

The best way of preventing avalanches is to remove unstable snow before it becomes a hazard. Skilled people set off small, controlled avalanches. Ski **rangers** regularly visit avalanche **terrain** after heavy snowfall. They look for overhangs of snow on ridges. They test the strength of snow cover by zigzagging across slopes on skis, and jumping up and down on the snow.

Army teams use rifles and cannons to 'shoot the slopes' with **explosives**. From up to 2 kilometres away they blow up suspect snow on large slopes and overhangs. Ski rangers and mountain patrol teams sometimes use avalaunchers – special cannons powered by gas. Unlike guns they make no noise when they fire, which is better as loud noise can **trigger** an avalanche. People also use helicopters and planes to shoot the slopes in less accessible areas.

These two explosions have started a controlled avalanche on a mountain. The explosives were set off by a team travelling by helicopter.

How do people prepare for avalanches?

Not all avalanches can be prevented. This means that people who live and work in areas threatened by avalanches have to be prepared when disaster strikes.

Many villages and towns build avalanche breakers on the slopes above them. These are strong barriers that can change the direction in which an avalanche is moving. The barriers are sometimes big heaps of rock and soil. Or they may be special V-shaped concrete structures about 4 metres high and 100 metres long.

When people build their houses on a mountain, they usually give them long sloping roofs. This is because avalanches are more likely to slide over a sloping roof than knock down the house.

Some roads and railway tracks are protected from smaller avalanches by special tunnels. These are called galleries. They stop the people and vehicles inside being buried in snow and rock.

These barriers will help to trap snow that falls in winter. Then it will not slip towards the buildings further down the valley.

Personal planning

People who want to travel on snowy mountains should follow a few simple rules. They should:

- learn about the area – its weather, **snow cover**, and any dangerous areas they should avoid
- tell someone where they are going and when they will be back
- pack the right items – lots of warm clothing, a shovel, a mobile phone or a **transceiver**, and some high-energy food
- look out for areas where avalanches could happen, including open slopes and valleys, and overhanging **snowdrifts** on ridges
- look out for signs of past avalanches such as damaged trees
- travel along valley floors, through dense (crowded) trees and on slopes that are not too steep
- turn back if they see signs of unsafe snow cover.

Some people carry special airbags in their rucksacks that inflate if an avalanche hits. This helps keep the wearer near the surface of the snow – a bit like wearing a rubber ring in water.

What about avalanches in the future?

In the future, as in the past, avalanches will depend on things people have little control over, such as **snow cover** and changes in the weather. However, people can avoid being caught in avalanches by being sensible. If they follow safety rules, build in safe areas and limit the number of mountain trees they cut down, fewer people will be hurt in future.

Scientists can also help. They are developing better systems to predict avalanches. In Switzerland, electronic monitors around the country measure things like snow temperature and wind speed. They automatically send this information to a computer. This computer produces accurate avalanche **forecasts** for each part of the country. Equipment like this will mean that fewer people will be caught in avalanches in the future.

This electronic snow probe is a new tool for measuring the strength of snow layers. It is a much quicker method than digging a snow pit.

Some avalanche disasters of the past

Thousands of big avalanches happen every year. These are some of the biggest and most crushing avalanches that have happened in the past 100 years.

1910, Wellington, Washington, USA
Three trains, several carriages and a station house were pushed over the edge of a 50-metre cliff into a canyon by a spring avalanche.

1915–1918, World War I, European Alps
Avalanches claimed the lives of over 60,000 soldiers fighting in the Alps. Most avalanches happened naturally, but some may have been triggered by one side shooting into the snow-covered slopes above their enemies.

1950–51, The Winter of Terror, European Alps
Warm air from the Atlantic Ocean caused unusually high amounts of snow and rain, resulting in over 600 major avalanches. In Austria alone, thousands of acres of forest and several small villages were destroyed. One hundred people were killed.

1962, Ranrahirca, Peru
An ice avalanche near Yungay buried several villages, killing over 3000 people. (See page 10.)

1970, Val d'Isère, France
A youth hostel was destroyed by an avalanche at breakfast time. Rescuers used dinner plates to help dig out the survivors.

1999, Galteur, Austria
A 500-metre-wide avalanche hit the village of Galteur. Rescuers could not reach the village for 16 hours. They found 23 buried survivors but another 31 people who were dead.

Glossary

bacteria tiny (microscopic) living things that can cause diseases

blizzard wind-blown snowstorm

climate weather conditions that normally affect a large area over a long period of time

electrocute kill by electric shock

explosive material that blows up, suddenly releasing energy

firewood wood burnt to provide heat, often for cooking

forecast prediction

glacier huge piece of ice formed after snow falls at high altitude

hypothermia when body temperature drops so much that the person becomes ill and could die without first aid

ice avalanche avalanche caused by a large moving lump of ice

institute group or organization of people who work together to learn and teach others about something

pie chart type of graph which divides a circle into slices of different sizes to show different amounts

pollution dirt or chemicals that spoil air, land or water

powerlines main electricity cables

ranger someone who looks after a natural area, such as a forest or a national park

satellite object put into space that can send TV signals or take photographs, for example

slab avalanche avalanche caused by the break-up of heavy, solid snow cover or a slab of snow

snow cover snow that has fallen and built up on land

snowdrifts where wind has blown snow into a very big pile

snowshoes shoes like tennis racquets. They have large nets for soles, which spread the wearer's weight to stop them sinking into snow.

terrain shape of land

timber wood used for building

topsoil upper layer of soil

tourism everything to do with holidays, from the holidaymakers to the places where they stay and eat

transceiver special machine that makes a signal or message. The signal can be detected using machines called receivers.

trigger set off or start

volunteer person who offers help without being paid

wind avalanche avalanche caused by thick clouds of snow powder in the air

Find out more

Books

Nature in Action: Avalanche, Stephen Kramer (Alaska Mountain Safety Centre, 2001)

Wild Earth: Avalanche!, Lorraine Jean Hopping (Cartwheel Books/Scholastic, 2002)

Websites

www.avalanche.org/~uac/Common-questions.html – this website contains the answers to lots of common questions about avalanches.

www.pbs.org/wgbh/nova/avalanche – the website of the US TV channel PBS, which has some good avalanche information, film and pictures.

www.comdens.com/SAR – this website contains an interesting description of avalanche dog training.

www.sais.gov.uk/about_avalanches – this website contains useful information about avalanches in the UK.

Disclaimer
All the Internet addresses (URLs) given in this book were valid at the time of going to press. However, due to the dynamic nature of the Internet, some addresses may have changed, or sites may have changed or ceased to exist since publication. While the author and publishers regret any inconvenience this may cause readers, no responsibility for any such changes can be accepted by either the author or the publishers.

Index